THE CENTENARY EDITION

Weir of Hermiston, 1995
edited by Catherine Kerrigan

The Ebb-Tide, 1995
edited by Peter Hinchcliffe and Catherine Kerrigan

Treasure Island, 1998
edited by Wendy R. Katz

The Collected Poems of Robert Louis Stevenson, 2003
edited by Roger Lewis

Strange Case of Dr Jekyll and Mr Hyde, 2004
edited by Richard Dury

The Collected Works of Robert Louis Stevenson

THE CENTENARY EDITION

General Editor
CATHERINE KERRIGAN

━━━━━━━━━━

Strange Case of Dr Jekyll and Mr Hyde

Last page of the incomplete autograph manuscript of Robert Louis Stevenson's *Strange Case of Dr Jekyll and Mr Hyde*. Reproduced by permission of the Pierpont Morgan Library, New York (*MA 628*, f. 62).

ROBERT LOUIS STEVENSON

Strange Case of Dr Jekyll and Mr Hyde

edited by
RICHARD DURY

EDINBURGH UNIVERSITY PRESS

© Richard Dury, 2004

Edinburgh University Press Ltd
22 George Square, Edinburgh

Typeset in Linotron Garamond
by Koinonia, Bury, and
printed and bound in Great Britain
by the University Press, Cambridge

A CIP record for this book is available
from the British Library

ISBN 0 7486 1518 0

Contents

Preface by the General Editor

Since his death in 1894, Robert Louis Stevenson's works have continued to find a global readership. His novels, poems, short stories, travel books, essays, criticism, journalism and letters have given countless readers many hours of entertainment and intellectual engagement. Yet the perception of Stevenson as a popular author has often obscured his contribution to world literature. Too often, Stevenson has been dismissed as simply a writer of stories and verses for children when in fact he was one of the most innovative writers of the late nineteenth century. His ideas on literature, language and their social relations are set out in a number of essays that chart his understanding of the technicalities of his craft and of the cultural currents of his day.

While many of Stevenson's works have remained in print, it has become increasingly apparent that these works are corrupted texts which impair the reader's full appreciation of the writer. The purpose of the Centenary Edition is to remedy this situation by producing the first authoritative editions of Stevenson's works. The new editions return to Stevenson's manuscripts, proofs and related materials to examine what the author actually wrote; they will correct long-standing errors and, on occasion, introduce material which Stevenson intended to include but which, for various reasons, was omitted from first editions. In accuracy, authority and authenticity the Centenary Edition improves on all previous editions of Stevenson's works.

No one understood better than Stevenson himself that a literary work does not exist in a cultural vacuum. His comments on copyright, censorship, commercial forces, printing innovations and relations between publishers and authors indicate that he was all too familiar with how such factors could affect the writing and reception of a work. Where appropriate, some account of these factors and their effects will be given so that the reader will have a sense of Stevenson's literary milieu and cultural constituency.

The new editions are clear texts, free from any editorial signals. An editorial commentary and explanatory notes accompany each edition and are designed to enhance the reader's understanding of the various stages of the work from its conception in Stevenson's mind (as recorded in his letters, notes and drafts) through to its production in manuscript and printed form, and on to the work's critical and public reception.

Stevenson began writing as a child in Edinburgh, and his first literary efforts were about the domestic and the local. From his birthplace, he travelled to many familiar and unfamiliar parts of the world and chronicled what he saw in factual and fictional forms. His great strength was that he never reduced the particular to the general, but struggled to articulate human circumstance in all its variety and contradiction.

In keeping with the spirit of Stevenson, the Centenary Edition is edited by a group of international scholars whose goal is to recapture the freshness of Stevenson's complex imagination, so that those familiar with his works may discover new pleasures, and those new to them may experience all the excitement of a first encounter with this most enduring 'teller of tales'.

CATHERINE KERRIGAN
University of Guelph

Acknowledgements

My thanks have to go first of all to the Beinecke Library, at Yale University, and to Vincent Giroud, Curator of Modern Books and Manuscripts, for invaluable help and support, and to all the staff there for creating the ideal study environment; thanks to Princeton University Library for permission to publish transcriptions of the two cancelled folios I have called *ND1*, and to Stephen Ferguson, Margaret Sherry and Margaret Rich and AnnaLee Pauls of the Rare Books and Special Collections department for their swift and efficient help; thanks to the Morgan Library, New York, for permission to publish the transcript of the incomplete final draft *MS* and to Eva Soas for efficient help; to Ann Kindred of the Silverado Robert Louis Stevenson Museum for generous help on various occasions; the Staff of the Berg Collection of the New York Public Library, of the British Library, and of the National Library of Scotland (especially Tom Hubbard); Mike Bott and Verity Andrews of the Archives Department of Reading University Library; Mme Veronique Leroux Hugon of the Bibliothèque Charcot of the Hôpital del la Salpêtrière, also Mme Bernadette Molitor and M. Henry Ferreira of the 'Histoire de la Médicine' section of the BIUM, Paris, for help with the 'French scientific journal'. A special thanks to the generous help provided by the members of the VICTORIA discussion list (among others, Paul Lewis, Keith Ramsey, Peter Shillingford, K. Eldron, Malcolm Shifrin, Kathleen McCormack, Chris Willis, Carol Thomas, Marysa Demoor). Sincere thanks are also due to many others for their help and advice: above all, to Ernest Mehew, world expert on Stevenson, for generous help in dating a letter to Henley and many other matters; to George

Addis for expert help with medical matters; Roger Lewis for help with the dedicatory poem; Frank de Glas of Utrecht University for help with dating a Dutch translation; John and Felicitas Macfie for a lodging for several nights in Heriot Row; Elizabeth Strong of McNaughton's Bookshop, Edinburgh, for letting me make notes from the Swanston Edition; Helen Beattie; Bob Stevenson; Martin A. Danahay; Andrew Nash; and Elaine Greig of the Writers' Museum, Edinburgh. Thanks also to my colleagues at Bergamo University, especially to Marina Dossena, with a scholarly interest in Scots and a personal interest in things Scottish, for help, photocopies and constant advice; and to Stefano Rosso for generous help in reading drafts at the last minute.

Four Stevensonian colleagues have given great and continual support with this project over the years and sustained me in the effort, these deserve my heartfelt thanks: Roger Swearingen for timely help with the Textual Notes and variant readings, for advice on scholarly editions, for supplying information about additional translations, and for innumerable acts of generous help over the years; Katherine Linehan for constant generous help, photocopies, and information as we prepared complementary editions of the text together; Jean-Pierre Naugrette for inspiration, constant help and friendly encouragement to speak and write; and Richard Ambrosini, co-convenor of the 2002 RLS conference, for help in reading drafts, for companionship and expert advice.

I would also like to thank Catherine Kerrigan, the General Editor of the Edition, who offered helpful advice, criticism and encouragement throughout the composition process, and my wonderful editors, especially Nicola Carr and Eddie Clark at EUP and Neil Curtis.

And extra special thanks to my wife Alda who accepted the necessary absences and shared in the joy as the project took shape.

RICHARD DURY

Abbreviations

	Heritage, London, Routledge & Kegan Paul, 1981
MS	Autograph manuscript of *JH*, Pierpont Morgan Library, New York (*MA 628*) and one folio in The Silverado Museum, California
Nabokov	New York Public Library, Berg Collection, *Nabokov 00–21*, 'Vladimir Nabokov's teaching copy [of *JH*], with his annotations and scorings'
ND1	'Notebook Draft 1': two cancelled folios, Princeton University Library
ND2	'Notebook Draft 2': Beinecke Library, Yale University, *B 6934*, with one additional folio at The R. L. Stevenson Silverado Museum, California
NLS	National Library of Scotland
OED	*The Oxford English Dictionary (2nd ed.) on CD-ROM*, Oxford University Press, 1992 (a following date, e.g. *OED* 1885, refers to the 1st edition and date of publication of the relevant volume)
RLS	Robert Louis Stevenson
TUS	*The Works of Robert Louis Stevenson*, Tusitala Edition, London, Heinemann, 1923–4
Veeder	William Veeder, 'The Texts in Question' and 'Collated Fractions of the Manuscript Drafts of *Strange Case of Dr Jekyll and Mr Hyde*', in *VH*, pp. 3–13, 14–56
VH	William Veeder and Gordon Hirsch (eds), *Dr Jekyll and Mr Hyde after One Hundred Years*, Chicago, 1988

Chronology

1850   Robert Louis Stevenson is born 13 November at 8 Howard Place, Edinburgh, the only child of Margaret Isabella Balfour and Thomas Stevenson of the famous engineering family.

1853   The family moves to 1 Inverleith Terrace.

1857   The family moves to 17 Heriot Row.

1858–67 A sickly child, he first attends school in September 1857. By 1964 his health has improved and in 1867 he is admitted to Edinburgh University, where he studies engineering and becomes a student of Professor Fleeming Jenkin.

1869   Tours the Orkney and Shetland islands on board the steamboat of the Commissioners of Northern Lights.

1871   Decides to abandon engineering and study law.

1873–4 Goes to Suffolk and stays with a Balfour cousin, Maud Babington, and her husband. Contributes to the *Cornhill Magazine*. At the end of the year he goes to Mentone, in the south of France, to spend the winter.

1875   Meets Henley in Edinburgh Royal Infirmary. RLS is called to the Scottish Bar but does not practise law. Joins his cousin Bob Stevenson in France.

1876–7 Takes a canoe trip around the canals of Northern France with Sir Walter Simpson recorded in *An Inland Voyage*. Meets Mrs Fanny Van de Grift Osbourne at Paris and Grez. Spends the winter in Edinburgh.

1878   Fanny Osbourne returns to America. RLS goes travelling in the Cevennes with a donkey called Modestine.
An Inland Voyage
Edinburgh: Picturesque Notes

1879	Spends time in Edinburgh, London and France.
1880	RLS, Fanny and Lloyd spend the winter of 1880–1 in Davos.
1881	At Pitlochry writes 'The Merry Men' and 'Thrawn Janet'. At Braemar develops the plot of *Treasure Island*.
1882	Returns from Davos to Scotland. Returns to France and moves to Hyères.
1883	*The Silverado Squatters* *Treasure Island*
1884	Returns to Hyères and in May has a major haemorrhage. After a brief visit to Royat returns to England. *Admiral Guinea* *Beau Austin* (both with W. E. Henley)
1885	RLS and Fanny settle at Bournemouth in Skerryvore, the house bought by Thomas Stevenson for Fanny. Henry James (among others) is a frequent visitor. *A Child's Garden of Verses* *Prince Otto* *More New Arabian Nights: The Dynamiter* (with Fanny Stevenson) *Macaire* (with W. E. Henley)
1886	*Strange Case of Dr Jekyll and Mr Hyde* *Kidnapped*
1887	Thomas Stevenson dies in May. RLS, his mother, Fanny and Lloyd sail for America. *The Misadventures of John Nicholson* *The Merry Men and other Tales and Fables* *Memories and Portraits* *Underwoods*
1888	*A Memoir of Fleeming Jenkin* *The Black Arrow* RLS plans a voyage on the *Casco* to the Marquesas, the Paumotus, Tahiti and Hawaii. The American publisher S. S. McClure agrees to syndicate the South Sea letters.
1889	The *Casco* arrives in Hawaii. Mrs Stevenson returns to Scotland. RLS, Fanny and Lloyd remain. RLS visits Father Damien's leper colony at Molokai, sails on the schooner *Equator* to the Gilbert Islands and Samoa,

where he buys an estate, Vailima, at Upolu.
The Wrong Box (with Lloyd Osbourne)
The Master of Ballantrae

1890 Sails in the *Janet Nicholl* to the Eastern and Western Pacific. Has a lung haemorrhage. For health reasons decides to live permanently in Samoa.
In the South Seas
Ballads
Father Damien

1891 Becomes involved in Samoan politics and writes letters to *The Times*.

1892 *A Footnote to History*
Across the Plains
The Wrecker (with Lloyd Osbourne)

1893 RLS is served with The Sedition (Samoa) Regulation 1892.
Island Nights' Entertainments
Catriona

1894 Civil order restored in Samoa. The supporters of Mataafa build 'The Road of Loving Hearts' in honour of RLS's help to them during the war.
The Ebb-Tide (with Lloyd Osbourne)
On 3 December, after working all morning on *Weir of Hermiston*, RLS collapses and dies of a brain haemorrhage. He is buried in Samoa.

1896 *Weir of Hermiston*

1897 *St Ives*

Introduction

Written in six weeks in the autumn of 1885, Stevenson's *Strange Case of Dr Jekyll and Mr Hyde* was published the following January to immediate popular and critical success. The period of writing was one of notable difficulty for the author: he had been unable to do much work for several months and, with bills to pay, he was acutely aware of the need to start writing again. Ill-health, with him since childhood, but more serious since his battering journey from Scotland to California in 1879, had dogged him through the year, starting with lung haemorrhaging over Christmas and the New Year and continuing with serious returns of the same condition in the second half of April and late August. In the same period he was also uneasy at being, after his Bohemian years, 'a beastly householder' (*LETBM*, vol. V, p. 85). The house in question (in the southern English coastal town of Bournemouth) was renamed 'Skerryvore' after the lighthouse off Tiree, one of the most elegant and arduous achievements of the Stevenson family firm of marine engineers.

In mid-September, as he recovered from his most recent attack of 'bloody Jack', he decided to write a story, probably for the Christmas 'ghost story' market, and 'For two days,' he says, 'I went about racking my brains for a plot of any sort' ('A Chapter on Dreams', *TUS*, vol. XXX, p. 52).

Important elements of *Dr Jekyll and Mr Hyde* can be seen separately in RLS's previous works. Ten years earlier he had told Andrew Lang of his idea for a story about 'a Man who was Two Men'.[1] The situation of a character who alternates between a normal and a sinful life (and attempts to justify this alternation to himself) had been the subject of a melodrama about Deacon

Brodie (respectable Edinburgh cabinet-maker by day, armed burglar by night) which he had begun as early as 1864, and then took up again in collaboration with W. E. Henley from 1878 to 1880 (Roger Swearingen, *The Prose Writings of Robert Louis Stevenson*, Hamden, CT, Archon Books, 1980, pp. 3, 36–8). In 'The Body Snatcher' (published as a 'Christmas story' in 1884), it is members of the medical profession (like Jekyll) who are involved in transgressive urban night-time activities. Another element found in *JH*, a character's feeling of alienation from the 'evil' part of the self (and a conviction of non-responsibility for its actions) was explored in 'Markheim' (another Christmas story, published 1885). Here, the dialogue between the protagonist and a mysterious double has some affinity with the arguments of Jekyll's final 'statement' (for example, Markheim's words 'My life is but a travesty and a slander on myself' and 'Evil and good run strong in me, haling me both ways'; *TUS*, vol. VIII, pp. 101, 104). Both *Brodie* and 'The Body Snatcher' are set in Edinburgh, but it is the dark labyrinth of London that provides the setting for the *New Arabian Nights* (1878) and *The Dynamiter* (1885) and their strange crimes involving respectable citizens. Affinities with *JH* can also be seen in one of his *Fables*, 'The House of Eld' (possibly written 1874; cf. Swearingen, *The Prose Writings*, pp. 15, 187), which tells the story of a young man who tries to free himself from an oppressive psychological burden only to find that the monsters of patriarchy he has killed are his own parents and uncle: a situation which in its insolubility resembles that in which Jekyll finds himself (suffering from both internal conflict and his solution to it).

Fanny Stevenson later claimed that two significant influences on *JH* were the story of Deacon Brodie and 'a paper he read in a French scientific journal on sub-consciousness', which had 'deeply-impressed' him ('Prefatory Note', *TUS*, vol. V, p. xvi). Stevenson himself admitted that Brodie was a subject of childhood fascination for him, due in part to the presence of a cabinet made by him in the room where he slept when a child in Edinburgh.[2]

It is impossible to identify the 'paper … in a French scientific journal', since there were numerous French scientific journals publishing articles on double personalities and related topics in the ten years before the writing of *JH*. That RLS would have a potential interest in such an article is clear from the interest in psychology that we see in all his writings, and indeed Jekyll's self-analytical anecdote of his attempts to understand why he feels he is waking in another house (p. 64) seems to show a familiarity with the personal anecdotes that we find in psychological papers on non-unitary consciousness at this period.[3] All that we can conclude, however, is that the idea of a single person changing from one personality to another, one of them more transgressive, could have been influenced by 'double consciousness' or 'double life' cases with similar alternations that were much discussed, especially in France, from 1876 onwards.[4]

After racking his brains for a story, RLS was finally helped by a nightmare. When Fanny heard him making cries in his sleep and woke him up, his first words were 'Why did you wake me? … I was dreaming a fine bogey tale' (Balfour, vol. II, p. 13). The dream supplied him with the image of a man 'pursued for some crime', who swallows a 'powder' and undergoes 'the change in the presence of his pursuers', and also 'the scene at the window', probably of a man at a window undergoing a transformation ('Dreams', *TUS*, vol. XXX, p. 52). Three elements that sparked off his imagination were apparently the potion,[5] something that could be taken at will, the metamorphosis, and the frightening idea of 'a voluntary change becoming involuntary' (ibid.).

RLS immediately set to work, writing mainly in bed, and in three days produced a part of the story and read it out aloud to his wife Fanny and his seventeen-year-old stepson, Lloyd. Fanny, in her role of unofficial editor and manager, was unhappy with the work (thinking it should be less sensational, more allegorical) and set out her criticism in writing. This led to an angry dispute, which RLS resolved by burning the draft and starting afresh – because (as he said, in accounts by Fanny and Lloyd) he had seen the justice of Fanny's remarks and didn't want to be influenced by the original.

After the burning, RLS may have written another short in-complete draft, again in three days (only attested by the accounts of Fanny and Lloyd, though the two cancelled pages on note-book paper, *ND1*, may date from this period), before tackling the first almost full version (*ND2*), which he broke off just before the end, followed by the final draft (*MS*). The latter is not simply a fair copy of *ND2* but a major reworking, including the substitution of one character ('Mr Lemsome') with another ('Sir Danvers Carew'), and with much new work on the final chapter (including its conclusion). Finished and sent off to Longman on or just before 28 October, the story had been written in about six weeks.

Before going further with the story of publication, let us look briefly at some of the ways in which the surviving manuscript drafts and revisions (transcribed in Appendix A) indicate significant evolution of the text during the composition process.[6] 1. *ND2* (f. 88) refers to 'the Lemsome murder' and young, weak-charactered Mr Lemsome is described in the cancelled *ND1* fragment when he comes to ask for help concerning Hyde (*ND1*, f. 33). The substitution of Carew as victim strengthens the theme of Hyde's opposition to patriarchal control and tones down the hints of homosexuality. 2. Revisions to the beginning of the last chapter (*MS*, f. 47) also show a move away from earlier veiled allusions to masturbation and homosexuality, contained in phrases such as 'From a very early age, however, I became in secret the slave of disgraceful pleasures', 'the iron hand of indurated habit' and 'vices ... criminal in the sight of the law and abhorrent in themselves' (*ND2*, ff. 76–7).[7] In addition, in a cancelled draft, Poole says that the mirror has seen 'some queer doings' (*MS*, cancelled f. 39), a phrase which might suggest homosexuality, altered to 'strange things' in *1886L*. Such changes have been seen as evidence of Stevenson conforming to Victorian proprieties, though they could also be seen as contributing to the indeterminate and multiple meaning of the text. 3. The description of the scene that Utterson and Poole find on forcing their way into the cabinet was considerably elaborated between *ND2* f. 58, the cancelled *MS* f. 39 and *1886L* (p. 49), with the addition of the 'pious work' annotated with blasphemies in Jekyll's hand and the dialogue in front of the mirror – details adding to the concentrated and complex symbolism of this scene. 4. The early drafts show Stevenson consciously working to create reversals of expectations of positive and negative polarity: in *MS* Stevenson originally wrote that the windows associated with the mysterious door 'are always shut and wonderfully dirty', but has crossed through the last three words and substituted 'but they're clean' (*MS*, f. 6). In *ND2* Hyde lives in 'somewhat dreary and exiguous rooms off the Gray's Inn Road' (*ND2*, f. 88), while in *1886L* this becomes a Soho apartment furnished in good taste. (For further 'complicated oppositions', see below, pp. xxxiv and li.) Other interesting passages from early versions include the end of Utterson's day with the detective and his 'horror of that monstrous seething mud-pot of a city, and of that kindred monster – man's soul' (*ND1*, f. 48), and his experience of urban alienation as he stares at shop-windows while waiting for Hyde (*MS*, f. 9).

Charles Longman acknowledged receipt of the *MS* on 31 October, and when he had received the report of his reader (Andrew Lang), he suggested that the story should not be serialised in the *Longman's Magazine* as originally planned but produced as a separate volume for the Christmas market. In a letter of 17 November to Scribner's in New York, he says enthusiastically 'We expect a considerable demand for the book in this country, as the story seems to be written in Mr Stevenson's best manner.'[8] The contract was signed on 3 November and on 6 November RLS received a welcome cheque as an advance on royalties. Then, at the end of November Longman decided to postpone publication until after Christmas.

The book was published in London and New York in two formats: a cheap edition in paper wrappers and a slightly more expensive hardback edition. Publication day was 5 January 1886 in New York (the text being set up from advance sheets of the London edition), and 9 January in London.

Sales took off within a few weeks of publication in Britain and in the United States, a helpful factor in Britain (according to Charles Longman) being the favourable review in *The Times* of 25 January (Balfour, vol. II, p. 14). Longman sold just under 40,000 by June 1886, a number considered 'enormous' by a trade magazine; Scribner's had sold almost 20,000 by April and 75,000 copies had been sold in the United States in all editions by June.[9]

The book was acclaimed in the US and British press in January and February 1886. One point often underlined was its originality: ⟵ 'Strikingly bold and original in design' (*The Brighton Telegraph*);[10]

'a story of extraordinary novelty' (*The Derby Mercury*); 'remarkable ... for the extreme and startling and wholly novel *motif* of the book' (*The Washington Post*); and 'a perfectly original production' (Julia Wedgwood in *The Contemporary Review*).

Reviewers repeatedly remarked on how the suspense is maintained: 'For the life of us, we cannot make out how such and such an incident can possibly be explained on grounds that are intelligible or in any way plausible' (*The Times*); 'It was not until we reached the Doctor's confession that we understood the mysterious power which bound him to Mr Hyde' (*Court and Society Review*); 'the denouement is concealed almost up to the end very cleverly' (*The Brighton Herald*).

One of the most frightening scenes for the book's first readers was where Utterson and Poole are listening outside Jekyll's cabinet and wondering what has happened inside: this is mentioned by Lang and by the reviewer of *Vanity Fair* in 1886 and by Henry James in 1888. Lang says that it 'produced such an emotion that I threw the manuscript on a chair, and scuttled apprehensively to the safety of bed' and that a friend in Scotland had the same reaction.[11]

Concerning its interpretation, critics were divided between a clear majority who identified a conventional moral message, others who saw it more as a psychological study, and a third group who saw no lesson or moral at all but a well-written story. For the first group (to which we may add the authors of sermons based on the book, cf. Balfour, vol. II, p. 14), the story was 'an allegory, illustrative of the two-sidedness of human nature, the constant struggle between good and bad, the higher and the lower being in man, and how when he yields to his natural inclination towards the latter, it gradually asserts itself more and more' (*The Brighton Telegraph*).

The *Times* reviewer mentions the 'intuitive psychological research' behind the tale, and a few others (from the United States) mentioned its 'psychological speculation' (*The Evening Telegram*), called it a 'psychological novel' (the San Francisco *Weekly Bulletin*), or saw how the story contains 'the germ of a remarkable psychological hypothesis' (*The Brooklyn Times*). The *Chicago Medical Standard* in 1886 pointed out affinities with cases of mental illness where there is a contrast of personality between 'the exalted state' and 'the depressed state'.[12]

Some writers had a doubt about the discernability of a moral in the story: Andrew Lang in 1905 (*Adventures Among Books*, p. 46) refers to 'the moral (whatever that may be)', and in 1886 he had said 'It is not a moral allegory, of course; but you cannot help reading the moral into it' (*The Saturday Review*). This is also the opinion of Henry James in 1888, who typically argues back and forth between the story's 'high philosophic intention ... the profundity of the idea' and its status as 'the most ingenious and irresponsible of fictions' characterised by its 'extremely successful form', before concluding that he finds the latter, the well-told narrative, most striking and (with a *fin-de-siècle* paradox) 'the most edifying thing' about the text (suggesting that any allegorical meaning would be less edifying).[13]

The new book became a common topic of conversation in the early months of 1886, when a correspondent of *The Court and Society Review* reported that the first question one is asked at dinner nowadays is 'Have you read Dr Jekyll and Mr Hyde?'. Its fame spread to India, and in early March *The Sind Gazette* reported that 'No book that has appeared for many months has produced such a sensation as Stevenson's little pamphlet of the strange case of Dr Jekyll. One hears of it everywhere.'

Another sign of notoriety was the derivative works that it immediately inspired: in less than a month from publication, *Punch* (February 6) produced a brief parody 'The Strange Case of Dr T. and Mr H.' (Maixner, pp. 208–10), and two other versions were published as pamphlets in London, *Strange Case of the Prime Minister and Mr Muldoon* (1886), a political satire, and *Stranger Case of Dr Hide and Mr Crushall* (n.d. but 1886–7), a nonsense parody (Harry M. Geduld, *The Definitive Dr Jekyll and Mr Hyde Companion*, New York, Garland, 1983, pp. 192–3, 137–52). The first stage adaptation was a 'political satire', *The Strange Case of a Hyde and Seekyll* by George Grossmith at Toole's Theatre in London in May 1886.[14]

The discussion and interpretation of the text, in critical analyses and derivative versions, have continued ever since. Indeed, the text itself encourages this: it foregrounds interpretative acts

(Utterson is continually trying to explain Jekyll's behaviour and attempting to define Hyde); it frames and repeats a series of oppositions (protagonist v. double, inside v. outside, right v. left, good v. evil, same v. different, pure v. impure) and a number of motifs with universal symbolism (door, hand, mirror, fire); and contains names that seem to have a meaning (Utterson, Hyde). But on close inspection, the motifs, the names and the unstable oppositions all have confusingly multiple interpretations.

Some early reviewers shared this feeling of a lack of a simple 'message', although most were happy to talk in terms of moral 'allegory' and 'parable'. Stevenson gestures in the direction of a moral interpretation in the use of biblical allusions and phrases in the speech and thoughts of the characters (as in Jekyll's reference to an inner 'war among my members', p. 59, his 'chastisement', p. 64, and his comparison of himself with 'any tempted and trembling sinner', p. 66). Jekyll also makes frequent use of words with a strong moral polarity: the repeated mentions of 'good' in his 'Statement' are typically in clear opposition to 'evil', e.g. 'good shone upon the countenance of the one, evil was written broadly … on the face of the other' (p. 61), 'his good qualities seemingly unimpaired; he would even make haste … to undo the evil done by Hyde' (p. 63). Such formulations (from the unreliable pen of Jekyll) probably lie behind the popular interpretation of Jekyll as 'good'.

When RLS writes 'as to a key, I conceive I could not make my allegory better, nay, that I could not fail to weaken it, if I tried. I have said my say as I was best able: others must look for what was meant' (*LETBM*, vol. V, p. 211), he must be using the term 'allegory' in the broad sense of 'narrative with symbolic interpretation'. It is true that the representation of inner conflict, *psychomachia*, is often expressed through a 'strong' allegory (as in the Good and Evil Angels of Marlowe's *Dr Faustus*) and that the text also borrows elements from the exaggerated melodramatic tradition that presents life in terms of simple moral oppositions. However, *JH* is only a marginal kind of allegory: there are no explicit personifications, only one possible 'characternym' ('Hyde'), no explicit moral at the end, and no simple code of equivalences providing a parallel meaning.

Rather than an allegory, *JH* could be seen as a kind of puzzle text: a fantastic 'weird tale' with elements of detective, science fiction and sensational tale, containing many signifying elements of multiple and changing values. Like a puzzle, the text forces the reader to interpret, to test ambiguities and recognise patterns. It resembles the labyrinth in being a fascinating structure in which the interpreter has to understand ambiguous situations while lacking a clear view of the whole. The text also has affinities with the verbal puzzle of the paradox, since the central enigma is that Jekyll and Hyde are two characters and one character, different and the same: they form a clear dualistic opposition yet are also seen as a complementary pair making a unity, so that boundaries disappear and fixed meaning (based on oppositions) is challenged. Stevenson's views on the unreality of strong linguistic opposi- tions is shown in his comment (in a letter to Colvin of February 1887): 'Everything is true; only the opposite is true too; *you must believe both equally or be damned*' (*LETBM*, vol. V, p. 359). And a further idea of the non-logical, chaotic nature of phenomena (which would make the good-v.-evil morality of Utterson and Jekyll unrealistic) is found in 'A Chapter on Dreams' (1888, *TUS*, vol. XXX, pp. 52–3) when he says that dreams give us hints of the sense 'we seem to perceive in the arabesques of time and space'.

The lack of any simple meaning to *JH* is suggested by the very multitude of interpretations that it has received. The following three sections will look at various threads of interpretation: first, of the characters Jekyll and Hyde; then, of the text's symbolic spaces and motifs; finally, of the tale as a mirror of Stevenson's society.

Jekyll and Hyde are linked by their names: if we consider the two initials 'H' and 'J', we see that Henry Jekyll, who is 'commingled out of good and evil' (p. 62), has a set of initials that combines them both, the more public 'J' and the more private 'H'.[15] Both 'Jekyll' and 'Hyde' contain the letter 'y', rare in the middle of a word, and a strange, sloping and divided letter that substitutes the 'straight' letter 'i' in 'hide' and 'kill' (Fabio Cleto, *Percorsi del dissenso*, Genova, ECIG, 2001, p. 207).[16] The two names also have elements of phonetic iconicity: two-syllable Jekyll against smaller, one-syllable Hyde; the close vowels in Jekyll (especially with the 1886 British pronunciation, see p. 78) against the diphthong /aɪ/ in Hyde with its open (sonorous, less-restrained) first element.

When we first meet the name Jekyll in the text it is followed by the initials of his high academic honours (p. 13). This self-presentation (Jekyll is the author of the quoted will) emphasises his established official and social identity as 'patriarch' and associates it with the fixed and formal language of the law. Yet it is immediately undermined by Utterson's evaluation of Jekyll's text as 'fanciful' and 'immodest' and by Jekyll's identification of Hyde (who for Utterson is a social outcast) as his 'friend and benefactor'.

The portrait of Jekyll that we are then given at the beginning of ch. 3 is a strange mixture of positive and negative qualities: he is 'a large, well-made, smooth-faced man of fifty' (p. 21). Here, the reader first interprets 'smooth-faced' as the third in a series of non-evaluative adjectives referring to physical appearance, but then begins to think that it must have the normal meaning of 'sly and persuasive' and that the narrator is deceptively attempting to make us accept a literal interpretation (and so acts like Jekyll in his 'Statement' when he tries to make us accept an etymological meaning of 'duplicity', p. 58). The complicity of the narrator is further suggested in the continuation of the description and its excessive down-toning and hedging: 'with something of a slyish cast perhaps'.

Linking the text with a long tradition of (mythical, biblical, Gothic-novel) warnings not to explore 'forbidden knowledge', Jekyll can be seen as the proud scientist who meddles with what should remain hidden: he sets a high value on 'the furtherance of knowledge' and appreciates the 'temptation of a discovery so singular and profound' which opens the way to 'a new province of knowledge' (pp. 58, 60, 56).

In a psychological approach that is also clearly encouraged, Jekyll symbolises a part of the human personality, what Freud (and his translators) would later call the ego (the conscious part of the mind), with Utterson and his paternal attributes as the superego (the part of the mind that regulates conduct according to society's norms), and with Hyde as the id (the instinctive and selfish mental force that seeks satisfaction of desires, suppressed or 'hidden' by civilisation).[17] Though welcomed by Jekyll for his 'energy of life', he is feared as a reminder of the body and of rejected sexuality and mortality (p. 72), the same fear that provokes instinctive repulsion among those who come near him.

Hyde is short (even 'dwarfish', p. 18), young, and is a gentleman, or passes as one. Otherwise he is described only in vague terms: deformed in some indefinable way ('gives a strong feeling of deformity', p. 12), vaguely diabolic ('hellish', p. 72), primitive ('Something troglodytic', p. 18), or animal-like ('ape-like', 'like a monkey', pp. 25, 46), possibly effeminate (see p. xxx), provoking in those near him 'loathing and fear' (p. 18).

He eludes interpretation – indeed, he seems to be a signifier for everything that is feared and so hidden and excluded from consciousness: instinctive drives, non-rational behaviour and motivation, homosexuality, the feminine, corporeality, materiality, decay and death, annihilation and meaninglessness; and also (on a sociological level) the urban poor and the criminal underclass.[18]

In a conventional moral interpretation Hyde is 'original sin', an innate tendency towards evil in everyone (when Jekyll first transforms into Hyde he sees himself as 'sold a slave to my original evil', p. 61), particularly emphasised in Scottish Calvinistic teaching of the time aiming to frighten into virtue by stressing the fateful ease of sin and damnation. Alternatively, Hyde can be seen as an external source of evil, a Mephistophelean double (he behaves 'like Satan', Jekyll refers to him as 'child of Hell'); or combination of the two, an internal devil (as when Jekyll refers to Hyde as 'my devil' and as the 'familiar that I called out of my own soul', pp. 67, 63).[19]

Hyde can also been interpreted as 'primitive man' (see below, p. xli) and as the angry artist (see below, pp. xlii), but, in truth, he is presented as subtly different from page to page, allowing a variety of moral, psychological, and sociological interpretations.

Hyde's activities remain deliberately hidden from the reader but it is legitimate to infer that they involve sexual excess: he is created to deal with Jekyll's 'impatient gaiety of disposition' and his concealed 'pleasures' (see Explanatory Notes to p. 58), and the first transformation is accompanied by 'a current of disordered sensual images running like a mill race in my fancy' (p. 60), after which Jekyll habitually changes into Hyde 'for his pleasures', at first merely 'undignified' but later sadistic (p. 63).

Substance-addiction (which RLS would have been familiar with in the alcoholism of his friend Walter Ferrier who died in 1883) is also hinted at. Jekyll is in a way 'addicted' to being Hyde: in an addict's typical fantasy of freedom he believes that 'the moment I choose, I can be rid of Mr. Hyde' (p. 22), only later to 'suffer smartingly in the fires of abstinence' (p. 66). In a way, Hyde too is tied to the potion that assures transformation back to Jekyll: his cry 'Have you got it? … Have you got it?' and his terrifying 'one loud sob of such immense relief' (p. 55) when Lanyon shows him the drawer of chemicals are perhaps the clearest suggestions of a frightening dependency.[20]

Of the socially condemned activities that Hyde is associated with, veiled allusions to homosexuality are particularly frequent. They are also appropriate since this hidden vice was often referred to indirectly as 'unspeakable' (so resembling the indescribable Hyde), and the double life of Jekyll as Hyde resembles the necessarily double life of the Victorian homosexual. The suspected blackmail of Jekyll for 'some of the capers of his youth' by his 'young man' 'favourite' (pp. 11, 19, 26), would make readers of the time think Jekyll might be a homosexual, one of the most common victims of blackmailers.

In addition, Jekyll and Hyde have some feminine characteristics: Hyde is 'closer than a wife' to Jekyll, walks 'with a certain swing' and weeps 'like a woman' (pp. 72, 47); Jekyll's hand is 'white and comely' and he is viewed in a typically female position: at a window by two male *flâneurs* (pp. 64, 38).[21]

The way in which Sir Danvers Carew, with his 'very pretty manner of politeness' (p. 24), 'accosts' Hyde in a lonely street in the small hours of the night, with a letter in his hand apparently 'inquiring his way' suggests a sexual proposition. Myers, in notes sent to RLS, says of this crime that 'the ground is ticklish' (i.e. 'delicate', 'risky') (in Maixner, p. 214). That Myers is thinking of homosexuality is shown by his mistaken query about Hyde's Soho house, 'What led you to specify Greek street?' (one of the principal streets of Soho), where the text does not mention any street name at all. Myers's Freudian slip undoubtedly derives from the text's hints of a link between Hyde and homosexuality, or 'Greek love' as it was often called.

The text's hints of homosexuality are also found in the way Hyde's door is given suggestive anal associations: it is a hidden 'back way to Dr. Jekyll's' (p. 38), reached by 'the back passage' (p. 65).[22] The London readers of 1886 would have also been aware of homosexuality as social phenomenon: *Reynolds News* in July 1885 attacked the corruption of youths by 'sated voluptuaries' in London (Judith R. Walkowitz, *City of Dreadful Delight, Narratives of Sexual Danger in Late-Victorian London*, London, Virago, 1992, pp. 278–9, note 123) and in the same year the 'Labouchère Amendment' to an Act of Parliament had made homosexual acts between men a criminal offence. Stevenson may have been acquainted with metropolitan homosexual communities via the Savile Club (after his election in 1874): its members included homosexuals such as Gosse and John Mahaffy, Wilde's Dublin tutor, whose *Social Life in Greece from Homer to Menander* (1874) was withdrawn because it dealt with male homosexuality.

The other characters in the story reflect Jekyll or Hyde, helping to create the typically chaotic structure of doubles narratives where, on various levels, doubles are doubled. Characters are linked in pairs by family relationship or old friendship, by the same profession and marital status, by common feelings, by repeating the same words or acting in a similar way, and by symmetrical spatial arrangement (see p. xxxvii).

Utterson emerges as a central character as he possesses the most equivalences with others: with Enfield (in family, shared feelings, echoed phrases and symmetrical configurations); Hyde (in symmetrical configurations, suspected/prospective blackmailing, and collocation in Jekyll's will); Jekyll (in symmetrical configurations, taste for books on divinity, giver/receiver of the Carew murder weapon, professional and marital status and repressed personality);[23] Lanyon (as unmarried professional men and Jekyll's two oldest friends); Poole (in symmetrical configurations and echoed phrases); and Guest (in symmetrical configuration).

Other important equivalences can be seen between Lanyon and Jekyll (both bachelor doctors, old friends, living in similar houses, both over-curious, and echoing each other in Lanyon's rejection of Jekyll and Jekyll's rejection of Hyde), and between Enfield and Hyde (both are gentlemen libertines who walk at night with a cane, and both are associated with an older man). Since Utterson in some way represents the reader (they learn the same things in the same order and read the last two chapters together), Utterson's affinities with Hyde suggest that Hyde has affinities with the reader too.[24] Utterson can also be seen as different from the other characters: he is the detached and taciturn bachelor observer and investigator, sympathetic to the faults of others, combining austerity with underplayed Caledonian self-irony. Undemonstrative, he is still brave enough to face the worst.[25] Nevertheless, this is an interpretation suggested in the first eight chapters, and it loses force as equivalences between Utterson and the two main characters multiply.

The setting is London, a symbolic 'city in a nightmare' that could be seen as similar to any modern town, but also gains additional meaning by being a world city, Imperial capital and the centre both of economic and political life and of criminality, vice and poverty. The idea that RLS makes his 'London' similar to Edinburgh was first proposed by Clayton Hamilton in 1915 (*On the Trail of Stevenson* [Garden City, Doubleday], p. 61), who says 'the tale might almost appropriately be conceived as happening among the gloomy doorways and narrow *wynds* of the Scottish capital', and most famously so by G. K. Chesterton in a typical languid paradox: 'it seems to me that the story of Jekyll and Hyde, which is presumably presented as happening in London, is all the time very unmistakably happening in Edinburgh' (*Robert Louis Stevenson*, London, Hodder & Stoughton, 1927, p. 72).[26] The idea has been repeated by various critics since then and also lies behind the interpretative choice of Edinburgh-inspired external sets and lighting for Stephen Frears's film *Mary Reilly* (1996).

The urban texture evoked in Stevenson's text is not strongly reminiscent of Edinburgh, however: there are no winding alleyways, no tall tenement buildings, no steep steps or slopes, no idea that the respectable and non-respectable parts of town can be viewed one from the other. Instead, references to Regent's Park, Cavendish Square and Soho place the action convincingly in the English capital, and the described city of the text fits clearly into the tradition of Victorian representations of London, in particular in its emphasis on vastness and repetitiveness ('street after street', p. 9; 'labyrinths of lamplighted city', p. 15), on the fog (that had already been given a symbolic meaning by Dickens),[27] and the closeness of respectable and non-respectable or poor areas (in Victorian London often just round the corner from one another).[28]

This is not to say, of course, that *JH* cannot be profitably studied in the important context of Scottish literature and cultural history. Jekyll's 'dissecting theatre' immediately brings to mind the notorious Edinburgh body-snatching crimes of Burke and Hare and the collusive Dr Knox; and we have seen that Stevenson was influenced by the double Edinburgh life of Deacon Brodie. Fears of the close association of good and evil and of the splitting and division of the personality can be seen repeatedly in Scottish writings, and are certainly present in an important Scottish literary influence on *JH*, James Hogg's *The Private Memoirs and Confessions of a Justified Sinner* (1824).[29] We can also see echoes of Stevenson's own Scottish upbringing in Jekyll's fear of the evil side of the self (remembered by RLS as such a source of anxiety that as a child he had sometimes been afraid to go to sleep lest he die and go to hell; cf. 'Memoirs of Myself', *TUS*, vol. XXIX, pp. 54–5), and also in Jekyll's strange experience of living a double life (which probably has some affinities with Stevenson's memories of his student days when he divided his time between an ultra-respectable home and the low life of nights in the Old Town).

The modern city in general was a source of nineteenth-century anxieties (since it was anonymous, home of vice, uncontrollable, labyrinthine, fragmented, the scene of isolated incidents, alienating, socially divided). In particular, London in the 1880s was significantly associated with 'representations of sexual danger' in two series of newspaper narratives: the investigation of child prostitution in W. T. Stead's articles on 'The Maiden Tribute of Modern Babylon' in *The Pall Mall Gazette* (July 1885) and (after *JH*) the reporting on Jack the Ripper (1888) (see Walkowitz, *City of Dreadful Delight*, p. 81 ff., p. 191 ff.).

While *JH* influenced reporting on the Ripper murders (explicit parallels were made between the two, and London performances of Sullivan and Mansfield's dramatisation of *Jekyll and Hyde* were suspended because it was thought to be providing a model for the murderer: Walkowitz, *City of Dreadful Delight*, p. 206 ff.), it seems itself to have been influenced by the earlier 'Maiden Tribute' articles, copies of which had been sent to RLS by his friend Henley (*LETBM*, vol. V, p. 119). The equivocal 'trampling' of the little girl in the dark labyrinthine city streets by the 'gentleman' Hyde would recall Stead's disclosures of the obsessive deflowering of young virgins by the retired doctor whom he called 'the London Minotaur'. Although Hyde's crimes remain unspecified, the anonymous reviewer of *The Court and Society Review* (4 February 1886) alludes to these reports when he says 'Hyde, it is probable, was a kind of "Minotaur" '.

In the centre of this labyrinthine city of contrasts is the house of Jekyll, a space central to the action and also one of the elements of the text most open to symbolic interpretation.[30] In this sense, *JH* can be seen in the tradition of the Gothic novel which associates the labyrinthine building with the mind of its perverse or degenerate inhabitant. With the front associated with Jekyll and back associated with Hyde, we are encouraged to interpret these characters, too, in terms of 'public side' of the self and 'nonsocial, private side'.[31]

The reader expects that front and back, outside and inside of the house will have opposite positive and negative connotations, but these oppositions are deliberately confused: Jekyll's 'square of ancient, handsome houses' also has the negative connotations of decay and 'obscure enterprises' (p. 18); the hall of his house seems to have positive connotations of traditional Englishness but, on closer examination, displays signs of superficial display and parvenu imitation (the cabinets are 'costly' and the apparently traditional décor is only 'a pet fancy' of Jekyll's); Hyde's bystreet door is in a 'dingy neighbourhood', but the actual street is prosperous-looking – though on closer examination it also has aggressive and sexual connotations (suggested by the words 'drove', 'thrust', 'coquetry ... invitation ... florid charms', p. 8).

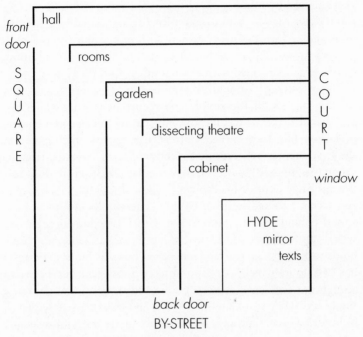

Figure 1. Jekyll's house

Just as Jekyll desires to hide a part of himself, so his house is arranged as a series of spaces around a mysterious centre (see Fig. 1).

This innermost part of his house (a raised space behind a 'blind forehead' and a red door; pp. 8, 29), clearly symbolises the most primitive, instinctive or hidden part of his mind, and contains Hyde (reminding us of the terrible secrets in the attics of *Jane Eyre* and *The Picture of Dorian Gray*).

The reader assumes, following the detective-story clues, that the cabinet will reveal an answer to the mysteries of the text, but the objects found there are enigmatic, self-reflexive, indeterminate: the dead body communicates nothing, but reminds us of mortality; the mirror merely reflects – other reflections, ourselves, itself (like our minds); and the series of envelopes in envelopes and texts in texts creates a new labyrinth.

The framing space surrounding this central area is significantly characterised by meaningless chaos: called 'laboratory', 'dissecting room', and 'theatre' – all spaces normally associated with divided or irregular forms – it is 'strewn with crates and littered with packing straw' and a 'lumber of crates and bottles'. In addition, below, is a cellar 'filled with crazy lumber' (pp. 29, 42, 48).

In an attempt to understand the text, readers have often focused on one of the simple and recurrent motifs, which not only help to give the text its fable-like nature but also invite interpretation. The door in the by-street, for example, highlighted in the first chapter and repeatedly referred to afterwards, is equivalent (or opposed) to others, in particular Jekyll's front door and the red baize door of his cabinet.[32] These doors (to which Utterson seems repeatedly to return) are generally locked and so the spaces behind gain an equivalence with the documents that are sealed in envelopes and locked away in safes. Doors are thresholds to knowledge and understanding but this house (and text) has two doors which 'correspond to two different interpretative sequences': the 'legal, correct, public and straight' that aims at a single and stable truth, and the 'secret and transgressive sequence of Hyde', a 'queer' process that produces a 'doubled knowledge', and is associated with the unrepresentable, with paradox, and with unstable meaning (Fabio Cleto, *Percorsi del dissenso*, Genova, ECIG, 2001, p. 203).

As we have seen, the back door could be associated with the anus, the part of the body that is denied, or more generally with anything that is hidden: the *OED* (1885), defines 'back-door' used adjectivally as 'unworthily secret, clandestine'.

The door is also associated with death: apart from the common phrase 'at death's door' (used in 'Across the Plains', *St. Ives*, and *LETBM*, vol. IV, p. 93), RLS repeatedly refers to death knocking at or opening the door: 'death is at the door' (*LETBM*, vol. II, p. 159), 'death will soon be rapping at the door' (*Ballantrae*, ch. 8), 'Death may be knocking at the door, like the Commander's statue' ('Aes Triplex'), 'Death, like a host, comes smiling to the door' (Roger C. Lewis, *The Collected Poems of Robert Louis Stevenson*, Edinburgh, Edinburgh University Press, 2003, p. 320). Stevenson refers to suicide as 'the open door' in 'Markheim' and *The Ebb-Tide*, and as 'the back stairs to liberty … Death's private door' in 'The Suicide Club'. Abandoned doors (like that in ch. 1 of *JH*) are particularly disturbing reminders of death: they have been seen as 'thresholds to nothing, the edge of an abyss' that nevertheless 'want to narrate their story'.[33]

Another repeated motif is that of the mirror, one of the uncanny objects found in the cabinet on 'the last night'.[34] Utterson and Poole look into its depths with 'involuntary horror', and see reflections of reflected firelight (rapidly changing, chaotic phenomena), and themselves.

The mirror naturally links up with the double, often given attributes of a mirror reflection, since the double is associated with the self-awareness that derives from self-contemplation. Jekyll refers to Hyde as 'that ugly idol in the glass' (p. 61), and Utterson is finally able to see Hyde's face when, after some hesitation, the latter suddenly turns to face him 'as if upon some sudden reflection' (p. 17). Indeed, in one sense, Jekyll's transformation (stimulated by thoughts that occur 'after I had reached years of reflection', p. 58) is achieved by looking in the mirror, which (in an ambiguous formulation) 'was brought here ... for the very purpose of these transformations' (p. 61). As in the mirror image, left and right are reversed, so Hyde's 'hand' slopes to the left ('backward', p. 64), while Jekyll's is 'differently sloped' (p. 33), so presumably to the right. Mirror reflections are also suggested by two characters arranged symmetrically (Utterson and Enfield side by side, ch. 1 and 7; two men on either side of a fire, pp. 21, 31, or divided by a bottle of wine, p. 31), staring at each other (pp. 17, 39 and 'giving look for look', p. 42), or echoing each other (see below p. 44).

Self-awareness is also produced by the act of writing, which makes the writer aware of the difference between the self directly experienced by the subject and the self as perceived through language by others. Jekyll could be seen as referring to the page of writing when he speaks of 'that [mirror] which stands beside me as I write' (p. 61). As a result of this kind of self-contemplation, the writer feels divided. In a letter to Auguste Rodin (December 1886) RLS admits to this feeling of doubleness: 'Je voudrais pouvoir vous écrire; mais ce n'est pas moi qui tient la plume – c'est l'autre, le bête, celui qui ne connaît pas le Français, celui qui n'aime pas mes amis comme je les aime ... celui que je renie' (*LETBM*, vol. V, pp. 333–4).[35] Here, it is the non-social writer, the stupid one (*le bête*, with an idea of 'beast') who is holding the pen. And in the same period (rather like Borges in 'Borges y yo') he says he is haunted by 'a Mr Stevenson the author ... who comes and goes and sometimes passes for me' (ibid., p. 106).

The mirror seems to confirm (by representing and framing) and at the same time question personal identity (by doubling). It also seems to reflect itself ('[It has] seen some strange things ... none stranger than itself', p. 49) and so becomes the symbol of textual narcissism, of the metafictional and the self-referential in this text 'that reflects itself, that alienates itself' (Cleto, *Percorsi del dissenso*, p. 201).

The centrality of 'the hand' as a motif has been pointed out by several critics.[36] The physical hand is a sign of identity, as is the writing it produces ('this is unquestionably the doctor's hand', p. 44), in part because of affinities with the personality of the writer ('an odd hand ... a very odd writer', p. 32). The hand is also symbolically connected with a socially dominant group because it guarantees possession, control, certainty ('I have him in my hand', p. 27; 'when I had walked with my father's hand', p. 68; 'to place in his hands the drawer', p. 52).

It is therefore disturbing that this conventional sign of identity and certainty should be associated with destabilised identity (with the detailed description of the hand placed next to the revelation of the first spontaneous change to Hyde, p. 64) and with falsification (Jekyll and Hyde forge each other's 'hand'). The fact that Jekyll does not sign his 'statement' shows that his 'hand' can no longer attest a single identity. (The *MS*, however, is signed by RLS – in a slightly different hand.)

The physical hand is also the most visible part of the body and so is a reminder of corporeality, sexuality and mortality, for which Hyde can be seen as a symbol. Sexual differences and bodily changes (including maturation and ageing) are also visible here and it is by seeing his changed hands that Jekyll knows that he has metamorphosed (pp. 64, 69). In particular, the hand is the part of the body most frequently viewed by a writer, the part of the body that writes (and in general 'makes'), and so is associated with the writer's feeling of doubleness that we have already mentioned.

The two hands are symmetrical and similar but culturally clearly distinguished, the left hand being traditionally associated in all cultures (and often in their religions) with the negative members of pairs of opposed terms like good v. bad, male v. female, familiar v. strange, alive v. dead, etc. Even Freud thought that in dreams 'left' stands for 'what is wrong, forbidden and sinful', such as 'masturbation carried out in childhood in the face of prohibition ... crime ... homosexuality, incest or perversion' (*Traumdeutung*, 1900, qu. Chris McManus, *Right Hand, Left Hand*, London, Weidenfeld & Nicholson, 2002, pp. 34–5). Unsurprisingly, Hyde is several times associated with the left hand: the door he uses is in a 'sinister' building 'on the left hand' of the street, and the chemicals for the transformation are 'on the left hand' of the cabinet (pp. 8, 51).

Jekyll in part recognises the merely conventional nature of these negative/positive moral oppositions (he initially finds Hyde's face 'natural' to him, feels 'happier in body' after the transformation, and recognises that 'This, too, was myself', pp. 60, 61), yet at the same time he also believes in the conventional evaluation since he wants to separate Hyde and his acts from himself, a view that in the end becomes dominant, leading to his desire to suppress his other self.

In a sociological approach, Stevenson's text has been seen as a protest against how the dominant professional classes define reality and defend their own social position. The class of professional gentlemen here form an exclusively male social network ('old friends, old mates both at school and college', p. 14) who control the membership of the group: Lanyon makes a move towards the professional exclusion of Jekyll by calling his medical work 'unscientific balderdash' (p. 14) and finally declaring 'I wish to see or hear no more of Doctor Jekyll' (p. 35). Utterson works to exclude Hyde, never calling him 'gentleman' and showing a distance from him in expressions such as 'that young man' (p. 19).

Jekyll himself is a representative of patriarchal society: a fifty-year-old member of an established profession with high academic honours and a large house and accustomed to imposing his view of reality (he scowls at Utterson and says 'I do not care to hear more ... This is a matter I thought we had agreed to drop', p. 22). Hyde can be seen as the son (he is smaller and younger than Jekyll, is in a way 'born' from him and has a 'son's indifference', p. 66); he rebels against the father by writing blasphemies in the pages of Jekyll's books (pp. 49, 72) and attacking other symbols of patriarchy, such as the white-haired Carew. The fact that he destroys the letters and portrait of Jekyll's own father (p. 72), and writes the blasphemies in Jekyll's hand suggests that he is also an expression of Jekyll's own hidden desires.

While Jekyll is the image of the self-defined non-deviant, Hyde possesses the physical and moral attributes of the excluded 'criminal type'. The fact that the two are the same person and that Jekyll is actively involved in the transgressions of Hyde, calls into question any kind of inherently different moral nature between upper and lower classes and, at the same time, suggests that the upper social class is necessarily constantly deceptive about itself.

The insufferable hypocrisy of middle-class claims to moral integrity is shown when Carew apparently makes a sexual proposition to a stranger in the street and reacts to the rejection with an accusatorial 'air of one very much surprised and a trifle hurt' (p. 25). Similar self-protective hypocrisy is adopted by Hyde when he assumes the tones of gentlemanly moderation after his undefined savage attack (p. 10). Even the apparently upright Utterson considers blackmail and frequently suppresses information in order to protect his fellow-gentleman Jekyll: he asks Enfield to keep quiet about the use of the back door by Hyde; he omits to tell the detective that the Carew murder weapon belonged to Jekyll; and he invites Guest to say nothing about Jekyll's forged note.

At the same time, Utterson wants to see, know, and understand Hyde, and so can be seen as similar to members of the late nineteenth-century scientific community and their desire to describe, categorise, and explain deviance of all kinds. Cesare Lombroso (in *L'uomo delinquente*, 1876; tr. *Criminal Man*, 1911) classified criminals and delinquents as distinctive biological and physiological types; Max Nordau extended Lombroso's model to the behaviour of Bohemian or 'decadent' artists (in *Entartung*, 1892; tr. *Degeneration*, 1895); Krafft-Ebbing's *Psychopathia Sexualis* (1886) classified pathological sexuality; and Francis Galton in *Inquiries into Human Faculty* (1883) tried to discover the essential facial form of criminality by means of superimposed 'composite photographs'. These describers, classifiers and controllers assumed a basic Darwin-derived model that criminals were similar to primitive humans, closer to their animal origins. Another widespread assumption was that such degeneration was greatest in large cities: in 1889 J. Milner Fothergill, for example, suggested that the East End cockney is 'a return to an earlier archaic type of man'.[37] Hyde (with his animal and primitive attributes) seems to express these late-Victorian anxieties of 'the aboriginal man within us' (RLS, 'Talk and Talkers', 1882, *TUS*, vol. XXIX, p. 83) and of atavistic degeneration back to a primitive level of existence among criminals and the urban poor.[38] Although early reviewers did not comment on this aspect of the text, it is implicit in the association of Hyde-equivalents (Mr Muldoon and Mr Crushall) with 'inferior races' in two early parodies (see p. xxv).

Stevenson's tale upsets this work of scientific definition of criminality, hysteria, and primitiveness by making the apparently neutral and detached scientist himself part of what is criminal, hysteric, and primitive. This is perhaps what shocks Lanyon to death – the impossibility of claiming to be uninvolved in what he defines and condemns.

A special aspect of conventional society for Stevenson was the literary market-place. His feelings about art and the market forces were not simple: on one hand he wanted to defend his art against social censorship (including internalised censorship, but also coming from his father, his friend Colvin, and his wife Fanny); on the other hand he was divided between pressure to write popular works (deriving in part from his own desire to be read and to be financially independent of his father, but also from an attraction to popular forms as a way of revitalising literature) and encouragement (from his own aspirations and from his artistic appreciators) to concentrate on works of high literature. In both complex situations he is like Jekyll suffering between the socially aware part of his personality on the one hand (aware of the requirements of society and the market and of the necessity of making a living, and also of the judgement of other artists) and, on the other hand, instinctive Hyde (wanting to express himself unrestrained, like the subconscious amoral 'Brownies' responsible for his artistic creations, according to 'A Chapter on Dreams'; though in other ways Hyde could represent the feared uneducated reader).

His resultant divided attitude towards the literary marketplace (alternately disdaining and enthusiastically embracing it)[39] is shown in his comparison of the writer to a (compassionately viewed) prostitute in a letter to Gosse of January 1886 (*LETBM*, vol. V, p. 171). These irresolvably opposed feelings are reflected in the eventual mutual dislike of Jekyll and Hyde, and in the text's proliferation of documents, including forged documents.[40] Hyde has been seen as an aspect of the writer, aware of ideas coming from an unconscious over which he has little control, and who feels that his writing self and normal self are different. His violent outbursts also have affinities with the rage of the artist at insincere writing; and indeed the most frightening appearances of Hyde seem to come after passages of excessive over-decorated prose: the descriptions of the by-street (ch. 1), the moonlit scene with Sir Danvers Carew (ch. 4), and the hand (ch. 10).

RLS is a writer always interested in technique and form: as Henry James remarked in 1888, he 'regards the literary form not simply as a code of signals, but as the keyboard of a piano and as so much plastic material' (qu. Maixner, p. 292). The following section looks at formal elements (punctuation, lexis, and discourse structure, as well as larger textual units) from the point of view of two basic techniques: repetition and heterogeneous juxtaposition. The first of these takes many forms: the echoing between conversational turns; the repetition, diffused through the text, of similar spatial configurations; the repetition of verbal formulas, passages of dense alliteration, densely patterned word repetitions; and the distribution through the text of references to mirrors, doubling, devils and death – these all give us the uncanny feeling of repeatedly returning to something familiar and already experienced.

Repeated words can create links between characters: we remember that Utterson lives in 'Gaunt Street' when we learn that Jekyll's dissecting theatre is 'gaunt' (pp. 17, 29); Hyde 'did not look the lawyer in the face' and speaks 'hoarsely' 'with a ... somewhat broken voice' (pp. 17–18), and later on Poole, too, 'had not once looked the lawyer in the face' and speaks 'hoarsely' and with a voice that is 'harsh and broken' (pp. 40–1).

As in fables, we find the repetition of verbal formulas used to underline a series of parallel situations. Examples of this are: 1. Jekyll's rejection of Hyde, 'I am done with him in this world ... I am quite done with him' (p. 30), and Lanyon's rejection of Jekyll, 'I am quite done with that person' (p. 35); 2. the similar formulations used by Enfield, Utterson, and onlookers in their attempts to describe Hyde (pp. 12, 18, 28); 3. Utterson's invocations not to speak: 'I wouldn't speak of this note' (p. 33), 'I would say nothing of this paper' (p. 50).

Sometimes the patterning of repetition attains poetic intensity, as in 'He, I say – I cannot say, I' (p. 70), where the attempt to distinguish between the first and last word is undermined by their formal equivalence (in the pattern of intonation and in the mirrored chiastic structure of the sentence); and where 'I cannot say, I' illustrates a division between the first 'I', which refers to the speaker, and the second, which is 'the word "I" ', or the 'I' represented in language. Another example of dense patterning is 'he resented the dislike with which he was himself regarded' (p. 72). Here, the context revitalises the prefix *re-* so that 'regarded' takes on the meaning 'looked at in return'. Meanwhile the active 'he' in the main clause is succeeded by the passive 'he' in the subordinate clause – a fascinating structure of syntactic mirroring, with 'he ... himself' the iconic representation of a doubled Jekyll.

Repetition betrays the obsessions of the characters, as when Utterson repeatedly speaks or thinks about Hyde's name and face (pp. 11–12, 15–16), or reveals their insecurity, as in Jekyll's nervous bluster during his confrontation with Utterson (pp. 21–2).

We also find a curious echoing across dialogue turns that seems to underline the equivalence of doubled characters:

'Did you ever come across a protégé of his – one Hyde?'
'Hyde?' repeated Lanyon. (p. 15)

'We have common friends,' said Mr. Utterson.
'Common friends?' echoed Mr. Hyde (p. 17)

'It seems much changed,' replied the lawyer, very pale, but giving
look for look.
'Changed? Well, yes, ...' (pp. 42–3)

'I've seen him!'
'Seen him?' repeated Mr. Utterson. (p. 44)

'This does not look like use', observed the lawyer.
'Use!' echoed Poole. (p. 48)

'This glass have seen some strange things, sir' whispered Poole.
'And surely none stranger than itself,' echoed the lawyer in the
same tones. (p. 49)

Similar echoes across speech-turns are also found without the
explicit verb ('he repeated' etc.) in 'odd hand ... odd writer' (p.
32), and 'rather quaint ... rather quaint' (p. 33).

The repeated sounds of alliteration characterise passages of
heightened description. Several of these are marked by Nabokov
in his copy of *JH* in the New York Public Library. They include:
'to drive away these random visitors or to repair their ravages' (p.
8); 'labyrinths of lamplighted city' (p. 15); 'the first fog ... the cab
crawled from street to street' (p. 26); the many s-sounds in
Jekyll's description of his first transformation, 'The most racking
pangs succeeded ... swiftly to subside ... something strange in my
sensations ... conscious of a heady recklessness, a current of
disordered sensual images running like a mill race in my fancy, a
solution ... sold a slave ... lost in stature' (pp. 60–1); 'an unknown
but not an innocent freedom of the soul' (p. 60, with the marginal
comment 'I like this little "n" alliteration'); 'the elderly and
discontented doctor ... the liberty, the comparative youth, the
light step, leaping pulses and secret pleasures' (p. 66, to which
Nabokov adds the note 'd=duty pl=pleasure'); 'the common
quarry of mankind, hunted, houseless' (p. 69).

Assonance is also used in significant patterns of repetition, as
when, at the meeting of Utterson and Hyde 'the pair stared at
each other pretty fixedly for a few seconds' (p. 17); here the two
stressed and juxtaposed words with the same vowel give us a
'picture' of the two characters standing face to face.

xliv

In addition to repeated words and sounds, the text is also notable for its patterned repetition of narrative situations, what Jean-Pierre Naugrette calls 'echoes' or 'parallels',[41] and what Stephen Arata calls 'structural rhyming' (*Fictions of Loss*, 1996, p. 41). Tension is created (as Naugrette observes) by associating the second example of these repeated situations with greater complexity or anxiety. The principal repeated acts and 'configurations' of characters and spaces are the following (arranged in the order in the text of the first member of each group):

1. Two men at a door: Utterson and Enfield, passing through a side street, stop opposite Jekyll's back door, (a) p. 8, (b) p. 38; a situation which is also echoed when Utterson and Poole stand at the door of the cabinet, p. 42 ff.

2. Women and children in sordid streets: (a) Jekyll's back street, with its shops 'like rows of smiling saleswomen' and the door where 'tramps slouched' and 'children kept shop', p. 8; (b) Hyde's street, with its prostitutes and 'children huddled in the doorways', p. 26.

3. Violent meeting on the streets at night: (a) two figures approach on the streets, Hyde tramples 'over' a little girl, observed by young *flâneur*, who then recounts the story, p. 9; (b) two figures approach on the streets, Hyde attacks and tramples 'under foot' an elderly *flâneur*, observed by a young woman, who then recounts the story, p. 24–5.

4. Investigative visits to a bank: (a) Enfield goes with Hyde and others to Jekyll's bank, p. 10; (b) Utterson goes with Newcomen to Hyde's bank, p. 27.

5. Pious works near the fire: (a) Utterson with his 'volume of some dry divinity on his reading desk', p. 13; (b) Jekyll's 'pious work' on his tea table, p. 49.

6. Characters near a fire: Utterson (pp. 13, 18–19), Utterson and Jekyll (p. 21), Utterson and Guest (p. 31), Utterson and Poole (p. 40), Jekyll (pp. 29, 71), Hyde (p. 70), Jekyll's servants (pp. 41, 50); there is also a cold hearth (p. 27) and a fire with an empty chair (p. 47, 49).

7. Utterson visits Lanyon to ask for advice about Jekyll, (a) p. 14, (b) p. 35.

8. The drinking of wine: by Lanyon (p. 14), Jekyll's old friends (p. 21), Utterson and Guest (p. 31), Utterson and Poole (p. 40).

9. Utterson talks confidentially to Jekyll: (a) in the front part of Jekyll's house, pp. 21–3, (b) in the cabinet, pp. 29–31.

10. Sleeping figures: (a) Utterson, unable to sleep in his 'curtained room' (p. 15) dreams of (b) Jekyll, in a curtained bed, woken by a mysterious figure (p. 15).

11. Utterson calls: (a) at Jekyll's house, but the male servant says that he is out, pp. 18–9; (b) at Hyde's house, but the female servant says that he is out, p. 27.

12. Horrifying scenes and windows: (a) a horrifying scene involving two men in the street is observed from above by a female witness at a window, pp. 24–5; (b) a horrifying scene at a window is observed from below by two male witnesses in the street, p. 39.

13. Forced entrances to Jekyll's cabinet: (a) p. 47, (b) p. 53.

14. Transformation scenes: (a) Hyde transforms into Jekyll (third-person narrative), ch. 9; (b) Jekyll transforms into Hyde (first-person narrative), ch. 10.

15. A transformed Jekyll crosses the courtyard: (a) after the first voluntary transformation, Hyde crosses the courtyard at night from the cabinet to his bedroom to look at himself in the mirror, p. 61; (b) after the first involuntary transformation, Hyde looks at himself in the mirror and then crosses the courtyard during the day from his bedroom to the cabinet, pp. 64–5.

Certain of these situations are combined in a kind of spiral structure:[42] Utterson and Enfield stand in front of the door in ch. 1 and 7; Utterson visits Lanyon in ch. 2 and 6; Utterson talks confidentially to Jekyll in ch. 3 and 5; leaving ch. 4 as a central point in this particular structure. In addition, where single episodes start and end in the same way (as ch. 2, with Utterson and the will, or Utterson's visit to Jekyll's house in ch. 8, which starts and ends with the servants huddled round the fire), the reader gets an idea of obsessive return or lack of progress. Even Utterson's dream has a circularity, beginning and ending with evocations of a wide expanse of lamplighted city and trampled girl(s).

There are several examples of the special doubling of *mise-en-abyme*, the mirroring of the text itself and of its composition or reading: Jekyll's 'version book' containing repetitions of the word 'double' (p. 53); the various embedded texts and narratives (accompanied by references to 'story', 'narrative', and 'incident' and 'case'); the mirror (with its 'hundred repetitions', and representation of those who look into it); Jekyll writing his 'statement' in parallel with the author writing the last chapter, with the same chapter being read by both Utterson and the reader; Utterson's dream of a sleeping Jekyll (which recalls Stevenson's own dream of scenes from *JH*).

Another aspect of the text's own strangeness apart from these many kinds of repetition, is the way that the linear textual sequence is fragmented. The chapters seem potentially separate documents (since they have no chapter numbers and contain words like 'Story' and 'Incident' which could be self-contained narratives); one genre modulates to another; literary and colloquial language are juxtaposed; dialogues have non-coherent turns; strange words and unusual meanings make short phrases stand out from the whole;[43] pronoun reference to Jekyll and Hyde in the last chapter ('I', 'he', 'it') shifts even within the same sentence; and characters are presented with contradictory attributes. The resultant divided-up text is particularly appropriate for *JH* and its central character, not only simply divided but fragmented (as Jekyll predicts, 'man will be ultimately known for a mere polity of multifarious, incongruous and independent denizens', p. 59).

One simple way that fragmentation is achieved is by the frequent use of the semicolon.[44] RLS typically places one before a conjunction, perhaps to render problematic the link between the two parts of the sentence. Early examples of this are: 'No doubt the feat was easy to Mr. Utterson; for he was undemonstrative at the best' (p. 7), 'And then there is a chimney which is generally smoking; so somebody must live there' (p. 11). The conjunction following the semicolon is frequently 'and': there are no fewer than 203 examples of this in the text. Nabokov seems to have noticed this, as in his teaching copy of the book he rings both semicolon and following 'and' in three examples in the first two chapters.[45]

Barry Menikoff observes that Stevenson's use of the semicolon creates uncertainty and ambiguity (*Robert Louis Stevenson and 'The Beach of Falesá'*, Edinburgh University Press, 1984, pp. 43–6). The semicolon juxtaposes and accumulates but does not promise a causal link (especially true when followed by 'and'), and it can also 'set up contrast within a sentence' (p. 44). Michele Mari, in a general study on punctuation (Alessandro Baricco et al., *Punteggiatura*, vol. 1, *I Segni*, Milan, BUR, 2001), refers to 'the ambiguous semicolon' which neither links like the comma nor divides like the full stop, but helps to give 'an idea of accumulation and unanalysed chaos'; indeed 'the semicolon has an antisemantic function, because it devalues the importance and independence of the syntactic unit that precedes and that which follows (where, in contrast, the stop "makes" the sentence like the frame makes the picture)' (Michele Mari, 'L'ambiguo punto-comma', pp. 85–92). According to Ernesto Franco in the same work ('Tutto il punto e tutta la virgola', pp. 93–4) 'what is juxtaposed' by the semicolon 'is both separated and united'; the semicolon requires the reader to interpret because 'the interpretation of the semicolon is not simple but open', it is 'a mark that raises doubts'.

Another kind of fragmentation is produced by different parts of the text seeming to belong to different genres: *JH* has been seen as similar to the Gothic novel, the detective story, the realistic novel, the fantastic tale, science fiction, horror story, doubles narrative, weird tale, fable, decadent nouvelle and sensational tale.[46] In a similar way, features of 'high' and 'low' literature are mixed together: 'shilling shocker' book format and sensational content (shocking urban crimes and guilty secrets of respectable middle-class people) combine with poetic formulation, foregrounded artfulness and use of archaic and literary language. This piling up of generic signals calls into question the unitary and consistent text (and the unitary and consistent author that lies behind it), just as Jekyll and his failed attempt at the simplification of personality call into question the single and consistent individual.

Another strange aspect of the language is the mixture of formal language with colloquial clichés. It is no surprise to find clichés and slang characterising the speech of man-about-town Enfield (see Explanatory Notes to p. 9) but we are surprised (at the beginning of ch. 2) to read that Jekyll's will 'provided … that the said Edward Hyde should step into the said Henry Jekyll's shoes without further delay and free from any burthen or obligation'. Here the free indirect reading of the will and its formal legal language is interrupted by the substitution of a colloquial 'step into someone's shoes', though we cannot tell if this comes from an indignant Utterson or a cool narrator who, like Enfield, has a taste for slang.

In some ways, reading *JH* is like reading a text in a familiar foreign language: the meaning is clear, but one is constantly aware of things being said in a slightly unfamiliar way. Stevenson encourages such a conscious reading experience through a foregrounded style in which familiar words are given a new meaning from their context of use, and which is characterised by occasional adapted and literally translated phrases, and archaic or Scots words. As a result *JH* contains many 'curious' expressions[47] where the reader is actively involved in producing meaning, some of which are deliberately lacking in final meaning. In such cases the language creates a patch of opacity (like a *tache* of mere paint in a painting). An early example of this technique (others are glossed in the Explanatory Notes) is at the very centre of Enfield's story in ch. 1: 'the man trampled calmly over the child's body and left her screaming on the ground' (p. 9). The strangeness of the language is suggested by the fact that an Internet search for 'trampled over' produced 3650 hits, with (apart from instances of this text) no other example used literally of a physical act with a single agent and a single person affected; all the thousands of others involved a crowd of people or animals as the subject and something like a flower-bed or a fallen body or bodies as the object, or were used metaphorically to mean 'humiliatingly defeat (another team)' or 'violate (the constitution etc.)'. Stevenson's expression suggests an unimaginable combination of 'repeatedly trod heavily over the whole surface and flattened' (which fits in with the crowd's reaction and with the verb 'trample' but not with the unhurt state of the girl afterwards nor with the physical possibilities of a single person and a small body) and 'stepped calmly over and went on his way' (which is physically possible, fits in with the idea of a simple line of movement for Hyde and the unhurt state of the girl but not with the reaction of the crowd nor with the verb 'trample'). The expression makes the reader 'curious' and creates an uncomfortable voyeuristic need to imagine the violent and erotically charged scene in order to understand it. And in the end it remains opaque.

The use of words with potentially transgressive meanings is found especially in the passages of campishly 'excessive' description, e.g. the by-street (ch. 1), Sir Danvers (ch. 4), the moon on her back (ch. 8), and the hand (ch. 10) (see, for example, the Explanatory Note on the by-street description, p. 8). Here, the reader feels responsible for importing an innovative equivocal *double entendre* meaning into the text, so becomes an accomplice in the destabilisation of the values and meanings of society.

Another odd feature is the presence of certain subtly aggressive exchanges, where the dialogue becomes non-coherent and opaque, underlining the impossibility of communication or the way conversation is filled with meaningless formulas. The two dialogues between Utterson and Enfield (ch. 1 and ch. 7) are notably dysfunctional in this respect.[48]

Another component of the text's linguistic oddness is the use of formulas that seem familiar but turn out to be unusual. Examples are: 'it was a nut to crack' (p. 8) where the normal idiom is 'it was a tough/hard nut to crack'; 'thrust forward its gable on the street' (taken from the French, see Explanatory Notes for p. 8), with the verb changed from 'have' to 'thrust forward'; 'as empty as a church' (p. 9) where the normal idiom would be 'as quiet as a church'; 'I would … have sacrificed … my left hand to [help you]' (p. 51, see Explanatory Notes), where the normal 'right hand' is changed to 'left'. In the phrase 'when I had walked with my father's hand' (see Explanatory Notes for p. 68) we have a phrase that evokes several formulaic expressions while remaining elusively different from them.

In other cases a phrase maintains its familiar form but it is its use that is strange: 'some place at the end of the world' (p. 9)

1

suggests a place reached after a journey through empty territory, not (as here) merely in a distant part of town; and 'I ... took to my heels' (p. 9) usually means 'I started running in order to escape' but here means 'in order to pursue'.

The sense of heterogeneous mixture is also found in the way Stevenson typically presents his characters as possessing opposed positive and negative elements which the reader will try in vain to reduce to a coherent synthesis. The first example is the description of Utterson: 'lean, long, dusty, dreary *and yet* somehow lovable' (p. 7, italics added). Others are the sequences joined by 'but' or 'yet' in the descriptions of Lanyon ('but it reposed on genuine feeling', p. 14), Carew ('yet with something high too', p. 24), Jekyll ('but every mark of capacity and kindness', p. 21) and Hyde's housekeeper ('but her manners were excellent', p. 27).[49] Both repetition and heterogeneous juxtaposition help to make interpretation difficult and give the text a fragmented nature.

Derivative works (which, as we have seen, started to appear immediately after publication) also explore the text's ambiguities and carry on the work of interpretation that the text itself encourages.[50] Indeed, Stevenson's *Strange Case* can be classed as a 'modern myth', a narrative repeatedly used by adapters and retellers to explain worrying or puzzling aspects of the human condition: non-unitary personality, humankind's animal nature, the problem of both social restraint and lack of restraint, the desire to indulge in instinctive impulses contrasted with fears of the breakdown of order, the threat of science, and the desire to escape from the socially defined personality. As Charles King says, 'What is remarkable about Stevenson's central plot premise is that it allows any number of variant themes to be constructed on its basic framework' (qu. in Katherine Linehan (ed.), *Strange Case of Dr. Jekyll and Mr. Hyde*, New York, Norton, 2003, p. 161). Most of the various derivative versions, however, simplify the circular and repetitive elements of the original text and do not maintain its linguistic strangeness, as well as lacking the subjective and evasive point of view of Jekyll found in the last chapter.

The names in the title have themselves become part of the language in the expression 'a Jekyll and Hyde', used to mean 'a person with two very different sides to their personality, one good and the other evil' (*Cambridge Advanced Learner's Dictionary*). The difficulty of resisting this simplification (which, contrary to the text, presents Jekyll as 'good') is shown by the fact that even RLS seems to make it in his correspondence: sending a copy of *JH* to Katherine de Mattos on 1 January 1886, he says in the accompanying letter that 'it is sent to you by one that loves you – Jekyll and not Hyde', and in April of the same year he calls his ailing father 'Hyde' or 'Jekyll' according to whether he is unreasonably bad tempered or not, and signs off 'Yours – (I think) Hyde – (I wish) Jekyll (*LETBM*, vol. V, pp. 168, 245–6).

Adaptations for performance on stage, screen, radio and television have been especially numerous.[51] The first serious stage version was the most successful: that by Thomas Russell Sullivan and Richard Mansfield, first performed in Boston on 9 May 1887 with actor-manager Mansfield in the title roles. Not only did Mansfield continue playing the role for twenty years, until just before his death in 1907, but the version with its added female parts and simplified melodramatic meaning (clearly distinguishing good and evil) was to influence many later stage and film adaptations. The circular plot is made linear, and the first transformation scene is placed near the beginning; Jekyll's self-deception and hypocrisy disappear and he becomes a good man involved in charitable work and desiring to benefit humanity through his scientific research; drawing-room scenes are added and Jekyll is given a fiancée whose father delays their marriage and who is killed by Hyde. Other significant stage versions are those by Daniel Bandman (1888), whose Hyde characterisation may have influenced later film interpretations,[52] and David Edgar (1991), which has two actors for the title roles and a Scottish Hyde.

Early film versions are clearly influenced by Sullivan's melodramatic stage version in their domestic sets, transformation scenes, and the addition of a fiancée placed between a noble Jekyll and a disapproving patriarch. They also usually add scenes in music halls and other elements reminiscent of the London of Jack the Ripper. A new convention found in many films is the dead Hyde transforming into Jekyll 'finally at peace'. In addition a dance-hall girl is usually added, whom Jekyll finds attractive, and who is later picked up by Hyde (clearly acting out Jekyll's desires) and is eventually killed by him. This new story element is first found in a film of 1912 and is adopted in three classic Hollywood versions, directed by J. S. Robertson (1920, with John Barrymore in the title roles), Rouben Mamoulian (1931, with Frederick March), and Victor Fleming (1941, with Spencer Tracy). Mamoulian's technically innovative version is ingenious in finding visual correspondences for the verbal repetitions, equivalences and oppositions of the original. It also tries to represent mental states by means of the subjective camera and rapid montage. Freudian ideas are clearly present (even more so in the 1941 remake), and new anxiety about science can be seen in the central place give to Jekyll's laboratory and to his long work of experimentation.

Other interesting film versions include those directed by Mario Soffici (*El hombre y la bestia*, 1950, with Soffici in the lead roles), Jean Renoir (*Le Testament du Docteur Cordelier*, 1959, with Jean-Louis Barrault), Terence Fisher (*The Two Faces of Dr Jekyll*, 1960, with Paul Massie), Jerry Lewis (*The Nutty Professor*, 1963), Charles Jarrot (1963, with Jack Palance), Stephen Weeks (*I, Monster*, 1973, with Christopher Lee), Roy Ward Baker, *Dr Jekyll and Sister Hyde*, 1971 with Ralph Bates and Martine Beswick), Alastair Reid (1980, with David Hemmings), David Wickes (1990, with Michael Caine), and Stephen Frears (*Mary Reilly*, 1996, with John Malkovich).

The musical-spectacle *Jekyll and Hyde* by Frank Wildhorn, with book and lyrics by Leslie Bricusse, (first performed in 1990) basically follows the Hollywood film versions (noble Jekyll, fiancée and dance-hall girl, etc.), adding a crowd chorus and (in the solo songs) a focus on pathos and individual feelings that is in strong contrast with other elements of Gothic excess.

There is no space here to discuss the wider influence of *Jekyll and Hyde* over later works in the areas of psychological fantasy (Wilde's *The Picture of Dorian Gray*, for example), science fiction (Wells's *The Island of Dr Moreau*), detective fiction (Doyle's Sherlock Holmes Stories, which share the London location and also highlight strange phenomena), horror fiction (Stoker's *Dracula*), and others.[53] Limiting ourselves to clearly derivative prose-narrative versions, these include the short story 'Doctor Jekyll' by Susan Sontag (in *I, Etcetera*, 1978, originally published in the *Partisan Review*, 1974), a present-tense, present-day, post-modern New York narrative with all the character names from *JH* and constant allusions to Stevenson's story. Two longer works are by Emma Tennant, *Two Women of London. The Strange Case of Ms Jekyll and Mrs Hyde* (1989), a modernised feminist version; and Valerie Martin, *Mary Reilly* (1990), a retelling of Stevenson's story from the point of view of a female servant, with descriptions of scenes that take place 'off-stage' in the original. Hyde is given a voice in the short monologue 'Habla Mr Hyde' by Fernando Savater (in *Criaturas de aire*, 1979), and in Jean-Pierre Naugrette's *Le crime étrange de Mr Hyde* (1998), a postmodern fantastic tale and detective-story version with many literary allusions, the first nine chapters a first-person narrative by Hyde (lacking in commas, colons or semicolons), the last a third-person narrative (so reversing Stevenson's structure).

JH was also an early choice for the US 'Classic Comics' series (called 'Classics Illustrated' from 1947): the 1943 version (number 13 in the series) derives from the films of 1931 and 1941 (with drawing-room scenes, a fiancée for Jekyll, and a final trans-formation after death from Hyde to Jekyll). It is also notable as the very first example of the American 'horror comic', the cover showing a huge monstrous Hyde and a fleeing crowd. The 1953 version follows Stevenson's text more closely (though the narrative is still linear), while the 1990 version in a revived series is notable for John K. Snyder's artwork evocative of German Expressionist cinema.[54]

The most interesting graphic-novel version is by Lorenzo Mattotti (art) and Jerry Kramsky (script), *Dr Jekyll et Mr Hyde* (Paris, Casterman, 2002) (then published in other countries). The version by Guido Crepax, (*Dr. Jekyll e Mr. Hyde*, Milano, Olympia Press, 1987) follows Stevenson's narrative sequence quite closely, adding several pages devoted to Hyde's sadistic sexual excesses. Of illustrated editions, the most interesting are perhaps those by S. G. Hulme Beaman (1930), Mervyn Peake (1948), and the limited edition with many interesting etchings by Raoul Livain (1947).

There also exists a number of retellings for younger readers and dramatised versions for school performance: undoubtedly this 'horror classic' appeals to adolescents on account of the metamorphosis (which could be mapped on to changes at puberty or troubling sexual or aggressive arousal), and for its themes of the uncertainty of identity and meaning, and for its dramatisation of the struggle between instinctive urges and social regulation.

The work has also been widely translated, and Appendix B.2 traces this cultural diffusion through the first fifty years after publication.

The last word of the text is 'end' – a final self-referential detail and a transparently deceptive declaration of closure to a narrative that has continued to stimulate unending interpretation and countless derivative works. The text seems to lack any simple and explicit symbolic meaning while at the same time encouraging interpretation: in this, it resembles texts of uncertain meaning by the Symbolists and by such authors as Hawthorne, Hogg, E. T. A. Hoffmann, and Franz Kafka. In the visual arts, we could see an affinity with other works that we feel 'must have a meaning' yet remain elusively enigmatic, like Botticelli's 'Primavera', Giorgione's 'Tempest', or Parmiganino's 'Self-Portrait in a Convex Mirror'. Another comparison might be with the works of Escher, some of which give a similar feeling of unease with their combination of the perturbing and the paradoxical, the contradictory and the irresolvable.

JH is built around the puzzle-concept that Jekyll and Hyde are both different and the same, accompanied by a kaleidoscope of potentially symbolic elements and patternings, unstable oppositions, repetitions and symmetries which the reader may rearrange infinitely. Like the house in Borges's 'Death and the Compass' (1943) the text abounds in 'superfluous symmetries and in maniacal repetitions' suggesting the idea that the world itself is a labyrinth from which it is impossible to flee. There is no definitive configuration of these elements, no promise of final meaning – instead, as we read this text, we are given the experience (unsettling yet also fascinating) of trying to understand a series of problematic aspects of the human condition.

Notes

1 See Textual Notes, p. 187, note 14.
2 *New York Herald*, 8 September 1887. The cabinet is now in The Writers' Museum, Edinburgh. See also Explanatory Notes for p. 29.
3 For example, Th. Galacier ('La conscience du moi', *Revue philosophique* 4 (1877), pp. 72–80) narrates how the author tried to work out why he was talking to himself. The personal anecdote continues to be a characteristic of psychological writings: Freud (at the beginning of 'Das Unheimliche', 1919) tells a personal story about trying to understand an uncanny repeated experience.
4 See Textual Notes p. 188, note 16.
5 'The powder – which I thought might be changed – he couldn't eliminate because he saw it so plainly in his dream' (Fanny Stevenson [May 1900], answer to Graham Balfour's 'list of questions' (Graham Balfour, *Balfour Biography Notebook*: NLS MS 9895, f. 157r; qu. Christopher Frayling, *Nightmare. The Birth of Horror*, BBC Books, p. 148).
6 For a further discussion of the significant changes during composition, see Veeder (pp. 7–11) and Katherine Linehan (ed.), *Strange Case of Dr. Jekyll and Mr. Hyde*, New York, Norton, 2003, pp. 64–5.
7 Contemporary medical opinion held that masturbation was harmful and led on to homosexuality (cf. Jeffrey Weeks, *Coming Out*, London, Quartet, 1977, p. 23). The final text still contains enough hints of masturbation (e.g. in the erotic contemplation of the hand, p. 64) for a contemporary to see Hyde as a typical onanist (see Mighall [ed.], *The Strange Case of Dr Jekyll and Mr Hyde*, p. 171, note 15).
8 Princeton University Library *C0101* (Scribner's Archives), Box 143, Folder 7: '6 letters and 2 telegrams … on *Dr Jekyll and Mr Hyde*, 1885–1887'.
9 See p. 190, note 43 and note 44.
10 Quotations from reviews are taken from Stevenson's Mother's Scrapbook 2 (1881–86), pp. 94–100 (Stevenson House, Monterey), with nine reviews from January and February 1886, and Scrapbook 3 (1886–87), pp. 1–19 (Stevenson Cottage, Saranac Lake), with thirty-seven reviews mainly from January and February 1886 and a few from March and April. RLS's mother annotates the pasted-in clippings with the title of the newspaper and usually an indication of the date (often just the month).
11 Andrew Lang, 'Recollections of Robert Louis Stevenson', *Adventures among Books*, Longman, 1905, p. 46, qu. R. C. Terry, *Robert Louis Stevenson. Interviews and Recollections*, Iowa U. P., 1996; pp. 57–61; also Andrew Lang, 'The Supernatural in Fiction', *Adventures among Books*, p. 278; and Andrew Lang, 'Introduction', Swanston Edition of Stevenson's *Works*, London, 1911, vol. 1, p. xxiv.
12 The 'double-personality' interpretation soon became common: in 1893 a New Zealand journalist tried repeatedly to make RLS discuss

the connection between *JH* and recent double-personality cases (*The Argus*, April 11). In the same period, the American journalist Robert Bridges wrote a dialogue between Jekyll and Hyde ('Jekyll Meets Hyde'), first published in *Life* and then collected in *Overheard in Arcady*, 1894, in which Jekyll says that his original 'guess' has now been 'scientifically demonstrated by the hypnotic investigations of Charcot, Binet, and the rest' (Harry M. Geduld, *The Definitive Dr Jekyll and Mr Hyde Companion*, New York, Garland, 1983, pp. 155–6).

13 *The Century Magazine* (April 1888), pp. 877–8; Linehan (ed.), *Strange Case of Dr. Jekyll and Mr. Hyde*, pp. 101–2.

14 A political satire by Grossmith based on *JH* is announced for Toole's Theatre in *The Daily News*, 16 May 1886, p. 3; Geduld (*The Definitive Dr Jekyll and Mr Hyde Companion*, p. 215) lists an anonymous *Strange Case of a Hyde and Seekyll* at Toole's Theatre on 18 May, but *The Daily News* of that day and the day after lists another play there; perhaps it was a curtain-raiser.

15 The two opposed brothers, Henry and James, in *The Master of Ballantrae* have the same opposed initials and it is possible that Stevenson was in part joking at the expense of his friend Henry James, since we know he liked to play on the opposition of 'familiar first name' and 'public surname' (cf. anecdotes in J. A. Hammerton, *Stevensoniana*, Edinburgh, Grant, 1910, pp. 80–1). In *Weir of Hermiston* (ch. 2), Frank Innes says of Archie Weir, 'I know *Weir*; but I never met *Archie*'.

16 A troubling substitution of 'y' for 'i' is also found in a letter of March 1885 when RLS writes that he is now 'a beastly householder' and so feels threatened by the socialist leader Hyndman: 'his step is beHynd me as I go' (*LETBM*, vol. V, p. 85).

17 The film versions of 1931 and 1941 show the influence of Freudian theories. For a brief summary of psychoanalytical studies of *JH*, see Martin A. Danahay, 'Introduction', in R. L. Stevenson (ed. Danahay), *The Strange Case of Dr Jekyll and Mr Hyde*, Broadview, 1999, p. 22. Also Jean-Pierre Naugrette, *L'aventure et son double*, Paris, Presses de l'Ecole Normale Supérieure, 1987, pp. 57–73.

18 For critical interpretations of Hyde, see Stephen Heath, 'Psychopathia Sexualis: Stevenson's Strange Case', *Critical Quarterly* 28, 1986, pp. 93–108 (Hyde and perverse male sexuality); Janice Doane and Devon Hodges, 'Demonic Disturbances of Sexual Identity: The Strange Case of Dr Jekyll and Mr/s Hyde', *Novel* 23(1), 1989, pp. 6–74 (Hyde and the contemporary blurring of gender categories); Judith Halberstein, *Skin Shows: Gothic Horror and the Technology of Monsters*, Duke University Press, 1995 (Hyde as product of medicalisation of sex); and M. K. Williams, ' "Down with the Door, Poole": Designating Deviance in Stevenson's *Strange Case of Dr Jekyll and Mr Hyde*', *English Literature in Transition* 39(4), 1996, pp. 413 and 426 note 6 (Hyde as troubling free-floating sign). For

Hyde and homosexuality, see note 22 below; for Hyde and the literary market-place, see note 40; for Hyde and addiction, see note 20; for Hyde and atavism, see note 38.

19 This was a conventional metaphor for internal temptation: Samuel Pepys (with a Puritan background) refers to 'my devil that is within me', *Diary*, 12 March 1669.

20 For *JH* and addiction, see Daniel L. Wright, ' "The Prisonhouse of My Disposition": A Study of the Psychology of Addiction in *Dr. Jekyll and Mr. Hyde*', *Studies in the Novel* 26(3), 1994, pp. 254–67.

21 On a more psychological level, Jekyll claims that Hyde views him as a 'cavern' of refuge, talks of 'the agonised womb of consciousness', describes the pains of the first transformation in a way that recalls childbirth, and in the end constantly feels Hyde 'struggle to be born' (pp. 66, 60, 72). The psychoanalytic aspects of this situation are examined by Naugrette, *Robert Louis Stevenson: L'aventure et son double*, pp. 63–6.

22 'A gentleman of the back door', is a 'practiser of an unmentionable vice', Albert Barrère & Charles G. Leland, *A Dictionary of Slang, Jargon and Cant*, London, 1889. Interpretations of *JH* in terms of homosexuality include: Wayne Koestenbaum 'The Shadow on the Bed: Dr Jekyll, Mr Hyde, and the Labouchère Amendment', *Critical Matrix* 1 (Spring 1988, Spec. Iss.), pp. 31–55; William Veeder, 'Children of the Night: Stevenson and Patriarchy', in *VH*, pp. 143–8; Showalter, *Sexual Anarchy*, 1990, pp. 106–9; Robert Mighall, 'Introduction', in R. L. Stevenson (ed. Mighall), *The Strange Case of Dr Jekyll and Mr Hyde and Other Tales of Terror*, Penguin, 2002, pp. xviii–xix.

23 In the graphic-novel version by Mattotti and Kramsky (see below, p. liv), Utterson metamorphoses into Jekyll before beginning the 'full statement' sequence.

24 For more on this patterning of equivalent characters, see Dury, pp. 51–3.

25 For more on divided views on Utterson, see Dury, p. 62.

26 In a review of Chesterton, T. S. Eliot comments ironically on this idea: 'How illuminating his observation that though his story is nominally set in London, it is really taking place in Edinburgh!' (1927, qu. Christopher Ricks, 'A Note on "The Hollow Men" and Stevenson's *The Ebb-Tide*', *Essays in Criticism* 51(1), p. 9). Chesterton does not say anything further about Edinburgh topography, however, justifying his paradox with references to the Scottishness of the characters and the community of respectable professional men, and to typical Calvinistic moral preoccupations. Even Hamilton discusses the Scottish-like characters and cultural climate as well as the urban texture, and goes on to say that the story 'might have been set, without the slightest loss of emphasis, in any other of the major cities of the world' (p. 62).

27 Gordon Hirsch ('*Frankenstein*, Detective Fiction, and *Jekyll and Hyde*, in *VH*, p. 244, note 13) notes several echoes between the

description of the Soho fog in *JH* and Dickens's description of the London fog in the first three paragraphs of *Bleak House*.

28 Friedrich Engels says 'In the immense tangle of [London] streets, there are hundreds and thousands of alleys and courts lined with houses too bad for anyone to live in, who can still spend anything whatsoever upon a dwelling fit for human beings. Close to the splendid houses of the rich such a lurking-place of the bitterest poverty may often be found' (Friedrich Engels, *Die Lage der arbeitenden Klasse in England*, 1845; English translation, *The Condition of the Working Class in England*, London, Swan, Sonnenschein & Co., 1895, ch. 4 'The Great Towns'); the West Central area included 'every grade of English Society living in every class of English dwelling from Buckingham Palace to Kennedy Court' (Charles Booth, *Life and Labour of the People in London*, 1892, vol. I, p. 188) and 'St Giles and St James's' (a notorious slum and the royal court) proverbially summed up the extreme contrasts in this small area. Asa Briggs also confirms that within the West End there were also areas of poverty, 'within the region of Belgrave Square, for example' (Asa Briggs, *Victorian Cities*, London, Odhams, 1963, p. 327) and Engels cites Portman Square as being close to an area of slum dwellings.

29 RLS says that Hogg's *Justified Sinner* 'has always haunted and puzzled me' (*LETBM*, vol. VII, p. 125). Its influence can be seen in 1. the juxtaposed third-person and self-revealing first-person narrative covering the same events; 2. the similar moonlit murders of George Colwan and Danvers Carew observed by a woman from a window; 3. the indeterminate theological, psychological and sociological symbolism; 4. the vague characterisation of the Hyde-equivalent Gil-Martin and his presentation as part of the alternating personality of the protagonist; 5. the strange linguistic style. For the Scottish context of *JH*, see Jenni Calder, 'Introduction', in R. L. Stevenson *Dr Jekyll and Mr Hyde and Other Stories*, Penguin, 1979, pp. 11–13; Caroline McCracken-Flesher, 'Multiplying Doubles', *Novel* 24(2), pp. 234–5; Douglas Mack, 'Dr Jekyll, Mr Hyde, and Count Dracula', in P. Liebregts and W. Tigges (eds), *Beauty and the Beast*, Amsterdam, Rodopi, 1996, pp. 149–56; Jean-Pierre Naugrette, 'Présentation', in R. L. Stevenson, *L'Étrange Cas du Dr Jekyll et de Mr Hyde*, Paris, Livre de Poche, 2000, pp. 11–17; Jean-Pierre Naugrette, '*The Strange Case of Dr Jekyll and Mr Hyde*: pour une relecture écossaise', *Cahiers Victoriens et Edouardiens*, 54, 2001, pp. 27–45. Canongate of Edinburgh included *JH* in a collection of RLS's narratives with the title *Shorter Scottish Fiction* in 1995 (reissued in 2001 as *Markheim, Jekyll and The Merry Men*).

30 'The human body as a whole is pictured by the dream imagination as a house, and the separate portions of the body as portions of a house' (Freud, *Standard Edition*, vol. 5, p. 225). The house can also represent the text: 'Le bâtiment ... joue toujours ... la fonction d'un métalangage incorporé', allowing the literary text 'de se penser

indirectement', (Philippe Hamon, 'Texte et architecture', *Poétique* 73, 1988, p. 25). In *JH*, the text opens with the door and reaches a climax as the central part of the building is entered.

31 The front v. back symbolism of the house has a long cultural history: in the second part of *Roman de la Rose* (1275–80; ll. 6063–88, 6115–17), the House of Fortune has one side of gold and silver, the other of cracked, dirty, broken mud and straw.

32 Studies and observations on the centrality of the door in *JH* include: Stephen Heath, 'Psychopathia Sexualis: Stevenson's Strange Case', *Critical Quarterly* 28(1–2), 1986, p. 95; Dury, pp. 74–5; Elaine Showalter, *Sexual Anarchy*, London, Bloomsbury, 1990, pp. 110; Shafquat Towheed, 'R. L. Stevenson's Sense of the Uncanny: "The Face in the Cheval-Glass"', *English Literature in Transition* 42(1), 1999, pp. 25–9.

33 From a commentary by Generoso Picono in the catalogue to an exhibition of photographs by Felice Nittolo of abandoned doors in the city of Avellino entitled 'Centoportemorte' (A-hundred-dead-doors), Avellino, Chiesa del Carmine, 12 August 2001–30 September 2001.

34 Scholars who have seen the mirror as a central symbol of the text include Attilio Brilli, 'La doppia vita', in R. L. Stevenson, *Lo strano caso del dottor Jekyll e del signor Hyde*, Milano, Mondadori, 1985, p. viii; Mario Trevi, 'Introduzione', in R. L. Stevenson, *Il Dottor Jekyll e Mr Hyde*, Milano, Feltrinelli, 1991, p. 12; Martin Tropp, '*Dr Jekyll and Mr Hyde*, Schopenhauer and the Power of Will', *Midwestern Quarterly* 32(2), 1991, p. 152; Dury, pp. 77–8; Richard Ambrosini, *R. L. Stevenson: la poetica del romanzo*, Roma, Bulzoni, pp. 200–7; Towheed, 'R. L. Stevenson's Sense of the Uncanny', pp. 23–38.

35 'I wish I could write to you, but it isn't me who holds the pen – it's the other one, the stupid one, who doesn't know French, who doesn't love my friends as I love them ... he whom I disavow.'

36 The main studies on the hand motif in *JH* are: Janice Doane and Devon Hodges, 'Demonic Disturbance of Sexual Identity: The Strange Case of Dr. Jekyll & Mr/s Hyde', *Novel* 23(1), 1989, pp. 70–2; Showalter, *Sexual Anarchy*, 1990, p. 114 ; Dury, pp. 78–80; Richard Dury, 'Variations sur la main de Hyde', in Jean-Pierre Naugrette (ed.), *Dr Jekyll & Mr Hyde*, Paris, Autrement, pp. 99–117; Richard Dury, 'The Hand of Hyde', in William B. Jones (ed.), *Robert Louis Stevenson Reconsidered: New Critical Perspectives*, Jefferson NC, McFarland, 2003, pp. 101–16.

37 Qu. Danahay, 'Introduction', *The Strange Case of Dr Jekyll and Mr Hyde*, 1999, p. 177.

38 For *JH* and fears of atavism and degeneration, see Guy Davidson, 'Sexuality and the Degenerate Body in Robert Louis Stevenson's *The Strange Case of Dr Jekyll and Mr Hyde*', *Australasian Victorian Studies Journal* 1, 1995; Stephen D. Arata, *Fictions of Loss in the Victorian Fin de Siècle*, Cambridge University Press, 1996, pp. 33ff and references in the notes; and Mighall (ed.), *The Strange Case of Dr Jekyll and Mr Hyde*, pp. xxiii–xxiv, 150–4.

39 'There must be something wrong in me, or I would not be popular' (*LETBM*, vol. V, p. 171); 'literature is a business, and must be followed as best a man can, above all, when his family is hard up ... Igh Artises can go to blazes. I love low art myself' (*LETBM*, vol. III, p. 290).

40 The reading of *JH* in terms of Stevenson's divided attitude towards his art can be found in Patrick Brantlinger and Richard Boyle, 'The Education of Edward Hyde: Stevenson's "Gothic Gnome" and the Mass Readership of Late-Victorian England', in *VH*, pp. 265–82; and Arata, *Fictions of Loss*, pp. 43–9. Arata sees *JH* as in part 'a symbolic working through' of his mixed feelings towards art, commerce and middle-class ideology.

41 Jean-Pierre Naugrette, notes to his *Livre de Poche* bilingual edition, 1985, and in *'Dr Jekyll and Mr Hyde*: dans le labyrinth', *Tropismes* 5, 1988, pp. 9–37.

42 Naugrette, *'Dr Jekyll and Mr Hyde*: dans le labyrinth', pp. 14–16.

43 See the Explanatory Notes for examples of archaic and Scots words and of familiar words with unusual meanings.

44 The ratio of semicolons to full stops in *JH* is just over 1 : 2 (for a quick comparison, it is 1 : 11 in Le Fanu's 'Green Tea'); Graham Good refers to Stevenson's 'near-addictive use of the semi-colon' ('Rereading Robert Louis Stevenson', *Dalhousie Review* 62(1), 1982, p. 51); Barry Menikoff remarks that 'There are indications, especially in Stevenson's correspondence, that his use of the semicolon was habitual in his writing, and not peculiar to his fiction' (*Robert Louis Stevenson and 'The Beach of Falesá'*, Edinburgh University Press, 1984, p. 43). For semicolons added at the proof stage, see Textual Notes p. 192.

45 To get a quick idea of how many this is, Le Fanu's 'Carmilla', slightly longer than *JH*, has eighty-six such cases of a semicolon followed by 'and', and his 'Green Tea', half the length, has only thirteen. This use of the semicolon is possibly influenced by RLS's youthful admiration for Baroque stylists such as Sir Thomas Browne; but even Browne's *Religio Medici*, a quarter longer than *JH*, with a similar frequency of 'and' and a slightly greater frequency of semicolons, has only 113 examples of '; and'. (Statistics for Le Fanu and Browne are based on e-texts of unknown reliability on the sites of the University of Pennsylvania and Oregon.) *JH* also has fifty-four examples of a semicolon followed by 'but'.

46 For a study of different generic characteristics of *JH*, see Dury, pp. 45–56.

47 Henry James says that RLS's style is 'a complexity of curious and picturesque garments' and 'curious of expression' ('Robert Louis Stevenson', *Century Magazine* (April 1888), in Janet Adam Smith, *Henry James and Robert Louis Stevenson. A Record of Friendship and Criticism*, Rupert Hart-Davis, 1948, p. 126).

48 See Explanatory Notes for pp. 12 and 38. Similar aggressive dialogue-turns disguised as politeness are found in *The New Arabian Nights*,

see Richard Dury, 'Le caractère *camp* des *Nouvelles mille et une nuits*', in Gilles Menegaldo and Jean-Pierre Naugrette (eds), *R. L. Stevenson & A. Conan Doyle. Aventures de la Fiction*, Rennes, Terre de Brume, 2003, p. 127.

49 This technique is also found in Hogg (e.g. a life 'of sorrow and vengeance'; James Hogg [ed. P. D. Garside], *The Private Memoirs and Confessions of a Justified Sinner*, Edinburgh, Edinburgh University Press, 2001, p. xxi); Dickens (a smile 'handsome but compressed'; Brian Rosenberg, 'Character and Contradictions in Dickens', *Nineteenth-Century Literature* 147(2), 1992, pp. 145–63); and Henry James ('he looked clever and ill'; cf. Dury, p. 40).

50 For derivative works, see the *RLS Web Site* at wwwesterni.unibg.it/rls/rls.htm, which lists films, stage versions, musicals and operas, sequels and retellings, comic books and graphic novels.

51 For studies and listings of performance adaptations, see Brian A. Rose: *Jekyll and Hyde Adapted: Dramatizations of Cultural Anxiety*, London, Greenwood, 1996; Harry M. Geduld, *The Definitive 'Dr Jekyll and Mr Hyde' Companion*, New York/London, Garland, 1983, pp. 195–217; Scott Allen Nollen, *Robert Louis Stevenson: Life, Literature and the Silver Screen*, New York, McFarland, 1994; Charles King, 'Dr Jekyll and Mr Hyde. A Filmography', *Journal of Popular Film and Television* 25(1), 1997, pp. 9–20; Roger Swearingen, 'Robert Louis Stevenson', in *The New Cambridge Bibliography of English Literature* (3rd edition), vol. 4: 1800–1900 (ed. Joanne Shattock), Cambridge University Press, 2000, p. 1697; Linehan (ed.), *Strange Case of Dr. Jekyll and Mr. Hyde*, pp. 150–74; Raymond T. McNally and Radu Florescu, *In Search of Dr. Jekyll and Mr. Hyde*, Los Angeles, Renaissance Books, 2000, pp. 163–214.

52 Cf. Pierce, 'Penny-Wise and Pound Foolish', p. 173.

53 For a brief note on such influence, see Mighall (ed.), *The Strange Case of Dr Jekyll and Mr Hyde*, pp. xxxiii–xxxv.

54 For more information and reproductions, see William B. Jones, Jnr, *Classics Illustrated: A Cultural History, with Illustrations*, Jefferson, NC, McFarland, 2002; also William B. Jones, 'Forty-Eight Pages and Speech Balloons', in Jones (ed.), *Robert Louis Stevenson Reconsidered*, pp. 229–32.

Strange Case of Dr Jekyll and Mr Hyde

STRANGE CASE

OF

DR JEKYLL AND MR HYDE

BY

ROBERT LOUIS STEVENSON

LONDON
LONGMANS, GREEN, AND CO.
1886

Title page of the first London edition of Robert Louis Stevenson's *Strange Case of Dr Jekyll and Mr Hyde* (1886). Reproduced by permission of the British Library (BL 12331.g.27).

It's ill to loose the bands that God decreed to bind;
Still will we be the children of the heather and the wind.
Far away from home, O it's still for you and me
That the broom is blowing bonnie in the north countrie.

Contents

Story of the Door

MR. Utterson the lawyer was a man of a rugged countenance, that was never lighted by a smile; cold, scanty and embarrassed in discourse; backward in sentiment; lean, long, dusty, dreary and yet somehow lovable. At friendly meetings, and when the wine was to his taste, something eminently human beaconed from his eye; something indeed which never found its way into his talk, but which spoke not only in these silent symbols of the after-dinner face, but more often and loudly in the acts of his life. He was austere with himself; drank gin when he was alone, to mortify a taste for vintages; and though he enjoyed the theatre, had not crossed the doors of one for twenty years. But he had an approved tolerance for others; sometimes wondering, almost with envy, at the high pressure of spirits involved in their misdeeds; and in any extremity inclined to help rather than to reprove. 'I incline to Cain's heresy,' he used to say quaintly: 'I let my brother go to the devil in his own way.' In this character, it was frequently his fortune to be the last reputable acquaintance and the last good influence in the lives of down-going men. And to such as these, so long as they came about his chambers, he never marked a shade of change in his demeanour.

No doubt the feat was easy to Mr. Utterson; for he was undemonstrative at the best, and even his friendships seemed to be founded in a similar catholicity of good-nature. It is the mark of a modest man to accept his friendly circle ready-made from the hands of opportunity; and that was the lawyer's way. His friends were those of his own blood or those whom he had known the longest; his affections, like ivy, were the growth of time, they implied no aptness in the object. Hence, no doubt, the bond that

7

united him to Mr. Richard Enfield, his distant kinsman, the well-known man about town. It was a nut to crack for many, what these two could see in each other or what subject they could find in common. It was reported by those who encountered them in their Sunday walks, that they said nothing, looked singularly dull, and would hail with obvious relief the appearance of a friend. For all that, the two men put the greatest store by these excursions, counted them the chief jewel of each week, and not only set aside occasions of pleasure, but even resisted the calls of business, that they might enjoy them uninterrupted.

It chanced on one of these rambles that their way led them down a by-street in a busy quarter of London. The street was small and what is called quiet, but it drove a thriving trade on the week-days. The inhabitants were all doing well, it seemed, and all emulously hoping to do better still, and laying out the surplus of their gains in coquetry; so that the shop fronts stood along that thoroughfare with an air of invitation, like rows of smiling sales-women. Even on Sunday, when it veiled its more florid charms and lay comparatively empty of passage, the street shone out in contrast to its dingy neighbourhood, like a fire in a forest; and with its freshly painted shutters, well-polished brasses, and general cleanliness and gaiety of note, instantly caught and pleased the eye of the passenger.

Two doors from one corner, on the left hand going east, the line was broken by the entry of a court; and just at that point, a certain sinister block of building thrust forward its gable on the street. It was two storeys high; showed no window, nothing but a door on the lower storey and a blind forehead of discoloured wall on the upper; and bore in every feature, the marks of prolonged and sordid negligence. The door, which was equipped with neither bell nor knocker, was blistered and distained. Tramps slouched into the recess and struck matches on the panels; children kept shop upon the steps; the schoolboy had tried his knife on the mouldings; and for close on a generation, no one had appeared to drive away these random visitors or to repair their ravages.

Mr. Enfield and the lawyer were on the other side of the by-street; but when they came abreast of the entry, the former lifted up his cane and pointed.

8

'Did you ever remark that door?' he asked; and when his companion had replied in the affirmative, 'It is connected in my mind,' added he, 'with a very odd story.'

'Indeed?' said Mr. Utterson, with a slight change of voice, 'and what was that?'

'Well, it was this way,' returned Mr. Enfield: 'I was coming home from some place at the end of the world, about three o'clock of a black winter morning, and my way lay through a part of town where there was literally nothing to be seen but lamps. Street after street, and all the folks asleep – street after street, all lighted up as if for a procession and all as empty as a church – till at last I got into that state of mind when a man listens and listens and begins to long for the sight of a policeman. All at once, I saw two figures: one a little man who was stumping along eastward at a good walk, and the other a girl of maybe eight or ten who was running as hard as she was able down a cross street. Well, sir, the two ran into one another naturally enough at the corner; and then came the horrible part of the thing; for the man trampled calmly over the child's body and left her screaming on the ground. It sounds nothing to hear, but it was hellish to see. It wasn't like a man; it was like some damned Juggernaut. I gave a view halloa, took to my heels, collared my gentleman, and brought him back to where there was already quite a group about the screaming child. He was perfectly cool and made no resistance, but gave me one look, so ugly that it brought out the sweat on me like running. The people who had turned out were the girl's own family; and pretty soon, the doctor, for whom she had been sent, put in his appearance. Well, the child was not much the worse, more frightened, according to the Sawbones; and there you might have supposed would be an end to it. But there was one curious circumstance. I had taken a loathing to my gentleman at first sight. So had the child's family, which was only natural. But the doctor's case was what struck me. He was the usual cut and dry apothecary, of no particular age and colour, with a strong Edinburgh accent, and about as emotional as a bagpipe. Well, sir, he was like the rest of us; every time he looked at my prisoner, I saw that Sawbones turn sick and white with the desire to kill him. I knew what was in his mind, just as he knew what was in mine;

and killing being out of the question, we did the next best. We told the man we could and would make such a scandal out of this, as should make his name stink from one end of London to the other. If he had any friends or any credit, we undertook that he should lose them. And all the time, as we were pitching it in red hot, we were keeping the women off him as best we could, for they were as wild as harpies. I never saw a circle of such hateful faces; and there was the man in the middle, with a kind of black, sneering coolness – frightened too, I could see that – but carrying it off, sir, really like Satan. "If you choose to make capital out of this accident," said he, "I am naturally helpless. No gentleman but wishes to avoid a scene," says he. "Name your figure." Well, we screwed him up to a hundred pounds for the child's family; he would have clearly liked to stick out; but there was something about the lot of us that meant mischief, and at last he struck. The next thing was to get the money; and where do you think he carried us but to that place with the door? – whipped out a key, went in, and presently came back with the matter of ten pounds in gold and a cheque for the balance on Coutts's, drawn payable to bearer and signed with a name that I can't mention, though it's one of the points of my story, but it was a name at least very well known and often printed. The figure was stiff; but the signature was good for more than that, if it was only genuine. I took the liberty of pointing out to my gentleman that the whole business looked apocryphal, and that a man does not, in real life, walk into a cellar door at four in the morning and come out of it with another man's cheque for close upon a hundred pounds. But he was quite easy and sneering. "Set your mind at rest," says he, "I will stay with you till the banks open and cash the cheque myself." So we all set off, the doctor, and the child's father, and our friend and myself, and passed the rest of the night in my chambers; and next day, when we had breakfasted, went in a body to the bank. I gave in the cheque myself, and said I had every reason to believe it was a forgery. Not a bit of it. The cheque was genuine.'

'Tut-tut,' said Mr. Utterson.

'I see you feel as I do,' said Mr. Enfield. 'Yes, it's a bad story. For my man was a fellow that nobody could have to do with, a really damnable man; and the person that drew the cheque is the very pink of the proprieties, celebrated too, and (what makes it worse) one of your fellows who do what they call good. Black mail, I suppose; an honest man paying through the nose for some of the capers of his youth. Black Mail House is what I call that place with the door, in consequence. Though even that, you know, is far from explaining all,' he added, and with the words fell into a vein of musing.

From this he was recalled by Mr. Utterson asking rather suddenly: 'And you don't know if the drawer of the cheque lives there?'

'A likely place, isn't it?' returned Mr. Enfield. 'But I happen to have noticed his address; he lives in some square or other.'

'And you never asked about – the place with the door?' said Mr. Utterson.

'No, sir: I had a delicacy,' was the reply. 'I feel very strongly about putting questions; it partakes too much of the style of the day of judgment. You start a question, and it's like starting a stone. You sit quietly on the top of a hill; and away the stone goes, starting others; and presently some bland old bird (the last you would have thought of) is knocked on the head in his own back garden and the family have to change their name. No, sir, I make it a rule of mine: the more it looks like Queer Street, the less I ask.'

'A very good rule, too,' said the lawyer.

'But I have studied the place for myself,' continued Mr. Enfield. 'It seems scarcely a house. There is no other door, and nobody goes in or out of that one but, once in a great while, the gentleman of my adventure. There are three windows looking on the court on the first floor; none below; the windows are always shut but they're clean. And then there is a chimney which is generally smoking; so somebody must live there. And yet it's not so sure; for the buildings are so packed together about that court, that it's hard to say where one ends and another begins.'

The pair walked on again for a while in silence; and then 'Enfield,' said Mr. Utterson, 'that's a good rule of yours.'

'Yes, I think it is,' returned Enfield.

'But for all that,' continued the lawyer, 'there's one point I want to ask: I want to ask the name of that man who walked over the child.'

'Well,' said Mr. Enfield, 'I can't see what harm it would do. It was a man of the name of Hyde.'

'Hm,' said Mr. Utterson. 'What sort of a man is he to see?'

'He is not easy to describe. There is something wrong with his appearance; something displeasing, something downright detestable. I never saw a man I so disliked, and yet I scarce know why. He must be deformed somewhere; he gives a strong feeling of deformity, although I couldn't specify the point. He's an extraordinary looking man, and yet I really can name nothing out of the way. No, sir; I can make no hand of it; I can't describe him. And it's not want of memory; for I declare I can see him this moment.'

Mr. Utterson again walked some way in silence and obviously under a weight of consideration. 'You are sure he used a key?' he inquired at last.

'My dear sir...' began Enfield, surprised out of himself.

'Yes, I know,' said Utterson; 'I know it must seem strange. The fact is, if I do not ask you the name of the other party, it is because I know it already. You see, Richard, your tale has gone home. If you have been inexact in any point, you had better correct it.'

'I think you might have warned me,' returned the other with a touch of sullenness. 'But I have been pedantically exact, as you call it. The fellow had a key; and what's more, he has it still. I saw him use it, not a week ago.'

Mr. Utterson sighed deeply but said never a word; and the young man presently resumed. 'Here is another lesson to say nothing,' said he. 'I am ashamed of my long tongue. Let us make a bargain never to refer to this again.'

'With all my heart,' said the lawyer. 'I shake hands on that, Richard.'

Search for Mr. Hyde

THAT evening, Mr. Utterson came home to his bachelor house in sombre spirits and sat down to dinner without relish. It was his custom of a Sunday, when this meal was over, to sit close by the fire, a volume of some dry divinity on his reading desk, until the clock of the neighbouring church rang out the hour of twelve, when he would go soberly and gratefully to bed. On this night, however, as soon as the cloth was taken away, he took up a candle and went into his business room. There he opened his safe, took from the most private part of it a document endorsed on the envelope as Dr. Jekyll's Will, and sat down with a clouded brow to study its contents. The will was holograph, for Mr. Utterson, though he took charge of it now that it was made, had refused to lend the least assistance in the making of it; it provided not only that, in case of the decease of Henry Jekyll, M.D., D.C.L., LL.D., F.R.S., &c., all his possessions were to pass into the hands of his 'friend and benefactor Edward Hyde,' but that in case of Dr. Jekyll's 'disappearance or unexplained absence for any period exceeding three calendar months,' the said Edward Hyde should step into the said Henry Jekyll's shoes without further delay and free from any burthen or obligation, beyond the payment of a few small sums to the members of the doctor's household. This document had long been the lawyer's eyesore. It offended him both as a lawyer and as a lover of the sane and customary sides of life, to whom the fanciful was the immodest. And hitherto it was his ignorance of Mr. Hyde that had swelled his indignation; now, by a sudden turn, it was his knowledge. It was already bad enough when the name was but a name of which he could learn no more. It was worse when it began to be clothed upon with detestable

13

attributes; and out of the shifting, insubstantial mists that had so long baffled his eye, there leaped up the sudden, definite present-ment of a fiend.

'I thought it was madness,' he said, as he replaced the obnoxious paper in the safe, 'and now I begin to fear it is disgrace.'

With that he blew out his candle, put on a great coat and set forth in the direction of Cavendish Square, that citadel of medicine, where his friend, the great Dr. Lanyon, had his house and received his crowding patients. 'If anyone knows, it will be Lanyon,' he had thought.

The solemn butler knew and welcomed him; he was subjected to no stage of delay, but ushered direct from the door to the dining-room where Dr. Lanyon sat alone over his wine. This was a hearty, healthy, dapper, red-faced gentleman, with a shock of hair prematurely white, and a boisterous and decided manner. At sight of Mr. Utterson, he sprang up from his chair and welcomed him with both hands. The geniality, as was the way of the man, was somewhat theatrical to the eye; but it reposed on genuine feeling. For these two were old friends, old mates both at school and college, both thorough respecters of themselves and of each other, and, what does not always follow, men who thoroughly enjoyed each other's company.

After a little rambling talk, the lawyer led up to the subject which so disagreeably preoccupied his mind.

'I suppose, Lanyon,' said he, 'you and I must be the two oldest friends that Henry Jekyll has?'

'I wish the friends were younger,' chuckled Dr. Lanyon. 'But I suppose we are. And what of that? I see little of him now.'

'Indeed?' said Utterson. 'I thought you had a bond of common interest.'

'We had,' was the reply. 'But it is more than ten years since Henry Jekyll became too fanciful for me. He began to go wrong, wrong in mind; and though of course I continue to take an interest in him for old sake's sake as they say, I see and I have seen devilish little of the man. Such unscientific balderdash,' added the doctor, flushing suddenly purple, 'would have estranged Damon and Pythias.'

This little spirt of temper was somewhat of a relief to Mr.

14

Utterson. 'They have only differed on some point of science,' he thought; and being a man of no scientific passions (except in the matter of conveyancing) he even added: 'It is nothing worse than that!' He gave his friend a few seconds to recover his composure, and then approached the question he had come to put. 'Did you ever come across a protégé of his – one Hyde?' he asked.

'Hyde?' repeated Lanyon. 'No. Never heard of him. Since my time.'

That was the amount of information that the lawyer carried back with him to the great, dark bed on which he tossed to and fro, until the small hours of the morning began to grow large. It was a night of little ease to his toiling mind, toiling in mere darkness and besieged by questions.

Six o'clock struck on the bells of the church that was so conveniently near to Mr. Utterson's dwelling, and still he was digging at the problem. Hitherto it had touched him on the intellectual side alone; but now his imagination also was engaged or rather enslaved; and as he lay and tossed in the gross darkness of the night and the curtained room, Mr. Enfield's tale went by before his mind in a scroll of lighted pictures. He would be aware of the great field of lamps of a nocturnal city; then of the figure of a man walking swiftly; then of a child running from the doctor's; and then these met, and that human Juggernaut trod the child down and passed on regardless of her screams. Or else he would see a room in a rich house, where his friend lay asleep, dreaming and smiling at his dreams; and then the door of that room would be opened, the curtains of the bed plucked apart, the sleeper recalled, and lo! there would stand by his side a figure to whom power was given, and even at that dead hour, he must rise and do its bidding. The figure in these two phases haunted the lawyer all night; and if at any time he dozed over, it was but to see it glide more stealthily through sleeping houses, or move the more swiftly and still the more swiftly, even to dizziness, through wider labyrinths of lamplighted city, and at every street corner crush a child and leave her screaming. And still the figure had no face by which he might know it; even in his dreams, it had no face, or one that baffled him and melted before his eyes; and thus it was that there sprang up and grew apace in the lawyer's mind a singularly strong, almost an inordinate, curiosity to behold the features of the real Mr. Hyde. If he could but once set eyes on him, he thought the mystery would lighten and perhaps roll altogether away, as was the habit of mysterious things when well examined. He might see a reason for his friend's strange preference or bondage (call it which you please) and even for the startling clauses of the will. And at least it would be a face worth seeing: the face of a man who was without bowels of mercy: a face which had but to show itself to raise up, in the mind of the unimpressionable Enfield, a spirit of enduring hatred.

From that time forward, Mr. Utterson began to haunt the door in the bystreet of shops. In the morning before office hours, at noon when business was plenty and time scarce, at night under the face of the fogged city moon, by all lights and at all hours of solitude or concourse, the lawyer was to be found on his chosen post.

'If he be Mr. Hyde,' he had thought, 'I shall be Mr. Seek.'

And at last his patience was rewarded. It was a fine dry night; frost in the air; the streets as clean as a ballroom floor; the lamps, unshaken by any wind, drawing a regular pattern of light and shadow. By ten o'clock, when the shops were closed, the bystreet was very solitary and, in spite of the low growl of London from all round, very silent. Small sounds carried far; domestic sounds out of the houses were clearly audible on either side of the roadway; and the rumour of the approach of any passenger preceded him by a long time. Mr. Utterson had been some minutes at his post, when he was aware of an odd, light footstep drawing near. In the course of his nightly patrols, he had long grown accustomed to the quaint effect with which the footfalls of a single person, while he is still a great way off, suddenly spring out distinct from the vast hum and clatter of the city. Yet his attention had never before been so sharply and decisively arrested; and it was with a strong, superstitious prevision of success that he withdrew into the entry of the court.

The steps drew swiftly nearer, and swelled out suddenly louder as they turned the end of the street. The lawyer, looking forth from the entry, could soon see what manner of man he had to deal with. He was small and very plainly dressed, and the look of him, even at that distance, went somehow strongly against the watcher's inclination. But he made straight for the door, crossing the road-way to save time; and as he came, he drew a key from his pocket like one approaching home.

Mr. Utterson stepped out and touched him on the shoulder as he passed. 'Mr. Hyde, I think?' *ANIMALISTIC*

Mr. Hyde shrank back with a hissing intake of the breath. But his fear was only momentary; and though he did not look the lawyer in the face, he answered coolly enough: 'That is my name. What do you want?'

'I see you are going in,' returned the lawyer. 'I am an old friend of Dr. Jekyll's – Mr. Utterson of Gaunt Street – you must have heard my name; and meeting you so conveniently, I thought you might admit me.'

'You will not find Dr. Jekyll; he is from home,' replied Mr. Hyde, blowing in the key. And then suddenly, but still without looking up, 'How did you know me?' he asked.

'On your side,' said Mr. Utterson, 'will you do me a favour?'

'With pleasure,' replied the other. 'What shall it be?'

'Will you let me see your face?' asked the lawyer.

Mr. Hyde appeared to hesitate, and then, as if upon some sudden reflection, fronted about with an air of defiance; and the pair stared at each other pretty fixedly for a few seconds. 'Now I shall know you again,' said Mr. Utterson. 'It may be useful.'

'Yes,' returned Mr. Hyde, 'it is as well we have met; and *à propos*, you should have my address.' And he gave a number of a street in Soho.

'Good God!' thought Mr. Utterson, 'can he too have been thinking of the will?' But he kept his feelings to himself and only grunted in acknowledgement of the address.

'And now,' said the other, 'how did you know me?'

'By description,' was the reply.

'Whose description?'

'We have common friends,' said Mr. Utterson.

'Common friends?' echoed Mr. Hyde, a little hoarsely. 'Who are they?'

'Jekyll, for instance,' said the lawyer.

'He never told you,' cried Mr. Hyde, with a flush of anger. 'I did not think you would have lied.'

17

'Come,' said Mr. Utterson, 'that is not fitting language.'

The other snarled aloud into a savage laugh; and the next moment, with extraordinary quickness, he had unlocked the door and disappeared into the house.

The lawyer stood awhile when Mr. Hyde had left him, the picture of disquietude. Then he began slowly to mount the street, pausing every step or two and putting his hand to his brow like a man in mental perplexity. The problem he was thus debating as he walked, was one of a class that is rarely solved. Mr. Hyde was pale and dwarfish, he gave an impression of deformity without any nameable malformation, he had a displeasing smile, he had borne himself to the lawyer with a sort of murderous mixture of timidity and boldness, and he spoke with a husky, whispering and somewhat broken voice; all these were points against him, but not all of these together could explain the hitherto unknown disgust, loathing and fear with which Mr. Utterson regarded him. 'There must be something else,' said the perplexed gentleman. 'There *is* something more, if I could find a name for it. God bless me, the man seems hardly human! Something troglodytic, shall we say? or can it be the old story of Dr. Fell? or is it the mere radiance of a foul soul that thus transpires through, and transfigures, its clay continent? The last, I think; for O my poor old Harry Jekyll, if ever I read Satan's signature upon a face, it is on that of your new friend.'

Round the corner from the bystreet, there was a square of ancient, handsome houses, now for the most part decayed from their high estate and let in flats and chambers to all sorts and conditions of men: map-engravers, architects, shady lawyers and the agents of obscure enterprises. One house, however, second from the corner, was still occupied entire; and at the door of this, which wore a great air of wealth and comfort, though it was now plunged in darkness except for the fan-light, Mr. Utterson stopped and knocked. A well-dressed, elderly servant opened the door.

'Is Dr. Jekyll at home, Poole?' asked the lawyer.

'I will see, Mr. Utterson,' said Poole, admitting the visitor, as he spoke, into a large, low-roofed, comfortable hall, paved with flags, warmed (after the fashion of a country house) by a bright, open fire, and furnished with costly cabinets of oak. 'Will you wait here by the fire, sir? or shall I give you a light in the dining-room?'

'Here, thank you,' said the lawyer, and he drew near and leaned on the tall fender. This hall, in which he was now left alone, was a pet fancy of his friend the doctor's; and Utterson himself was wont to speak of it as the pleasantest room in London. But to-night there was a shudder in his blood; the face of Hyde sat heavy on his memory; he felt (what was rare with him) a nausea and distaste of life; and in the gloom of his spirits, he seemed to read a menace in the flickering of the firelight on the polished cabinets and the uneasy starting of the shadow on the roof. He was ashamed of his relief, when Poole presently returned to announce that Dr. Jekyll was gone out.

'I saw Mr. Hyde go in by the old dissecting room door, Poole,' he said. 'Is that right, when Dr. Jekyll is from home?'

'Quite right, Mr. Utterson, sir,' replied the servant. 'Mr. Hyde has a key.'

'Your master seems to repose a great deal of trust in that young man, Poole,' resumed the other musingly.

'Yes, sir, he do indeed,' said Poole. 'We have all orders to obey him.'

'I do not think I ever met Mr. Hyde?' asked Utterson.

'O, dear no, sir. He never *dines* here,' replied the butler. 'Indeed we see very little of him on this side of the house; he mostly comes and goes by the laboratory.'

'Well, good night, Poole.'

'Good night, Mr. Utterson.'

And the lawyer set out homeward with a very heavy heart. 'Poor Harry Jekyll,' he thought, 'my mind misgives me he is in deep waters! He was wild when he was young; a long while ago to be sure; but in the law of God, there is no statute of limitations. Ay, it must be that; the ghost of some old sin, the cancer of some concealed disgrace: punishment coming, *pede claudo*, years after memory has forgotten and self-love condoned the fault.' And the lawyer, scared by the thought, brooded awhile on his own past, groping in all the corners of memory, lest by chance some Jack-in-the-Box of an old iniquity should leap to light there. His past was fairly blameless; few men could read the rolls of their life with less apprehension; yet he was humbled to the dust by the many ill things he had done, and raised up again into a sober and fearful gratitude by the many that he had come so near to doing, yet avoided. And then by a return on his former subject, he conceived a spark of hope. 'This Master Hyde, if he were studied,' thought he, 'must have secrets of his own: black secrets, by the look of him; secrets compared to which poor Jekyll's worst would be like sunshine. Things cannot continue as they are. It turns me cold to think of this creature stealing like a thief to Harry's bedside; poor Harry, what a wakening! And the danger of it; for if this Hyde suspects the existence of the will, he may grow impatient to inherit. Ay, I must put my shoulder to the wheel – if Jekyll will but let me,' he added, 'if Jekyll will only let me.' For once more he saw before his mind's eye, as clear as a transparency, the strange clauses of the will.

Dr. Jekyll was Quite at Ease

A fortnight later, by excellent good fortune, the doctor gave one of his pleasant dinners to some five or six old cronies, all intelligent, reputable men and all judges of good wine; and Mr. Utterson so contrived that he remained behind after the others had departed. This was no new arrangement, but a thing that had befallen many scores of times. Where Utterson was liked, he was liked well. Hosts loved to detain the dry lawyer, when the light-hearted and the loose-tongued had already their foot on the threshold; they liked to sit awhile in his unobtrusive company, practising for solitude, sobering their minds in the man's rich silence after the expense and strain of gaiety. To this rule, Dr. Jekyll was no exception; and as he now sat on the opposite side of the fire – a large, well-made, smooth-faced man of fifty, with something of a slyish cast perhaps, but every mark of capacity and kindness – you could see by his looks that he cherished for Mr. Utterson a sincere and warm affection.

'I have been wanting to speak to you, Jekyll,' began the latter. 'You know that will of yours?'

A close observer might have gathered that the topic was distasteful; but the doctor carried it off gaily. 'My poor Utterson,' said he, 'you are unfortunate in such a client. I never saw a man so distressed as you were by my will; unless it were that hide-bound pedant, Lanyon, at what he called my scientific heresies. O, I know he's a good fellow – you needn't frown – an excellent fellow, and I always mean to see more of him; but a hide-bound pedant for all that; an ignorant, blatant pedant. I was never more disappointed in any man than Lanyon.'

'You know I never approved of it,' pursued Utterson, ruthlessly disregarding the fresh topic.

'My will? Yes, certainly, I know that,' said the doctor, a trifle sharply. 'You have told me so.'

'Well, I tell you so again,' continued the lawyer. 'I have been learning something of young Hyde.'

The large handsome face of Dr. Jekyll grew pale to the very lips, and there came a blackness about his eyes. 'I do not care to hear more,' said he. 'This is a matter I thought we had agreed to drop.'

'What I heard was abominable,' said Utterson.

'It can make no change. You do not understand my position,' returned the doctor, with a certain incoherency of manner. 'I am painfully situated, Utterson; my position is a very strange – a very strange one. It is one of those affairs that cannot be mended by talking.'

'Jekyll,' said Utterson, 'you know me: I am a man to be trusted. Make a clean breast of this in confidence; and I make no doubt I can get you out of it.'

'My good Utterson,' said the doctor, 'this is very good of you, this is downright good of you, and I cannot find words to thank you in. I believe you fully; I would trust you before any man alive, ay, before myself, if I could make the choice; but indeed it isn't what you fancy; it is not so bad as that; and just to put your good heart at rest, I will tell you one thing: the moment I choose, I can be rid of Mr. Hyde. I give you my hand upon that; and I thank you again and again; and I will just add one little word, Utterson, that I'm sure you'll take in good part: this is a private matter, and I beg of you to let it sleep.'

Utterson reflected a little looking in the fire.

'I have no doubt you are perfectly right,' he said at last, getting to his feet.

'Well, but since we have touched upon this business, and for the last time I hope,' continued the doctor, 'there is one point I should like you to understand. I have really a very great interest in poor Hyde. I know you have seen him; he told me so; and I fear he was rude. But I do sincerely take a great, a very great interest in that young man; and if I am taken away, Utterson, I wish you to promise me that you will bear with him and get his rights for him.

I think you would, if you knew all; and it would be a weight off my mind if you would promise.'

'I can't pretend that I shall ever like him,' said the lawyer.

'I don't ask that,' pleaded Jekyll, laying his hand upon the other's arm; 'I only ask for justice; I only ask you to help him for my sake, when I am no longer here.'

Utterson heaved an irrepressible sigh. 'Well,' said he. 'I promise.'

The Carew Murder Case

NEARLY a year later, in the month of October 18—, London was startled by a crime of singular ferocity and rendered all the more notable by the high position of the victim. The details were few and startling. A maid servant living alone in a house not far from the river, had gone upstairs to bed about eleven. Although a fog rolled over the city in the small hours, the early part of the night was cloudless, and the lane, which the maid's window overlooked, was brilliantly lit by the full moon. It seems she was romantically given, for she sat down upon her box, which stood immediately under the window, and fell into a dream of musing. Never (she used to say, with streaming tears, when she narrated that experience) never had she felt more at peace with all men or thought more kindly of the world. And as she so sat she became aware of an aged and beautiful gentleman with white hair, drawing near along the lane; and advancing to meet him, another and very small gentleman, to whom at first she paid less attention. When they had come within speech (which was just under the maid's eyes) the older man bowed and accosted the other with a very pretty manner of politeness. It did not seem as if the subject of his address were of great importance; indeed, from his pointing, it sometimes appeared as if he were only inquiring his way; but the moon shone on his face as he spoke, and the girl was pleased to watch it, it seemed to breathe such an innocent and old-world kindness of disposition, yet with something high too, as of a well-founded self-content. Presently her eye wandered to the other, and she was surprised to recognise in him a certain Mr. Hyde, who had once visited her master and for whom she had conceived a dislike. He had in his hand a heavy cane, with which he was

24

trifling; but he answered never a word, and seemed to listen with an ill-contained impatience. And then all of a sudden he broke out in a great flame of anger, stamping with his foot, brandishing the cane, and carrying on (as the maid described it) like a madman. The old gentleman took a step back, with the air of one very much surprised and a trifle hurt; and at that Mr. Hyde broke out of all bounds and clubbed him to the earth. And next moment, with ape-like fury, he was trampling his victim under foot, and hailing down a storm of blows, under which the bones were audibly shattered and the body jumped upon the roadway. At the horror of these sights and sounds, the maid fainted.

It was two o'clock when she came to herself and called for the police. The murderer was gone long ago; but there lay his victim in the middle of the lane, incredibly mangled. The stick with which the deed had been done, although it was of some rare and very tough and heavy wood, had broken in the middle under the stress of this insensate cruelty; and one splintered half had rolled in the neighbouring gutter – the other, without doubt, had been carried away by the murderer. A purse and a gold watch were found upon the victim; but no cards or papers, except a sealed and stamped envelope, which he had been probably carrying to the post, and which bore the name and address of Mr. Utterson.

This was brought to the lawyer the next morning, before he was out of bed; and he had no sooner seen it, and been told the circumstances, than he shot out a solemn lip. 'I shall say nothing till I have seen the body,' said he; 'this may be very serious. Have the kindness to wait while I dress.' And with the same grave countenance he hurried through his breakfast and drove to the police station, whither the body had been carried. As soon as he came into the cell, he nodded.

'Yes,' said he, 'I recognise him. I am sorry to say that this is Sir Danvers Carew.'

'Good God, sir,' exclaimed the officer, 'is it possible?' And the next moment his eye lighted up with professional ambition. 'This will make a deal of noise,' he said. 'And perhaps you can help us to the man.' And he briefly narrated what the maid had seen, and showed the broken stick.

Mr. Utterson had already quailed at the name of Hyde; but

when the stick was laid before him, he could doubt no longer: broken and battered as it was, he recognised it for one that he had himself presented many years before to Henry Jekyll.

'Is this Mr. Hyde a person of small stature?' he inquired.

'Particularly small and particularly wicked-looking, is what the maid calls him,' said the officer.

Mr. Utterson reflected; and then, raising his head, 'If you will come with me in my cab,' he said, 'I think I can take you to his house.'

It was by this time about nine in the morning, and the first fog of the season. A great chocolate-coloured pall lowered over heaven, but the wind was continually charging and routing these embattled vapours; so that as the cab crawled from street to street, Mr. Utterson beheld a marvellous number of degrees and hues of twilight; for here it would be dark like the back-end of evening; and there would be a glow of a rich, lurid brown, like the light of some strange conflagration; and here, for a moment, the fog would be quite broken up, and a haggard shaft of daylight would glance in between the swirling wreaths. The dismal quarter of Soho seen under these changing glimpses, with its muddy ways, and slatternly passengers, and its lamps, which had never been extinguished or had been kindled afresh to combat this mournful reïnvasion of darkness, seemed, in the lawyer's eyes, like a district of some city in a nightmare. The thoughts of his mind, besides, were of the gloomiest dye; and when he glanced at the companion of his drive, he was conscious of some touch of that terror of the law and the law's officers, which may at times assail the most honest.

As the cab drew up before the address indicated, the fog lifted a little and showed him a dingy street, a gin palace, a low French eating house, a shop for the retail of penny numbers and twopenny salads, many ragged children huddled in the doorways, and many women of many different nationalities passing out, key in hand, to have a morning glass; and the next moment the fog settled down again upon that part, as brown as umber, and cut him off from his blackguardly surroundings. This was the home of Henry Jekyll's favourite; of a man who was heir to a quarter of a million sterling.

26

An ivory-faced and silvery-haired old woman opened the door. She had an evil face, smoothed by hypocrisy; but her manners were excellent. Yes, she said, this was Mr. Hyde's, but he was not at home; he had been in that night very late, but had gone away again in less than an hour; there was nothing strange in that; his habits were very irregular, and he was often absent; for instance, it was nearly two months since she had seen him till yesterday.

'Very well then, we wish to see his rooms,' said the lawyer; and when the woman began to declare it was impossible, 'I had better tell you who this person is,' he added. 'This is Inspector Newcomen of Scotland Yard.'

A flash of odious joy appeared upon the woman's face. 'Ah!' said she, 'he is in trouble! What has he done?'

Mr. Utterson and the inspector exchanged glances. 'He don't seem a very popular character,' observed the latter. 'And now, my good woman, just let me and this gentleman have a look about us.'

In the whole extent of the house, which but for the old woman remained otherwise empty, Mr. Hyde had only used a couple of rooms; but these were furnished with luxury and good taste. A closet was filled with wine; the plate was of silver, the napery elegant; a good picture hung upon the walls, a gift (as Utterson supposed) from Henry Jekyll, who was much of a connoisseur; and the carpets were of many plies and agreeable in colour. At this moment, however, the rooms bore every mark of having been recently and hurriedly ransacked; clothes lay about the floor, with their pockets inside out; lockfast drawers stood open; and on the hearth there lay a pile of gray ashes, as though many papers had been burned. From these embers the inspector disinterred the butt end of a green cheque book, which had resisted the action of the fire; the other half of the stick was found behind the door; and as this clinched his suspicions, the officer declared himself delighted. A visit to the bank, where several thousand pounds were found to be lying to the murderer's credit, completed his gratification.

'You may depend upon it, sir,' he told Mr. Utterson: 'I have him in my hand. He must have lost his head, or he never would have left the stick or, above all, burned the cheque book. Why, money's life to the man. We have nothing to do but wait for him at the bank, and get out the handbills.'

This last, however, was not so easy of accomplishment; for Mr. Hyde had numbered few familiars – even the master of the servant maid had only seen him twice; his family could nowhere be traced; he had never been photographed; and the few who could describe him differed widely, as common observers will. Only on one point, were they agreed; and that was the haunting sense of unexpressed deformity with which the fugitive impressed his beholders.

28

Incident of the Letter

IT was late in the afternoon, when Mr. Utterson found his way to Dr. Jekyll's door, where he was at once admitted by Poole, and carried down by the kitchen offices and across a yard which had once been a garden, to the building which was indifferently known ✳ as the laboratory or the dissecting rooms. The doctor had bought the house from the heirs of a celebrated surgeon; and his own tastes being rather chemical than anatomical, had changed the destination of the block at the bottom of the garden. It was the first time that the lawyer had been received in that part of his friend's quarters; and he eyed the dingy windowless structure with curiosity, and gazed round with a distasteful sense of strangeness as he crossed the theatre, once crowded with eager students and now lying gaunt and silent, the tables laden with chemical apparatus, the floor strewn with crates and littered with packing straw, and the light falling dimly through the foggy cupola. At the further end, a flight of stairs mounted to a door covered with red baize; and through this, Mr. Utterson was at last received into the doctor's cabinet. It was a large room, fitted round with glass presses, furnished, among other things, with a cheval-glass and a business table, and looking out upon the court by three dusty windows barred with iron. The fire burned in the grate; a lamp was set lighted on the chimney shelf, for even in the houses the fog began to lie thickly; and there, close up to the warmth, sat Dr. Jekyll, looking deadly sick. He did not rise to meet his visitor, but held out a cold hand and bade him welcome in a changed voice.

'And now,' said Mr. Utterson, as soon as Poole had left them, 'you have heard the news?'

The doctor shuddered. 'They were crying it in the square,' he said. 'I heard them in my dining room.'

'One word,' said the lawyer. 'Carew was my client, but so are you, and I want to know what I am doing. You have not been mad enough to hide this fellow?'

'Utterson, I swear to God,' cried the doctor, 'I swear to God I will never set eyes on him again. I bind my honour to you that I am done with him in this world. It is all at an end. And indeed he does not want my help; you do not know him as I do; he is safe, he is quite safe; mark my words, he will never more be heard of.'

The lawyer listened gloomily; he did not like his friend's feverish manner. 'You seem pretty sure of him,' said he; 'and for your sake, I hope you may be right. If it came to a trial, your name might appear.'

'I am quite sure of him,' replied Jekyll; 'I have grounds for certainty that I cannot share with anyone. But there is one thing on which you may advise me. I have – I have received a letter; and I am at a loss whether I should show it to the police. I should like to leave it in your hands, Utterson; you would judge wisely I am sure; I have so great a trust in you.'

'You fear, I suppose, that it might lead to his detection?' asked the lawyer.

'No,' said the other. 'I cannot say that I care what becomes of Hyde; I am quite done with him. I was thinking of my own character, which this hateful business has rather exposed.'

Utterson ruminated awhile; he was surprised at his friend's selfishness, and yet relieved by it. 'Well,' said he, at last, 'let me see the letter.'

The letter was written in an odd, upright hand and signed 'Edward Hyde': and it signified, briefly enough, that the writer's benefactor, Dr. Jekyll, whom he had long so unworthily repaid for a thousand generosities, need labour under no alarm for his safety as he had means of escape on which he placed a sure dependence. The lawyer liked this letter well enough; it put a better colour on the intimacy than he had looked for; and he blamed himself for some of his past suspicions.

'Have you the envelope?' he asked.

'I burned it,' replied Jekyll, 'before I thought what I was about.

But it bore no postmark. The note was handed in.'

'Shall I keep this and sleep upon it?' asked Utterson.

'I wish you to judge for me entirely,' was the reply. 'I have lost confidence in myself.'

'Well, I shall consider,' returned the lawyer. 'And now one word more: it was Hyde who dictated the terms in your will about that disappearance?'

The doctor seemed seized with a qualm of faintness; he shut his mouth tight and nodded.

'I knew it,' said Utterson. 'He meant to murder you. You have had a fine escape.'

'I have had what is far more to the purpose,' returned the doctor solemnly: 'I have had a lesson – O God, Utterson, what a lesson I have had!' And he covered his face for a moment with his hands.

On his way out, the lawyer stopped and had a word or two with Poole. 'By the by,' said he, 'there was a letter handed in to-day: what was the messenger like?' But Poole was positive nothing had come except by post; 'and only circulars by that,' he added.

This news sent off the visitor with his fears renewed. Plainly the letter had come by the laboratory door; possibly, indeed, it had been written in the cabinet; and if that were so, it must be differently judged, and handled with the more caution. The newsboys, as he went, were crying themselves hoarse along the footways: 'Special edition. Shocking murder of an M.P.' That was the funeral oration of one friend and client; and he could not help a certain apprehension lest the good name of another should be sucked down in the eddy of the scandal. It was, at least, a ticklish decision that he had to make; and self-reliant as he was by habit, he began to cherish a longing for advice. It was not to be had directly; but perhaps, he thought, it might be fished for.

Presently after, he sat on one side of his own hearth, with Mr. Guest, his head clerk, upon the other, and midway between, at a nicely calculated distance from the fire, a bottle of a particular old wine that had long dwelt unsunned in the foundations of his house. The fog still slept on the wing above the drowned city, where the lamps glimmered like carbuncles; and through the muffle and smother of these fallen clouds, the procession of the town's life was still rolling in through the great arteries with a sound as of a mighty wind. But the room was gay with firelight. In the bottle the acids were long ago resolved; the imperial dye had softened with time, as the colour grows richer in stained windows; and the glow of hot autumn afternoons on hillside vineyards, was ready to be set free and to disperse the fogs of London. Insensibly the lawyer melted. There was no man from whom he kept fewer secrets than Mr. Guest; and he was not always sure that he kept as many as he meant. Guest had often been on business to the doctor's; he knew Poole; he could scarce have failed to hear of Mr. Hyde's familiarity about the house; he might draw conclusions: was it not as well, then, that he should see a letter which put that mystery to rights? and above all since Guest, being a great student and critic of handwriting, would consider the step natural and obliging? The clerk, besides, was a man of counsel; he would scarce read so strange a document without dropping a remark; and by that remark Mr. Utterson might shape his future course.

'This is a sad business about Sir Danvers,' he said.

'Yes, sir, indeed. It has elicited a great deal of public feeling,' returned Guest. 'The man, of course, was mad.'

'I should like to hear your views on that,' replied Utterson. 'I have a document here in his handwriting; it is between ourselves, for I scarce know what to do about it; it is an ugly business at the best. But there it is; quite in your way: a murderer's autograph.'

Guest's eyes brightened, and he sat down at once and studied it with passion. 'No, sir,' he said; 'not mad; but it is an odd hand.'

'And by all accounts a very odd writer,' added the lawyer.

Just then the servant entered with a note.

'Is that from Doctor Jekyll, sir?' inquired the clerk. 'I thought I knew the writing. Anything private, Mr. Utterson?'

'Only an invitation to dinner. Why? do you want to see it?'

'One moment. I thank you, sir;' and the clerk laid the two sheets of paper alongside and sedulously compared their contents. 'Thank you, sir,' he said at last, returning both; 'it's a very interesting autograph.'

There was a pause, during which Mr. Utterson struggled with himself. 'Why did you compare them, Guest?' he inquired suddenly.

'Well, sir,' returned the clerk, 'there's a rather singular resemblance; the two hands are in many points identical: only differently sloped.'

'Rather quaint,' said Utterson.

'It is, as you say, rather quaint,' returned Guest.

'I wouldn't speak of this note, you know,' said the master.

'No, sir,' said the clerk. 'I understand.'

But no sooner was Mr. Utterson alone that night, than he locked the note into his safe where it reposed from that time forward. 'What!' he thought. 'Henry Jekyll forge for a murderer!' And his blood ran cold in his veins.

Remarkable Incident of
Dr. Lanyon

TIME ran on; thousands of pounds were offered in reward, for the death of Sir Danvers was resented as a public injury; but Mr. Hyde had disappeared out of the ken of the police as though he had never existed. Much of his past was unearthed, indeed, and all disreputable: tales came out of the man's cruelty, at once so callous and violent, of his vile life, of his strange associates, of the hatred that seemed to have surrounded his career; but of his present whereabouts, not a whisper. From the time he had left the house in Soho on the morning of the murder, he was simply blotted out; and gradually, as time drew on, Mr. Utterson began to recover from the hotness of his alarm, and to grow more at quiet with himself. The death of Sir Danvers was, to his way of thinking, more than paid for by the disappearance of Mr. Hyde. Now that that evil influence had been withdrawn, a new life began for Dr. Jekyll. He came out of his seclusion, renewed relations with his friends, became once more their familiar guest and entertainer; and whilst he had always been known for charities, he was now no less distinguished for religion. He was busy, he was much in the open air, he did good; his face seemed to open and brighten, as if with an inward consciousness of service; and for more than two months, the doctor was at peace.

On the 8th of January Utterson had dined at the doctor's with a small party; Lanyon had been there; and the face of the host had looked from one to the other as in the old days when the trio were inseparable friends. On the 12th, and again on the 14th, the door was shut against the lawyer. 'The doctor was confined to the house,' Poole said, 'and saw no one.' On the 15th, he tried again, and was again refused; and having now been used for the last two

months to see his friend almost daily, he found this return of
solitude to weigh upon his spirits. The fifth night, he had in Guest
to dine with him; and the sixth he betook himself to Dr. Lanyon's.

There at least he was not denied admittance; but when he came
in, he was shocked at the change which had taken place in the
doctor's appearance. He had his death-warrant written legibly
upon his face. The rosy man had grown pale; his flesh had fallen
away; he was visibly balder and older; and yet it was not so much
these tokens of a swift physical decay that arrested the lawyer's
notice, as a look in the eye and quality of manner that seemed to
testify to some deep-seated terror of the mind. It was unlikely
that the doctor should fear death; and yet that was what Utterson
was tempted to suspect. 'Yes,' he thought; 'he is a doctor, he must
know his own state and that his days are counted; and the knowledge is more than he can bear.' And yet when Utterson remarked
on his ill-looks, it was with an air of great firmness that Lanyon
declared himself a doomed man.

'I have had a shock,' he said, 'and I shall never recover. It is a
question of weeks. Well, life has been pleasant; I liked it; yes, sir, I
used to like it. I sometimes think if we knew all, we should be
more glad to get away.'

'Jekyll is ill, too,' observed Utterson. 'Have you seen him?'

But Lanyon's face changed, and he held up a trembling hand. 'I
wish to see or hear no more of Doctor Jekyll,' he said in a loud,
unsteady voice. 'I am quite done with that person; and I beg that
you will spare me any allusion to one whom I regard as dead.'

'Tut-tut,' said Mr. Utterson; and then after a considerable
pause, 'Can't I do anything?' he inquired. 'We are three very old
friends, Lanyon; we shall not live to make others.'

'Nothing can be done,' returned Lanyon; 'ask himself.'

'He will not see me,' said the lawyer.

'I am not surprised at that,' was the reply. 'Some day, Utterson,
after I am dead, you may perhaps come to learn the right and
wrong of this. I cannot tell you. And in the meantime, if you can
sit and talk with me of other things, for God's sake, stay and do
so; but if you cannot keep clear of this accursed topic, then, in
God's name, go, for I cannot bear it.'

As soon as he got home, Utterson sat down and wrote to

35

Jekyll, complaining of his exclusion from the house, and asking the cause of this unhappy break with Lanyon; and the next day brought him a long answer, often very pathetically worded, and sometimes darkly mysterious in drift. The quarrel with Lanyon was incurable. 'I do not blame our old friend,' Jekyll wrote, 'but I share his view that we must never meet. I mean from henceforth to lead a life of extreme seclusion; you must not be surprised, nor must you doubt my friendship, if my door is often shut even to you. You must suffer me to go my own dark way. I have brought on myself a punishment and a danger that I cannot name. If I am the chief of sinners, I am the chief of sufferers also. I could not think that this earth contained a place for sufferings and terrors so unmanning; and you can do but one thing, Utterson, to lighten this destiny, and that is to respect my silence.' Utterson was amazed; the dark influence of Hyde had been withdrawn, the doctor had returned to his old tasks and amities; a week ago, the prospect had smiled with every promise of a cheerful and an honoured age; and now in a moment, friendship, and peace of mind and the whole tenor of his life were wrecked. So great and unprepared a change pointed to madness; but in view of Lanyon's manner and words, there must lie for it some deeper ground.

A week afterwards Dr. Lanyon took to his bed, and in something less than a fortnight he was dead. The night after the funeral, at which he had been sadly affected, Utterson locked the door of his business room, and sitting there by the light of a melancholy candle, drew out and set before him an envelope addressed by the hand and sealed with the seal of his dead friend. 'PRIVATE: for the hands of J. G. Utterson ALONE and in case of his predecease *to be destroyed unread*,' so it was emphatically superscribed; and the lawyer dreaded to behold the contents. 'I have buried one friend to-day,' he thought: 'what if this should cost me another?' And then he condemned the fear as a disloyalty, and broke the seal. Within there was another enclosure, likewise sealed, and marked upon the cover as 'not to be opened till the death or disappearance of Dr. Henry Jekyll.' Utterson could not trust his eyes. Yes, it was disappearance; here again, as in the mad will which he had long ago restored to its author, here again were the idea of a disappearance and the name of Henry Jekyll bracketed. But in the will, that idea had sprung from the sinister suggestion of the man Hyde; it was set there with a purpose all too plain and horrible. Written by the hand of Lanyon, what should it mean? A great curiosity came on the trustee, to disregard the prohibition and dive at once to the bottom of these mysteries; but professional honour and faith to his dead friend were stringent obligations; and the packet slept in the inmost corner of his private safe.

It is one thing to mortify curiosity, another to conquer it; and it may be doubted if, from that day forth, Utterson desired the society of his surviving friend with the same eagerness. He thought of him kindly; but his thoughts were disquieted and fearful. He went to call indeed; but he was perhaps relieved to be denied admittance; perhaps, in his heart, he preferred to speak with Poole upon the doorstep and surrounded by the air and sounds of the open city, rather than to be admitted into that house of voluntary bondage, and to sit and speak with its inscrutable recluse. Poole had, indeed, no very pleasant news to communicate. The doctor, it appeared, now more than ever confined himself to the cabinet over the laboratory, where he would sometimes even sleep; he was out of spirits, he had grown very silent, he did not read; it seemed as if he had something on his mind. Utterson became so used to the unvarying character of these reports, that he fell off little by little in the frequency of his visits.

Incident at the Window

IT chanced on Sunday, when Mr. Utterson was on his usual walk with Mr. Enfield, that their way lay once again through the by-street; and that when they came in front of the door, both stopped to gaze on it.

'Well,' said Enfield, 'that story's at an end at least. We shall never see more of Mr. Hyde.'

'I hope not,' said Utterson. 'Did I ever tell you that I once saw him, and shared your feeling of repulsion?'

'It was impossible to do the one without the other,' returned Enfield. 'And by the way what an ass you must have thought me, not to know that this was a back way to Dr. Jekyll's! It was partly your own fault that I found it out, even when I did.'

'So you found it out, did you?' said Utterson. 'But if that be so, we may step into the court and take a look at the windows. To tell you the truth, I am uneasy about poor Jekyll; and even outside, I feel as if the presence of a friend might do him good.'

The court was very cool and a little damp, and full of premature twilight, although the sky, high up overhead, was still bright with sunset. The middle one of the three windows was half way open; and sitting close beside it, taking the air with an infinite sadness of mien, like some disconsolate prisoner, Utterson saw Dr. Jekyll.

'What! Jekyll!' he cried. 'I trust you are better.'

'I am very low, Utterson,' replied the doctor drearily, 'very low. It will not last long, thank God.'

'You stay too much indoors,' said the lawyer. 'You should be out, whipping up the circulation like Mr. Enfield and me. (This is my cousin – Mr. Enfield – Dr. Jekyll.) Come now; get your hat and take a quick turn with us.'

38

'You are very good,' sighed the other. 'I should like to very much; but no, no, no, it is quite impossible; I dare not. But indeed, Utterson, I am very glad to see you; this is really a great pleasure; I would ask you and Mr. Enfield up, but the place is really not fit.'

'Why then,' said the lawyer, good-naturedly, 'the best thing we can do is to stay down here and speak with you from where we are.'

'That is just what I was about to venture to propose,' returned the doctor with a smile. But the words were hardly uttered, before the smile was struck out of his face and succeeded by an expression of such abject terror and despair, as froze the very blood of the two gentlemen below. They saw it but for a glimpse, for the window was instantly thrust down; but that glimpse had been sufficient, and they turned and left the court without a word. In silence, too, they traversed the bystreet; and it was not until they had come into a neighbouring thoroughfare, where even upon a Sunday there were still some stirrings of life, that Mr. Utterson at last turned and looked at his companion. They were both pale; and there was an answering horror in their eyes.

'God forgive us, God forgive us,' said Mr. Utterson.

But Mr. Enfield only nodded his head very seriously, and walked on once more in silence.

The Last Night

MR. Utterson was sitting by his fireside one evening after dinner, when he was surprised to receive a visit from Poole.

'Bless me, Poole, what brings you here?' he cried; and then taking a second look at him, 'What ails you?' he added, 'is the doctor ill?'

'Mr. Utterson,' said the man, 'there is something wrong.'

'Take a seat, and here is a glass of wine for you,' said the lawyer. 'Now, take your time, and tell me plainly what you want.'

'You know the doctor's ways, sir,' replied Poole, 'and how he shuts himself up. Well, he's shut up again in the cabinet; and I don't like it, sir – I wish I may die if I like it. Mr. Utterson, sir, I'm afraid.'

'Now, my good man,' said the lawyer, 'be explicit. What are you afraid of?'

'I've been afraid for about a week,' returned Poole, doggedly disregarding the question, 'and I can bear it no more.'

The man's appearance amply bore out his words; his manner was altered for the worse; and except for the moment when he had first announced his terror, he had not once looked the lawyer in the face. Even now, he sat with the glass of wine untasted on his knee, and his eyes directed to a corner of the floor. 'I can bear it no more,' he repeated.

'Come,' said the lawyer, 'I see you have some good reason, Poole; I see there is something seriously amiss. Try to tell me what it is.'

'I think there's been foul play,' said Poole, hoarsely.

'Foul play!' cried the lawyer, a good deal frightened and rather inclined to be irritated in consequence. 'What foul play? What does the man mean?'

'I daren't say, sir,' was the answer; 'but will you come along with me and see for yourself?'

Mr. Utterson's only answer was to rise and get his hat and great coat; but he observed with wonder the greatness of the relief that appeared upon the butler's face, and perhaps with no less, that the wine was still untasted when he set it down to follow.

It was a wild, cold, seasonable night of March, with a pale moon, lying on her back as though the wind had tilted her, and a flying wrack of the most diaphanous and lawny texture. The wind made talking difficult, and flecked the blood into the face. It seemed to have swept the streets unusually bare of passengers, besides; for Mr. Utterson thought he had never seen that part of London so deserted. He could have wished it otherwise; never in his life had he been conscious of so sharp a wish to see and touch his fellow-creatures; for struggle as he might, there was borne in upon his mind a crushing anticipation of calamity. The square, when they got there, was all full of wind and dust, and the thin trees in the garden were lashing themselves along the railing. Poole, who had kept all the way a pace or two ahead, now pulled up in the middle of the pavement, and in spite of the biting weather, took off his hat and mopped his brow with a red pocket-handkerchief. But for all the hurry of his coming, these were not the dews of exertion that he wiped away, but the moisture of some strangling anguish; for his face was white and his voice, when he spoke, harsh and broken.

'Well, sir,' he said, 'here we are, and God grant there be nothing wrong.'

'Amen, Poole,' said the lawyer.

Thereupon the servant knocked in a very guarded manner; the door was opened on the chain; and a voice asked from within, 'Is that you, Poole?'

'It's all right,' said Poole. 'Open the door.'

The hall, when they entered it, was brightly lighted up; the fire was built high; and about the hearth the whole of the servants, men and women, stood huddled together like a flock of sheep. At the sight of Mr. Utterson, the housemaid broke into hysterical whimpering; and the cook, crying out 'Bless God! it's Mr. Utterson,' ran forward as if to take him in her arms.

'What, what? Are you all here?' said the lawyer peevishly. 'Very irregular, very unseemly; your master would be far from pleased.'

'They're all afraid,' said Poole.

Blank silence followed, no one protesting; only the maid lifted up her voice and now wept loudly.

'Hold your tongue!' Poole said to her, with a ferocity of accent that testified to his own jangled nerves; and indeed, when the girl had so suddenly raised the note of her lamentation, they had all started and turned towards the inner door with faces of dreadful expectation. 'And now,' continued the butler, addressing the knife-boy, 'reach me a candle, and we'll get this through hands at once.' And then he begged Mr. Utterson to follow him, and led the way to the back garden.

'Now, sir,' said he, 'you come as gently as you can. I want you to hear, and I don't want you to be heard. And see here, sir, if by any chance he was to ask you in, don't go.'

Mr. Utterson's nerves, at this unlooked-for termination, gave a jerk that nearly threw him from his balance; but he recollected his courage and followed the butler into the laboratory building and through the surgical theatre, with its lumber of crates and bottles, to the foot of the stair. Here Poole motioned him to stand on one side and listen; while he himself, setting down the candle and making a great and obvious call on his resolution, mounted the steps and knocked with a somewhat uncertain hand on the red baize of the cabinet door.

'Mr. Utterson, sir, asking to see you,' he called; and even as he did so, once more violently signed to the lawyer to give ear.

A voice answered from within: 'Tell him I cannot see anyone,' it said complainingly.

'Thank you, sir,' said Poole, with a note of something like triumph in his voice; and taking up his candle, he led Mr. Utterson back across the yard and into the great kitchen, where the fire was out and the beetles were leaping on the floor.

'Sir,' he said, looking Mr. Utterson in the eyes, 'was that my master's voice?'

'It seems much changed,' replied the lawyer, very pale, but giving look for look.

'Changed? Well, yes, I think so,' said the butler. 'Have I been twenty years in this man's house, to be deceived about his voice? No, sir; master's made away with; he was made away with, eight days ago, when we heard him cry out upon the name of God; and who's in there instead of him, and why it stays there, is a thing that cries to Heaven, Mr. Utterson!'

'This is a very strange tale, Poole; this is rather a wild tale, my man,' said Mr. Utterson, biting his finger. 'Suppose it were as you suppose, supposing Dr. Jekyll to have been – well, murdered, what could induce the murderer to stay? That won't hold water; it doesn't commend itself to reason.'

'Well, Mr. Utterson, you are a hard man to satisfy, but I'll do it yet,' said Poole. 'All this last week (you must know) him, or it, or whatever it is that lives in that cabinet, has been crying night and day for some sort of medicine and cannot get it to his mind. It was sometimes his way – the master's, that is – to write his orders on a sheet of paper and throw it on the stair. We've had nothing else this week back; nothing but papers, and a closed door, and the very meals left there to be smuggled in when nobody was looking. Well, sir, every day, ay, and twice and thrice in the same day, there have been orders and complaints, and I have been sent flying to all the wholesale chemists in town. Every time I brought the stuff back, there would be another paper telling me to return it, because it was not pure, and another order to a different firm. This drug is wanted bitter bad, sir, whatever for.'

'Have you any of these papers?' asked Mr. Utterson.

Poole felt in his pocket and handed out a crumpled note, which the lawyer, bending nearer to the candle, carefully examined. Its contents ran thus: 'Dr. Jekyll presents his compliments to Messrs. Maw. He assures them that their last sample is impure and quite useless for his present purpose. In the year 18—, Dr. J. purchased a somewhat large quantity from Messrs. M. He now begs them to search with the most sedulous care, and should any of the same quality be left, to forward it to him at once. Expense is no consideration. The importance of this to Dr. J. can hardly be exaggerated.' So far the letter had run composedly enough, but here with a sudden splutter of the pen, the writer's emotion had broken loose. 'For God's sake,' he had added, 'find me some of the old.'

43

'This is a strange note,' said Mr. Utterson; and then sharply, 'How do you come to have it open?'

'The man at Maw's was main angry, sir, and he threw it back to me like so much dirt,' returned Poole.

'This is unquestionably the doctor's hand, do you know?' resumed the lawyer.

'I thought it looked like it,' said the servant rather sulkily; and then, with another voice, 'But what matters hand of write,' he said. 'I've seen him!'

'Seen him?' repeated Mr. Utterson. 'Well?'

'That's it!' said Poole. 'It was this way. I came suddenly into the theatre from the garden. It seems he had slipped out to look for this drug or whatever it is; for the cabinet door was open, and there he was at the far end of the room digging among the crates. He looked up when I came in, gave a kind of cry, and whipped upstairs into the cabinet. It was but for one minute that I saw him, but the hair stood upon my head like quills. Sir, if that was my master, why had he a mask upon his face? If it was my master, why did he cry out like a rat, and run from me? I have served him long enough. And then...' the man paused and passed his hand over his face.

'These are all very strange circumstances,' said Mr. Utterson, 'but I think I begin to see daylight. Your master, Poole, is plainly seized with one of those maladies that both torture and deform the sufferer; hence, for aught I know, the alteration of his voice; hence the mask and his avoidance of his friends; hence his eagerness to find this drug, by means of which the poor soul retains some hope of ultimate recovery – God grant that he be not deceived! There is my explanation; it is sad enough, Poole, ay, and appalling to consider; but it is plain and natural, hangs well together and delivers us from all exorbitant alarms.'

'Sir,' said the butler, turning to a sort of mottled pallor, 'that thing was not my master, and there's the truth. My master' – here he looked round him and began to whisper – 'is a tall fine build of a man, and this was more of a dwarf.' Utterson attempted to protest. 'O, sir,' cried Poole, 'do you think I do not know my master after twenty years? do you think I do not know where his head comes to in the cabinet door, where I saw him every morning of my life? No, sir, that thing in the mask was never Doctor Jekyll – God knows what it was, but it was never Doctor Jekyll; and it is the belief of my heart that there was murder done.'

'Poole,' replied the lawyer, 'if you say that, it will become my duty to make certain. Much as I desire to spare your master's feelings, much as I am puzzled by this note which seems to prove him to be still alive, I shall consider it my duty to break in that door.'

'Ah, Mr. Utterson, that's talking!' cried the butler.

'And now comes the second question,' resumed Utterson: 'Who is going to do it?'

'Why, you and me, sir,' was the undaunted reply.

'That is very well said,' returned the lawyer; 'and whatever comes of it, I shall make it my business to see you are no loser.'

'There is an axe in the theatre,' continued Poole; 'and you might take the kitchen poker for yourself.'

The lawyer took that rude but weighty instrument into his hand, and balanced it. 'Do you know, Poole,' he said, looking up, 'that you and I are about to place ourselves in a position of some peril?'

'You may say so, sir, indeed,' returned the butler.

'It is well, then, that we should be frank,' said the other. 'We both think more than we have said; let us make a clean breast. This masked figure that you saw, did you recognise it?'

'Well, sir, it went so quick, and the creature was so doubled up, that I could hardly swear to that,' was the answer. 'But if you mean, was it Mr. Hyde? – why, yes, I think it was! You see, it was much of the same bigness; and it had the same quick light way with it; and then who else could have got in by the laboratory door? You have not forgot, sir, that at the time of the murder he had still the key with him? But that's not all. I don't know, Mr. Utterson, if ever you met this Mr. Hyde?'

'Yes,' said the lawyer, 'I once spoke with him.'

'Then you must know as well as the rest of us that there was something queer about that gentleman – something that gave a man a turn – I don't know rightly how to say it, sir, beyond this: that you felt it in your marrow kind of cold and thin.'

'I own I felt something of what you describe,' said Mr. Utterson.

'Quite so, sir,' returned Poole. 'Well, when that masked thing like a monkey jumped from among the chemicals and whipped into the cabinet, it went down my spine like ice. O, I know it's not evidence, Mr. Utterson; I'm book-learned enough for that; but a man has his feelings, and I give you my bible-word it was Mr. Hyde!'

'Ay, ay,' said the lawyer. 'My fears incline to the same point. Evil, I fear, founded – evil was sure to come – of that connection. Ay, truly, I believe you; I believe poor Harry is killed; and I believe his murderer (for what purpose, God alone can tell) is still lurking in his victim's room. Well, let our name be vengeance. Call Bradshaw.'

The footman came at the summons, very white and nervous.

'Pull yourself together, Bradshaw,' said the lawyer. 'This suspense, I know, is telling upon all of you; but it is now our intention to make an end of it. Poole, here, and I are going to force our way into the cabinet. If all is well, my shoulders are broad enough to bear the blame. Meanwhile, lest anything should really be amiss, or any malefactor seek to escape by the back, you and the boy must go round the corner with a pair of good sticks, and take your post at the laboratory door. We give you ten minutes, to get to your stations.'

As Bradshaw left, the lawyer looked at his watch. 'And now, Poole, let us get to ours,' he said; and taking the poker under his arm, he led the way into the yard. The scud had banked over the moon, and it was now quite dark. The wind, which only broke in puffs and draughts into that deep well of building, tossed the light of the candle to and fro about their steps, until they came into the shelter of the theatre, where they sat down silently to wait. London hummed solemnly all around; but nearer at hand, the stillness was only broken by the sound of a footfall moving to and fro along the cabinet floor.

'So it will walk all day, sir,' whispered Poole; 'ay, and the better part of the night. Only when a new sample comes from the chemist, there's a bit of a break. Ah, it's an ill-conscience that's such an enemy to rest! Ah, sir, there's blood foully shed in every step of it! But hark again, a little closer – put your heart in your ears, Mr. Utterson, and tell me, is that the doctor's foot?'

The steps fell lightly and oddly, with a certain swing, for all they went so slowly; it was different indeed from the heavy creaking tread of Henry Jekyll. Utterson sighed. 'Is there never anything else?' he asked.

Poole nodded. 'Once,' he said. 'Once I heard it weeping!'

'Weeping? how that?' said the lawyer, conscious of a sudden chill of horror.

'Weeping like a woman or a lost soul,' said the butler. 'I came away with that upon my heart, that I could have wept too.'

But now the ten minutes drew to an end. Poole disinterred the axe from under a stack of packing straw; the candle was set upon the nearest table to light them to the attack; and they drew near with bated breath to where that patient foot was still going up and down, up and down, in the quiet of the night.

'Jekyll,' cried Utterson, with a loud voice, 'I demand to see you.' He paused a moment, but there came no reply. 'I give you fair warning, our suspicions are aroused, and I must and shall see you,' he resumed; 'if not by fair means, then by foul – if not of your consent, then by brute force!'

'Utterson,' said the voice, 'for God's sake, have mercy!'

'Ah, that's not Jekyll's voice – it's Hyde's!' cried Utterson. 'Down with the door, Poole.'

Poole swung the axe over his shoulder; the blow shook the building, and the red baize door leaped against the lock and hinges. A dismal screech, as of mere animal terror, rang from the cabinet. Up went the axe again, and again the panels crashed and the frame bounded; four times the blow fell; but the wood was tough and the fittings were of excellent workmanship; and it was not until the fifth, that the lock burst in sunder and the wreck of the door fell inwards on the carpet.

The besiegers, appalled by their own riot and the stillness that had succeeded, stood back a little and peered in. There lay the cabinet before their eyes in the quiet lamplight, a good fire glowing and chattering on the hearth, the kettle singing its thin strain, a drawer or two open, papers neatly set forth on the business table, and nearer the fire, the things laid out for tea: the quietest room, you would have said, and, but for the glazed presses full of chemicals, the most commonplace that night in London.

Right in the midst there lay the body of a man sorely contorted and still twitching. They drew near on tiptoe, turned it on its back and beheld the face of Edward Hyde. He was dressed in clothes far too large for him, clothes of the doctor's bigness; the cords of his face still moved with a semblance of life, but life was quite gone; and by the crushed phial in the hand and the strong smell of kernels that hung upon the air, Utterson knew that he was looking on the body of a self-destroyer.

'We have come too late,' he said sternly, 'whether to save or punish. Hyde is gone to his account; and it only remains for us to find the body of your master.'

The far greater proportion of the building was occupied by the theatre, which filled almost the whole ground story and was lighted from above, and by the cabinet, which formed an upper story at one end and looked upon the court. A corridor joined the theatre to the door on the bystreet; and with this, the cabinet communicated separately by a second flight of stairs. There were besides a few dark closets and a spacious cellar. All these they now thoroughly examined. Each closet needed but a glance, for all were empty and all, by the dust that fell from their doors, had stood long unopened. The cellar, indeed, was filled with crazy lumber, mostly dating from the times of the surgeon who was Jekyll's predecessor; but even as they opened the door, they were advertised of the uselessness of further search, by the fall of a perfect mat of cobweb which had for years sealed up the entrance. Nowhere was there any trace of Henry Jekyll, dead or alive.

Poole stamped on the flags of the corridor. 'He must be buried here,' he said, hearkening to the sound.

'Or he may have fled,' said Utterson, and he turned to examine the door in the bystreet. It was locked; and lying near by on the flags, they found the key, already stained with rust.

'This does not look like use,' observed the lawyer.

'Use!' echoed Poole. 'Do you not see, sir, it is broken? much as if a man had stamped on it.'

'Ay,' continued Utterson, 'and the fractures, too, are rusty.' The two men looked at each other with a scare. 'This is beyond me, Poole,' said the lawyer. 'Let us go back to the cabinet.'

They mounted the stair in silence, and still with an occasional awestruck glance at the dead body, proceeded more thoroughly to examine the contents of the cabinet. At one table, there were traces of chemical work, various measured heaps of some white salt being laid on glass saucers, as though for an experiment in which the unhappy man had been prevented.

'That is the same drug that I was always bringing him,' said Poole; and even as he spoke, the kettle with a startling noise boiled over.

This brought them to the fireside, where the easy chair was drawn cosily up, and the tea things stood ready to the sitter's elbow, the very sugar in the cup. There were several books on a shelf; one lay beside the tea things open, and Utterson was amazed to find it a copy of a pious work, for which Jekyll had several times expressed a great esteem, annotated, in his own hand, with startling blasphemies.

Next, in the course of their review of the chamber, the searchers came to the cheval glass, into whose depths they looked with an involuntary horror. But it was so turned as to show them nothing but the rosy glow playing on the roof, the fire sparkling in a hundred repetitions along the glazed front of the presses, and their own pale and fearful countenances stooping to look in.

'This glass have seen some strange things, sir,' whispered Poole.

'And surely none stranger than itself,' echoed the lawyer in the same tones. 'For what did Jekyll' – he caught himself up at the word with a start, and then conquering the weakness: 'what could Jekyll want with it?' he said.

'You may say that!' said Poole.

Next they turned to the business table. On the desk among the neat array of papers, a large envelope was uppermost, and bore, in the doctor's hand, the name of Mr. Utterson. The lawyer unsealed it, and several enclosures fell to the floor. The first was a will, drawn in the same eccentric terms as the one which he had returned six months before, to serve as a testament in case of death and as a deed of gift in case of disappearance; but in place of the name of Edward Hyde, the lawyer, with indescribable amazement, read the name of Gabriel John Utterson. He looked at Poole, and then back at the paper, and last of all at the dead malefactor stretched upon the carpet.

'My head goes round,' he said. 'He has been all these days in possession; he had no cause to like me; he must have raged to see himself displaced; and he has not destroyed this document.'

He caught up the next paper; it was a brief note in the doctor's hand and dated at the top. 'O Poole!' the lawyer cried, 'he was alive and here this day. He cannot have been disposed of in so short a space, he must be still alive, he must have fled! And then, why fled? and how? and in that case, can we venture to declare this suicide? O, we must be careful. I foresee that we may yet involve your master in some dire catastrophe.'

'Why don't you read it, sir?' asked Poole.

'Because I fear,' replied the lawyer solemnly. 'God grant I have no cause for it!' And with that he brought the paper to his eyes and read as follows.

> 'My dear Utterson, —When this shall fall into your hands, I shall have disappeared, under what circumstances I have not the penetration to foresee, but my instinct and all the circumstances of my nameless situation tell me that the end is sure and must be early. Go then, and first read the narrative which Lanyon warned me he was to place in your hands; and if you care to hear more, turn to the confession of
>
>   'Your unworthy and unhappy friend,
>   'HENRY JEKYLL.'

'There was a third enclosure?' asked Utterson.

'Here, sir,' said Poole, and gave into his hands a considerable packet sealed in several places.

The lawyer put it in his pocket. 'I would say nothing of this paper. If your master has fled or is dead, we may at least save his credit. It is now ten; I must go home and read these documents in quiet; but I shall be back before midnight, when we shall send for the police.'

They went out, locking the door of the theatre behind them; and Utterson, once more leaving the servants gathered about the fire in the hall, trudged back to his office to read the two narratives in which this mystery was now to be explained.

Dr. Lanyon's Narrative

ON the ninth of January, now four days ago, I received by the evening delivery a registered envelope, addressed in the hand of my colleague and old school-companion, Henry Jekyll. I was a good deal surprised by this; for we were by no means in the habit of correspondence; I had seen the man, dined with him, indeed, the night before; and I could imagine nothing in our intercourse that should justify the formality of registration. The contents increased my wonder; for this is how the letter ran:

> '10th December 18—
> 'Dear Lanyon, —You are one of my oldest friends; and although we may have differed at times on scientific questions, I cannot remember, at least on my side, any break in our affection. There was never a day when, if you had said to me, "Jekyll, my life, my honour, my reason, depend upon you," I would not have sacrificed my fortune or my left hand to help you. Lanyon, my life, my honour, my reason, are all at your mercy; if you fail me to-night, I am lost. You might suppose, after this preface, that I am going to ask you for something dishonourable to grant. Judge for yourself.
> 'I want you to postpone all other engagements for to-night – ay, even if you were summoned to the bedside of an emperor; to take a cab, unless your carriage should be actually at the door; and with this letter in your hand for consultation, to drive straight to my house. Poole, my butler, has his orders; you will find him waiting your arrival with a locksmith. The door of my cabinet is then to be forced; and you are to go in alone; to open the glazed press (letter E) on the left hand, breaking the lock if it be shut; and to draw out, *with all its contents as they stand*, the fourth drawer from the top or (which is the same thing) the third from the bottom. In my extreme distress of mind, I have a morbid fear of misdirecting you; but even if I am in error, you may know the right drawer by its contents: some powders, a phial and a paper book. This drawer I

beg of you to carry back with you to Cavendish Square exactly as it stands.

'That is the first part of the service: now for the second. You should be back, if you set out at once on the receipt of this, long before midnight; but I will leave you that amount of margin, not only in the fear of one of those obstacles that can neither be prevented nor foreseen, but because an hour when your servants are in bed is to be preferred for what will then remain to do. At midnight, then, I have to ask you to be alone in your consulting room, to admit with your own hand into the house a man who will present himself in my name, and to place in his hands the drawer that you will have brought with you from my cabinet. Then you will have played your part and earned my gratitude completely. Five minutes afterwards, if you insist upon an explanation, you will have understood that these arrangements are of capital importance; and that by the neglect of one of them, fantastic as they must appear, you might have charged your conscience with my death or the shipwreck of my reason.

'Confident as I am that you will not trifle with this appeal, my heart sinks and my hand trembles at the bare thought of such a possibility. Think of me at this hour, in a strange place, labouring under a blackness of distress that no fancy can exaggerate, and yet well aware that, if you will but punctually serve me, my troubles will roll away like a story that is told. Serve me, my dear Lanyon, and save

'Your friend,
'H. J.

'P.S. I had already sealed this up when a fresh terror struck upon my soul. It is possible that the post office may fail me, and this letter not come into your hands until to-morrow morning. In that case, dear Lanyon, do my errand when it shall be most convenient for you in the course of the day; and once more expect my messenger at midnight. It may then already be too late; and if that night passes without event, you will know that you have seen the last of Henry Jekyll.'

Upon the reading of this letter, I made sure my colleague was insane; but till that was proved beyond the possibility of doubt, I felt bound to do as he requested. The less I understood of this farrago, the less I was in a position to judge of its importance; and an appeal so worded could not be set aside without a grave responsibility. I rose accordingly from table, got into a hansom, and drove straight to Jekyll's house. The butler was awaiting my arrival; he had received by the same post as mine a registered letter of instruction, and had sent at once for a locksmith and a

[handwritten margin notes: "like Stevenson's Greshott unmarked powders etc"]

carpenter. The tradesmen came while we were yet speaking; and we moved in a body to old Dr. Denman's surgical theatre, from which (as you are doubtless aware) Jekyll's private cabinet is most conveniently entered. The door was very strong, the lock excellent; the carpenter avowed he would have great trouble and have to do much damage, if force were to be used; and the locksmith was near despair. But this last was a handy fellow, and after two hours' work, the door stood open. The press marked E was unlocked; and I took out the drawer, had it filled up with straw and tied in a sheet, and returned with it to Cavendish Square.

Here I proceeded to examine its contents. The powders were neatly enough made up, but not with the nicety of the dispensing chemist; so that it was plain they were of Jekyll's private manu-facture; and when I opened one of the wrappers, I found what seemed to me a simple, crystalline salt of a white colour. The phial, to which I next turned my attention, might have been about half-full of a blood-red liquor, which was highly pungent to the sense of smell and seemed to me to contain phosphorus and some volatile ether. At the other ingredients, I could make no guess. The book was an ordinary version book and contained little but a series of dates. These covered a period of many years, but I observed that the entries ceased nearly a year ago and quite abruptly. Here and there a brief remark was appended to a date, usually no more than a single word: 'double' occurring perhaps six times in a total of several hundred entries; and once very early in the list and followed by several marks of exclamation, 'total failure!!!' All this, though it whetted my curiosity, told me little that was definite. Here were a phial of some tincture, a paper of some salt, and the record of a series of experiments that had led (like too many of Jekyll's investigations) to no end of practical usefulness. How could the presence of these articles in my house affect either the honour, the sanity, or the life of my flighty colleague? If his messenger could go to one place, why could he not go to another? And even granting some impediment, why was this gentleman to be received by me in secret? The more I reflected, the more convinced I grew that I was dealing with a case of cerebral disease; and though I dismissed my servants to bed, I loaded an old revolver that I might be found in some posture of self-defence.

[handwritten margin note: "degeneration worse one / time"]

Twelve o'clock had scarce rung out over London, ere the knocker sounded very gently on the door. I went myself at the summons, and found a small man crouching against the pillars of the portico.

'Are you come from Dr. Jekyll?' I asked.

He told me 'yes' by a constrained gesture; and when I had bidden him enter, he did not obey me without a searching backward glance into the darkness of the square. There was a policeman not far off, advancing with his bull's eye open; and at the sight, I thought my visitor started and made greater haste.

These particulars struck me, I confess, disagreeably; and as I followed him into the bright light of the consulting room, I kept my hand ready on my weapon. Here, at last, I had a chance of clearly seeing him. I had never set eyes on him before, so much was certain. He was small, as I have said; I was struck besides with the shocking expression of his face, with his remarkable combination of great muscular activity and great apparent debility of constitution, and – last but not least – with the odd, subjective disturbance caused by his neighbourhood. This bore some resemblance to incipient rigor, and was accompanied by a marked sinking of the pulse. At the time, I set it down to some idiosyncratic, personal distaste, and merely wondered at the acuteness of the symptoms; but I have since had reason to believe the cause to lie much deeper in the nature of man, and to turn on some nobler hinge than the principle of hatred.

This person (who had thus, from the first moment of his entrance, struck in me what I can only describe as a disgustful curiosity) was dressed in a fashion that would have made an ordinary person laughable: his clothes, that is to say, although they were of rich and sober fabric, were enormously too large for him in every measurement – the trousers hanging on his legs and rolled up to keep them from the ground, the waist of the coat below his haunches, and the collar sprawling wide upon his shoulders. Strange to relate, this ludicrous accoutrement was far from moving me to laughter. Rather, as there was something abnormal and misbegotten in the very essence of the creature that now faced me – something seizing, surprising and revolting – this fresh disparity seemed but to fit in with and to reïnforce it; so that to

my interest in the man's nature and character, there was added a
curiosity as to his origin, his life, his fortune and status in the
world.

These observations, though they have taken so great a space to
be set down in, were yet the work of a few seconds. My visitor
was, indeed, on fire with sombre excitement.

'Have you got it?' he cried. 'Have you got it?' And so lively
was his impatience that he even laid his hand upon my arm and
sought to shake me.

I put him back, conscious at his touch of a certain icy pang
along my blood. 'Come, sir,' said I. 'You forget that I have not yet
the pleasure of your acquaintance. Be seated, if you please.' And I
showed him an example, and sat down myself in my customary
seat and with as fair an imitation of my ordinary manner to a
patient, as the lateness of the hour, the nature of my prëoccupations,
and the horror I had of my visitor, would suffer me to muster.

'I beg your pardon, Dr. Lanyon,' he replied civilly enough.
'What you say is very well founded; and my impatience has
shown its heels to my politeness. I come here at the instance of
your colleague, Dr. Henry Jekyll, on a piece of business of some
moment; and I understood...' he paused and put his hand to his
throat, and I could see, in spite of his collected manner, that he
was wrestling against the approaches of the hysteria – 'I understood, a drawer...'

But here I took pity on my visitor's suspense, and some perhaps
on my own growing curiosity.

'There it is, sir,' said I, pointing to the drawer, where it lay on
the floor behind a table and still covered with the sheet.

He sprang to it, and then paused, and laid his hand upon his
heart; I could hear his teeth grate with the convulsive action of his
jaws; and his face was so ghastly to see that I grew alarmed both
for his life and reason.

'Compose yourself,' said I.

He turned a dreadful smile to me, and as if with the decision of
despair, plucked away the sheet. At sight of the contents, he uttered
one loud sob of such immense relief that I sat petrified. And the
next moment, in a voice that was already fairly well under control,
'Have you a graduated glass?' he asked.

I rose from my place with something of an effort and gave him what he asked.

He thanked me with a smiling nod, measured out a few minims of the red tincture and added one of the powders. The mixture, which was at first of a reddish hue, began, in proportion as the crystals melted, to brighten in colour, to effervesce audibly, and to throw off small fumes of vapour. Suddenly and at the same moment, the ebullition ceased and the compound changed to a dark purple, which faded again more slowly to a watery green. My visitor, who had watched these metamorphoses with a keen eye, smiled, set down the glass upon the table, and then turned and looked upon me with an air of scrutiny.

'And now,' said he, 'to settle what remains. Will you be wise? will you be guided? will you suffer me to take this glass in my hand and to go forth from your house without further parley? or has the greed of curiosity too much command of you? Think before you answer, for it shall be done as you decide. As you decide, you shall be left as you were before, and neither richer nor wiser, unless the sense of service rendered to a man in mortal distress may be counted as a kind of riches of the soul. Or, if you shall so prefer to choose, a new province of knowledge and new avenues to fame and power shall be laid open to you, here, in this room, upon the instant; and your sight shall be blasted by a prodigy to stagger the unbelief of Satan.'

'Sir,' said I, affecting a coolness that I was far from truly possessing, 'you speak enigmas, and you will perhaps not wonder that I hear you with no very strong impression of belief. But I have gone too far in the way of inexplicable services to pause before I see the end.'

'It is well,' replied my visitor. 'Lanyon, you remember your vows: what follows is under the seal of our profession. And now, you who have so long been bound to the most narrow and material views, you who have denied the virtue of transcendental medicine, you who have derided your superiors – behold!'

He put the glass to his lips and drank at one gulp. A cry followed; he reeled, staggered, clutched at the table and held on, staring with injected eyes, gasping with open mouth; and as I looked there came, I thought, a change – he seemed to swell – his face became suddenly black and the features seemed to melt and alter – and the next moment, I had sprung to my feet and leaped back against the wall, my arm raised to shield me from that prodigy, my mind submerged in terror.

'O God!' I screamed, and 'O God!' again and again; for there before my eyes – pale and shaken, and half fainting, and groping before him with his hands, like a man restored from death – there stood Henry Jekyll!

What he told me in the next hour, I cannot bring my mind to set on paper. I saw what I saw, I heard what I heard, and my soul sickened at it; and yet now when that sight has faded from my eyes, I ask myself if I believe it, and I cannot answer. My life is shaken to its roots; sleep has left me; the deadliest terror sits by me at all hours of the day and night; I feel that my days are numbered, and that I must die; and yet I shall die incredulous. As for the moral turpitude that man unveiled to me, even with tears of penitence, I cannot, even in memory, dwell on it without a start of horror. I will say but one thing, Utterson, and that (if you can bring your mind to credit it) will be more than enough. The creature who crept into my house that night was, on Jekyll's own confession, known by the name of Hyde and hunted for in every corner of the land as the murderer of Carew.

HASTIE LANYON.

Henry Jekyll's Full Statement of the Case

I was born in the year 18— to a large fortune, endowed besides with excellent parts, inclined by nature to industry, fond of the respect of the wise and good among my fellow-men, and thus, as might have been supposed, with every guarantee of an honourable and distinguished future. And indeed the worst of my faults was a certain impatient gaiety of disposition, such as has made the happiness of many, but such as I found it hard to reconcile with my imperious desire to carry my head high, and wear a more than commonly grave countenance before the public. Hence it came about that I concealed my pleasures; and that when I reached years of reflection, and began to look round me and take stock of my progress and position in the world, I stood already committed to a profound duplicity of life. Many a man would have even blazoned such irregularities as I was guilty of; but from the high views that I had set before me, I regarded and hid them with an almost morbid sense of shame. It was thus rather the exacting nature of my aspirations than any particular degradation in my faults, that made me what I was and, with even a deeper trench than in the majority of men, severed in me those provinces of good and ill which divide and compound man's dual nature. In this case, I was driven to reflect deeply and inveterately on that hard law of life, which lies at the root of religion and is one of the most plentiful springs of distress. Though so profound a double-dealer, I was in no sense a hypocrite; both sides of me were in dead earnest; I was no more myself when I laid aside restraint and plunged in shame, than when I laboured, in the eye of day, at the furtherance of knowledge or the relief of sorrow and suffering. And it chanced that the direction of my scientific studies, which led wholly towards the mystic and the transcendental, rëacted and shed a strong light on this consciousness of the perennial war among my members. With every day, and from both sides of my intelligence, the moral and the intellectual, I thus drew steadily nearer to that truth, by whose partial discovery I have been doomed to such a dreadful shipwreck: that man is not truly one, but truly two. I say two, because the state of my own knowledge does not pass beyond that point. Others will follow, others will outstrip me on the same lines; and I hazard the guess that man will be ultimately known for a mere polity of multifarious, incongruous and independent denizens. I for my part, from the nature of my life, advanced infallibly in one direction and in one direction only. It was on the moral side, and in my own person, that I learned to recognise the thorough and primitive duality of man; I saw that, of the two natures that contended in the field of my conscious-ness, even if I could rightly be said to be either, it was only because I was radically both; and from an early date, even before the course of my scientific discoveries had begun to suggest the most naked possibility of such a miracle, I had learned to dwell with pleasure, as a beloved daydream, on the thought of the separation of these elements. If each, I told myself, could but be housed in separate identities, life would be relieved of all that was unbearable; the unjust might go his way, delivered from the aspirations and remorse of his more upright twin; and the just could walk stead-fastly and securely on his upward path, doing the good things in which he found his pleasure, and no longer exposed to disgrace and penitence by the hands of this extraneous evil. It was the curse of mankind that these incongruous faggots were thus bound together – that in the agonised womb of consciousness, these polar twins should be continuously struggling. How, then, were they dissociated?

I was so far in my reflections when, as I have said, a side light began to shine upon the subject from the laboratory table. I began to perceive more deeply than it has ever yet been stated, the trembling immateriality, the mist-like transience, of this seemingly so solid body in which we walk attired. Certain agents I found to have the power to shake and to pluck back that fleshly vestment, even as a wind might toss the curtains of a pavilion. For two good reasons, I will not enter deeply into this scientific branch of my confession. First, because I have been made to learn that the doom and burthen of our life is bound forever on man's shoulders, and when the attempt is made to cast it off, it but returns upon us with more unfamiliar and more awful pressure. Second, because as my narrative will make alas! too evident, my discoveries were incomplete. Enough, then, that I not only recognised my natural body for the mere aura and effulgence of certain of the powers that made up my spirit, but managed to compound a drug by which these powers should be dethroned from their supremacy, and a second form and countenance substituted, none the less natural to me because they were the expression, and bore the stamp, of lower elements in my soul.

I hesitated long before I put this theory to the test of practice. I knew well that I risked death; for any drug that so potently controlled and shook the very fortress of identity, might by the least scruple of an overdose or at the least inopportunity in the moment of exhibition, utterly blot out that immaterial tabernacle which I looked to it to change. But the temptation of a discovery so singular and profound, at last overcame the suggestions of alarm. I had long since prepared my tincture; I purchased at once, from a firm of wholesale chemists, a large quantity of a particular salt which I knew, from my experiments, to be the last ingredient required; and late one accursed night, I compounded the elements, watched them boil and smoke together in the glass, and when the ebullition had subsided, with a strong glow of courage, drank off the potion.

The most racking pangs succeeded: a grinding in the bones, deadly nausea, and a horror of the spirit that cannot be exceeded at the hour of birth or death. Then these agonies began swiftly to subside, and I came to myself as if out of a great sickness. There was something strange in my sensations, something indescribably new and, from its very novelty, incredibly sweet. I felt younger, lighter, happier in body; within I was conscious of a heady reck-lessness, a current of disordered sensual images running like a mill race in my fancy, a solution of the bonds of obligation, an unknown but not an innocent freedom of the soul. I knew myself, at the first breath of this new life, to be more wicked, tenfold more wicked, sold a slave to my original evil; and the thought, in that moment, braced and delighted me like wine. I stretched out my hands, exulting in the freshness of these sensations; and in the act, I was suddenly aware that I had lost in stature.

There was no mirror, at that date, in my room; that which stands beside me as I write, was brought there later on and for the very purpose of these transformations. The night, however, was far gone into the morning – the morning, black as it was, was nearly ripe for the conception of the day – the inmates of my house were locked in the most rigorous hours of slumber; and I determined, flushed as I was with hope and triumph, to venture in my new shape as far as to my bedroom. I crossed the yard, wherein the constellations looked down upon me, I could have thought, with wonder, the first creature of that sort that their unsleeping vigilance had yet disclosed to them; I stole through the corridors, a stranger in my own house; and coming to my room, I saw for the first time the appearance of Edward Hyde.

I must here speak by theory alone, saying not that which I know, but that which I suppose to be most probable. The evil side of my nature, to which I had now transferred the stamping efficacy, was less robust and less developed than the good which I had just deposed. Again, in the course of my life, which had been, after all, nine tenths a life of effort, virtue and control, it had been much less exercised and much less exhausted. And hence, as I think, it came about that Edward Hyde was so much smaller, slighter and younger than Henry Jekyll. Even as good shone upon the countenance of the one, evil was written broadly and plainly on the face of the other. Evil besides (which I must still believe to be the lethal side of man) had left on that body an imprint of deformity and decay. And yet when I looked upon that ugly idol in the glass, I was conscious of no repugnance, rather of a leap of welcome. This, too, was myself. It seemed natural and human. In my eyes it bore a livelier image of the spirit, it seemed more express and single, than the imperfect and divided countenance, I had been hitherto accustomed to call mine. And in so far I was doubtless right. I have observed that when I wore the semblance of Edward Hyde, none could come near to me at first without a visible misgiving of the flesh. This, as I take it, was because all human beings, as we meet them, are commingled out of good and evil: and Edward Hyde, alone in the ranks of mankind, was pure evil.

I lingered but a moment at the mirror: the second and conclusive experiment had yet to be attempted; it yet remained to be seen if I had lost my identity beyond redemption and must flee before daylight from a house that was no longer mine; and hurrying back to my cabinet, I once more prepared and drank the cup, once more suffered the pangs of dissolution, and came to myself once more with the character, the stature and the face of Henry Jekyll.

That night I had come to the fatal cross roads. Had I approached my discovery in a more noble spirit, had I risked the experiment while under the empire of generous or pious aspirations, all must have been otherwise, and from these agonies of death and birth, I had come forth an angel instead of a fiend. The drug had no discriminating action; it was neither diabolical nor divine; it but shook the doors of the prisonhouse of my disposition; and like the captives of Philippi, that which stood within ran forth. At that time my virtue slumbered; my evil, kept awake by ambition, was alert and swift to seize the occasion; and the thing that was projected was Edward Hyde. Hence, although I had now two characters as well as two appearances, one was wholly evil, and the other was still the old Henry Jekyll, that incongruous compound of whose reformation and improvement I had already learned to despair. The movement was thus wholly toward the worse.

Even at that time, I had not yet conquered my aversion to the dryness of a life of study. I would still be merrily disposed at times; and as my pleasures were (to say the least) undignified, and I was not only well known and highly considered, but growing towards the elderly man, this incoherency of my life was daily growing more unwelcome. It was on this side that my new power tempted me until I fell in slavery. I had but to drink the cup, to doff at once the body of the noted professor, and to assume, like a thick cloak, that of Edward Hyde. I smiled at the notion; it seemed to me at the time to be humorous; and I made my preparations with the most studious care. I took and furnished that house in Soho, to which Hyde was tracked by the police; and engaged as housekeeper a creature whom I well knew to be silent and unscrupulous. On the other side, I announced to my servants that a Mr. Hyde (whom I described) was to have full liberty and power about my house in the square; and to parry mishaps, I even called and made myself a familiar object, in my second character. I next drew up that will to which you so much objected; so that if anything befell me in the person of Doctor Jekyll, I could enter on that of Edward Hyde without pecuniary loss. And thus fortified, as I supposed, on every side, I began to profit by the strange immunities of my position.

Men have before hired bravos to transact their crimes, while their own person and reputation sat under shelter. I was the first that ever did so for his pleasures. I was the first that could thus plod in the public eye with a load of genial respectability, and in a moment, like a schoolboy, strip off these lendings and spring headlong into the sea of liberty. But for me, in my impenetrable mantle, the safety was complete. Think of it – I did not even exist! Let me but escape into my laboratory door, give me but a second or two to mix and swallow the draught that I had always standing ready; and whatever he had done, Edward Hyde would pass away like the stain of breath upon a mirror; and there in his stead, quietly at home, trimming the midnight lamp in his study, a man who could afford to laugh at suspicion, would be Henry Jekyll.

The pleasures which I made haste to seek in my disguise were, as I have said, undignified; I would scarce use a harder term. But in the hands of Edward Hyde, they soon began to turn towards the monstrous. When I would come back from these excursions, I was often plunged into a kind of wonder at my vicarious depravity. This familiar that I called out of my own soul, and sent forth alone to do his good pleasure, was a being inherently malign and villainous; his every act and thought centred on self; drinking pleasure with bestial avidity from any degree of torture to another; relentless like a man of stone. Henry Jekyll stood at times aghast before the acts of Edward Hyde; but the situation was apart from ordinary laws, and insidiously relaxed the grasp of conscience. It was Hyde, after all, and Hyde alone, that was guilty. Jekyll was no worse; he woke again to his good qualities seemingly unimpaired; he would even make haste, where it was possible, to undo the evil done by Hyde. And thus his conscience slumbered.

Into the details of the infamy at which I thus connived (for even now I can scarce grant that I committed it) I have no design of entering; I mean but to point out the warnings and the successive steps with which my chastisement approached. I met with one accident which, as it brought on no consequence, I shall no more than mention. An act of cruelty to a child aroused against me the anger of a passer by, whom I recognised the other day in the person of your kinsman; the doctor and the child's family joined him; there were moments when I feared for my life; and at last, in order to pacify their too just resentment, Edward Hyde had to bring them to the door, and pay them in a cheque drawn in the name, of Henry Jekyll. But this danger was easily eliminated from the future, by opening an account at another bank in the name of Edward Hyde himself; and when, by sloping my own hand backward, I had supplied my double with a signature, I thought I sat beyond the reach of fate.

Some two months before the murder of Sir Danvers, I had been out for one of my adventures, had returned at a late hour, and woke the next day in bed with somewhat odd sensations. It was in vain I looked about me; in vain I saw the decent furniture and tall proportions of my room in the square; in vain that I recognised the pattern of the bed curtains and the design of the mahogany frame; something still kept insisting that I was not where I was, that I had not wakened where I seemed to be, but in the little room in Soho where I was accustomed to sleep in the body of Edward Hyde. I smiled to myself, and, in my psychological way, began lazily to inquire into the elements of this illusion, occasionally, even as I did so, dropping back into a comfortable morning doze. I was still so engaged when, in one of my more wakeful moments, my eye fell upon my hand. Now the hand of Henry Jekyll (as you have often remarked) was professional in shape and size: it was large, firm, white and comely. But the hand which I now saw, clearly enough, in the yellow light of a mid-London morning, lying half shut on the bed clothes, was lean, corded, knuckly, of a dusky pallor and thickly shaded with a swart growth of hair. It was the hand of Edward Hyde.

I must have stared upon it for near half a minute, sunk as I was in the mere stupidity of wonder, before terror woke up in my breast as sudden and startling as the crash of cymbals; and bounding from my bed, I rushed to the mirror. At the sight that met my eyes, my blood was changed into something exquisitely thin and icy. Yes, I had gone to bed Henry Jekyll, I had awakened Edward Hyde. How was this to be explained? I asked myself; and then, with another bound of terror – how was it to be remedied? It was well on in the morning; the servants were up; all my drugs were in the cabinet – a long journey, down two pair of stairs, through the back passage, across the open court and through the anatomical theatre, from where I was then standing horror-struck. It might indeed be possible to cover my face; but of what use was that, when I was unable to conceal the alteration in my stature? And then with an overpowering sweetness of relief, it came back upon my mind that the servants were already used to the coming and going of my second self. I had soon dressed, as well as I was able, in clothes of my own size: had soon passed through the house, where Bradshaw stared and drew back at seeing Mr. Hyde at such an hour and in such a strange array; and ten minutes later, Dr. Jekyll had returned to his own shape and was sitting down, with a darkened brow, to make a feint of breakfasting.

Small indeed was my appetite. This inexplicable incident, this reversal of my previous experience, seemed, like the Babylonian finger on the wall, to be spelling out the letters of my judgment; and I began to reflect more seriously than ever before on the issues and possibilities of my double existence. That part of me which I had the power of projecting, had lately been much exercised and nourished; it had seemed to me of late as though the body of Edward Hyde had grown in stature, as though (when I wore that form) I were conscious of a more generous tide of blood; and I began to spy a danger that, if this were much prolonged, the balance of my nature might be permanently overthrown, the power of voluntary change be forfeited, and the character of Edward Hyde become irrevocably mine. The power of the drug had not been always equally displayed. Once, very early in my career, it had totally failed me; since then I had been obliged on more than one occasion to double, and once, with infinite risk of death, to treble the amount; and these rare uncertainties had cast hitherto the sole shadow on my contentment. Now, however, and in the light of that morning's accident, I was led to remark that whereas, in the beginning, the difficulty had been to throw off the body of Jekyll, it had of late, gradually but decidedly transferred itself to the other side. All things therefore seemed to point to this: that I was slowly losing hold of my original and better self, and becoming slowly incorporated with my second and worse.

Between these two, I now felt I had to choose. My two natures had memory in common, but all other faculties were most unequally shared between them. Jekyll (who was composite) now with the most sensitive apprehensions, now with a greedy gusto, projected and shared in the pleasures and adventures of Hyde; but Hyde was indifferent to Jekyll, or but remembered him as the mountain bandit remembers the cavern in which he conceals himself from pursuit. Jekyll had more than a father's interest; Hyde had more than a son's indifference. To cast in my lot with Jekyll, was to die to those appetites which I had long secretly indulged and had of late begun to pamper. To cast it in with Hyde, was to die to a thousand interests and aspirations, and to become, at a blow and forever, despised and friendless. The bargain might appear unequal; but there was still another consideration in the scales; for while Jekyll would suffer smartingly in the fires of abstinence, Hyde would be not even conscious of all that he had lost. Strange as my circumstances were, the terms of this debate are as old and commonplace as man; much the same inducements and alarms cast the die for any tempted and trembling sinner; and it fell out with me, as it falls with so vast a majority of my fellows, that I chose the better part and was found wanting in the strength to keep to it.

Yes, I preferred the elderly and discontented doctor, surrounded by friends and cherishing honest hopes; and bade a resolute farewell to the liberty, the comparative youth, the light step, leaping pulses and secret pleasures, that I had enjoyed in the disguise of Hyde. I made this choice perhaps with some unconscious reservation, for I neither gave up the house in Soho, nor destroyed the clothes of Edward Hyde, which still lay ready in my cabinet. For two months, however, I was true to my determination; for two months, I led a life of such severity as I had never before attained to, and enjoyed the compensations of an approving conscience.

But time began at last to obliterate the freshness of my alarm; the praises of conscience began to grow into a thing of course; I began to be tortured with throes and longings, as of Hyde struggling after freedom; and at last, in an hour of moral weakness, I once again compounded and swallowed the transforming draught.

I do not suppose that, when a drunkard reasons with himself upon his vice, he is once out of five hundred times affected by the dangers that he runs through his brutish, physical insensibility; neither had I, long as I had considered my position, made enough allowance for the complete moral insensibility and insensate readiness to evil, which were the leading characters of Edward Hyde. Yet it was by these that I was punished. My devil had been long caged, he came out roaring. I was conscious, even when I took the draught, of a more unbridled, a more furious propensity to ill. It must have been this, I suppose, that stirred in my soul that tempest of impatience with which I listened to the civilities of my unhappy victim; I declare at least, before God, no man morally sane could have been guilty of that crime upon so pitiful a provocation; and that I struck in no more reasonable spirit than that in which a sick child may break a plaything. But I had voluntarily stripped myself of all those balancing instincts, by which even the worst of us continues to walk with some degree of steadiness among temptations; and in my case, to be tempted, however slightly, was to fall.

Instantly the spirit of hell awoke in me and raged. With a transport of glee, I mauled the unresisting body, tasting delight from every blow; and it was not till weariness had begun to succeed, that I was suddenly, in the top fit of my delirium, struck through the heart by a cold thrill of terror. A mist dispersed; I saw my life to be forfeit; and fled from the scene of these excesses, at once glorying and trembling, my lust of evil gratified and stimulated, my love of life screwed to the topmost peg. I ran to the house in Soho, and (to make assurance doubly sure) destroyed my papers; thence I set out through the lamplit streets, in the same divided ecstasy of mind, gloating on my crime, light-headedly devising others in the future, and yet still hastening and still hearkening in my wake for the steps of the avenger. Hyde had a song upon his lips as he compounded the draught, and as he drank it, pledged the dead man. The pangs of transformation had not done tearing him, before Henry Jekyll, with streaming tears of gratitude and remorse, had fallen upon his knees and lifted his clasped hands to God. The veil of self-indulgence was rent from head to foot, I saw my life as a whole: I followed it up from the days of childhood, when I had walked with my father's hand, and through the self-denying toils of my professional life, to arrive again and again, with the same sense of unreality, at the damned horrors of the evening. I could have screamed aloud; I sought with tears and prayers to smother down the crowd of hideous images and sounds with which my memory swarmed against me; and still, between the petitions, the ugly face of my iniquity stared into my soul. As the acuteness of this remorse began to die away, it was succeeded by a sense of joy. The problem of my conduct was solved. Hyde was thenceforth impossible; whether I would or not, I was now confined to the better part of my existence; and O, how I rejoiced to think it! with what willing humility, I embraced anew the restrictions of natural life! with what sincere renunciation, I locked the door by which I had so often gone and come, and ground the key under my heel!

The next day, came the news that the murder had been overlooked, that the guilt of Hyde was patent to the world, and that the victim was a man high in public estimation. It was not only a crime, it had been a tragic folly. I think I was glad to know it; I think I was glad to have my better impulses thus buttressed and guarded by the terrors of the scaffold. Jekyll was now my city of refuge; let but Hyde peep out an instant, and the hands of all men would be raised to take and slay him.

I resolved in my future conduct to redeem the past; and I can say with honesty that my resolve was fruitful of some good. You know yourself how earnestly in the last months of last year, I laboured to relieve suffering; you know that much was done for others, and that the days passed quietly, almost happily for myself. Nor can I truly say that I wearied of this beneficent and innocent life; I think instead that I daily enjoyed it more completely; but I was still cursed with my duality of purpose; and as the first edge of my penitence wore off, the lower side of me, so long indulged, so recently chained down, began to growl for license. Not that I dreamed of resuscitating Hyde; the bare idea of that would startle me to frenzy: no, it was in my own person, that I was once more tempted to trifle with my conscience; and it was as an ordinary secret sinner, that I at last fell before the assaults of temptation.

There comes an end to all things; the most capacious measure is filled at last; and this brief condescension to my evil finally destroyed the balance of my soul. And yet I was not alarmed; the fall seemed natural, like a return to the old days before I had made my discovery. It was a fine, clear, January day, wet under foot where the frost had melted, but cloudless overhead; and the Regent's park was full of winter chirruppings and sweet with Spring odours. I sat in the sun on a bench; the animal within me licking the chops of memory; the spiritual side a little drowsed, promising subsequent penitence, but not yet moved to begin. After all, I reflected I was like my neighbours; and then I smiled, comparing myself with other men, comparing my active goodwill with the lazy cruelty of their neglect. And at the very moment of that vainglorious thought, a qualm came over me, a horrid nausea and the most deadly shuddering. These passed away, and left me faint; and then as in its turn the faintness subsided, I began to be aware of a change in the temper of my thoughts, a greater boldness, a contempt of danger, a solution of the bonds of obligation. I looked down; my clothes hung formlessly on my shrunken limbs; the hand that lay on my knee was corded and hairy. I was once more Edward Hyde. A moment before I had been safe of all men's respect, wealthy, beloved – the cloth laying for me in the dining room at home; and now I was the common quarry of mankind, hunted, houseless, a known murderer, thrall to the gallows.

My reason wavered, but it did not fail me utterly. I have more than once observed that, in my second character, my faculties seemed sharpened to a point and my spirits more tensely elastic; thus it came about that, where Jekyll perhaps might have suc-cumbed, Hyde rose to the importance of the moment. My drugs were in one of the presses of my cabinet; how was I to reach them? That was the problem that (crushing my temples in my hands) I set myself to solve. The laboratory door I had closed. If I sought to enter by the house, my own servants would consign me to the gallows. I saw I must employ another hand, and thought of Lanyon.

How was he to be reached? how persuaded? Supposing that I escaped capture in the streets, how was I to make my way into his presence? and how should I, an unknown and displeasing visitor, prevail on the famous physician to rifle the study of his colleague, Dr. Jekyll? Then I remembered that of my original character, one part remained to me: I could write my own hand; and once I had conceived that kindling spark, the way that I must follow became lighted up from end to end.

Thereupon, I arranged my clothes as best I could, and summoning a passing hansom, drove to an hotel in Portland street, the name of which I chanced to remember. At my appearance (which was indeed comical enough, however tragic a fate these garments covered) the driver could not conceal his mirth. I gnashed my teeth upon him with a gust of devilish fury; and the smile withered from his face – happily for him – yet more happily for myself, for in another instant I had certainly dragged him from his perch. At the inn, as I entered, I looked about me with so black a countenance as made the attendants tremble; not a look did they exchange in my presence; but obsequiously took my orders, led me to a private room, and brought me wherewithal to write. Hyde in danger of his life was a creature new to me: shaken with inordinate anger, strung to the pitch of murder, lusting to inflict pain. Yet the creature was astute; mastered his fury with a great effort of the will; composed his two important letters, one to Lanyon and one to Poole; and that he might receive actual evidence of their being posted, sent them out with directions that they should be registered.

Thenceforward, he sat all day over the fire in the private room, gnawing his nails; there he dined, sitting alone with his fears, the waiter visibly quailing before his eye; and thence, when the night was fully come, he set forth in the corner of a closed cab, and was driven to and fro about the streets of the city. He, I say – I cannot say, I. That child of Hell had nothing human; nothing lived in him but fear and hatred. And when at last, thinking the driver had begun to grow suspicious, he discharged the cab and ventured on foot, attired in his misfitting clothes, an object marked out for observation, into the midst of the nocturnal passengers, these two base passions raged within him like a tempest. He walked fast, hunted by his fears, chattering to himself, skulking through the less frequented thoroughfares, counting the minutes that still divided him from midnight. Once a woman spoke to him, offering, I think, a box of lights. He smote her in the face, and she fled.

When I came to myself at Lanyon's, the horror of my old friend perhaps affected me somewhat: I do not know; it was at least but a drop in the sea to the abhorrence with which I looked back upon these hours. A change had come over me. It was no longer the fear of the gallows, it was the horror of being Hyde that racked me. I received Lanyon's condemnation partly in a dream; it was partly in a dream that I came home to my own house and got into bed. I slept after the prostration of the day, with a stringent and profound slumber which not even the nightmares that wrung me could avail to break. I awoke in the morning shaken, weakened, but refreshed. I still hated and feared the thought of the brute that slept within me, and I had not of course forgotten the appalling dangers of the day before; but I was once more at home, in my own house and close to my drugs; and gratitude for my escape shone so strong in my soul that it almost rivalled the brightness of hope.

I was stepping leisurely across the court after breakfast, drinking the chill of the air with pleasure, when I was seized again with those indescribable sensations that heralded the change; and I had but the time to gain the shelter of my cabinet, before I was once again raging and freezing with the passions of Hyde. It took on this occasion a double dose to recall me to myself; and alas, six hours after, as I sat looking sadly in the fire, the pangs returned, and the drug had to be re-administered. In short, from that day forth it seemed only by a great effort as of gymnastics, and only under the immediate stimulation of the drug, that I was able to wear the countenance of Jekyll. At all hours of the day and night, I would be taken with the premonitory shudder; above all, if I slept, or even dozed for a moment in my chair, it was always as Hyde that I awakened. Under the strain of this continually impending doom and by the sleeplessness to which I now condemned myself, ay, even beyond what I had thought possible to man, I became, in my own person, a creature eaten up and emptied by fever, languidly weak both in body and mind, and solely occupied by one thought: the horror of my other self. But when I slept, or when the virtue of the medicine wore off, I would leap almost without transition (for the pangs of transformation grew daily less marked) into the possession of a fancy brimming with images of terror, a soul boiling with causeless hatreds, and a body that seemed not strong enough to contain the raging energies of life. The powers of Hyde seemed to have grown with the sickliness of Jekyll. And certainly the hate that now divided them was equal on each side. With Jekyll, it was a thing of vital instinct. He had now seen the full deformity of that creature that shared with him some of the phenomena of consciousness, and was co-heir with him to death: and beyond these links of community, which in themselves made the most poignant part of his distress, he thought of Hyde, for all his energy of life, as of something not only hellish but inorganic. This was the shocking thing; that the slime of the pit seemed to utter cries and voices; that the amorphous dust gesticulated and sinned; that what was dead, and had no shape, should usurp the offices of life. And this again, that that insurgent horror was knit to him closer than a wife, closer than an eye; lay caged in his flesh, where he heard it mutter and felt it struggle to be born; and at every hour of weakness, and in the confidence of slumber, prevailed against him, and deposed him out of life. The hatred of Hyde for Jekyll, was of a different order. His terror of the gallows drove him continually to commit temporary suicide, and return to his subordinate station of a part instead of a person; but he loathed the necessity, he loathed the despondency into which Jekyll was now fallen, and he resented the dislike with which he was himself regarded. Hence the apelike tricks that he would play me, scrawling in my own hand blasphemies on the pages of my books, burning the letters and destroying the portrait of my father; and indeed, had it not been for his fear of death, he would long ago have ruined himself in order to involve me in the ruin. But his love of life is wonderful; I go further: I, who sicken and freeze at the mere thought of him, when I recall the abjection and passion of this attachment, and when I know how he fears my power to cut him off by suicide, I find it in my heart to pity him.

It is useless, and the time awfully fails me, to prolong this description; no one has ever suffered such torments, let that suffice; and yet even to these, habit brought – no, not alleviation – but a certain callousness of soul, a certain acquiescence of despair; and my punishment might have gone on for years, but for the last calamity which has now fallen, and which has finally severed me from my own face and nature. My provision of the salt, which had never been renewed since the date of the first experiment, began to run low. I sent out for a fresh supply, and mixed the draught; the ebullition followed, and the first change of colour, not the second; I drank it and it was without efficiency. You will learn from Poole how I have had London ransacked; it was in vain; and I am now persuaded that my first supply was impure, and that it was that unknown impurity which lent efficacy to the draught.

About a week has passed, and I am now finishing this statement under the influence of the last of the old powders. This, then, is the last time, short of a miracle, that Henry Jekyll can think his own thoughts or see his own face (now how sadly altered!) in the glass. Nor must I delay too long to bring my writing to an end; for if my narrative has hitherto escaped destruction, it has been by a combination of great prudence and great good luck. Should the throes of change take me in the act of writing it, Hyde will tear it in pieces; but if some time shall have elapsed after I have laid it by, his wonderful selfishness and circumscription to the moment will probably save it once again from the action of his apelike spite. And indeed the doom that is closing on us both, has already changed and crushed him. Half an hour from now, when I shall again and forever reindue that hated personality, I know how I shall sit shuddering and weeping in my chair, or continue, with the most strained and fearstruck ecstasy of listening, to pace up and down this room (my last earthly refuge) and give ear to every sound of menace. Will Hyde die upon the scaffold? or will he find the courage to release himself at the last moment? God knows; I am careless; this is my true hour of death, and what is to follow concerns another than myself. Here then, as I lay down the pen and proceed to seal up my confession, I bring the life of that unhappy Henry Jekyll to an end.

Explanatory Notes

Explanatory Notes

The numbers preceding the various explanatory notes are page references.

Title

Strange: One of the most frequent words in the text, 'strange' and words derived from it occur twenty-two times (and 'odd' and 'oddly' eight times). The word, which can mean 'uncanny', is repeated often and so creates an uncanny feeling in the reader: 'strange' becomes strange.

A traditional epithet for a story, we find 'my story is a strange story' as an enticing introductory formula in the *Arabian Nights*. The word had also acquired the meaning of 'mysterious' and 'uncanny': in the vampire tale 'Carmilla' by Le Fanu (1872), a text slightly longer than *JH*, 'strange' and its derivations occur no fewer than forty times.

Le Fanu also uses 'strange' to allude to feelings of disturbing sexual attraction (which, as Freud explained in 'das Unheimliche' [1919], are associated with the uncanny because familiar yet repressed): after Carmilla's 'foolish embraces' (Chapter 4), the female narrator admits, 'I experienced a strange tumultuous excitement that was pleasurable, ever and anon mixed with a vague sense of fear and disgust'. We find the same usage in Wilde and other *fin-de-siècle* writers.

The adjective of the title therefore prepares the reader for a 'case' that may involve the disturbingly paranormal or repressed yet disturbingly familiar sexuality.

Case: could refer ambiguously either to a criminal or to a medical/psychoanalytical case, and indeed Stevenson's narrative is both: it apparently starts as a detective story related to 'The Carew Murder Case', but there are continual indications of disturbing and unrealistic phenomena that move the narrative towards that of a medical, psychological, or paranormal 'case history'. The distancing from the detective story becomes clear in the last two chapters as the 'detective' Utterson disappears and the expected final denouement is replaced by the unreliable confession of the guilty party (cf. Jean-

Pierre Naugrette, '*The Strange Case of Dr Jekyll and Mr Hyde* est-il un roman policier?', *Confluences* 20, 2002, pp. 85–111).

RLS was himself referred to as 'the case' for a time: in a joint letter of January 1884 Fanny remarks that the nurse they had hired in the south of France 'refuses to call him anything but the "case", never "Mr Stevenson"' (*LETBM*, vol. IV, p. 235). The word could also have a more general meaning of 'condition': in a letter of January 1894, RLS refers to his wife's recent mental illness: 'she was in a strange case for some while after she came back' (*LETBM*, vol. VIII, p. 176).

'The strange case of …' has become a fixed collocation often used in titles: thirty examples are listed in the New York Public Library catalogue from 1901 onwards; an Internet search in February 2003 found over 800 different uses of the phrase.

Dr. Jekyll: The name Jekyll should be pronounced /'dʒiːk ɪl/, the normal pronunciation of that surname and the one that RLS used ('let the name be pronounced as though spelt "jee-kill"; not "jek-ill"', interview in the San Francisco *Examiner*, 8 June 1888), and it is also the pronunciation used in the 1931 Mamoulian film (while the 1941 Fleming film uses the pronunciation that has become more widespread). Apparently of Breton or Cornish origin, it is found in south-west England, East Anglia, and Yorkshire (D. L. Gould, *A Dictionary of Surnames*, Oxford, OUP, 1988; Nabokov's speculation on a Scandinavian origin would therefore seem to be unfounded). A 'Jekyl' (*sic*) is found in Walter Scott's novel *St. Ronan's Well* (1823, ch. 39) as well as in Le Fanu's *Wylder's Hand* (1864, ch. 72).

The title of 'Dr' possibly reminds the reader of a long literary and cultural tradition of deviant doctors: Dr Faustus, Dr Frankenstein, Stevenson's own Dr K— (in 'The Body Snatcher') and Dr Noel (in *The New Arabian Nights*), and Dr D—, the London pervert obsessed with possessing virgins in the 'Maiden Tribute' scandal published in June 1885 (Judith Walkowitz, *City of Dreadful Delight*, London, Virago, 1992, pp. 97–102, 131, 199). The negative associations of the title have continued in characters such as Wells's Dr Moreau, Dr Raymond (in Machen's *The Great God Pan*), Dr Fu Manchu, Dr Strangelove, and Dr Filth (in Bob Dylan's 'Desolation Row'). RLS's choice of a doctor to exemplify hypocrisy seems to find an anticipation in the comment of Wilkie Collins (in the 'Epilogue' to *Armadale*, 1866): 'We live in an age eminently favourable to the growth of all roguery which is careful enough to keep up appearances. In this enlightened nineteenth century, I look upon the doctor as one of our rising men.' In Stevenson's case we have the professional title and a name containing the word 'kill', a reminder of aggressivity behind the social surface.

Hyde: This character who 'hides' from respectable society, uses a back door, disappears, clearly symbolises what people hide of themselves (their body, their sexual and aggressive desires) and from themselves (their animal nature and their mortality), and those things that society has silenced and made invisible.

'Hide' also means 'animal skin', a sign of animal nature. In Scots the word is applied pejoratively to 'a female domestic animal', 'a woman', or (rarely) 'a man, a disagreeable fellow' (*Scottish National Dictionary*), meanings which reinforce the hints of female nature of both protagonists and the status of Hyde as social outcast.

On eight occasions (five of them in the last chapter) a sentence ends with 'Hyde' and the next sentence begins with 'I', bringing the two words into juxtaposition, separated by the full stop, linked by their assonant vowels.

Dedication

Katherine De Mattos: Stevenson's cousin (daughter of his father's elder brother Alan and the sister of Bob Stevenson, RLS's youthful companion).

It's ill ... : The original verses (as transcribed in Colvin's edition of the *Letters*, see p. 173) were the following:

Ave!

Bells upon the city are ringing in the night;
High above the gardens are the houses full of light;
On the heathy Pentlands is the curlew flying free;
And the broom is blowing bonnie in the north countrie.

We cannae break the bonds that God decreed to bind,
Still we'll be the children of the heather and the wind;
Far away from home, O, it's still for you and me
That the broom is blowing bonnie in the north countrie!

In the full poem, 'the bonds' are clearly the ties with identity and childhood experience (the latter associated with images of freedom: houses 'full of light', curlews 'flying free', 'wind'). The epigraph version adds an idea of moral judgement: 'We cannae' becomes 'It's ill to'. It also creates an ambiguity involving the first and second lines: in the epigraph they are separated by a semicolon and 'we'll' becomes 'will we', shifting the beat from *Still* to *will* (still WILL we BE). This means that a paraphrase of the second line as '*and so* (by refusing to break natural ties) we will both always feel intimately connected to the Scottish hill country of the Pentlands', valid both for the original and the epigraph version, is, in the case of the latter, shadowed by another possible interpretation: '*and yet* (despite acknowledging that it's wrong to break divinely ordained restrictions), we *must* be part of the free and natural world'. This ambiguity introduces us to Jekyll's double bind: he suffers from the constraints of social convention and is punished because he aims at too much freedom. The first two lines of the epigraph start with what seems the 'moral' of the story ('It's wrong to interfere with Nature by trying to separate the two aspects of the personality') but then mix together the ideas of restraint and freedom in a way that puts the reader (like Jekyll) in a situation of uncertainty as to whether the text means that we should accept restraint, aim for freedom, or see freedom in restraint.

loose the bands: 'Canst thou ... loose the bands of Orion?', Job 38: 31.

wind: this is clearly intended to have the traditional poetic pronunciation rhyming with *kind* (*OED* 1926, though this pronunciation is no longer listed in *The Longmans Pronunciation Dictionary*, 1990). The rhyme of 'bind' and 'wind' links words associated with the two contraries, 'restraint' and 'freedom', involved in the fate of Jekyll.

7   *Utterson*: the name, composed of two apparently meaningful elements 'utter' and 'son', holds itself out as a key to interpretation. Yet in the first paragraph perhaps the most obvious meaning of 'utter' ('speak') is apparently contradicted by the description of a taciturn man who spends much time alone – creating not only a connotation of mystery around the name and the character but also around the intentions and co-operativeness of the author. It is true that Utterson does become more talkative and, indeed, in his detective-like role offers a continuous series of (clearly inadequate) interpretations of events and discoveries, but then he stops talking as he reads the last two chapters along with the reader and silently disappears.

Looking for some further meaning in the name, it could suggest the limitations of the human condition, bound by language (which might even be meaningless, since the verb 'utter' can be used equally of speech or of meaningless words and cries, as in 'utter cries and voices', the only occurrence of the word in the text), and by social and biological relationships ('son').

The first part of the name could also be the adjective 'utter', meaning 'complete' or 'absolute', which almost always qualifies something negative, rejected or unknown (it derives significantly from the same word as 'outer'): utter ruin, utter failure, utter disgrace. In Stevenson's works we find no positive terms after this adjective, but 'utter desolation' ('Pavilion on the Links'), 'utter blackness' ('The Merry Men'), 'utter stranger' ('The Suicide Club'), etc. The 'utter son' could therefore be the outer, that is, 'rejected' son (just as in Scots 'outerling' means 'the black sheep of the family, a reprobate', *Concise Scots Dictionary*).

The whole name might also be seen as a variant on the obsolete and biblical phrase 'the utter (outer, or outward) man' meaning 'the body' (as opposed to the soul). This would link up with Utterson's equivalence with Jekyll as a representative of all sinners, or of all men seen as merely material with no transcendental soul.

All these possible meanings (the [taciturn] proclaimer; the restricted and limited human being; the reprobate; the body) bring us back to our starting point of a name that seems to provide a key, but which frustrates our search for meaning.

Like all surnames ending in –*son* ('Stevenson' being another) it is a Scandinavian formation and so much more frequent in north-eastern England and southern Scotland than in the rest of Britain (we find it in G. F. Black, *The Surnames of Scotland*, New York, New York Public Library; 1946). With this name as the only clue to place, a reader could easily imagine the first paragraph to be about an Edinburgh lawyer.

Stevenson re-uses Utterson the lawyer in the draft of a melodrama written in December 1886: 'We will tell this tale to Utterson ... he's honest, but he's clever; he'll find a way to clear me' ('The King's Rubies', Beinecke Uncat. MS, acc. No. 20010222-I; cf. *LETBM*, vol. V, p. 175–6).

to mortify a taste for vintages: 'to dominate and punish a liking for good wine' (an example of Utterson's repression, or possibly – since it is so excessive – of his self-monitoring irony).

approved: 'tried and tested' ('obsolete' use for the *OED*, 1885).

I incline to Cain's heresy: Cain, Adam's son, murdered his brother Abel, and when God asked him 'Where is Abel thy brother?', Cain said 'I know not: Am I my brother's keeper?' (i.e. he claimed he did not know and anyway felt no responsibility for the other's acts and movements; Genesis 4: 9). Apart from the frivolity with which Utterson 'quaintly' makes his remark about feeling an affinity with the first murderer, it is a rather inaccurate allusion, since it is Cain not his brother who 'goes to the devil' through sin. Such inaccurate biblical references (of which there are further examples in the text) give the narrative a superficial air of a conventional moralising text while showing a provocative indifference to accurate citation of the book on which that morality is supposed to be based. Utterson's lack of involvement can also be seen as self-censorship to 'protect the caste' (Stephen Arata, *Fictions of Loss in the Victorian Fin de Siècle*, Cambridge, CUP, 1996, p. 40) as is also his later comment on not interfering when an affair looks like 'Queer Street' (p. 11).

It is the mark of a modest man to accept his friendly circle ready-made from the hands of opportunity and that was the lawyer's way ... his affections ... implied no aptness in the object.: Utterson accepts friends supplied by chance, circumstance or expedience ('opportunity' here is used in an ambiguous way). RLS had a different idea of friendship: in *An Inland Voyage* (1878) he praises the spontaneous enthusiasms of the individual who has the ability to 'love his friends with an elective, personal sympathy, and not accept them as an adjunct of the station to which he has been called' (*TUS*, vol. XVII, p. 14).

8 *Enfield*: The name was probably suggested by Henry Enfield, a minor painter and friend of both RLS and his cousin Bob from the period of the visits to Grez (1876–8). Fanny's daughter, Belle, says 'There was the Englishman, Enfield, a hearty jovial soul with a "haw, haw" accent, who always wore a monocle' (Isobel Field, *This Life I've Loved*, New York, Scribner's, 1937, p. 110). The name comes from the Middlesex village (now part of North London) that has associations with the British army (the Enfield Royal Small Arms Factory and the Enfield Riflemen). The odd couple of Utterson and Enfield are therefore further contrasted by the Scottish and English associations of their names.

It was a nut to crack for many: 'many found it difficult to understand'. Stevenson alters a familiar saying ('a tough/hard nut to crack'), creating an expression that is partly familiar, partly strange.

rambles: 'wanderings'. Johnson's Dictionary (1755) and the *Concise Oxford Dictionary of English Etymology* (ed. T. F. Hoad, 1986) derive *ramble* from a Dutch verb meaning 'to wander loosely in lust' (Johnson). This transgressive meaning is clearly present in Rochester's licentious 'A Ramble in St. James's Park' and in John Dunton's *Voyage Round the World* (1691), where the word becomes a running joke, appearing repeatedly in a wide variety of grammatical and typographic forms. We also see it in the 'evening ramble' of Florizel and Colonel Geraldine in 'The Suicide Club' (1878, *TUS*, vol. I, p. 1), which involves dressing in shabby clothes and going to one of the oyster bars near Leicester Square (known as haunts of prostitutes), ready for any 'adventure' that might present itself. It was also known by the author of an early parody *The Stranger Case of Dr Hyde and Mr Crushall* (*c.* 1886–7, Harry M. Geduld, *The Definitive 'Dr Jekyll and Mr Hyde' Companion*, New York, Garland, 1983, p. 137), in which a 'Mr Utterduffer' goes on Sunday walks in town to 'a mansion ... decorated with a red lamp over the hall door'.

coquetry: 'attractive decorations', but the reader will also think of the usual meaning ('behaviour [in a woman] designed to attract sexual attention by being playful and charming'), especially in the context of other equivocal expressions in the same paragraph: the shops have 'an air of invitation' like smiling women; on Sunday the street veils its 'charms' ('attractions', but also a euphemism for 'sexually attractive parts of a woman's body') and so is 'comparatively empty of passage'. The winking complicity of the description creates a doubling of both narrator and reader (since both recognise the transgressive meaning but do not fully acknowledge it); at the same time it associates bourgeois commerce with prostitution (as Stevenson also compares professional authors to prostitutes in a letter to Gosse in the same period, *LETBM*, vol. V, p. 171, and in 'A Letter to a Young Gentleman who Proposes to Embrace the Career of Art', 1888, *TUS*, vol. XXVIII, p. 8).

The fictional by-street resembles the 'by-paragraph' that describes it: both are characterised by distracting excess, by carefully wrought effect and by sexual suggestiveness. The passage can also be seen as a parody of the obsessive detail of the conventional 'descriptive paragraph' which attempts to give a coherent picture of elusive reality.

passenger: 'passer-by, pedestrian' ('now rare', *OED* 1904).

on the left hand going east: the door is located on the north side, associated (in cultures north of the tropic of Cancer) with night and death; also associated with the left hand, since 'orientation' was achieved by facing the direction of the rising sun (Chris McManus, *Right Hand, Left Hand*, London, Weidenfeld & Nicholson, 2002, pp. 22, 23). Right and left have symbolic associations in all human cultures and (independently of latitude) it is always the right that is good and the left that is bad (ibid., pp. 26–35). As an illustration of this, later in the sentence we have the alliterative 'a certain sinister block of building', where 'evil' and 'leftness' are suggested by the same word. The suggestion of 'going east' is also that Jekyll's house is towards the eastern part of town (more explicitly stated in *MS*, f. 8), the poorer (and less-regulated) part of London. This symbolism of 'east' and 'north' and 'left' is never confirmed, however, and the excess of signs leads to ambiguity, uncertainty and a sense of 'uncanniness'.

thrust forward its gable on the street: an adaptation of the French *avoir pignon sur rue* (literally, 'to have your gable on the street'), meaning 'to have a house of your own', 'to be well off', 'to achieve a social position'. Stevenson's change of the verb ('have' becomes 'thrust') undermines the ideology of the cliché, suggesting that social status is achieved by brutally pushing others aside (in addition, the gable itself is dirty and repulsive). The literally translated French idiom was a characteristic of Stevenson's early style noted by a contemporary critic (cf. Maixner, p. 118); here it creates an appropriate reading experience that combines familiarity with unfamiliarity.

a blind forehead: Stevenson would have pronounced the noun as /'fɒr ɪd/, the only form given in the *OED* (1897). The house resembles Hyde in being 'deformed', 'amorphous', and with 'no shape'. The top of a building also corresponds to Hyde because of traditional associations of this part of a house with the unconscious and instinctive (e.g. Stevenson says the 'Brownie' that creates stories while he sleeps is kept 'locked in a back garret', 'A Chapter on Dreams', *TUS*, vol. XXX, p. 51).

distained: 'discoloured' ('archaic' use for the *OED*, 1896).

9   *'It is connected in my mind,' added he, 'with a very odd story'*: A conventional lead-in to an embedded narrative. Italo Calvino in Chapter XI of *Se una notte d'inverno un viaggiatore* (1979) writes 'Novels all started like this once. There was someone walking along a lonely street who saw something that attracted his attention, something that seemed to hide a mystery, or a premonition; so he asked for an explanation and someone else told him a long story.'

stumping along: 'walking along with heavy steps' – marked 'slang' in the *OED* (1919). Enfield sprinkles his speech with slang expressions: 'my gentleman' ('the gentleman I had to deal with'), 'Sawbones' ('doctor'), p. 9; 'make his name stink' ('ruin his reputation'), 'pitching it in red hot' ('attacking [him] verbally with great vehemence'), 'screwed him up' ('forced him up'), 'stick out' ('persist in resistance'), 'apocryphal' ('of doubtful authenticity'), 'one of your fellows who ...' ('one of the well-known types who ...'), p. 10; 'bland old bird' ('harmless old man'), 'Queer Street' ('a situation of debt or suspicious difficulties'), p. 11. He also uses numerous phrasal verbs, associated with informal speech: these (apart from those already quoted) include 'turned out', 'put in his appearance', 'carrying it off'. Another London type who uses similar 'flash' language (including 'sawbones') is John Finsbury in *The Wrong Box*, 'a gentleman with a taste for the banjo, the music-hall, the Gaiety Bar, and the sporting papers' (*TUS*, vol. XI, p. 5).

naturally enough: 'of course'; a strange phrase since a collision in the circumstances would be *un*expected, but either Enfield (the cool observer) was able to judge the (spatial or sexual) trajectories with an expert eye, or he means (with languid detachment) that 'it's something you would expect in a narrative' (just as Umberto Eco starts *Il nome della rosa* [1980] with a preface entitled 'Naturalmente, un manoscritto').

the man trampled calmly over the child's body and left her screaming on the ground: Gerard Manley Hopkins says 'The trampling scene is perhaps a convention: he was thinking of something unsuitable for fiction' (letter to Robert Bridges 28 October 1886; qu. Maixner, p. 229) and the reaction of the crowd and the compensation offered (see the note on 'a hundred pounds' below) combined with the opacity of the language (cf. pp. xlix–l) suggest something like rape (the equivalent scene is referred to by Jekyll as 'an act of infamy' in *ND2*, f. 87).

Juggernaut: 'great force that destroys everything in its path'. Devotees (especially women) of the Hindu god Vishnu, also called Jugannatha, would throw themselves in front of the heavy carriage carrying the image of the god and be crushed to death.

view halloa: the second word is pronounced /'hæl əʊ/ (the older pronunciation) or /hə 'ləʊ/; a hunter's cry to tell the others that he has seen the fox breaking out from cover; *I gave a view halloa*, 'I gave a cry to call the others to follow me in the chase after him'. A sudden change back to languid slang after the indignant 'damned Juggernaut'.

cut and dry apothecary: 'doctor with brisk, unemotional manner'. Stevenson uses 'cut and dry' to mean 'brisk' ('his charming cut-and-dry, here we are again kind of manner', *LETBM*, vol. I, p. 497), 'plain' ('my bald prose ... my cut and dry literature', *LETBM*, vol. VII, p. 211), 'pre-formed' ('language is ready shaped to his purpose; he speaks out of a cut and dry vocabulary' ('The Truth of Intercourse', *TUS*, vol. XXV, p. 32), and 'conventional', 'unimaginative' (all 'cut-and-dry professions' are opposed to the life of the artist, 'Letter to a Young Gentleman', *TUS*, vol. XXVIII, p. 4). The use of 'apothecary' for '(non-University-trained) doctor' is jokingly archaic in this period.

10 *harpies ... hateful faces*: Harpies, monsters of ancient Greek and Roman mythology, are rapacious birds with the head of a woman. The two men are protecting Hyde from the women (perhaps from a general male fear of the violent potential of oppressed women: Dickens in *A Tale of Two Cities*, for example, refers to the women *sans culottes* as 'gorgons', 'furies' and 'monsters'). 'Hateful faces' is ambiguous: it could mean 'faces expressing hate' or (the more normal modern meaning) 'repulsive faces', the latter making the women similar to Hyde, and suggesting that their reaction is a rejection of something in themselves.

a hundred pounds: a London artisan in this period earned about £80 a year (Charles Booth, *Life and Labour of the People of London*, London, Macmillan, 1892, vol. I, p. 50); domestic servants (who received board and lodgings as part of their remuneration) were paid considerably less: a lower servant living in would get £10 a year and an upper servant, like Poole, £50 (VICTORIA discussion list, 11 December 2001 and following days). A hundred pounds is therefore a huge sum for knocking over a child who is basically unhurt. Combined with the murderous reaction of the bystanders it leaves the reader with the strong suspicion that the actual offence was more serious and is being hidden either by Enfield (perhaps to protect Hyde, a fellow gentleman 'about town') or by the elusive narrator of this first part of the text.

struck: 'surrendered', 'accepted terms'; either an extension of the nautical term meaning 'to lower topsail or flag as a sign of surrender', or an obsolete intransitive use of the verb meaning 'agree to terms' (similar to transitive uses such as 'to strike an agreement'). The *OED* (STRIKE 17c) cites this very passage as an illustration of the former meaning, but it could be seen as ambiguous (between 'surrender' and 'reach an agreement'), in line with Enfield's ambiguous stance towards Hyde.

Coutts's: 'The most elite bank in Great Britain, catering to a wealthy, respectable clientèle' (Linehan [ed.], *Strange Case of Dr. Jekyll and Mr. Hyde*, p. 10 note 4).

fellow: an ambiguous word, it could be a deprecatory term for 'man' but was also used by public schoolboys and upper-class young men to refer to one of their own class and age-group. We may imagine the flash-talking Enfield using a reduced vowel in the second syllable (as Pope rhymes *fellow* and *prunella*) (K. C. Phillipps, *Language and Class in Victorian England*, Oxford, Blackwell, 1985, pp. 45–7).

11 *the very pink of the proprieties ... and ... one of your fellows who do what they call good*: 'the flower of social correctness, and one of those well-known types who ...'; notice that although Hyde is 'damnable', Jekyll is not good, just very respectable and someone who sees himself as a 'do-gooder'.

Black mail: Blackmail plots were popular in Victorian fiction (cf. Alexander Welsh, *George Eliot and Blackmail*, Harvard University Press, 1985), though novels avoided mentioning the blackmailing of male homosexuals, in reality one of the most important types of such extortion in Britain from the eighteenth century onwards (Angus McLaren, *Sexual Blackmail*, Harvard University Press, 2002).

12 *I can make no hand of it*: 'I can't understand it' (probably derived from card games).

I know it already: Utterson (we learn in the next chapter) knows that Hyde is somehow connected with Jekyll, and that the door leads into the dissection theatre and then to Jekyll's house.

My dear sir ... : 'Meaning: do you take me for a liar?' (Nabokov), although there is no justification for this offended reply as Utterson has asked Enfield only to confirm a detail. Other incoherent and aggressive elements in Enfield's contributions include (below) 'you might have warned me' (where it is impossible to identify what source of danger or difficulty Enfield thinks he should have been *warned* about) and 'I have been pedantically exact, as you call it' (where Utterson has not used the words 'exact' or 'pedantically exact').

has gone home: 'has been fully understood', 'has hit its target', 'has affected me intimately'. The normal subject would be something with a 'point' (a joke, a lesson, an idea). Here, however, Enfield is not aiming to produce any particular effect and so the phrase is puzzlingly inappropriate. As S. Towheed has pointed out ('R. L. Stevenson's Sense of the Uncanny', *English Literature in Transition* 42(1), 1999, p. 26), the use of 'home' can be seen as hinting at an inner confrontation with the familiar but suppressed, associated with the 'uncanny' (Freud's *unheimlich*).

long tongue: 'loquacity', 'gossiping'. 'Long-Tongue: A tale bearer' (*Dictionary of the Vulgar Tongue*, 1811).

13   *a volume of some dry divinity on his reading desk*: 'dry' here means 'uninteresting' or 'austere'; notice that we have no assurance that the lawyer actually reads the volume. Utterson's habitual choice of a volume of divinity makes him similar to Jekyll (with his 'pious work, for which [he] had several times expressed a great esteem', p. 49), and also to Stevenson's father: 'Lactantius, Vossius, and Cardinal Bona were his chief authors. The first he must have read for twenty years, uninterruptedly, keeping it near him in his study, and carrying it in his bag on journeys. Another old theologian, Brown of Wamphray, was often in his hands' (RLS, 'Thomas Stevenson, Civil Engineer', 1887, *TUS*, vol. XXX, p. 68–9).

holograph: 'handwritten by the person who signed it'.

M.D., D.C.L., LL.D., F.R.S.: 'Doctor of Medicine, Doctor of Civil Laws, Doctor of Laws, Fellow of the Royal Society' – Jekyll is clearly an eminent intellectual figure, a member of the powerful professional class. Like Faustus, he is both a man of the law and of medicine (so has affinities with both Lanyon and Utterson).

the fanciful was the immodest: 'the non-rational was indecorous', that is, should not be made public (with the additional connotation that it is 'morally wrong').

14 *presentment*: 'image' or 'idea' (the latter a metaphysical and psychological term, cf. *OED* 7b).

Cavendish Square: north of Oxford Street, the starting point for Harley Street, where the most eminent members of the English medical profession have their practices. On Charles Booth's sociological map of London (*Life and Labour of the People in London*, London, vol. I, 1892) all four sides of the square are marked 'Upper-middle and Upper classes. Wealthy'. There are numerous courts ('mews' and 'places') in the area.

Lanyon: a name of English origin, possibly suggested by Sir Charles Lanyon, civil engineer and acquaintance of Stevenson's mentor Fleeming Jenkin (Gillian Cookson, 'Engineering Influences on *Jekyll and Hyde*', *Notes and Queries*, vol. 244 No. 4 [Dec. 1999]: 487–91).

Damon and Pythias: loyal friends of antiquity (when Damon was sentenced to death for attempting to kill the tyrant Dionysus of Syracuse, Pythias took his place in prison to allow him one last visit to his family, agreeing to be executed himself if his friend failed to return). Often referred to in classical literature, the story is also the subject of a play by Richard Edwards (1571).

for old sake's sake: 'out of consideration for old friendship'.

spirt of temper: 'short and sudden outburst of anger' (the normal modern spelling is 'spurt').

15 *conveyancing*: the preparation of documents for the transfer of property (Utterson is therefore a solicitor). Nabokov annotates (referring also to the preceding 'passions'): 'dreary deeds – (i.e. irony)'.

in mere darkness: 'in absolute darkness' (a use of *mere* with no *OED* examples after 1703).

Six o'clock struck on the bells of the church that was so conveniently near to Mr. Utterson's dwelling: The closeness of Utterson's house to the church could remind readers of the proverb 'The nearer the church, the farther from God' (John Simpson, *The Concise Oxford Dictionary of Proverbs*, Oxford, OUP, 1982). The phrase 'so conveniently near' could mean 'so near that Utterson could get to church easily and often', or 'so near that he could get there with the minimum effort' (and this latter might correspond to Utterson's private thoughts – either Utterson the hypocrite, or Utterson the amused self-observer). A third possibility is that Utterson ironically calls the church 'conveniently near' though he finds the closeness of its loud bells very *in*convenient. Stevenson himself, in *An Inland Voyage* (*TUS*, vol. VII, p. 51), says he dislikes the sound of most bells, and remarks: 'There is often a threatening note, something blatant and metallic, in the voice of bells, that I believe we have fully more pain than pleasure from hearing them' (qu. Leonard Wolf, *The Essential Dr. Jekyll & Mr. Hyde*, New York, Plume, 1995, p. 46, note 15).

the curtains of the bed plucked apart, the sleeper recalled: A similar situation is found in Mary Shelley's *Frankenstein* (1818, ch. 5): 'I started from my sleep with horror ... I beheld the wretch ... he held up the curtain of the bed', and also in Richardson's *Pamela* (1740; Dent, 1962, vol. I, p. 145): 'When I went to bed, I could think of nothing but this hideous person, and my master's more hideous actions ... When I dropt asleep, I dreamed they were both coming to my bedside with the worst designs.'

to whom power was given: 'and power was given unto him [the beast]', Revelations 14: 5.

16   *without bowels of mercy*: 'without any inner capacity for mercy'; this use of 'bowels' as 'feeling' is biblical (e.g. Colossians 3: 12) and 'now somewhat archaic' (*OED* 1887). The bowels were traditionally seen as 'the seat of compassion and mercy' (Wolf, *The Essential Dr. Jekyll & Mr. Hyde*, p. 47, note 23).

the rumour of the approach of any passenger preceded him by a long time: 'rumour' for 'noise' is an archaic use (*OED* 1910), or a Gallicism (from the French *rumeur*). Footsteps amid silence are noted by RLS in a letter of 1873: 'Everything here is utterly silent. I can hear men's footfalls streets away' (*LETBM*, vol. I, p. 289); the situation is perhaps an 'urban Gothic' convention: in Le Fanu's 'The Familiar' (1872) Mr Barton walks home alone through streets in 'that utter silence which has in it something indefinably exciting' and which 'made the sound of his steps, which alone broke it, unnaturally loud and distinct'.

superstitious prevision: 'irrational presentiment' (this, at any rate, is an acceptable translation into 'normal English' based on contextual clues, though 'superstitious' is not normally used in this sense, nor does it accord well with a word usually meaning 'knowing in advance').

17 *Gaunt Street*: an appropriate address for the 'lean, long, dusty, dreary' Utterson.

blowing in the key: 'blowing through the head of the key'; this was probably done to save locks from getting blocked with dust ('This wind blows the memory out of me, as you can whistle dust out of a key', *LETBM*, vol. V, p. 383) as well as being an idle affectation ('he stood whistling in the key, with his back to the garden railings', *The Dynamiter*, 1885, *TUS*, vol. III, p. 99). Hyde's gesture shows insolent detachment (cf. his 'sneering coolness', p. 10).

fronted about: 'turned round suddenly to face' ('front!' is normally only a military command; 'front about' in this sense was not found in any other text on an Internet search and has only this citation in the *OED*).

18 *something troglodytic*: 'something reminiscent of a primitive caveman'.

can it be the old story of Dr. Fell: 'can my reaction just be one of those inexplicable dislikes that we have for people sometimes?' A seventeenth-century Oxford student, punished with the task of translating a Latin epigram by Martial about an inexplicable dislike ('Non amo te, Sabidi ...'), produced the following close translation (wittily substituting the name of the Dean who issued the punishment for the original name): 'I do not love thee, Dr Fell / The reason why I cannot tell / But this alone I know full well, / I do not love thee Dr Fell'. Perhaps with 'Dr. Fell' Utterson has unconsciously seen a connection between Dr Jekyll and Hyde (both 'fell' and 'hide' mean 'animal skin').

clay continent: 'material container'; man is made from 'dust' (Genesis 2: 7) or 'clay' (Job 10: 9 etc.) and the latter is used to mean 'the body'. The *OED* (1893) classes this use of 'continent' as 'rare or arch.' and the expression 'clay continent' seems to be Stevenson's invention (and is used as the title of a 1998 American stage adaptation of *JH* by Bob Fisher).

my poor old Harry Jekyll: 'Old Harry' is a name for the Devil.

Round the corner from the bystreet, there was a square of ancient, handsome houses: The decadent square, the respectable large house and its private back entrance are possibly influenced by Gaunt Square and Lord Steyne's 'town palace' in Thackeray's *Vanity Fair* (1848, Chapter 47): most of the houses are no longer inhabited by families with liveried servants but 'brass plates have penetrated into the Square', belonging to doctors and a branch of the Diddlesex

Bank (where 'diddle' suggests Stevenson's 'shady operations'). 'A few yards down' the street leading from the square and at the entrance to a stable court is 'a modest back door' leading to Lord Steyne's 'famous petits appartements' (qu. in Alan Sandison, *Stevenson and the Appearance of Modernism*, London, Macmillan, 1996, p. 217). A contrast of 'faded and stagnant square' and the road with its 'fine shops' behind it and just round the corner is also later found in Conan Doyle's 'The Red-Headed League' (1891).

estate: 'status', 'standing' (archaic usage for the *OED*, 1891).

all sorts and conditions of men: phrase from the Book of Common Prayer (1662); also the title of a novel by Walter Besant (1882).

occupied entire: 'occupied as one house, not divided up' (an unusual use of the adverb).

Poole: a port near Bournemouth; the name (suggesting 'pool') could also be associated with the frightening connotations of water in the text ('in deep waters', p. 19; London is like a 'drowned city', p. 31; 'the shipwreck of my reason' p. 52; the courtyard is a 'deep well', p. 46; 'a dreadful shipwreck', p. 59), cf. Jean-Pierre Naugrette, '*The Strange Case of Dr. Jekyll and Mr. Hyde*: Essai d'onomastique', *Cahiers Victoriens et Edouardiens* 40, 1994, p. 83 and note. The one-syllable name that is also a common noun or adjective seems to be part of a tradition of whimsical humour in the representation of servants (cf. 'Cool' in Boucicault's *London Assurance*, 1841; 'Bowls' in Thackeray's *Vanity Fair*, 1848 ; 'Lane' in Wilde's *The Importance of Being Earnest*, 1895; as well as 'Guest', Utterson's clerk).

flags: 'flagstones', large square paving stones.

19 *statute of limitations*: law that defines the number of years after a crime beyond which no one can be tried.

punishment coming pede claudo: a reference to a line by Horace (*Odes* III. ii. 32) 'raro antecedentem scelestum / deseruit pede Poena claudo', 'seldom has Punishment, on limping foot, abandoned a wicked man, even when he has a start on her'. Punishment comes, slowly but surely, in the form of the deformed Hyde. The 'limping foot' also associates Hyde once again with the devil: Mephistopheles, in the German tradition, is represented as limping (because of hoofs hidden in boots), e.g. Goethe *Faust*, l. 2499; Vélez de Guevara's *El Diablo cojuelo* (1641), imitated and adapted by Le Sage in *Le diable boiteux* (1707, 1726), is about the limping devil Asmodeus who sees into houses and reveals the secrets and vices of private lives. Asmodeus is referred to by Carlyle in *The French*

Revolution, Book 6, Chapter 6, and is alluded to by Dickens in *The Old Curiosity Shop* (Chapter 33, 'Zambullo and his familiar').

Jack-in-the-Box: another possible diabolic allusion since in French this toy is called *le Diable*.

20 *transparency*: a painting on paper or glass, shown back-lit in a darkened room (popular from *c*. 1780) or as part of a large diorama (from *c*. 1820), both of which gave impressive suggestions of reality.

21 *expense*: 'expenditure of effort' (obsolete usage), unusually associated here with entertainment.

smooth-faced ... with something of a slyish cast perhaps: 'with a plausible manner', and 'with a suggestion of an appearance of deceptiveness, perhaps'.

hide-bound: 'bigoted', with the suggestion that Jekyll sees Lanyon as foolishly bound to the Hyde part of his personality, or to his body (his 'hide' or 'skin'), when he might free himself from it like Jekyll.

24 *living alone in a house*: 'left alone in a house' – or such is the likely meaning ('living in her own house by herself' is not possible: maids usually 'lived in' and anyway would not have a two-storey house of their own).

accosted: 'went up to and spoke to'. A secondary meaning of the verb 'go up to and ask for money or suggest a sexual adventure' is not recognised by the *OED* (1884) but is recorded in the *OED* Supplement (1972–86) with a first example from 1887 (though suggestions of this meaning can be seen in Sir Toby Belch's well-known words from *Twelfth Night* (I, iii): '"Accost" is front her, board her, woo her, assail her'). Additional suggestions of a homosexual approach are provided by Carew's effeminate characteristics ('beautiful gentleman', 'with a very pretty manner of politeness'), by his calculated and excessive politeness, and by the apparently superficial nature of his enquiry (Stevenson refers to men and women passengers pairing up together on board ship with the help of various stratagems, including 'the sham desire for information', *LETBM*, vol. VI, p. 3).

26 *A great chocolate-coloured pall lowered over heaven*: 'a heavy dark-brown-coloured layer [of fog] threateningly covered the sky, like a pall over a coffin'. The fog 'lowered' (pronounced / laʊə(r)d/ and now usually spelt 'loured') either 'from one side to the other' or 'above and outside' the sky or heaven. The expression 'great chocolate-coloured pall', together with 'rich, lurid brown' and 'as

brown as umber' emphasise a type of colour which Stevenson tells us recurred in his own nightmares ('His dreams ... would be haunted ... by nothing more definite than a certain hue of brown, which he did not mind in the least when he was awake, but feared and loathed while he was dreaming', 'A Chapter on Dreams', *TUS*, vol. XXX, p. 42).

that terror of the law and the law's officers, which may at times assail the most honest: The daughter of Edward Burne-Jones gives an account of Stevenson's conversation on the afternoon of 10 August 1886 when W. B. Richmond was painting his portrait: 'He said he was afraid of nothing & nobody in the world till Father said he was afraid of policemen; then Mr Stevenson confessed he was, & Mr Richmond chimed in & added his terror' (NLS MS 9894, *Balfour Biography Notebook*, f. 256).

a shop for the retail of penny numbers and twopenny salads: 'a shop selling penny story magazines and twopenny lettuces' (with 'twopenny' pronounced /'tʌp(ə)ni/). The magazines are 'penny dreadfuls', carrying serialised sensational narratives. The sale of story papers and vegetables in the same shop shows the poor nature of the area, where the shopkeeper sells any combination of cheap things. The shop in a poor quarter in Coketown (*Hard Times* [1854], Book I, Chapter 10) displays 'wretched little toys, mixed up in its window with cheap newspapers and pork'. In 1858, Wilkie Collins (*Household Words*, 21 August) mentions, as a new pheno-menon, 'penny-novel journals', which he finds displayed in the windows of almost every kind of shop, 'especially in the second and third rate neighbourhoods'. The incongruous mixture of goods also reflects the wider chaos in Soho.

many women of many different nationalities passing out, key in hand, to have a morning glass: A woman with a key (held in hand for lack of pockets in women's clothes) was not a lady (who had a servant to open the door) but a servant or lower-class woman. Here the suggestion is that these women are prostitutes: they have a key allowing freedom of movement, they have disorderly lives (drinking alcohol in the morning). Soho was well known for its foreign prostitutes: Charles Booth observes that most central-London prostitutes did not live there 'except for the foreign women, many of whom live in the Soho neighbourhood' (*Life and Labour of the People of London*, London, Macmillan, 1892, vol. I, p. 186). In his early poem 'My brain swims empty and light' (Roger C. Lewis, *The Collected Poems of Robert Louis Stevenson*, Edinburgh, EUP, 2003, p. 260), Stevenson the *flâneur* mentions female figures seen in the street in the early morning, including 'A slavey [a maidservant] with lifted dress and the key in her hand'.

27 *of many plies*: 'made from thick yarn' (from yarn made of several single threads twisted together).

   lockfast: 'with a lock', 'lockable' ('Chiefly Scottish', *OED*).

28 *handbills*: small printed notices distributed by hand.

29 *offices*: 'the parts of a house ... devoted to household work or services' (*OED*).

   destination: 'assigned use'.

   cabinet: 'private room' (archaic or obsolete use for the *OED*, 1888). Interestingly, in the dream origin of the story, the act of transformation is associated with a 'cabinet' in its normal sense: Stevenson says that he dreamed of 'one man ... being pressed into a cabinet, when he swallowed a drug and changed into another being' (1887 interview, in J. A. Hammerton [ed.], *Stevensoniana*, 2nd ed., 1907, p. 85). That this was not a room is confirmed by Andrew Lang's report (based on correspondence with Stevenson): 'He saw Hyde chased into a mysterious recess, saw him take the drug, and was awakened by the terror of what followed' (*Longman's Magazine*, February 1886, p. 441). In a later account he says 'he saw Hyde pursued, take refuge in a closet, swallow ... the mysterious powder or potion – and change horribly into Jekyll' ('Introduction' to R. L. Stevenson, *Works*, Swanston Edition, 1911, vol. I, p. xxxiii).

   glass presses: 'glass-fronted cupboards'.

   cheval-glass: a full-length mirror balanced half-way along the sides in a standing frame and adjustable by tilting; normally found in a bedroom or dressing-room (which is why Utterson is puzzled to see it in the cabinet, p. 49).

30 *I want to know what I am doing*: 'I want to know from you what I (as your legal representative) am getting involved in' – this, at any rate, is the paraphrase that neatly fits the context, though 'what I am doing' cannot normally mean 'what I am getting involved in', but 'what acts I am now performing', and Utterson does not need someone else to tell him this. The unusual and opaque phrase has produced a range of interpretations from translators, several taking it as equivalent to the more normal 'I want to know what I'm *to do*' or '*I'd like to know* what I'm doing', and Stevenson's sentence seems to be a puzzling hybrid of these two sentences.

31 *circulars*: printed business letters.

carbuncles: name given to various kinds of red precious stone (especially ruby and garnet) and to a mythical red stone that emits its own light (*OED*).

32 *imperial dye*: purple colouring (a reference to Tyrian purple, the costly dye used for the robes of Roman emperors).

There was no man from whom he kept fewer secrets than Mr. Guest; and he was not always sure that he kept as many as he meant: The first part of the sentence implies that Utterson wishes to hide few things from Guest; the second part that he intends to hide more things than he actually does. These conflicting wishes could suggest Utterson's divided will, or that the author wants to test the reader with puzzling, insoluble linguistic sequences.

in your way: 'up your street', 'corresponding to your interests' (the *OED*, for WAY 18c, says the phrase is usually used in the negative).

33 *the two hands are in many points identical: only differently sloped*: Jekyll forges for Hyde, just as Hyde has forged Jekyll's signature on the cheque. Interestingly, Stevenson himself adopted two very different styles of writing in his maturity, partly in order to overcome writer's cramp, and has to warn correspondents that he has himself written the passages in both 'hands': 'I have changed my hand' (March 1883, *LETBM*, vol. IV, p. 251), 'I have been obliged to lean my hand the other way, which makes it unrecognisable; the hand is the hand of Esau' (March 1884, *LETBM*, vol. VIII, p. 417, with an allusion to the Hyde-like hairy hand of Isaac's more primitive brother), 'I have two hand-writings' (July 1885, *LETBM*, vol. V, p. 122).

quaint: 'strange' (a use marked obsolete in the *OED*, 1902).

his blood ran cold in his veins: This exaggerated expression is underlined by Nabokov; like the similar 'froze the very blood of ...' (p. 39), it is a cliché of sensational texts. In Walpole's *Castle of Otranto* (1765, Chapter 5) we find 'Frederic's blood froze in his veins'; in *Oliver Twist* (1838, Chapter 18), 'Oliver's blood ran cold'.

34 *resented*: 'felt', an obsolete usage or a Gallicism (from the French *ressentir*).

ken: 'knowledge', 'sight' ('now rare' for the *OED*, 1901; also Scots).

35 *ask himself*: 'ask the man himself', 'ask the man in question' – a usage found in both Irish and Scottish English.

36 *the chief of sinners*: biblical echo, 'Christ Jesus came into the world to save sinners of which I am chief' (1 Timothy 1: 5); also a phrase found in the General Confession of the Church of Scotland and in the title of John Bunyan's spiritual autobiography *Grace Abounding to the Chief of Sinners* (1666).

J. G. Utterson: Here 'J. G.' but, later (p. 49) 'Gabriel John': a discrepancy overlooked in the haste of preparing the text for publication.

38 *It was partly your own fault that I found it out, even when I did*: The sentence has an opaque meaning: first, there can be no 'fault' about helping someone overcoming stupidity (to get round the problem some translators have chosen the equivalent of 'It was partly thanks to you'); then, although 'even when I did' means 'when I finally did', it is normally used in a completely different way (e.g. 'I rarely went to meetings, and never spoke, even when I did'). Understandably some translators have chosen not to translate the final clause.

like some disconsolate prisoner: Perhaps here Stevenson is making use of his own experience and feelings: in this period he felt himself to be a prisoner of his illness, of Skerryvore, and of the bourgeois role of householder. His stepson remembers that one day he entered the dining-room ready for a walk in the garden after being kept indoors several days by rain, only to be stopped by his wife, who firmly pointed out the dangers of going out and getting his feet wet, 'He made no protest, ... but such a look of despair crossed his face that it remains with me yet' (Lloyd Osbourne, *An Intimate Portrait of R.L.S.*, New York, Scribner's, 1924, p. 60).

39 *the smile was struck out of his face and succeeded by an expression of such abject terror and despair*: Stevenson may again be re-using personal experience: he himself seems to have been occasionally overwhelmed by despair which expressed itself memorably in his features. Lloyd mentions such an incident (see previous note) and Colvin on another occasion came up unexpectedly on him in the garden in Skerryvore, when he 'turned round upon me a face such as I never saw on him save that once – a face of utter despondency, nay tragedy, upon which seemed stamped for one concentrated moment the expression of all he had ever had, or might yet have, in life to suffer or renounce' (*Memories and Notes of Persons and Places 1852–1912*, London, Arnold, 1921, pp. 142–3). A similar experience and at a window is subjectively described in 'Some College Memories' (1886), where RLS tells the story of 'a student' (probably himself) who studied for an exam all night then looked out of the window to see the dawn breaking 'and at the sight, nameless terror

seized upon his mind' which causes him to flee into the street and fear its return all day long (*TUS*, vol. XXIX, p. 17).

God forgive us: After his diagnosis of Lady Macbeth's sickness, the doctor says 'God, God forgive us all' (*Macbeth* V, i, 72), before adding 'I think, but dare not speak' (the same reaction of Utterson and Enfield).

41 *a flying wrack of the most diaphanous and lawny texture*: 'strips of wind-blown cloud like fine, transparent cloth'. The description is anticipated in an early poem: 'Wild was the night; the charging rack / Had forced the moon upon her back' ('The Builder's Doom', written 1870; Lewis, *The Collected Poems of Robert Louis Stevenson*, p. 231).

42 *we'll get this through hands*: 'we'll deal with this', 'we'll investigate this matter' (Scots).

43 *to his mind*: 'to his liking'.

this week back: 'for the past week'. Stevenson has made Poole's language generically colloquial and dialectal: 'wanted bitter bad' (p. 43, 'wanted very badly'); 'main angry' (p. 44, 'very angry'); 'that's talking!' (p. 45); 'with that upon my heart' (p. 47, 'with so much on my heart', northern and Scottish English); 'this glass have seen ...' (p. 49); 'you may say that!' (p. 49).

44 *hand of write*: 'handwriting' (Scots).

stood upon my head like quills: 'And each particular hair to stand on end / Like quills upon the fearful porpentine', *Hamlet* I, v, 19–20.

every morning of my life: This must be an emphatic 'every single morning', as in 'goodness and mercy shall follow me all the days of my life' (Psalm 23), yet here the past verb seems to force the meaning (opaque because untrue) 'every morning since I was born'.

46 *The scud had banked over the moon*: 'the light, wind-driven cloud had built up over the moon'.

47 *in sunder*: 'asunder', 'apart' (now poetical for the *OED*, 1917).

48 *smell of kernels*: 'smell resembling that of bitter almond kernels', the typical smell of the cyanide in highly poisonous prussic acid. The unusual inferential leap (from 'smell of kernels' to reach 'smell of prussic acid') leaves the reader thinking that this may be an idiomatic phrase that he or she hasn't come across before.

49   *Gabriel John*: the unusual first name reminds us of the archangel (the second could be Baptist, apostle, author of Revelations, or just a common name), associating Utterson with powerful moral forces of the Universe. Interestingly, Sidney Colvin was privately called 'the archangel' by Stevenson and Henley (*LETBM*, vol. V, pp. 51 note, 106, 199), and Utterson seems to share some of Colvin's taciturnity ('few of words' in the poem 'I knew thee strong', Lewis, *The Collected Poems of Robert Louis Stevenson*, pp. 181–2), and some of his slightly oppressive paternalistic qualities: 'something arbitrary, something a little official, in manner and character ... He always had the air of a man accustomed to obedience' (as Stevenson describes him in 'Memoirs of Himself', *TUS*, vol. XXIX, p. 165).

50   *caught up*: 'took up' (marked obsolete in the *OED*, 1889).

   nameless situation: 'situation that social decorum forbids me from naming' (cf. Enfield's refusal to disclose 'a name that I can't mention', p. 10; Jekyll's previous reference to 'a punishment and a danger that I cannot name', p. 36; and Lanyon's declaration that he cannot 'set on paper' what Jekyll told him, p. 57). This is an unusual use of 'nameless', but Stevenson elsewhere uses the word in the related sense of 'legally un-nameable' (as in the 'proscribed, nameless ... clan of the Macgregors', *Kidnapped*, *TUS*, vol. VI, p. 179). Alternatively, the phrase could have the normal meaning of 'a situation so horrible that it cannot be described'. The note shows Jekyll still trying to use language to control and define, however, and conscious too of social relationships, so the first paraphrase would correspond more closely to his intentions.

   save his credit: 'save his good name or reputation'.

51   *10ᵗʰ December*: Lanyon says he received the letter 'On the ninth of January ... by the evening delivery', so the date at the top of the letter must be a mistake for '9ᵗʰ January'. The tale was originally conceived for the Christmas market and since 'Christmas stories' often set their supernatural events on Christmas Eve (a window of opportunity for evil spirits before a holy day, like Halloween) this December date may be a leftover from such a temporal collocation in an earlier version.

   I would ... have sacrificed ... my left hand to help you: The normal idiom is 'I would give my right hand for (something)', meaning 'I would be prepared to make a great sacrifice to obtain (something) for myself'. Stevenson's idiom-like phrase refers to making a sacrifice for the benefit of another person, with the unusual sacrifice of the *left* hand (the *OED* lists 'to give (a person or a thing) the left hand of friendship' with the meaning 'to deal unfriendly with'). The substitution of 'right' with 'left' suggests that for Jekyll the left (with all its 'sinister' and negative connotations) is now the normal and more valued side. Nabokov rings 'left' and adds a doubly underlined marginal comment: 'good'.

52 *This drawer I beg of you to carry back with you*: Stevenson here seems to be recycling part of his own experiences: in April 1885 (*LETBM*, vol. V, pp. 99–100) he wrote to his friend Charles Baxter asking him to go to his parents' home in Edinburgh (his parents then staying with him in Bournemouth), open his business table with the keys that he probably has (otherwise have it opened by a locksmith), and to put the contents (and those of a box with blank books and manuscripts) 'into a cheap portmanteau and send off here'. In a later letter (ibid., p. 102) he says he is sure that Baxter understood the 'delicacy' of the operation when he 'opened a certain drawer and came upon my arsenal! These shall now go into the heaving deep, I guess.' The visit of the friend to the house, the admittance by servants, the proposed intervention of a locksmith, and the transport of the contents all seem to be similar to the incident in *JH*. The contents of this 'certain drawer' likewise seem to belong to an area of Stevenson's life that he wants to keep hidden.

punctually: 'accurately', 'in every detail' (meanings marked 'archaic' and 'obsolete' in the *OED*, 1909).

my troubles will roll away like a story that is told: Usually it is life that is said to pass in this way: 'Our life is … like the shadow that departed; or like a tale that is told, or as a dream when one waketh' (Jeremy Taylor, *Holy Dying*, Chapter 1, Section I); and the last words of Charles Dickens's *The Old Curiosity Shop* (1840), 'and so do things pass away, like a tale that is told!'

I made sure: 'I was convinced'. This seems to be the common nineteenth-century usage; although the first *OED* quote for the phrase is Stevenson's *Kidnapped* (1886), we also find it in Dickens (e.g. 'made quite sure' in *David Copperfield* (1850), Chapter 24).

53 *old Dr. Denman's surgical theatre*: 'Denman' could suggest 'den man' (J.-P. Naugrette, in R. L. Stevenson, *L'Étrange Cas du Dr Jekyll et de Mr Hyde*, Livre de Poche, 2000, p. 14), with the 'den' as a primitive 'cavern' (p. 66) or 'refuge' (p. 68) for Hyde. It might also suggest 'dead man' (in pronunciations of this phrase with assimilation of the consonant before the 'm'). The surgical theatre here reminds one of the notorious crimes of Burke and Hare (who stole corpses to supply teachers of anatomy) in Edinburgh in the 1820s, which inspired Stevenson's horrific tale 'The Body Snatcher' (1884).

version book: exercise book (Scottish English), for 'versions' (school translations from English to Latin). Here, the book is used to record Jekyll's 'con-versions' and 're-versions'.

54 *bull's eye*: 'bull's-eye lantern', a lantern with a thick hemispherical lens and with a shutter allowing the main beam to be hidden.

incipient rigor: 'the beginning of a sudden feeling of chillness'; in *MS* Stevenson had written 'incipient rigor or what is called goose-flesh'. Stevenson gives some other medical terminology to Lanyon ('acuteness of the symptoms', p. 54; 'injected eyes', p. 56) but, when correcting the proofs, decided not to overdo this because he also substituted 'tickling the cacchinatory impulse' with 'moving me to laughter' and 'the hysteric ball' with 'the hysteria' (*MS*, ff. 44, 45).

a disgustful curiosity: either 'a curiosity mixed with disgust' or 'a curiosity that is in itself disgusting and disturbing' (so similar to the double meaning of 'hateful faces', p. 10). Underlined by Nabokov.

of rich and sober fabric: either 'made from *a* rich and sober fabric (i.e. cloth)', or 'of rich and sober quality or fabrication', the second being an obsolete usage.

55 *the hysteria*: The use of the article here is unusual: names for illnesses had usually been preceded by the article before the nineteenth century (K. C. Phillipps, *Language and Class in Victorian England*, Oxford, Blackwell, 1985, pp. 76–7) but, with much technical medical writing still in Latin even in the eighteenth century, the term *hysteria* is not used in English texts until late (first *OED* citation, 1801), and so apparently always in the new style, without the article. From the mouth of Dr Lanyon, it shows an insistent attachment to old-fashioned usage; from the pen of Stevenson, we can see it as one of the archaic and French-influenced forms that help to make the language of this strange tale in itself strange.

56 *minims*: 'drops' (or the equivalent amount).

stagger the unbelief of Satan: Hyde says he will produce evidence that will reveal divine truth and would convert even Satan himself from atheism (and Lanyon we learn a little later is firmly 'incredulous' or atheistic). Hyde means that the transformation, as proof of diabolic forces, will serve as negative proof of the existence of God. George Sinclair in *Satan's Invisible World Discovered* (Glasgow, 1685) says that his account of 'The Devil of Glenluce' is of value for its 'usefulness for refuting Atheism'. This is quoted by Andrew Lang (*Adventures Among Books*, Longman, 1905, p. 285), who adds (p. 292) that 'in Sinclair's day, people who did not believe in bogies believed in nothing'. It is strange, though, that Satan is here presented as an atheist (when, as God's antagonist he must believe in the existence and power of God), and that the proof of God's existence is promised by a character who is here clearly speaking and acting like Satan himself: Satan promises to reveal the truth of something that he says he does not believe in.

under the seal of our profession: 'covered by the Hypocratic Oath imposing silence on what a doctor learns of a patient'. Since this can only be Jekyll speaking, his claims of separating Hyde from himself seem questionable.

transcendental medicine: medicine that is open to non-material, apparently irrational or supernatural explanations. In Le Fanu's 'Green Tea' (*In a Glass Darkly*, 1872, Chapter 1), the narrator Dr Hesselius makes a declaration that might be shared by Dr Jekyll: 'when I ... speak of medical science, I do so, and I hope some day to see it more generally understood, in a much more comprehensive sense than its generally material treatment would warrant. I believe the entire natural world is but the ultimate expression of that spiritual world from which, and in which alone, it has its life. I believe that ... the material body is, in the most literal sense, a vesture.' Dr Frankenstein also confesses that 'still my inquiries were directed to the metaphysical, or in its highest sense, the physical secrets of the world' (*Frankenstein*, Chapter 2).

injected eyes: 'bloodshot eyes'.

57 *and yet I shall die incredulous*: Lanyon's refusal to believe could refer to revealed religion or to Hyde's metamorphosis (seen as 'impossible'). The first interpretation depends on use of the word 'incredulous' that the *OED* (1900) declares obsolete ('no longer applicable'), yet this seems to be the meaning intended, since *ND2* has: 'the shock of that moment ... has not bowed the pride of my scepticism; I shall die, but I shall die incredulous', that is, although the transformation might be seen by some as proof of the truth of revealed religion, or anyway of non-material forces at work in the world, 'I will nevertheless continue proudly and stubbornly not to believe'. This atheistical resistance would link up with Hyde's vaunt that the transformation will 'stagger the unbelief of Satan' (p. 56).

even with tears of penitence ... even in memory: the first 'even' has the rather archaic meaning of 'at the same moment with' (cf. Shakespeare's Sonnet 71: 'Let your love even with my life decay' – together with my life). The reader has difficulty identifying this meaning and rejecting the concessive 'even though with', and is further confused because the sentence continues immediately afterwards with a phrase that has the deceptive appearance of a parallel construction: '*even* with tears of penitence, I cannot, *even* in memory, dwell on it without a start of horror' – where the second 'even' actually has the more normal meaning of 'including, surprisingly'. Disorientation continues, however, because this very phrase is of the riddling kind: for how can you 'dwell on' something in the past (that is, think about it at length), if not 'in memory'?

Hastie: A Scottish surname, here apparently used as a first name. It was the maiden name of the mother of Stevenson's nurse, Cummie, and Alison Hastie is the lass who helps David and Alan cross the Firth of Forth and whose name we learn in *Catriona*. A more negative personal association is the Reverend William Hastie, a tactless and irascible Scottish minister, after whom Stevenson temporarily named his dog in 1884 (*LETBM*, vol. IV, pp. 302–3). Lanyon's first name 'nicely indicates his fatal characteristic' (Arata, *Fictions of Loss*, p. 41), his rash desire to see Hyde's transformation ('I have gone too far ... to pause before I see the end', p. 56). The adjective 'hasty' can also mean 'quick tempered' (*OED* 4), which also fits Lanyon's outbursts against Jekyll ('scientific balderdash', p. 14; 'I am quite done with that person', p. 35), a habit of thoughtless and absolute rejection that makes him similar to Jekyll (who uses the same words as Lanyon when he twice repeats that he is 'done with' Hyde, p. 30).

58 *gaiety of disposition*: 'of a gay disposition', where 'gay' was frequently used in the nineteenth century to mean 'addicted to social pleasures and dissipations. Often euphemistically: Of loose or immoral life' (*OED*).

a profound duplicity of life: Jekyll would like to impose the scientific and morally neutral meaning for *duplicity* of 'doubleness'. The reader, however, cannot forget its normal meaning of 'deception' (reinforced when Jekyll admits to being a 'profound ... double-dealer' a few lines later). Thus, Jekyll the narrator tries to present his life as morally neutral by deceptively manipulating the meaning of the word 'duplicity', which itself normally means 'deception'. The phrase is underlined by Nabokov.

blazoned: 'boasted of', 'made public'.

I was in no sense a hypocrite: Although Jekyll means that he was not a hypocrite to himself, the word is generally used of an individual's deliberately false presentation of himself (as more virtuous than he really is) to *others*, and Jekyll has just told us that he 'concealed' his pleasures in order to 'wear a ... grave countenance

before the public' (p. 58). Hence Jekyll here is being hypocritical
about not being hypocritical. In a letter Stevenson writes that 'The
harm was in Jekyll, because he was a hypocrite ... The Hypocrite let
out the beast Hyde' (*LETBM*, vol. VI, p. 56).

59 *war among my members*: 1. 'conflict between different parts of
   myself'; 2. 'rebellion diffused through my body (and directed
   against my mind)'. The first interpretation depends on an
   interpretation of 'members' to include the mind (though it usually
   means 'parts of the body'); the second on an unusual interpretation
   of 'war among' to mean 'war waged by'. The reader certainly
   expects 'war between my body and my mind', recalling the biblical
   phrases that lie behind Stevenson's choice of words (in which
   'members' refers to the body and 'war' (as a verb) means 'to act with
   the force of the sexual instinct'): 'your lusts that war in your
   members' (James 4: 1), 'I see another law in my members, warring
   against the law of my mind' and 'the law of sin which is in my
   members' (Romans 7: 23). These are phrases that we also find
   echoed in RLS's comment, in an essay of 1884, that 'The person,
   man or dog, who has a conscience is eternally condemned to some
   degree of humbug; the sense of the law in their members fatally
   precipitates either towards a frozen and affected bearing' ('On the
   Character of Dogs', *TUS*, vol. XXIX, p. 96). The association of
   awareness of sexuality ('law in their members') and hypocrisy (the
   pretence of 'humbug') is similar to that confessed by Jekyll in the
   first part of ch. 10.

   a mere polity of ... independent denizens: 'a veritable association of
   independent inhabitants' (though 'mere' could also have the modern
   meaning of 'simple', 'nothing more than'). In 'Crabbed Age and
   Youth' (1878, *TUS*, vol. XXV, p. 43) Stevenson had already
   expressed the same idea: 'we cannot even regard ourselves as
   constant; in this flux of things, our identity itself seems in a
   perpetual variation' and in 1893 he repeats it in an interview: 'My
   profound conviction is that there are many consciousnesses in a
   man. I have no doubt about it – I can feel them working in many
   directions' (*The Argus* [New Zealand], 11 April 1893). The sentence
   is marked by a double vertical line in the margin by Nabokov.

   suggest the most naked possibility: 'Naked possibility' is a rare legal
   term meaning 'mere possibility', 'remote possibility', especially of
   acquiring a property (*West's Law & Commercial Dictionary*, Eagan,
   MN, West Publishing, 1985). The whole phrase here sounds strange
   because *naked* is not normally gradable (we cannot normally say
   'this is the most naked of the three Venuses') and not at all in legal
   use. Using our skills at repairing scrambled messages or in
   interpreting odd collocations in familiar foreign languages, we will

probably read the phrase here as 'suggest *even* the *merest* possibility'. It is also legitimate to infer, from the normal meaning of *naked*, an additional connotation of 'defiantly or shamelessly revealed' – producing a riddling phrase, since it would seem impossible to 'suggest' a 'defiantly revealed possibility'. Translators, understandably, have often omitted 'most naked'.

faggots: 'bundles of sticks'.

that in the agonised womb of consciousness, these polar twins should be continuously struggling: an allusion to the twins Jacob and Esau in the womb of Rebecca, 'And the children struggled together within her' (Genesis 25: 22). Esau, the disinherited 'hairy' hunter, can be seen as similar to Hyde.

How, then, were they dissociated?: This does not mean 'In what manner were they then dissociated?' but continues Jekyll's free indirect thoughts: 'What would happen, then, if they were dissociated?' It is possible that Stevenson actually intended to write 'How, then, were they *to be* dissociated?': in *ND2*, Stevenson comes to the bottom of the page with 'were they' and starts the new page with 'dissociated' (*ND2* ff. 79–80), perhaps forgetting to write 'to be'; this could have then been copied unthinkingly into *MS* and *1886L*.

60 *I ... recognised my natural body for the mere aura and effulgence of certain of the powers that made up my spirit*: 'I identified my physical body as the pure (or simple) emanation and radiation of certain elements of my spirit'. Schopenhauer sees the body as the will 'made visible' (and Stevenson read Schopenhauer in 1874, *LETBM*, vol. II, p. 71); for the criminologist Lombroso, too, the body revealed the spirit within (cf. Martin Tropp, '*Dr Jekyll and Mr Hyde*, Schopenhauer, and the Power of Will', *Midwest Quarterly* 32(2), 1991, pp. 141–5). We have already seen (notes to p. 56) that Le Fanu's Dr Heselius also saw the material body as 'a vesture'.

exhibition: 'administration' (pharmacological term).

tabernacle: in the Old Testament the 'tabernacle' is a portable tent sanctuary, the 'place where God lives'; in the New Testament it is used metaphorically for the body, the temporary and material house of the immaterial soul (2 Corinthians 5: 1–4, 2 Peter 1: 13–14).

solution of the bonds of obligation: 'a release from social ties and restraints' (this use of 'solution' is marked 'obsolete' in the *OED*, 1913).

61 *a stranger in my own house*: a phrase which seems to have originated with Stevenson. We find an interesting echo in Freud's 'The Ego feels ill at ease ... inside its own house' ('Eine Schwierig- keit der Psychoanalyse' ['A Problem in Psychoanalysis'], 1917). It has appealed to recent songwriters, as a title (Foreigner 1984, Roine Stolt 1989) or in the lyrics (Cattle Company 1994, Bruce Cockburn 1999, The Slugs 2000, Ronan Keating 2002). Stevenson's essay 'The Foreigner at Home' portrays the Scot in England as in a similar ill- at-ease position as Hyde in Jekyll's house (cf. Jean-Pierre Naugrette, 'Le texte et son double', *Otrante*, 1995–6, p. 154).

the stamping efficacy: 'the faculty of producing a form, such as a coin, by forceful impression on receptive material', cf. (a few lines below) 'evil ... had left on that body an imprint of deformity and decay'; both phrases derive from the idea (which we also find in Wilde's *Dorian Gray*, 1891) that evil leaves its mark on the body and the face. Stevenson here uses 'efficacy' in an unusual way as 'power to do something' (cf. 'the exalting Efficacy of this kind of distillation', Boyle, 1665, qu. in the *OED*) rather than with the normal meaning of 'effectiveness in producing an intended result'.

idol: 1. 'incorporeal phantom'; 2. 'object of false worship' (*OED*).

express: 1. 'perfectly representational' (as Christ is 'the express image' of God, Hebrews 1: 3); 2. 'well-formed' ('What a piece of work is man! ... In form and moving, how express and admirable,' *Hamlet* II, ii, 317).

a visible misgiving of the flesh: fear and foreboding visible in the instinctive reaction of the body.

62 *the captives of Philippi*: reference to Acts 16: 24, 26: the apostles Paul and Silas, imprisoned in Philippi, sang hymns of praise to God and an earthquake opened all the doors of the prison. Here, the prison is 'my disposition', the liberating earthquake is 'the drug', the captives are 'my evil'. By his comparison with the apostle, Jekyll seems to see Hyde as somehow divinely approved. In the Bible story, however, the two apostles do not escape ('that which stood within ran forth' is a biblical-sounding phrase not actually in the Bible). Jekyll thinks Hyde ran free from his prison (and invents a biblical phrase to justify it) but, in fact, Hyde remains linked to Jekyll just as Paul actually remained inside the prison.

my evil, kept awake by ambition: Stevenson's correspondent Myers says 'I don't understand the phrase ... I thought the stimulus was a different one' (Maixner, pp. 216–17), but the context excludes the normal meaning of 'ambition' ('a desire for social eminence or for something advantageous') and forces us to look for a more appropriate one. Stevenson probably intends an etymological meaning from the Latin *ambitio* 'going around' (cf. the note on 'rambles', p. 8): Jekyll's evil is 'stimulated by urban rambles'.

63   *bravos*: 'irregular soldiers at the service of a powerful individual'.

lendings: 'clothes' (cf. 'Off, off, you lendings!', *King Lear* III, iv, 114); sometimes Jekyll presents the change to Hyde as the removal of habits/clothes in order to jump naked into the 'sea of liberty', sometimes as the donning of a concealing cloak in order to move around in disguise.

familiar: 1. 'intimate friend'; 2. 'attendant evil spirit' (with the suggestion of demonic possession – a traditional explanation of multiple-personality symptoms).

to do his good pleasure: 'to do whatever he wanted and considered right'; a phrase used frequently in the Authorised Version of the Bible (e.g. 'It is God which worketh in you both to will and to do of His good pleasure', Philippians 2: 13); it is a legal phrase of French origin and related to phrases (*selon son bon plaisir* etc.) that are common in modern French. Here, the word 'pleasure' has a second, punning meaning of 'sensual indulgence'.

64   *swart*: 'dark' or 'black' with connotations of 'rough'.

65   *seemed, like the Babylonian finger on the wall, to be spelling out the letters of my judgment*: King Balshazzar of Babylon (in Daniel 5: 5) saw a mysterious hand writing on the wall of his palace. Daniel was later able to interpret the writing as a prediction of the end of the king's empire as a punishment for having raised himself up against God.

66   *I chose the better part and was found wanting in the strength to keep to it*: An expression similar to 'the good that I would I do not; but the evil which I would not, that I do' (Romans 7: 19) – an experience not confined to Judaeo-Christian tradition, as is shown by Ovid's 'video meliora proboque, deteriora sequor' ('I see the better and approve it, but I follow the worse'), *Metamorphoses* VII, 20–1. Nabokov annotates this sentence with 'this is the allegorical note'.

67   *the leading characters*: 'the leading characteristics' (an archaic usage).

My devil had been long caged, he came out roaring: Cf. 1 Peter 5: 8 'be vigilant; because your adversary the devil, as a roaring lion, walketh about'. Although 'my devil' could be fitted into the traditional idea of demonic possession, the new element of an internal devil gaining extra power from confinement, and almost inevitably breaking out, looks forward to Freud's similar concept of 'the return of the repressed' (in 'Das Unheimliche', 1919).

morally sane: 'Moral insanity was proposed as a category of medical diagnosis by Dr. James Prichard in 1835 ... and subsequently was sometimes used in court as a criminal defense plea' (Linehan [ed.], *Strange Case of Dr. Jekyll and Mr. Hyde*, p. 56 note); for more information, see Mary Rosen, 'A Total Subversion of Character: Dr. Jekyll's Moral Insanity', *The Victorian Newsletter* 93 (spring 1998), pp. 27–31.

screwed to the topmost peg: 'Raised to the greatest degree of tension' (like a string on a violin etc.); an unusual phrase but understandable.

68   *The veil of self-indulgence was rent from head to foot*: 'and the veil of the temple was rent in the midst' (Luke 23: 45).

when I had walked with my father's hand: This sounds like a set phrase but is not. It seems to be a combination of 'when I walked holding my father's hand' and 'when I was in my father's hand' (i.e. under his control) or 'when I behaved in accordance with my father's hand' (i.e. in accordance with the 'right hand' of social conventions).

overlooked: 'observed from above'; an unusual but understandable use.

city of refuge: An Old Testament institution (Numbers 35: 9, 11).

the hands of all men would be raised to take and slay him: 'And he [Ishmael] will be a wild man; his hand will be against every man, and every man's hand against him' (Genesis 16: 12).

license: The *OED* refers to the spelling rule of *-ce* for noun, *-se* for verb in pairs of words like 'practice' and 'practise', but adds that 'Late 19th–c Dicts., however, almost universally have *license* both for n. and vb., either without alternative or in the first place'.

70   *Portland street*: a small street off Wardour Street in Soho; Stevenson probably intended Portland Place, the continuation of Regent Street north of Oxford Street, or Great Portland Street, just east of this, both of them near to Lanyon's house in Cavendish Square.

72   *This was the shocking thing; that the slime of the pit seemed to utter*

cries and voices; that the amorphous dust gesticulated and sinned; that what was dead, and had no shape, should usurp the offices of life: 'This was the shocking thing: that repulsive and formless Sin seemed to try to communicate; that Death communicated in gestures and sinned, that a dead and formless (therefore meaningless) Thing took over the functions belonging to life.' This, at any rate, is one simple paraphrase of a dense structure of variations of biblical and moralistic language in which Hell ('the pit'), death ('dust', 'what was dead'), the repulsive ('slime'), and the formless ('amorphous', 'had no shape' and, just previously, 'inorganic') are associated in opposition to 'life' (and beings that can feel and communicate) and to things with shape (and that are therefore knowable). The shocking thing is that what is rejected from life by Jekyll is found to be associated with life. Stevenson, unlike Jekyll, saw formlessness as an essential aspect of life itself: it is 'infinite in complication', 'infinite, illogical' ('A Humble Remonstrance', 1884, *TUS*, vol. XXIX, pp. 134, 136), and has a 'sort of sense which we seem to perceive in the arabesques of time and space' ('A Chapter on Dreams', *TUS*, vol. XXX, p. 53).

73   *reindue*: 'put on'; an obsolete use of the verb.

I am careless: 'I don't care'; an unusual use of the adjective.

end: The last chapter/document does not end with a signature (though most translations have changed the word order to make the last words 'Henry Jekyll', one even putting this on a separate line and in capitals), as we might expect from the signature at the end of ch. 9 and at the end of the letter from Jekyll within that chapter. There can be no signature here because there is no single and non-changing identity which it can attest.

Appendices

APPENDIX A

Manuscript Drafts

There exist two fragmentary preparatory 'notebook drafts' of *Jekyll and Hyde* (*ND1*, two cancelled leaves, and *ND2*, probably the remains of an almost-complete draft) and the fragmentary final manuscript (*MS*), all of which are described in full in the Textual Notes. The present appendix includes the transcription of all these fragments. The only other complete transcription, by Veeder (1988), includes numerous mistakes, such as 'the star' for 'the stair', 'dearly liked' for 'clearly liked', 'proudly supposed' for 'fondly supposed' and 'that kindred monster-man's soul' for 'that kindred monster – man's soul'. It also includes two short underlined sequences (one followed by a question mark) not in the manuscripts, clearly taken over by mistake from working notes.

The transcriptions below are in parallel passages on the same page, *ND* at the top and *MS* below, followed by an indication of the page and line of corresponding passages in the present edition (*EUP*). Where a parallel passage is lacking there are three dots in that part of the page. The beginning of a new manuscript page is indicated in the body of the transcription by a vertical line |, with the new page number in the margin.

A problem for the transcriber is presented by Stevenson's apparently strange forms like 'mis-gives' (*MS*, f. 12.29) and 'dis-course' (*MS*, f. 1.5), which are transcribed by Veeder with hyphens (and are also perceived as hyphens in his letters, though not transcribed thus, by Booth and Mehew, *LETBM*, vol. I, p. 19). They have not been so transcribed here: there are no historical examples of thus hyphenating these prefixes (so it is not an archaic affectation) and none of them was interpreted as a hyphen by the printer. In fact, Stevenson almost never has a continuous linking line to his word-internal small 'c' (except for 'oc'): he usually leaves a space between it and the previous letter but, when it follows an 's' (so after 'dis-' or 'mis-'), he almost always lifts the pen from the bottom of the 's', adds a short horizontal linking line, then lifts the pen again to start the following 'c'. The result is often a short line not actually touching one or both letters (so with the appearance of a hyphen). We find a similar hyphen-like link between an 's' and the small-bowl letters 'g' and 'd' but, on other occasions, he leaves a space (which can be quite wide, as in 'disguise', *ND2*, f. 52.19) or uses a continuous linking line.

Stevenson's occasional wide gaps when he lifts his pen in the middle of a word can present problems for the transcription of compounds as one or two words: these have been resolved by appealing to nearby examples of the same word: '[I gave in the cheque] myself' (*MS*, f. 4), not 'my self', since there are two examples of 'myself' immediately afterwards; a similar case is 'bystreet' (at the beginning of *MS*, f. 9), rather than a possible 'by street' because of the single-word form on the same page. On the other hand, 'great coat' (*MS*, ff. 7, 8) has been kept as two words, since there is a space on both occasions.

Any transcription includes an element of interpretation, and this has been unavoidable in the case of altered punctuation, where the following procedures have been followed: 1. a punctuation mark overwritten by a new one is shown (as with overwritten letters) by the cancelled mark (in angle brackets) followed immediately by the new mark with no intervening space (where a comma etc. is overwritten by a bracket, the former has been separated from the preceding word by a space in order to bring it next to the mark that overwrites it); 2. a punctuation mark written immediately after a cancellation, or squeezed into an existing space after a cancellation during revision, is separated by a space from the preceding cancellation (to avoid confusion with the above transcription convention for overwritten elements); 3. where a punctuation mark has been crossed out and a new punctuation mark then squeezed in *before* it, in this transcription the inserted punctuation has nevertheless been placed *second*, separated by a space (as in point 2. above). For example, where a full stop has been cancelled and an exclamation mark squeezed in front of it, I have not transcribed it as 'Yes!<.>' but (in the interests of readability) as 'Yes<.> !' Similarly, where a passage has been cancelled and, unusually, an inserted passage has been located *before* it, I have nevertheless placed the insert afterwards, again in order to reflect the temporal order of writing.

The manuscripts show revealing early versions of parts of the text as well as merely mechanical scribal errors (words skipped, repeated or anticipated). An interesting aspect of Stevenson's self-dictation (as he copied from *ND2* to *MS*) are two cases of mistaken homophones: 1. *The figure in these two <faces> ^phases^* (*MS*, f. 8A), which shows that the two words must have had the same sound for Stevenson, *phases* (whose singular until the nineteenth century was *phasis*) undoubtedly retaining a Latinate /s/ as its middle consonant; 2. *and <the fall of their favourite crew>* (*MS*, f. 57) where the last word must be meant for *Carew*, suggesting Stevenson's pronunciation of the name with a typically Scots elision of the vowel in an unstressed first syllable (as in 'c'rrect' and 'c'llapse'). Another mistake, *trouses* (*MS* p. 44), if not purely mechanical, could indicate that /r/ was not very prominent for Stevenson in a word-final -*rs* sequence.

SYMBOLS

{ }	Editor's insertion
< >	Deletion (<< >> for a deleted section containing deletions)
<?>	Unclear cancelled letter
^ ^	Insertion (also ^^ ^^ as for deletions)
<x>y	(no space after deletion) x deleted by being overwritten by y
x .	(space before punctuation) Inserted punctuation
|	Page break in the manuscript
8.7	page 8, line 7
~~8B~~	cancelled page 8B

ND ...

MS 1   Strange Case of Dr Jekyll and Mr Hyde

—

Story of the door.

Mr Utterson the lawyer was a man of a rugged countenance,
<and> that ^was^ never lighted by a smile; cold, scanty and
embarrassed in discourse; backward in sentiment; lean, long,
dusty, dreary and yet somehow loveable. At friendly meetings,
and when the wine was to his taste, something <evid> eminently
human beaconed from his eye; something indeed which never
found its way into his talk, but which spoke not only in these
silent symbols of the afterdinner face, but more often and loudly
in the acts of his life. He was austere with himself; drank gin when
he was alone, to mortify a taste for vintages; and though he
enjoyed the theatre, had not crossed the doors of one for twenty
years. But he had an approved tolerance for others, sometimes
wondering, almost with envy, at the ^high^ pressure of <high>
spirits involved in their misdeeds, and in any extremity inclined to
help rather than to reprove. "I rather incline to Cain's heresy," he
used to say quaintly: "I let my brother go to the devil in h{is} own
way." In this character, it was frequently his fortune to be the last
reputable acquaintance and the last good influence in the lives of
down-going men. And to these, as long as they came about his
chambers, he never marked a shade of change in his demeanour.

No doubt the feat was easy to Mr Utterson, for he was
undemonstrative at the best, and even his friendships seemed to be
founded in a similar catholicity of good nature. It is the mark of a
modest man to accept his friendly circle ready-made from the
hands of opportunity; and that was the lawyer's way. His friends
were those of his own blood or those whom he had known the
longest; his affections, like ivy, were the growth of time, <and>
they implied no aptness in the object. Hence, no doubt, the bond
that united him to Mr Richard Enfield, his distant kinsman, the
well known man about town. It was a nut to crack for many, what
these two could see in each other or what subject they could find
in common. It was <encountered> ^reported^ by those who encountered them in their Sunday walks, that they said nothing, looked
| 2   singularly dull, and would | hail with obvious relief the appearance
of a friend. For all that, the two men set the greatest store by these
excursions, counted them the chief jewel of each week, and not
only set ^aside^ occasions of pleasure, but even resisted the calls
of business, that they ^might^ enjoy them uninterrupted.

EUP 7–8.10

ND ...

MS It <changed> ^chanced^ on one of these rambles that their
way led them down a by-street in a busy quarter of London. The
street was small and what is called quiet, but it drove a thriving
trade on the weekdays. The inhabitants were all doing well, it
seemed, ^and all^ emulously hoping to do better still, and laying
out the surplus of their gains in coquetry; so that the shop fronts
^stood^ along that thoroughfare with an air of invitation, like
rows of smiling saleswomen. Even on Sunday, when it veiled its
more florid charms and lay comparatively empty of passage, the
street shone out in contrast to its dingy nieghbourhood, like a fire
in a forest; and with its freshly painted shutters, well polished
brasses, and general cleanliness and gaiety of note, instantly
caught and pleased the eye of the passenger.

Two doors from one corner, on the left hand going east, the
line was broken by the entry of a court; and just at that point, a
certain sinister block of building thru{st} forward its gable on the
street. It was two storeys high; showed no window, nothing but a
door on the lower storey and a blind forehead of discoloured wall
on the upper; and bore in every feature, the marks of ^prolonged
and^ sordid negligence. The door, which was equipped with
niether bell nor knocker, was blistered and distained. Tramps
slouched into its shelter and struck matches on the panels;
children kept shop <on> ^upon^ the steps; the schoolboy had
tried his knife on the mouldings; and for close on a generation, no
one had appeared to drive away these random visitors or to repair
their ravages.

Mr Enfield and the lawyer were on the other side of the
bystreet; but when they came abreast of the entry, the former
lifted up his cane and pointed.

"Did you ever remark that door?" he asked; and when his
companion had replied in the affirmative, "It is connected in my
mind," added he, "with a very odd story."

"Indeed?" said Mr Utterson, with a slight change of voice.
"And what was that?"

"Well, it was this way," returned Mr Enfield: "I was coming
| 3 home | from some place at the end of the world, about three
o'clock of a black winter morning, and my way lay through a part
of town where there was literally nothing to be seen but lamps.
Street after street, and all the folks asleep – street after street, all
lighted <bu> up as if for a procession and all as empty as a church
– till at last I got into that state of mind when a man listens and
listens and begins to <weary> ^long^ for the sight of a policeman.
All at once, I saw two figures: one a little man who was stumping

ND ...

MS along eastward at a <d> good walk, and the other a girl of maybe
eight or ten who was running <down> ^as^ hard as she was able
down a cross street. Well, sir, the two ran into one another
naturally enough ^at the corner^; and then came the horrible part
of the thing; for the man trampled calmly over the child's body and
left her screaming on the ground. It sounds nothing to hear, but it
was hellish to see. ^It wasn't like a man; it was like some damned
Juggernaut^ I gave a view halloa, took to my heels, collared <the>
^my^ gentleman, and brought him back to where there was
already quite a group about the screaming child. He was perfectly
cool and made no resistance, but gave me one look so ugly that it
brought out the sweat on me like running. The people who had
turned out were the girl's own family; and pretty soon, the doctor,
for whom she had been sent, put in his appearance. Well, the child
was not much the worse, more frightened, according to the
<s>Sawbones; and there you might have supposed would be an
end to it. But there was one curious circumstance. I had taken a
loathing to my gentleman at first sight; so had the child's family,
which was only natural. But the doctor's case was <the> what
struck me. He was the usual cut and dry apothecary, of no
particular age and colour, with a strong Edinburgh accent, and
about as emotional as a bagpipe. Well, sir, he was like the rest of us;
every time he looked at my prisoner, I saw that Sawbones turn sick
and white with the desire to kill him. I knew what was in his mind,
just as he knew what was in mine; and killing being out of the
question, we did the next best. We told <him> ^the man^ we could
and would make such a scandal out of this, as should make his
name stink from one end of London to the other. If he had any
friends or any credit, we undertook that he should lose them. And
all the time, as we were pitching it in red hot, we were keeping the
women off him as best <they> ^we^ could, for they were as wild
as harpies. <All the> I never saw a circle of such hateful faces; <I
| 4   declare we looked like fiends> and there was the | man in the middle,
with a kind of black, sneering coolness, <that> – frightened<,> too,
I could see that – but carrying it off, sir, really like Satan. <">'If
you choose to make capital out of this accident,<">' said he, <">'I
am naturally helpless. No gentleman but wishes to avoid a
scene,<">' says he. 'Name your figure.' Well, we screwed him
<do> up to a <thousand> ^hundred^ pounds for the child's
family; he would have clearly liked to stick out; but there was
something about the lot of us that meant mischief, and at last he
struck. The next thing was to get the money; and where do you
think he carried us but that place with the door? <I pointed out> –

ND ...

MS whipped out a key, went in, and presently came back with the
matter of <fifty> ^ten^ pounds in gold and a cheque for the
balance on Coutts's, drawn payable to bearer and signed with a
name that I can't mention, though it's one of the points of my
story, but it was a name at least very well known and often printed.
The figure was stiff; but the signature was good for more than that,
if it was only genuine. I took the liberty of pointing out to my
gentleman that the whole business looked apocryphal, and that a
man does not, in real life, walk into a cellar door at four in the
morning and come out of it with another man's cheque for close
upon a <thousand> ^hundred^ pounds. But he was quite easy and
sneering. '<L>Set your mind at rest,' says he. 'I will stay with you
till the banks open and cash the cheque myself.' So we all <went>
^set^ off, the doctor, and the child's father, and our friend and
myself, and passed the rest of the night in my chambers; and next
day, when we had breakfasted, <set off> ^went^ in a body <for>
^to^ the bank. I gave in the cheque myself, and said I had every
reason to believe it was a forgery. Not a bit of it, sir. The cheque
was genuine."

"Tut-tut," said Mr Utterson.

"I see you feel as I do," said Mr Enfield. "Yes, it's a bad story.
For my man was a fellow that nobody could have to do with, a
really damnable man; and the person that drew the cheque is the
very pink of the proprieties, celebrated too, and (what makes it
worse) one of your fellows who do what they call good. Black
mail, I suppose<;>: an honest man paying <for> through the nose
for some of the capers of his youth. Black Mail House is what I
call that place with the door, in consequence. Though<,> even
that, you know, is far from explaining all," he added, and with the
words fell into a vein of musing.

| 5 | From this he was recalled by Mr Utterson asking rather
suddenly: "And you don't know if the drawer of the cheque lives
there?"

"A likely place, isn't it?" returned Mr Enfield. "But I happen to
have noticed his address; he lives in some square or other."

"And you never asked about – the place with <a> ^the^ door?"
said Mr Utterson.

"No, sir: I had a delicacy," was the reply. "I feel very strongly
about putting questions; it partakes too much of the style of the
day of judgement. You start a question, and it's like starting a
stone. You sit quietly on the top of a hill; and away the stone goes,
starting others; and presently some bland old bird (the last you
would have thought of) is knocked on the head in his own back

ND ...

MS garden and the family have to change their name. No, sir<;>, I
make it a rule of mine: the more it looks like Queer Street, the less
I ask."

"A very good rule, too," said the lawyer.

"But I have studied the place for myself," continued Mr
Enfield. "It seems scarcely a house. There is no other door, and
nobody goes in or out of that one but, once in a great while, <my>
^the^ gentleman of my adventure. There are three windows
looking on the court on the first floor; none below; the windows
are always shut <and wonderfully dirty> ^but they're clean^. And
then there is a chimney which is generally smoking; so somebody
must live there. And yet it's not so sure; for the buildings are so
packed together about that court, that it's hard to say where one
ends and another begins."

The pair walked on again ^for a while^ in silence; and then
"Enfield," said Mr Utterson, "that's a good rule of yours."

"Yes, sir, I think it is," returned Enfield.

"But for all that," continued the lawyer, "there's one point I
want to ask: I want to ask the name of <that> ^<t>^ that¹ man
who walked over the child."

"Well," said Mr Enfield, "I can't see what harm it would do. It
was a man of the name of Hyde."

"Hm," said Mr Utterson. "What sort of a man is he to see?"

"He is not easy to describe. There is something wrong with his
appearance; something displeasing, something downright
detestable. I never saw a man I so disliked, and yet I scarce know
why. He must be deformed somewhere; he gives a strong feeling of
deformity, although I couldn't specify the point. He's an
extraordinary looking man, and yet I really can name nothing out
| 6   of the way. No, sir; I can make no | hand of it; I can't describe him.
And it's not want of memory; for I declare I can see him at this
moment."

Mr Utterson again walked some way in silence and obviously
under a weight of consideration. "You are sure he used a key?" he
inquired at last.

"My dear sir ..." <cried> ^began^ Enfield, surprised out of
himself.

"Yes, I know," said Utterson; "I know it must seem strange.
The fact is, <I know something about this> ^if I do not ask you
the name of the^ other party, it is because I know it already. You
see, Richard, your tale has gone home. If you have been inexact in
any point, you had better correct it."

"I think you might have warned me," returned the other with a

ND ...

MS   touch of sullenness. "But I have been pedantically exact, as you call it. The fellow had a key; and what's more, he << <must have been> ^<is>^ in the habit of using it, for I have seen him go in again in the same way.>> he has it still. I saw him use it, not a week ago."

Mr Utterson sighed deeply but said never a word; and the young man presently resumed. "<This> ^Here^ is another lesson to say nothing," said he. "I am ashamed of my long tongue. Let us make a bargain never to refer to this again."

"With all my heart," said the lawyer. "I shake hands on that, Richard."

<u>Search for Mr Hyde</u>

That evening, Mr Utterson came home to his bachelor house in sombre spirits and sat down to dinner without relish. It was his custom of a sunday, when this meal was over, to sit close by the fire, a volume of some dry divinity on his reading desk, until the clock of the neighbouring church rang out the hour of twelve when he would go soberly and gratefully to bed. On this night, however, as soon as the cloth was taken away, he took up a candle and went into his business room. There he opened his safe, took from the most private part of it a document endorsed on the envelope as Dr Jekyll's Will, and sat down with a clouded brow to study its contents. The will was holograph, for Mr Utterson, though he took charge of it now that it was made, had refused to

| 7   lend the least assistance in the making of it; and it provided | not only that, in case of the decease of Henry Jekyll, M.D., D.C.L., L.L.D., F.R.S., &c, all his possessions were to pass into the hands of his "friend and benefactor Edward Hyde," but that in case of Dr Jekyll's "disappearance or unexplained absence for any period exceeding three calendar months", the said Edward Hyde should step into the said Henry Jekyll's shoes without further delay and free from any burthen or obligation, beyond the <immediate> payment of <the> a few small sums to the members of the doctor's household. This document had long been the lawyer's eyes<hu>ore. It offended him as a lawyer and as a lover of the sane and customary sides of life, to whom the fanciful was the immodest. And hitherto it was his ignorance of Mr Hyde that had swelled his indignation; now, by a sudden turn, it was his knowledge. It was already bad enough<,> when the name was but a name<,> of which he could learn <nothing further> ^no more^<,> . <i>It was

ND ...

MS worse when it began to be clothed upon with detestable attributes;
and out of the shifting, insubstantial mists that had so long baffled
his eye, there leaped up the sudden, definite presentment of a fiend.

"I thought it was madness" he said, as he replaced the obnoxious paper in the safe. "and now I begin to fear it is disgrace." <And
still there was no rest for the solicitor; and instead of taking his
place by the fire, he> ^<And thereupon>^ ^With that he blew out
his candle,^ put on <his> ^a^ great coat and set forth in the
direction of Cavendish Square, ^that citadel of medicine,^ where
his friend, the great Dr. Lanyon, had his house and received his
crowding patients. "If anyone knows, it will be Lanyon," he
^had^ thought.

The solemn butler <received> ^knew and^ welcomed him; he
was subjected to no stage of delay, but ushered direct from the
door to the dining room where Dr Lanyon sat alone over his wine.
This was a hearty, healthy, dapper, red-faced gentleman, with a
shock of hair prematurely white^, and a boisterous and decided
manner^. At sight of Mr Utterson, he sprang up from his chair and
welcomed him with both hands. The geniality, as was the
<manner> ^way^ of the man, was somewhat theatrical to the eye;
but it reposed on genuine feeling. For these two were old friends,
old mates both at school and college, both thorough respecters of
themselves and of each other, and, <(> what does not always
follow, men who thoroughly enjoyed each other's company.

| 8 | After a little rambling talk, the lawyer led up to the subject
which so disagreeably preoccupied his mind.

"I suppose, Lanyon," said he "you and I will be the two oldest
friends that Henry Jekyll has?"

"I wish the friends were younger," chuckled Dr Lanyon. "But I
suppose we are. And what of that? I see little of him now."

"Indeed?" said Utterson. "I thought you had a bond of
^common^ interest."

"We had," was the reply. "But it is more than ten years since
Henry Jekyll became too fanciful for me. He began to go wrong,
wrong in mind; and though of course I continue to take an interest
in him for old sake's sake as they say, I see and I have seen devilish
little of the man. Such unscientific balderdash," added the doctor,
flushing suddenly purple, "would have estranged Damon and
Pythias."

This little spirt of temper was somewhat of a relief to Mr Utterson. "They have only differed on some point of science," he
thought; and <even> ^being^ a man of no scientific passions
(except in the matter of conveyancing) he even added: "It is

ND ...

MS nothing worse than that!" He gave his friend a few seconds to
recover his composure, and then approached the question he had
come to put. "Did you ever come across a protégé of his – one
Hyde?" he asked.

"Hyde?" repeated Lanyon. "No. Never heard of him. Since my
time."

That was the amount of information that <the lawyer> ^<Mr
Utterson>^ the lawyer² carried back with him to the great, dark
bed on which he tossed to and fro, until the small hours of the
morning began to grow large. It was a night of little ease to his
toiling mind, toiling in mere darkness and besieged by questions.
<How could such a man as Henry Jekyll be bound up with such a
man as Edward Hyde? How should he have chosen as his heir one
who was unknown to his oldest intimates? If it were a case of
terrorism, why the will? Or again, if Hyde were Jekyll's son, why
the proviso of the disappearance?> Six o'clock struck on the bells
of the church that was so conveniently near to Mr Utterson's
dwelling, and still he was digging at the problem<;> . <<And for
all that, he had no sooner swallowed his breakfast, than he must
put on his hat and great coat and set forth eastward <of a> ^in^
the teeth of a fine, driving rain, coming iced out of Siberia, with no
more sensible purpose than to stand <awhile> on the opposite
pavement and look awhile at the door without the knocker.>>

| 8A   <| This>³ | ^^Hitherto <the matter> ^it^ had touched him on
the intellectual side alone; but now his imagination also was
engaged or rather enslaved; and as he lay and tossed in the gross
darkness of the night and the curtained room, Mr Enfield's tale
went by before his mind in a scroll of lighted pictures. He would
<see> ^be aware of^ the great field of lamps of the nocturnal city;
then of <a> the figure of a man walking swiftly; then of a child
running from the doctor's; and then these met, and that human
Juggernaut trod the child down and passed on regardless of her
screams. Or else he would see a room in a rich house, where his
friend lay asleep, dreaming and smiling at his dreams; and then the
door of that room would be opened, the curtains of the bed
plucked apart, the sleeper recalled, and lo! there would stand by
his side a figure to whom power was given, and even at that dead
hour <of the night>, he must rise and do its bidding. The figure in
these two <faces> ^phases^ haunted the lawyer all night; and if at
any time he dozed over, it was but to see it <glide> ^<stalk>^
^glide^ more stealthily through sleeping houses, or move the
more swiftly<,> and still the more swiftly, even to <diziness>
^dizziness^, through wider labyrinths of lamplighted city, and at

ND ...

MS every street corner<,> crush a child and leave her screaming.
<Still> ^And still^ the figure had no face by which he might know
it; even in his dreams, it had no face, or one that baffled him and
melted before his eyes; and thus it <came> ^was^ that<, whether
he was asleep or awake> ^there sprang up and grew apace in^ the
lawyer's mind, a singularly strong, ^<and>^ almost ^an^
inordinate, curiosity to behold the features of the real Mr Hyde. If
he could but once set eyes on him, he thought the mystery would
lighten and perhaps roll altogether away, as was the habit of
mysterious things when well examined. He might see a reason for
his friend's strange preference or bond^a^ge (<or>call it which
you please) and even for the startling clauses of the will. And at
least it would be a face worth seeing: the face of a man who was
without bowels of mercy: a face which ^had^ but to show itself to
raise up, in the mind of the unimpressionable Enfield, a spirit of
enduring hatred.

From that time forward, Mr Utterson began to haunt the door
in the by street of shops. In the morning before office hours, at
noon when <time> ^business^ was <scarce> ^plenty^ and
<business plenty> ^time scarce^, at night under the <fogged face
of the> ^<face of the fogged>^ fogged face of the⁴ city moon, by
all lights and at all hours of solitude <of> or concourse, the lawyer

| 9 was to be found on his chosen post. <Now> <| he>⁵ | <<This⁶
excursion, once taken, seemed to have laid a spell on the
methodical gentleman. In the morning before office hours, at noon
when business was plenty and time scarce, at night under the
glimpses of the fogged city moon or by the cheap glare of the
lamps, a spirit in his feet kept still drawing and guiding the lawyer
to that door in the bystreet of shops. <He saw it thus under all
sorts of illumination, and occupied by all kinds of passing
tenants.> He made long stages on the pavement opposite, studying
the bills of fare stuck on the sweating windows of the cookshop,
reading the labels on the various lotions or watching the bust of
the proud lady swing stonily round upon him on her ^velvet^
pedestal at the perfumers; but <all the time> ^still^ with one eye
over his shoulder, spying at the door. And all the time the door
remained inexorably closed; none entered in, none came forth;
<it> the high tides of the town swarmed close by, but did not
touch it. Yet the lawyer was not to be beaten. He had made a
solemn agreement with himself, <and> ^to^ penetrate this
mystery of Mr Hyde.>> "If he be Mr Hyde," he had thought
^<with grim pleasantry>^, "I shall be Mr Seek." <Let him but set
eyes upon the man, and he could judge him.>

EUP 15.34–16.16

ND ...

MS   And at last his patience was rewarded. It was a fine dry night; frost in the air; the streets as clean as a ballroom floor; the lamps, unshaken by any wind, drawing a regular pattern of light and shadow. By ten o'clock, when the shops were closed, the bystreet was very solitary and, in spite of the low growl of London from all round, very silent <to the ear>. Small sounds carried far; domestic sounds out of the houses were clearly audible on either side of the roadway; and the rumour of the approach of any passenger preceded him by a long <way> ^time^. Mr Utterson had been some minutes at his post, when he was aware of an odd, light footstep drawing <rapidly> near. In the course of his nightly patrols, he had long grown accustomed to the quaint effect with which the footfalls of a single person, while he is still a great way off, <spring> ^suddenly^ spring out distinct from the vast hum and clatter of the city. Yet his attention had never before been so sharply and decisively arrested; and it was with a strong, superstitious prevision of success that he withdrew into the entry of the court.

    The steps drew swiftly nearer, and swelled out suddenly louder as they turned the end of the street. The lawyer, looking forth from the | entry, could soon see what manner of man he had to deal with. He was small and very plainly dressed, and the look of him, even at that distance, went <st> somehow strongly against the watcher's inclination. But he made straight for the door, crossing the roadway to save time; and as he came, he drew a key from his pocket like one approaching home.

    Mr Utterson stepped out and touched him on the shoulder as he passed. "Mr Hyde, I think?"

    Mr Hyde shrank back with a hissing intake of the breath. But his fear was only momentary; and though he did not look the lawyer in the face, he answered coolly enough: "That is my name<," said he>. <">What do you want?"

    "I see you are going in," returned the lawyer. "I am an old friend of Dr Jekyll's – Mr Utterson of Gaunt Street – you must have heard my name; and meeting you so conveniently, I thought you might admit me."

    "You will not find Dr Jekyll; he is from home," replied Mr Hyde, blowing in the key. And then suddenly, but still without looking up, "How did you know me?" he asked.

    "On your side," said Mr Utterson, "will you do me a favour?"

    "With pleasure," replied the other. "What shall it be?"

    "Will you look me in the face?" asked the lawyer.

    Mr Hyde appeared to hesitate<;> , and then, as if <op> upon

EUP 16.17–17.20

ND ...

MS   some sudden reflection, fronted about with an air of defiance; and
the pair stared at each other pretty fixedly for <some> ^a few^
seconds. "Now I shall know you again," said Mr Utterson. "It
may be useful."

"Yes," returned Mr Hyde, "^it is as well we have met;^ and à
propos, you should have my address." And he gave a number of a
street in Soho.

"Good God," thought Mr Utterson, "can he too have been
thinking of the will<,>?" <discounting the inheritance> <But he
merely thanked the other and promised to remember it> ^But he
kept his feelings to himself and only grunted in acknowledge-
ment<.> of the address.^

"And now," said the other, "how did you know me?"

"By description," was the reply.

"Whose description?"

"We have common friends," said Mr Utterson.

"Common friends?" echoed ^Mr^ Hyde, a little hoarsely.
"Who are they?"

"Jekyll, for instance," said the lawyer.

"He never told you," cried Mr Hyde, "never, never told you. I |
| 11   <I d> did not think you would have lied."

"Come, <come,>" said Mr Utterson, "that is not fitting
language."

The other <laugh> snarled aloud into a savage laugh; and the
next moment, with extraordinary quickness, he had unlocked the
door and disappeared into the house.

The lawyer stood awhile when Mr Hyde had left him, the
picture of disquietude. Then he began slowly to mount the street,
pausing every step or two and putting his hand to his brow like a
man in mental perplexity. The problem he was thus debating as he
walked, was one of a class that is rarely solved. Mr Hyde was pale
and dwarfish, he gave an impression of deformity without any
nameable malformation, he had a displeasing smile, he had borne
himself to the lawyer with a <somewhat> ^sort of^ murderous
<mixture of cowardice and savagery> ^mixture of timidity and
boldness^, and he spoke with a husky, whispering and somewhat
broken voice; all these were points against him, but not all of these
together could explain the hitherto unknown disgust, loathing and
fear with which Mr Utterson regarded him. "There must be something else," said the perplexed gentleman. "There is something
more, if I could find a name for it. God bless me, the man seems
hardly human! Something troglodytic, shall we say? or can it be
the old story of Dr. Fell? or is ^it^ the mere radiance of a foul soul

_ND_ ...

_MS_ that thus transpires through, and transfigures, its clay continent? The last, I think; for O my poor old Harry Jekyll, if ever I read Satan's signature upon a face, it is on that of your new friend.

Round the corner from the bystreet, there was a square of ancient, handsome houses, now for the most part decayed from their high estate and let in flats and chambers to all sorts and conditions of men: map-engravers, architects, shady lawyers and the agents of obscure enterprises. One house, however, second from the corner, was still occupied entire; and at the door of this, which wore a great air of wealth and comfort, though it was now plunged in darkness except for the fanlight, Mr Utterson stopped and knocked. A well-dressed, elderly servant opened the door.

"Is Dr Jekyll at home, Poole?" asked the lawyer.

"I will see, Mr Utterson," said Poole, admitting the visitor, as he spoke, into a large, low-roofed, comfortable hall, paved with flags, warmed (after the fashion of a country house) by a bright,
| 12 open | fire, and furnished with costly cabinets of oak. "Will you wait here by the fire, sir? or shall I give you a light in the dining room?"

"Here, thank you," said the lawyer, and he drew near and leaned on the tall fender. This hall, in which he was now left alone, was a pet fancy of his friend the doctor's; and Utterson himself was wont to speak of it as the pleasantest room in London. But tonight there was a shudder in his blood; <his encounter with> ^the face of^ Hyde <had thrown him out of gear> ^sat heavy on his memory^; he felt (what was rare with him) a nausea and distaste of life; and in the gloom of his spirits, he seemed to read a menace in the flickering of the firelight on the polished cabinets and the uneasy starting of the shadow on the roof. He was ashamed of his relief, when Poole presently returned to <say> ^announce^ that Dr Jekyll was gone out.

"I saw Mr Hyde go in by the old dissecting room door, Poole," he said. "Is that right, when Dr Jekyll is from home?"

"Quite right, Mr Utterson, sir," replied the servant. "Mr Hyde has a key."

"Your master seems to repose a great deal of trust in that young man, Poole," resumed the other musingly.

"Yes, sir, he do indeed," said Poole. "We have all orders to obey him."

"I do not think I ever met Mr Hyde?" asked Utterson.

"O, dear no, sir. He never <u>dines</u> here," replied the butler. "Indeed we see very little of him on this side of the house; he mostly comes and goes by the laboratory."

EUP 18.21–19.25

ND ...

MS "Well, good night, Poole."
"Good night, Mr Utterson."
And the lawyer set out homeward with a very heavy heart.
"Poor Harry Jekyll," he thought, "my mind misgives me <you
are> ^he is^ in deep waters! <That could never be the face of his
son, never in this world. No, there is a secret at the root of it;
Jekyll> ^He^ was wild when he was young; a long while ago to be
sure; but in the law of God, there is no statute of limitations. Ay, it
must be that; the ghost of some old sin, the cancer of some
concealed disgrace: punishment coming, <u>pede claudo</u>, years after
memory has forgotten and self-love condoned the fault." And the

| 13 lawyer, scared by the | thought, brooded awhile on his own past,
groping in all the corners of memory, lest by chance some Jack-in-
the-Box of an old iniquity should leap to light there. His past was
fairly blameless; few men could read the rolls of their life with less
apprehension; yet he was humbled to the dust by the many ill
things he had done, and raised up again into a sober and fearful
gratitude by the many that he had so near to doing yet avoided.
And then by a return on his former subject, he conceived a spark
of hope. "This Master Hyde, if he were studied," thought he,
"must have secrets of his own: black secrets, by the look of him;
secrets compared to which poor Jekyll's worst would be like
sunshine. <I think we might turn the tables; I am sure, if Harry
will but let me, that I ought to try. For> <t>Things cannot continue as they are. It turns me cold to think of this creature stealing
like a thief to Harry's bedside <and>; poor Harry, what a wakening! And the danger of it; for if this Hyde suspects the existence of
the will, he may grow impatient to inherit. Ay, I must put my
<hand> ^shoulder^ to the wheel, if Jekyll will but let me," he
added, "if Jekyll will only let me." For once more he saw before his
minds eye, as clear as a transparency, the strange clauses of the will.
<<But he made up his mind <to> even to stretch friendship in
so good a cause, and on the first occasion>>

Dr Jekyll was quite at ease

A fortnight later, by excellent good fortune, the doctor gave one of
his pleasant dinners to some five or six old cronies, all intelligent,
reputable men and all judges of good wine; and Mr Utterson so
contrived that he remained behind after the others had departed.
This was no new arrangement, but a thing that had befallen many
scores of times. Where Utterson was liked, he was liked well.

EUP 19.26–21.7

ND ...

MS Hosts loved to detain the dry lawyer, when the light-hearted and
13   the loose-tongued had already their foot on the threshold; they
liked to sit awhile in his unobtrusive company, practising for
solitude, sobering their minds in the man's rich silence after the
expense and strain of gaiety. To this rule, Dr Jekyll was no
exception; and as he now sat on the opposite side |

EUP 21.7–21.12

ND1 | ten years old. For ten years he had kept that preposterous
33[7] document in his safe; and here was the first <external proof >
^independent sign^ that such a man as Mr Hyde existed<,>– here,
<on> ^from^ the lips of a creature who had come to him bleating
for help under the most ignoble and deserved misfortunes, he
<found> ^heard^ the name of the man to whom Henry Jekyll had
left everything and whom<, in that> he named his "friend and
benefactor." He studied Mr Lemsome[8] covertly. He was <still> a
<youngish> man of about twenty eight, with a fine forehead and
good features; anæmically pale; shielding a pair of <faint>
suffering eyes under blue spectacles; and dressed with that sort of
<external> ^outward^ decency that implies ^both^ a lack of
means and a defect of taste. By his own confession, Mr Utterson
knew him to be a bad fellow<,>; << <a> in this short scrutiny, he
<read him through and through> ^made <out very plainly that>^
him out to be a bad fellow of the>> he now saw for himself that he
was an incurable cad.

  "Sit down," said <I>he, "I will take your business."

  No one was more astonished than the client; but as he had been
speaking uninterruptedly for some three minutes, he set down the
success to the score of his own eloquence<;> . <and> There never
was a client who did less credit to his lawyer; but still Mr Utterson
stuck to him on the chance that something might |

MS ...

EUP ...

ND1 | Thereupon, Mr Utterson, conceiving he had done <the> all and
48 more than could be asked of him, went home to his rooms and lay
down upon his bed, <mentally> ^like one^ sick. <<The last words
of the <public> officer had been the last straw on his overtaxed
endurance<; there was something in> . <t>The beaming air, ^as of
a man who said a pleasant and witty thing,^ with which that
deadly truth had been communicated <that> finally unmanned the
lawyer.>> He had been dragged all day through scenes and among
characters that made his gorge rise; hunting a low murderer, and
himself hag-ridden by the thought that this murderer was the
chosen heir ^and^ the secret ally <<and the so-called benefactor
of the <good,> learned and well beloved Henry Jekyll >> ^of his
friend^; and now, at the end of that experience, an honest man and
active public servant <tells him with a smile> ^spoke out in words
what had been for Mr Utterson the haunting moral and unspoken
refrain of the day's journeyings:^ that all men, high and low, are of
the same ^pattern^. He lay on the outside <side> ^of^ his bed in
the fall of the foggy night; and <he> heard the pattering of
countless thousands of feet, all, as he now told himself, making
haste to do evil, and the rush of the wheels of countless cabs and
carriages conveying men <to deadly> <yet> ^<still> yet^ more
expeditiously to sin and punishment; and the horror of that
monstrous seething mud-pot of a city, and of that kindred
<monster> monster – man's soul, rose up within ^him^ to the |

MS ...

EUP 28.3–28.10

ND2 | alive.

58   "He must be buried underneath the flags," said Poole

"<He may> <," replied the lawyer>; "or he may have fled ^," replied the lawyer^[9]. <<O!" he cried suddenly, "<in what blind man's buff is this> in what>> This is beyond me, Poole. Let us return to the cabinet." <They mounted>

<Upstairs, all was as it was>

They mounted the stair in silence, and looked on every side. At a long table, there were traces of chemical experiments. Various measured heaps of some ^white^ salt, apparently the same, were laid out in glass saucers<: and>[10] , <these Poole recognised> as if for some purpose in which the unhappy man had been interrupted. On the desk of the business table, among the <n?i> neat array of papers, a very large envelope was uppermost and bore, in Doctor Jekyll's hand, the name of Mr Utterson. The lawyer tore it open<.>, <Then> <e>and as his hand was shaking with emotion, the enclosures fell to the floor. The first <that he> was a will, drawn in the same strange terms as the first one, to act as a testament in case of |

...

MS | <experiments> ^work^, various measured heaps of some white
39[11] salt, apparently the same, being laid out on glass saucers, as if for <some> ^an^ experiment in which the unhappy man had been prevented. <At another, as has been said, tea was set out> The kettle had by this time boiled over, and they were obliged to take it off the fire; but the tea things were still set forth with a comfortable orderliness that was in strange contrast to the tumbled corpse upon the floor. <Indeed the> Several books were on a shelf <beside> ^near^ the fire; one lay <beside> ^beside^ the tea things open<;> , and Utterson was <amazed> ^<somewhat surprised> ^amazed^ to find it <???> ^pious^. Next, in the course of their review of the chamber, the searchers came to the cheval glass.

"This glass have seen some queer doings, ^sir,^ no doubt," whispered Poole.

"And none stranger than itself," echoed the lawyer ^in the same tones^. "What did – what did Jekyll do with a glass?"

"<I can't tell you> ^That's what I have^ often asked myself," returned the butler.

Then they found a prayer in the doctor's writing, very eloquently put in words, but breathing a spirit of despair and horror worthy of the cells of Bedlam; the sight of this so |

ND2 | conclusion of <what still appeared to me a thing too freakish and
| 67   irrational> ^the adventure. As the hours dragged on, and I sat
alone in^ my consulting room, trying to compose my spirits over a
medical journal, <an odd> I found myself <grow steadi> more and
more attracted to the drawer and at last, undoing the sheet, I proceeded to examine the contents. There was first of all a considerable number of powders, <neatly> ^securely^ enough made up
but <still> not with the nicety of <a> ^the^ dispensing chemist; it
was therefore plain that they were of Jekyll's private manufacture;
and when I opened the wrappers ^<I per>^, I found what seemed
to me a simple crystalline salt of a white colour. The only other
objects in the drawer <was> ^were^ a small phial, about half filled
with a ^blood^ red liquor, and a paper ^book^ with a series of
dates. I took out the glass stopper of the phial and smelt ^<,
tasted>^ the contents; it was highly pungent, aromatic and burning, <too strong a> and I seemed to detect the presence of ^both^
ether and phosphorous: <of> ^at^ the other ingredients I <had>
could make no guess. The dates in the version ^book^ covered <a
consider> many years, fifteen I think or twenty, but I observed
| 68   that they had ceased | some months before ^that day or about
April 1884^. Here and there <there> were remarks appended,
usually not longer than a word: "Double" occurring perhaps
six times <out> ^in the course^ of several hundred entries; and
once very early in the list, and followed by several marks
of exclamation, "Total Failure!!!" All this, though I confess it

---

MS | Square.
| 43   Here I proceeded to examine its contents. The powders ^<(of
which there were but 3 or 4)>^ were neatly enough made up, but
not with the nicety of the dispensing chemist; so that it was plain
they were of Jekyll's private manufacture; and when I opened one
of the wrappers, I found what seemed to me a simple, crystalline
salt of a white colour. The phial, to which I next turned my
attention, might have been about half-full of a blood-red liquor,
which was highly pungent to the sense of smell and seemed ^to
me^ to contain phosphorus and some volatile ether. At the other
ingredients, I could make no guess. The book was an ordinary
version book and contained little but a series of dates. These
covered a period of many years, but I observed that the entries
ceased nearly a year ago and quite abruptly. Here and there a brief
remark was appended to a date, usually no more than a single
word: "double" occurring perhaps six times in a total of several
hundred entries; and once very early in the list and followed by
several marks of exclamation, "total failure!!!" All this, though it

---

EUP 53.10–53.27

ND2 whetted my curiosity, told me little that was definite. <<If the book were not left in the drawer by accident, it <see> seemed to prove ^indeed^ that Jekyll had been long engaged>> <What could> ^Here <was> were^ a phial of some tincture, a few papers of salts, and a record apparently of a series of experiments that had ^<probably>^ led (like too <my> ^many^ of Jekyll's investigations) to no end of practical usefulness<;> . <but> <h>How could the presence of these articles in my house affect either the honour, the sanity or the life of my flighty colleague? I own I began to have misgivings that I had been wrong directed and had brought a different drawer from the one required.

| 69   Two o'clock had scarce <struck before> rung over London, ere the <bell> knocker sounded very gently on | the door<; and I, when I had opened it found myself> According to my reading of Jekyll's letter, I had long ago sent the servants to bed, <and was alone> and I now <anse> answered the summons myself and led into the light of the consulting room, a small man whom I had certainly never seen before that night. He was small, I have said; he

---

MS whetted my curiosity, told me little that was definite. Here were a
| 43   phial of some tincture, a papers of some salt, and <a> ^the^ record of a series of experiments that had led (like too many of Jekyll's investigations) to no end of practical usefulness. How could the presence of these articles in my house affect either the honour, the sanity or the life of my flighty colleague? <and> if his messenger could go to one place, why could he not go to another? and even granting some impediment<, so that> , why was this gentleman to be received by me in secret? The more I reflected, the more convinced I grew that I was dealing with a case of cerebral disease; and though I dismissed my servants to bed, I loaded an old revolver that I might ^be found^ be in some posture of self-defence.

    Twelve o'clock had scarce rung out over London, ere the knocker sounded very gently on the door. I opened it, of course, myself, and found <almost> ^a small man^ crouching against the pillars of <a> ^the^ portico.

    "Are you come from Doctor Jekyll?" I asked

    He told me "yes" by a constrained gesture; and when I had bidden him enter, he did not obey me without a search backward glance into the darkness of the square. There was a policeman not far off, advancing with his bull's eye open; and at the sight, I thought my visitor started and made greater haste.

| 44 | These particulars struck me, ^I confess,^ disagreeably; and as I followed him into the bright light of the consulting room, I kept my hand ready on my weapon. Here, at last, I had <the> ^a^ chance of clearly seeing him. I had never set eyes on him before; so

---

ND2 had besides a slight shortening of some of the cords of the neck
which tilted his head upon one side; I was struck by his disagreeable expression, by <the great> ^his^ remarkable combination of
^great^ muscular activity and ^great, apparent^ constitutional
debility<;>, and, ^–^ last but not least<,>– by the <unu> odd subjective disturbance caused by his nieghbourhood. <I do not quite
kno> This <ma> bore some resemblance to incipient rigor, <and>
it was accompanied by a marked sinking of the pulse; <and> at the
time I set it down to some idiosyncratic personal distaste, and
merely wondered at the acuteness of the symptoms; <but>
^though^ I have <now> ^since had^ reason to believe <that> the
cause to lie much deeper in the nature of man, and to turn on
^some^ nobler <principles than> hinge than the principle of hatred.

| 70 | This person <,>(who had, from the first moment of his
entrance, fascinated me ^with^ what I can only describe as a
disgustful curiosity<,>) was dressed in a fashion that would have
made an ordinary person laughable: his clothes, that is to say,
^although they were made of the richest and soberest materials,^ were
enormously too large for him in every measurement<,>– the
trousers hanging about his legs and <turned> ^rolled^ up to keep
them from the ground<,>– the waist of his coat below his haunches
and the collar <low down> ^sprawling wide^ upon his shoulders.

MS much was certain. He was small, as I have said; I was struck
besides with the shocking expression of his face, with his remarkable combination of great muscular activity <and lightness> ^and
great,^ apparent debility of constitution, and – last but not least –
with the odd, sujective disturbance caused by his nieghbourhood.
This bore some resemblance to incipient rigor or what is called
goose-flesh; <it> ^and^ was accompanied by a marked sinking of
the pulse<;> . <a>At the time, I set it down to some idiosyncratic,
personal distaste, and merely wondered at the acuteness of the
symptoms; but I have since had reason to believe the cause to lie
much deeper in the nature of man, and to turn on some nobler
hinge than the principle of hatred.

This person (who had thus, from the first moment of his
entrance, struck in me what I can only describe as a disgustful
curiosity) was dressed in a fashion that would have made an
ordinary person laughable: his clothes, that is to say, although they
were of rich and sober fabric, were enormously too large for him
in every measurement – the trouses hanging on his legs and rolled
up to keep them from the ground, the waist of the coat below his
haunches, and the collar sprawling wide upon his shoulders.

EUP 54.14–54.33

ND2 Strange to <say> ^relate^, this ludicrous accoutrement <was> did not tickle in my chest the nerves of laughter. Rather, as there was something abnormal and misbegotten in the very essence of the creature that now faced me<,>– something seizing, surprising and revolting – this <second> fresh disparity seemed but to fit in with and to reinforce it; ^so that,^ to <the curiosity as to my visitor's> ^my interest in the man's^ nature and character, <this very> ^was now^ added a curiosity as to his origin, his life, his fortune and his status in the world.

These observations, <flashed across me> ^though they have taken so great a space^ to be set down in, were yet the work of a few seconds. My visitor was, indeed, <aflame> ^on fire^ with sombre excitement.

| 71 | "Have you got it?" he cried. "Have you got it?" and so lively was his impatience that he even laid his hand upon my sleeve and tried to shake me.

I put him back; conscious, at his touch of a certain icy pang along my blood. "Come, sir," said I. "I have not yet the pleasure of your acquaintance. Be seated, if you please." And I showed him an example and sat down myself in my customary seat and with as fair an imitation of my ordinary bearing to a patient, as the lateness of the hour, the nature of my preoccupations, and the horror I had of my visitor, would suffer me to muster.

MS Strange to relate, this ludicrous accoutrement <f> was far from tickling the cacchinatory impulse. Rather, as there was something abnormal and misbegotten in the very essence of the creature that now faced me – something siezing, surprising and revolting – this fresh disparity seemed but to fit in with and to reinforce it; so that to my interest in the man's nature and character, there was added a curiosity as to his origin, his life, his fortune and status in the world.

These observations, though they have taken so great a space to be set down in, were yet the work of a few seconds. My visitor was, indeed, on fire with somb<e>re excitement.

"Have you got it?" he cried, "Have you got it?" And so lively was his impatience that he even laid his hand upon my arm and sought to shake me.

I put him back, conscious at his touch of a certain icy pang along my blood. "Come, sir," said I. "You forget ^that^ I have not yet | 45 the pleasure of your | acquaintance. Be seated, if you please." And I showed him an example, and sat down myself in my customary seat and with as fair an imitation of my ordinary manner to a patient, as the lateness of the hour, the nature of my preoccupations, and the horror I had of my visitor, would suffer me to muster.

EUP 54.34–55.16

134

ND2   "I beg your pardon," Dr Lanyon," he replied civilly enough. "My impatience has shown its heels to my politeness. I come here <on behalf> ^at the instance^ of your colleague, Dr Henry Jekyll, on a piece of business of very considerable moment, and I understand –" he paused and put his hand to his throat, and I could see, in sp<a>ite of his very collected manner, that he was wrestling against the approaches of <u>globus hystericus</u> ^the hysteric ball^[12] – "I understand, a drawer..."

| 72 | <I declare> But here I took pity on <the v> my visitor's suspense, and some perhaps on my own growing curiosity "There it is, sir," said I, pointing to the drawer where it lay <still covered by the sheet> ^<on the floor again and co>^ on the floor behind a table and once again covered with the sheet.

He <ran> ^sprang^ to it, and then paused, and laid his hand upon his heart; I could hear his teeth grate together <??? in his jaws> with the ^convulsive action^ of his jaws<:>; and his face was ghastly to see.

"Compose yourself," <said> I cried.

He turned a dreadful smile to me, and <plucke> as if with the decision of despair, plucked away the sheet. At the sight of the contents, he uttered one loud sob of such immense relief that I sat petrified; And the next moment, in a voice which was already

MS   "I beg your pardon, Dr Lanyon," he replied civilly enough. "What you say is very well founded; and my impatience has shown its heels to my politeness. I come here at the instance of your colleague, Dr Henry Jekyll, on a piece of business of some moment; and I understood..." he paused and put his hand to his throat, and I could see, in spite of his collected manner, that he was wrestling against the approaches of the hysteric ball[12] – "I understood, a drawer..."

But here I took pity on my visitors surspense, and some perhaps on my own growing curiosity. "There it is, sir," said I, pointing to the drawer, where it lay on the floor behind a table and still covered with <a> the sheet.

He sprang to it, and then paused, and laid his hand upon his heart; I could here his teeth grate with the convulsive action of his jaws; and his face was ^so^ ghastly to see that I grew alarmed both for his life and reason.

"Compose yourself," said I.

He turned a dreadful smile to me, and as if with the decision of despair, plucked away the sheet. At sight of the contents, he uttered one loud sob of such immense relief that I sat petrified. And the next moment, in a voice that was already

EUP 55.17–55.37

ND2 fairly well under control, "Can you lend me a graduated glass?" he asked.

I rose from my place with something of an effort, and gave him what he asked.

| 73 He thanked me with a smiling nod, <and poure> ^measured^ | out a few minims of the red tincture, and added one of the powders. <<The mixture <ha> ^<which was at first of a reddish co>^ effervesced and threw off a little vapour, <while> ^<and>^ he stood and <looked> watched its metamor>> The mixture, which was at first of a reddish <colour> ^hue^, began, in proportion as the crystals melted, to <c> brighten in colour, to effervesce ^audibly^, and to throw off small fumes of vapour<;> . <s>Suddenly, ^and^ at the same moment, the ebullition ceased and the compound changed to a dark purple, which faded again more slowly to a waterish green. My visitor, who had watched these metamorphoses with a keen eye, smiled, set down the glass upon the table, and then turned and looked at me with a great air of scrutiny and hesitation.

"And now," said he, "to settle what remains. Will you be wise? will you be guided <by m>? will you suffer me to take this glass in my hand and to go forth from your house without more parley? or has the <evil> greed of curiosity too much command ^of^ you? <Spea> Think before you answer, for it shall be done as you decide<;> . <a>As you shall

---

MS fairly well under control, "Have you a graduated glass?" he asked

I rose from my place with something of an effort and gave him what he asked.

He thanked me with a smiling nod, measured out a few minims of the red tincture and added one of the powders. The mixture, which was at first of a reddish hue, began, in proportion as the crystals melted, to brighten in colour, to effervesce audibly, and to throw off small fumes of vapour. Suddenly and at the same moment, the ebullition ceased and the compound changed to a dark purple, which faded again more slowly to a watery green. My visitor, who had watched these metamorphoses with a keen eye, smiled, set down the glass upon the table, and then turned and looked upon me with an air of scrutiny.

"And now," said he, "to settle what remains. Will you be wise? will you be guided? will you suffer me to take this glass in my

| 46 hand and | to go forth from your house without further parley? or has the greed of curiosity too much command of you? Think before you answer, for it shall be done as you decide. As you

---

EUP 55.37–56.17

ND2 decide, you shall be left here ^as you were before <and> and^ niether wiser nor <unhappier<.>,> ^richer,^ <or you may>
| 74 ^unless the sense^ | ^<the>^ of a great service ^rendered^ to a man in mortal distress may be counted as a kind of riches of the soul<;> <o>Or, if you shall so prefer to choose, a new province of knowledge and new avenues to power and fame shall be laid open to you here, in this room, <and> upon the instant, and your sight shall be blasted by a ^prodigy to^ stagger the unbelief of Satan."

"Sir," said I, <"I a> affecting a coolness that I was far from <really> ^truly^ possessing, "I have gone rather too far in this most inexplicable piece of work, to pause before I see the end."

"It is well<;>," replied my visitor. "Lanyon, you remember your vows: what follows is under the seal of our profession. And now, sir, you who have been so long bound to the most narrow and material views, you who have <so obstinat> denied the virtue of transcendental medicine, you ^who^ have derided your superiors – behold!"

He put the glass to his lips and drank at one gulp. A cry followed, he reeled, staggered, clutched at the table and held on,
| 75 staring before | him with <congested> ^injected^ eyes, gasping with open mouth; and as I looked, there came, I thought, a change – he seemed to swell – his face became suddenly black and the

MS decide, you shall be left as you were before, and niether richer nor wiser, unless the sense of <a great> service rendered to a man in mortal distress may be counted as a kind of riches of the soul. <"> Or, if you shall so prefer to choose <?>, a new province of knowledge and new avenues to fame and power shall be laid open to you, here, in this room, upon the instant; and your sight shall be blasted by a prodigy to stagger the unbelief of Satan"

"Sir," said I, affecting a coolness that I was far from truly possessing, "you speak enigmas, and you will perhaps not wonder that I hear you with no very strong impression of belief<,> . But I have gone too far in the way of inexplicable services, to pause before I see the end.

"It is well," replied my visitor<,>. <with a kind of> "Lanyon, you remember your vows: what follows is under the seal of our profession. And now, you who have so long been bound to the most narrow and material views, you who have denied the virtue of transcendental medicine, you who have derided your superiors – behold!"

He put the glass to his lips and drank at one gulp. A cry followed; he reeled, staggered, clutched at the table and held on, staring with <congested> ^injected^ eyes, gasping with open

EUP 56.18–56.37

ND2   features seemed to melt and change – and the next moment, I had
sprung to my feet and <leaped> ^staggered^ back against the wall,
<with> my arm raised as if to shield me from that prodigy, my
mind submerged in consternation <and> .

"O God!" I screamed and "O God!" again and again; for there
before my eyes, <a little> ^ – ^ pale, and shaken, and half fainting,
and goping before him with his hands, like a man restored from
death – there stood <with his firm stature and> Henry Jekyll! The
other, <the ghost,> the double, the unutterable spectre that had
drunk the potion, was gone from before me, and there, in his place,
was Henry Jekyll!

What he told me in the next hour, I cannot bring my mind to
place on paper. In spite of what I saw, my mind revolts <from>
against belief; the shock of that moment has, I feel sure, struck at
the very roots of my life, but it has not <a> bowed the pride of my
| 76 | scepticism; I shall die, but I shall die incredulous. As for the moral
turpitude that man unveiled to me, it is matter that I disdain to
handle. He found me an elderly, a useful and a happy man; that he

MS   mouth; and as I looked there came, I thought, a change – he
seemed to swell – his face became suddenly black and the features
seemed to melt and alter – and the next moment, I had sprung to
my feet and leaped back against the wall, my arm raised to to shield
me from that prodigy, my mind submerged in <consternation>
^terror^.

"O God!" I screamed, and "O God!" again and again; for there
before my eyes – pale and shaken, and half fainting, and groping
before him with his hands, like a man restored from death – there
stood Henry Jekyll!

What he told me in the next hour, I cannot bring my mind to
set on paper. I saw what I saw, I heard what I heard, and my soul
sickened at it; and yet now when that sight has melted from my
eyes, I ask myself if I believe it, and I cannot answer. My life is
shaken to its roots; sleep has left me; the deadliest terror <of the>
sits by me at all hours of the day and night; I feel that my days are
numbered, and that I <shall> ^must^ die; and yet I shall die
incredulous. As for the moral turpitude that man unveiled to me,
| 47 | even with tears | of penitence, <even kneeling at my feet, and
covering my hands with his abhorred caresses>, I cannot, even in
memory, dwell on it without a start of horror. I will say but one
thing, Utterson, and that (if you can bring your mind to credit it)
will be more than enough. The creature who crept into my house
that night was, on Jekyll's own confession, known by the name of

EUP 56.37–57.21

138

ND2 has blighted and shortened what remains to me of life, is but a small addendum to the monstrous tale of his misdeeds.

Hastie Lanyon.

Henry Jekyll's Full Statement of the Case

I was born in the year 1830 to a good fortune, endowed ^besides^ with good parts <and much application, but with such as might justify the highest flights of ambition>, inclined by nature to industry, fond of the respect of <my fellow m> ^the wise and good^ among <crea> ^my^ fellow men, and thus, ^as^ it might have been supposed, with every <g> promise and guarantee of an honourable and distinguished future. From a very early age, however, I became <add> ^in secret^ the slave of disgraceful pleasures; <<my life was double; <outwardly> absorbed in scientific toil, <and^,^ not by a> never indifferent to any noble <opinion> cause or>> and when I <f> reached years of reflection, and began to look round me and I take note of my progress and position in the world, I <found myself> stood <al> <deeply> committed to a profound duplicity of life. On the one side, I was

| 77

MS Hyde and now hunted for in every corner of the land as the murderer of Carew.

Hastie Lanyon.

Henry Jekyll's Full Statement of the Case

I was born in the year 18– to a large fortune, endowed besides with excellent parts, inclined by nature to industry, fond of the respect of the wise and good among my fellow men, and thus, as might have been supposed, with every guarantee of an honourable and distinguished future. <From an early age, however, I became in secret the slave of certain appetites> ^[13]And indeed the worst of my faults was a certain impatient gaiety of disposition, such as has made the happiness of many, but such as I found it hard to reconcile with my imperious desire to carry my head high, and wear a more than commonly grave countenance before the public. Hence it came about that I concealed my pleasures<,>;^ ; and ^that when^ I reached years of reflection, and began to look round me and take <note> ^stock^ of my progress and position in the world, I stood already committed to a profound duplicity of life. <<On the one side, I was

EUP 57.21–58.13

ND2 what you have known me, a man of distinction, immersed in toils, open to generous sympathies, never slow to befriend struggling virtue, never backward in an honourable cause; on the other, as soon as night had fallen and I could shake off my friends, the iron hand of indurated habit plunged me once again into the mire of my vices. I will trouble you with these no further than to say that they were at once criminal in the sight of the law and abhorrent in themselves. They cut me off from the sympathy of those whom I otherwise respected; and with even a deeper trench than in the majority of men, severed <the> ^those^ provinces of good and ill which divide and compound man's dual nature. In <these>this case, I was driven to reflect <more> deeply and inveterately upon that hard law of life, which lies at the root of all religions and is the spring of all suffering. Though so profound a double-dealer, I was in no sense a hypocrite<:>; Both sides of me were in dead earnest;

| 78 I was no more | myself when I <fing> laid aside restraint and wallowed in shame, than when I laboured, in the eye of day, at the furtherance of knowledge or the relief of sorrow and suffering.

MS what you have known me, a man of some note, immersed in toils, open to ^all^ generous sympathies, never slow to befriend struggling virtue, never backward in <an honour> ^the cause^ of honour; on the other, as soon as night released me from my engagements and <covered> ^hid^ me from the <espial> ^notice^ of my friends, <the iron hand> indurated habit plunged me again into the mire of my vices. I will trouble you with these no further than to say that they were, at that period, no worse than those of many who have lived and died with credit<,> . It was rather the somewhat high aspirations of my life by daylight>>

   ^^[14]Many a man would have even blazoned such irregularities as I was guilty of; but from the high views <of conduct> ^that I had^ set before me I regarded and hid them with an almost morbid sense of shame,[15] and it was thus rather the exacting nature of my aspirations^^ than <t>any particular degradation in my faults, that made me what I was; and with even a deeper trench than in the majority of men, severed ^in me^ those provinces of good and ill which divide and compound man's dual nature. In this case, I was driven to reflect deeply and inveterately on that hard law of life, which lies at the root of religion and is the <t> one of the most plentiful springs of distress. Though so profound a double-dealer, I was in no sense a hypocrite; both sides of me were in dead earnest; I was no more myself when I laid aside restraint and plunged in shame, than when I laboured, in the eye of day, at the furtherance of knowledge or the relief of sorrow and suffering.

EUP 58.13–58.27

ND2 And it chanced that the <very> direction of my scientific
investigations, which led <entirely> ^wholly^ towards the
transcendental and the mystic, reacted and shed a strong light on
this consciousness of the perennial war among my members. With
every day, and from both sides of my intelligence, the moral and
the intellectual, I drew steadily nearer to that great truth, by
<whose> ^whose^ partial discovery <of which> I have been
<sent> ^doomed^ to such a dreadful shipwreck: that man is not
truly one, but truly two. I say two, because ^the state of^ my
^own^ knowledge does not pass beyond that point; others will
follow, others will outstrip me on the same lines; and I hazard the
guess that man will be ultimately known for a mere polity of
multifarious <and>, incongruous and independent denizens. I,
<upon> ^for^ my part, under the impulse of <my own> experi-
ences and sufferings, <leaned> to <the moral side, and leaned>
^advanced^ infallibly in one direction<;> ^and in one direction
| 79   only:^ | it was on the moral side ^and in my own case,^ that I
^learned to^ recognise<d> the thorough and primitive duality of
man; I saw that, of the two natures that contended in the field of
my consciousness, even if I could be rightly said to be either, it was
only because I was radically both; and from an early date, even
before the course of my scientific discoveries had begun to suggest
the <most> ^most naked^ possibility of such a miracle, I had

MS   And it chanced that the direction of my scientific studies, which
| 48   led wholly towards | the mystic and the transcendental, r<ë>eacted
and shed a strong light on this consciousness of the perennial war
among my members. With every day, and both sides of my
intelligence, the moral and the intellectual, I ^thus^ drew steadily
nearer to that truth, by whose partial discovery I have been
doomed to such a dreadful shipwreck: that man is not truly one,
but truly two. I say two, because the state of my own knowledge
does not pass beyond that point. Others will follow, others will
outstrip me on the same lines; and I hazard the guess that man will
^be^ ultimately <be> known for a mere polity of multifarious,
incongruous and independant denizens. I for my part, from the
nature of my life, advanced infallibly in one direction and in one
direction only. It was on the moral side, and in my own person,
that I learned to recognise the thorough and primitive duality of
man; I saw that, of the two natures that contended in the field of
my consciousness, even if I could rightly be said to be either, it
was only because I was radically both; and from an early date,
even before the course of my scientific discoveries had begun
to suggest the most naked possibility of such a miracle, I had

ND2   <begun> ^learned^ to dwell with pleasure ^as a beloved day-dream^ on the thought of the separation of these elements. If each, I told myself, could but be housed in separate identities, life would be relieved of all that was unbearable; the unjust might go his way, delivered from the aspirations and the remorse of his more perfect twin; and the just could walk steadfastly and securely on his upward path, <no longer> doing the good things in which he found his pleasure, and no longer exposed to disgrace and penitence <through> ^by^ the hands of this extraneous evil. It was the curse of mankind that these incongruous faggots were thus bound together – that, in the <sensitive> ^agonised^ womb of <our> consciousness, these polar twins should be continuously

| 80   struggling. How, then, were they | dissociated?

    I was so far in my reflections when, as I have said, a side-light began to shine upon the subject from <my> ^the^ laboratory table. I began to perceive, more deeply than it has ever yet been stated, the trembling immateriality, the mist-like transience, of this seemingly so solid body in which we walk <ha> walk attired. Certain <potent> agents I found to have the power to <make> shake and to pluck back that fleshly vestment, even as a wind might toss the curtains of a <tent> pavilion. For two good reasons, I will not enter deeply into this scientific branch of my confession.

MS   learned to dwell with pleasure, as a beloved daydream, on the thought of the separation of these elements. If each, I told myself, could but be housed in separate identities, life would be relieved of all that was unbearable<:>; the unjust might go his way, delivered from the aspirations and remorse of his more upright twin; and the just could walk steadfastly and securely on his upward path, doing the good things in which he found his pleasure, and no longer exposed to disgrace and penitence by the hands of this extraneous evil. It was the curse of mankind that these incongruous faggots were thus bound together – that in the agonised womb of consciousness, these polar twins should be continuously struggling. How, then, were they dissociated.

    I was so far in my reflections when, as I have said, a side light began to shine upon the subject from the laboratory table. I began to perceive more deeply than it has ever yet been stated, the trembling immateriality, the mist-like transience, of this seemingly so solid body in which we walk attired. Certain agents I found to have the power to shake and to pluck back that fleshly vestment, even as a wind might toss the curtains of a pavilion. For two good reasons, I will not enter ^deeply^ into this scientific branch of my confession. First, because I have been made to learn that the doom

---

ND2 First, because I have been made to learn that the doom and burthen of our life is rivetted forever on man's shoulders, and <that> when the attempt is made to cast it off, it but returns upon us with more unfamiliar and more awful pressure. Second, because, as my narrative will make alas! too evident, my discover-
| 81 ies were incomplete<, and my action> . Enough, then, that I not | only recognised my natural body for the mere aura and effulgence of certain of the powers that made up my spirit, but discovered an agent by which these powers might be dethroned from their supremacy, and <an>a second form and countenance substituted, none the less natural to me<,> although it was the expression, and bore the mark, of lower elements in my soul. <The efficacy of this drug was but to shake the immaterial and ineffable>

    I hesitated long before I put this theory to the dire test of practise. I knew well that I risked death, for any drug that so potently controlled and shook the <immaterial> ^frail^ pillars of identity, might, <at> ^by^ the least scruple of an overdose or at the least inopportunity in the <ti> moment of exhibition, utterly <destroy> ^blot out^ that <thin> ^immaterial^ tabernacle which I looked to it to change. But the temptation was too great. I had long since prepared my tincture<;> , though it was the work of years of killing study; I purchased at once from a <great> ^firm of^ wholesale chemists, a large quantity of a particular salt which I

MS and burthen of <man's> ^our^ life is bound forever on man's
| 49 shoulders, | and when the attempt is made to cast <if> ^it^ off, it but returns upon us with more unfamiliar and more awful pressure. Second, because as my narrative will make alas! too evident, my discoveries were incomplete. Enough, then, that I not only recognised my natural body for the mere aura and effulgence <at>of certain of the powers that made up my spirit, but managed to compound a drug by which these powers should be dethroned from their supremacy, and a second form and countenance substi- tuted, none the less natural to me because they were the expression, and bore the stamp, of lower elements in my soul.

    I hesitated long before I put this theory to the test of practise. I knew well that I risked death; for any drug that so potently con- trolled and shook the very fortress of identity, might by the least scruple of an overdose or at the least inopportunity in the moment of exhibition, utterly blot out that immaterial tabernacle which I looked to it to change. But the temptation of a discovery so singular and profound, ^at last^ overcame the suggestions of alarm. I had long since prepared my tincture; I purchased at once, from a firm of wholesale chemists, a large quantity of a particular salt which I

ND2 knew, by my | experiments to be the last ingredient ^required^;
| 82 and late one accursed night, I compounded the elements, watched
them boil and smoke together in the glass, and when the ebullition
had subsided, with a strong glow of courage, drank off the potion.

The most <deadly> ^racking^ pangs succeeded: a grinding in
the bones, <an unexampled sickness> deadly nausea, ^and^ a
horror of the spirit that cannot be exceeded at the hour of birth or
death; then these agonies began rapidly to subside, and I came to
myself, as if out of a great sickness<,>. There was something
strange in my sensations, something incredibly new<,> and, from
its very novelty, incredibly sweet. I felt <younger,> younger, <I
felt> lighter, happier in body; <in mind> ^within^, I was conscious of a heady recklessness, a current of disordered ^sensual^
images running like a mill race ^in my <imagination> fancy^, a
solution of the bonds of obligation, an unknown but not an
innocent freedom of the soul. I knew myself, at the first touch of
this new life, to be more wicked, tenfold more wicked, sold a slave
| 83 to my original evil<:>; and the thought, in that moment, | braced
and delighted me like wine. I stretched out my hands, and <lo>
then I was suddenly aware that I had lost in stature.

There was no mirror, at that date, in my cabinet; but the night

---

MS knew, from my experiments, to be the last ingredient required; and
late one accursed night, I compounded the elements, watched
them boil and smoke together in the glass, and when the ebullition
had subsided, with a strong glow of courage, drank off the potion.

The most racking pangs succeeded: a grinding in the bones,
deadly nausea, and a horror of the spirit that cannot be exceeded at
the hour of birth or death. Then these agonies began swiftly to
subside, and I came to myself as if out of a great sickness. There
was something strange in my sensations, something indescribably
new and, from its very novelty, incredibly sweet. I felt younger,
lighter, happier in body; within I was conscious of a heady
recklessness, a current of disordered sensual images running like a
mill race in my fancy, a solution of the bonds of obligation, an
unknown but not an innocent freedom of the soul. I knew myself,
at the first breath of this new life, to be more wicked, tenfold more
wicked, sold a slave to my original evil; and the thought, in that
moment, braced and delighted me like wine. I stretched out my
hands, exulting in the freshness of these sensations; and in the act, I
was suddenly aware that I had lost in stature.

There was no mirror, at that date, in my room; <but the night
| 50 was | far gone> ^that which stands | beside me^ as I write, was
brought there later on and for the very purpose of these

ND2 was far gone <into> into the morning<.><,> – the morning, black as it was, was nearly ripe for the conception of the day – the inmates of my house were locked in the most rigorous <hours> ^hours^ of slumber; and I determined, flushed as I was with hope and triumph, to venture in my new shape <into> ^as far as to^ my bedroom. I crossed the yard, <and I remember well with what a> wherein the constellations looked down upon me, I could have thought, with wonder, the first creature of the sort that their eternal vigilance had yet disclosed to them; I stole through the corridors, a thief in my own house; and coming <at last> to my room, I saw for the first time the appearance of Edward Hyde.

I speak now by theory. The evil side of my nature, to which I

| 84 had now transferred the stamping efficacy, was probably less robust and less developed | than the good, which I had just deposed<;>. <that> On the other hand, in my life which had been, after all, nine tenths a life of effort, virtue and control, it had been much less exercised and much less exhausted. And hence, as I think, it came ^about^ that Edward Hyde was so much smaller, slighter and younger than Henry Jekyll. Even as <the> good shone upon the countenance of the one, evil was <written> written

MS transformations. The night, however, was far gone into the morning – the morning, black as it was, was nearly ripe for the conception of the day – the inmates of my house were locked in the most rigorous hours of slumber; and I determined, flushed as I was with hope and triumph, to venture in my new shape as far as to my bedroom. I crossed the yard, wherein the constellations looked down upon me, I could have thought, with wonder, the first creature of that sort that their <eternal> ^unsleeping^ vigilance had yet disclosed to them; I stole through the corridors, a stranger in my own house; and coming to my room, I saw for the first time the appearance of Edward Hyde.

<What here follows is not so much a narrati> ^I must here speak by theory alone, saying not that which^ I know, but that which I suppose to be most probable. The evil side of my nature to which I ^had^ now transferred the stamping efficacy was less robust and less developed than the good which I had just deposed. And again, in the course of my life which had been after all, nine tenths a life of effort, virtue and control, it had been much less exercised and much less exhausted. And hence, as I think, it came about that Edward Hyde was so much smaller, slighter and younger than Henry Jekyll. Even as good shone upon the countenance of the one, evil was written

EUP 61.7–61.27

ND2 broadly and plainly on the face of the other. Evil<,> besides<,>–
which I must still believe to be the infernal and the <mortal>
^lethal^ side of man – had <printed> ^left^ on <the> ^that^ body
<the> evidences of deformity and decay. And yet when I looked
upon that ugly <and> <image> ^idol^ in the glass, I was conscious
of no repugnance, rather of a ^leap of^ welcome<;> . <t>This, too,
was myself<:> <i>It seemed natural and human<;> . <to me>
<i>In my eyes, it <was> ^<bore>^ <, and I still consider it to be>
bore <an> a livelier image of the spirit, it seemed more express and
single, than the imperfect and divided countenance <that> I <was>
| 85   had been hitherto accustomed to call mine. And in so far I was |¹⁶
[doubtless right.] I have observed that when I wore the semblance
of Edward Hyde, none could come near to me at first without
visible misgiving of the flesh. ...

MS   broadly and plainly on the face of the other. Evil, besides (which I
must still believe to be the lethal side of man) had left on that body
an imprint of deformity and decay. And yet when I looked upon
that ugly idol in the glass, I was conscious of no repugnance, rather
of a leap of welcome. This, too, was myself. It seemed natural and
human. In my eyes it bore a livelier image of the spirit, it seemed
more express and single, than the imperfect and divided countenance, I had been hitherto accustomed to call mine. And in so far I
was doubtless right. I have observed that when I wore the semblance
of Edward Hyde, none could come near to me at first without a
visible misgiving of the flesh. This, as I take it, was because all human
beings, as we meet them, are commingled out of good and evil; and
Edward Hyde, alone in the ranks of mankind, was pure evil.

I lingered but a moment at the mirror: the second and conclusive experiment had yet to be attempted; it yet remained to be
seen if I had lost my identity beyond redemption and must flee
before daylight from a house that was no longer mine; and hurrying back to my cabinet, I once more prepared and drank the cup,
| 51   once more suffered | the pangs of dissolution, and came to myself
once more with the character, the stature and the face of Henry
Jekyll.

That night I had come to the fatal crossroads. Had I approached
my discovery in a more noble spirit, had I risked the experiment
while under the empire of generous or pious aspirations, all
<might> ^must^ have been otherwise, and from these agonies of
death and birth, I had come forth <i>an angel instead of a fiend.
The drug had no discriminating action; it was niether diabolic
<and> nor divine; it but shook the doors <of the prison and let
forth > ^<and broke the seals, and >^ of the prisonhouse of my

EUP 61.27–62.17

ND2 | side unchastened; and although I had now indeed two characters
| 86   as well as two appearances, the one was wholly evil, and the other
was still the old Henry Jekyll of the past, that incongruous
compound of whose reformation and improvement I had already
learned to despair. You can see now what was the result; for days, I
would <be> <?><tu> ^, as of yore,^ pursue and obey my better
<nature> ^instincts^; and then when evil triumphed, I would
again drink the cup and, impenetrably disguised as <Henry>
^Edward^ Hyde, pass ^privately^ out of the laboratory door and
roll myself in infamy.

    The temptation of my present power can hardly be over-
estimated. As <Henry> ^Edward^ Hyde <,>(for I had so dubbed
<myself> ^my second self <(>– God help me! – ^ in pleasantry), I
was secure of an immunity that never <man> before was attained
by any criminal<;> . <t>Think of it[17] – I did not exist! Let me but
escape into my laboratory door, give me but a second to ^mix &^
swallow <that> the draught that I had always standing ready, and
| 87   whatever <I>he had done, Edward Hyde had vanished like a
wreath of smoke, and there in his stead, quietly at home and | trim-
ming[18] the midnight lamp in his laborious study, was the well-
known, the spotless, the benevolent and the beloved Dr Jekyll!

<hr>

MS   disposition; and like the <prisoners> ^captives^ of Philippi, that
which <lay> ^stood^ within <in tur> ran forth. At that <time>
^hour^ my virtue slumbered; my evil, kept awake by ambition,
was ale<r>rt and swift to sieze the occasion; and the thing that was
projected was <thus> Edward Hyde. Hence, although I had now
two characters as well as two appearances, one was wholly evil, and
the other was still the old Henry Jekyll, that incongruous compound of whose reformation and improvement I had already
learned to despair. The movement was thus wholly toward the
worse.

    Even at that time, I had not yet conquered my aversion to the
dryness of a life of study<,>. I would still be merrily disposed at
times; and as my pleasures were (to say the least) undignified,
<they had become> ^^and I was <both> ^not only^ well known^^
and highly considered, but growing towards the elderly man, this
incoherency of my life was daily growing more unwelcome. It was
<by this that> ^on this side^ that my new power tempted me until
I fell in slavery. <I had now at hand an impenetrable disguise;> I
had but to drink <my> ^the^ cup, to doff at once the <too well-
known and too> ^body of the noted professor^, and to assume
<that>, like a thick cloak, that of Edward Hyde. I smiled at the
notion; it seemed <at> to me at the time to be humorous; and I

<hr>

EUP 62.17–62.35

ND2 I made my preparations with the most studious care. I
announced to my servants that a Mr. Hyde <had full li> (whom I
described) had full liberty and power about the house; and to
parry mishaps, I even called and introduced <myself> ^and made
myself a familiar object,^ in my second character. I drew up the
will to which you so much objected; so that if anything befell me
in the character of Doctor Jekyll, I could enter upon that of Edward Hyde without pecuniary loss. And thus fortified as I fondly
supposed on every side, I began to plunge into a career of cruel,
soulless and degrading vice.

MS made my preparations with the most studious care. I took <th>
and furnished that house in Soho, to which Hyde was tracked by
the police; and engaged as housekeeper a creature whom I well
knew to be silent and unscrupulous. On the other side, <to parry>
^I announced^ to my servants that a Mr Hyde (whom I described)
was to have full liberty and power about my house in the square;
and to parry mishaps, I even called and made myself a familiar
object, in my second character. I next drew up that will to which
you so much objected; so that if anything befell me in the person
| 52 of | Doctor[19] Jekyll, I could enter on that of Edward Hyde without
pecuniary loss. And thus fortified, as I supposed, on every side, I
began to profit by the strange immunities of my position.

Men have before hired bravos to transact their crimes, while
their own person and reputation sat under shelter. I was the first
that ever did so for his pleasures<:>; <I was the first that
reconciled liberty and respectability.> ^^<<plodding ^the while^
in the public eye, with my load of <respectab> ^genial
respectability^[20]>>^^. I was the first that could thus plod in the
^public^ eye with a load of genial respectability, and in a moment,
like a schoolboy, strip off these lendings and spring headlong into
the sea of liberty. But for me, in my impenetrable mantle, the
safety was complete, and I could snap my fingers <at the>. Think
of it – I did not even exist! Let me but escape into my laboratory
door, give me but a second or two to mix and swallow the draught
that I had always standing ready; and whatever he had done,
Edward Hyde would pass away like the stain of breath upon a
mirror, and there in his stead, quietly at home <and>, trimming
the midnight lamp in his <laborious> study, a man who could
afford to laugh at suspicion, would be Henry Jekyll.

The pleasures which I made haste to seek in my disguise<,>
were, as I have said, undignified. <But I was now trusting ^<to the
guidance>^ the foul part of me abroad> I would scarce use a
harder term; but in the hands of Edward Hyde, they soon began to

ND2   Into the details of <this> my shame, I scorn to enter; I mean but to point out the warnings and the ^successive^ steps <of my chastisement> with which my chastisement approached me. I met with an accident<,> which <I>, as it brought on no consequence, I mention only in passing: detected in an act of infamy, I had to bribe a party of young fools to set me free, and in order to <find

| 88   the money> ^satisfy their demands,^ | <I had> Edward Hyde had to bring them to the door, and pay them with a cheque drawn in the name, of Henry Jekyll. But this danger was easily eliminated for the future, by opening an account at another bank in the name of

---

MS   turn towards the monstrous. <Into the details of this fall, I will not> When I <returned> ^would come back^ from these excursions, I soon began to be plunged into a kind of wonder at my vicarious depravity. This familiar that I called out of my own soul, and sent forth alone to ^do^ his <good> good pleasure, was a being inherently malign and villainous<:>; his every act and thought <self> centred <; and that on the lowest> ^on self; drinking pleasure^ with bestial avidity from any degree of torture to another; relentless like a man of stone. <I cannot deny that> Henry Jekyll <was> ^stood^ at times aghast <and at times swore to> <;>^before the acts of Edward Hyde;^ but the situation was apart from ordinary laws<;>, and <as time went I grew more and more> ^insidiously relaxed the grasp of conscience^. It was Hyde, after all, and Hyde alone, that was guilty. Jekyll was no worse; he <a>woke again to his good qualities seemingly unimpaired; he <woke to a fresh> ^would even make^ haste, where it was possible, to <rep> undo the evil <of the other> ^done by Hyde^. And thus his conscience slumbered.

    Into the details of the infamy at which I thus connived (for
| 53   even | now I can scarce grant that I committed it) I have no design of entering; I mean but to point out the warnings and the successive steps with which my chastisement approached <, and the halter of moral responsibility, which I had so long eluded, ^was^ once more tightened about my neck>. I met with one accident which, as it <led to> ^brought on^ no consequence, I mention only in passing. An act of cruelty to a child aroused against me the anger of a passer by, <(> whom I recognised <but> the other day in the person of your kinsman <)> ; the doctor and the child's family joined him <in>; there were moments when I feared for my life; and at last, in order to pacify their too just resentment, Edward Hyde had to bring them to the door, and pay them in a cheque drawn in the name, of Henry Jekyll. But this danger was easily eliminated from the future, by opening an account at another bank in the name of

ND2 Edward Hyde himself. And my true punishment lay in a far different direction.

About <five> ^a^ month<s> before the Lemsome murder, I had been out on one of my excursions, ^<and>^ had returned <about three in the morning> at a late hour, and woke the next day in my bed with somewhat strange sensations. It was in vain I looked about me; in vain I saw the handsome furniture and tall proportions of my room in the square, in vain that I recognised the <carving> pattern of the ^bed^ curtains and the carving of the <bed> ^mahogany posts^ <of Henry Jekyll's bed>; something still kept insisting that I was not where I thought I was, that I had not awakened where I seemed to be, but in the <l> iron bed and the somewhat dreary and exiguous rooms off Gray's Inn Road, where I was sometimes accustomed to sleep in my character of

| 89 <Henry Jekyll> Edward Hyde. I smiled | to myself and, in my psychological way, began lazily to examine into the elements of this <el> illusion, <dropp> occasionally, even as I did so, dropping back into a comfortable morning doze. I was still so engaged when, in one of my more wakeful moments, my eyes fell upon my hand. Now the hand of Henry Jekyll, as we have often jocularly said, was eminently professional in shape and size; it was large, firm, white and comely, the hand of a lady's doctor, in a word. <Now> ^But^ the hand which I now saw, clearly enough<,>

MS Edward Hyde himself; and when, by sloping my own hand backward, I had supplied my double with a signature, <me> ^I^ thought²¹ I sat beyond the reach of fate.

Some two months before the murder of Sir Danvers, I had been out <for so> ^on one^ of my adventures, had returned at a late hour, and woke the next day in bed with somewhat odd sensations. It was in vain I looked about me; in vain I saw the decent furniture ^and^ tall proportions of my room in the square; in vain that I recognised the pattern of the bed curtains and the design of the mahogany frame<;>: something still kept insisting that I was not where I was, that I had not wakened where I seemed to be, but in the little room <where> in <the> Soho where I was accustomed to sleep in the <character> ^body^ of Edward Hyde. I smiled to myself and <began>, in my psychological way, began lazily to <ex>inquire into the elements of this illusion, occasionally, even as I did so, dropping back into a comfortable morning doze. I was still so engaged when, in one of my more wakeful moments, my eye fell upon my hand. Now the hand of Henry Jekyll (as you have often remarked) was professional in shape and size: it was large, firm, white and comely. But the hand which I now saw, clearly enough,

---

ND2 in the yellow light of a mid-London morning, lying half-shut
<on> among the bed clothes, was lean, corded, knuckly, of a
dusky pallour and thickly shaded with a swart growth of hair. It
was the hand of Edward Hyde.

I think I must have stared upon it for near a minute, sunk as I
was into the mere stupidity of wonder; before terror woke up in
my breast ^as^ sudden and startling as the crash of cymbals; and
bounding from my bed, I rushed to the mirror. My blood was
| 90 changed into something | exquisitely cold and yet alive. Yes: I had
gone to bed Henry Jekyll, I had ^a^wakened <up> Edward Hyde.
How was this to be explained? I asked myself; and then, with a
another bound of terror – how was it to be remedied? It was well
on in the morning; the servants were up; and all my drugs were in
the cabinet ^ – a long journey^ down two pair of stairs, through the
back passage, across the open court and through the anatomical
theatre, from where I was then standing<,> horror-struck. To
conceal my face <were> ^might, indeed, be^ possible; but of what
use was that, when I was unable to dissemble the alteration in my
stature? And then I remembered <,>(and how I thanked God for
it!) that I had <prepared> ^accustomed^ my servants to the haunting presence of my second self. I had soon dressed, had soon

MS in the yellow light of a mid-London morning, lying half shut
<upon> ^on^ the bed clothes, was lean, corded, knuckly, of a
dusky pallor and thickly shaded with a swart growth of hair. It was
the hand of Edward Hyde.

I must have stared upon it for near half a minute, sunk as I was
in the mere stupidity of wonder, before terror woke up in my
| 54 breast | as sudden and startling as the crash of cymbals; and bound-
ing from my bed, I rushed to the mirror. At the sight that met my
eyes, my blood was changed into something exquisitely thin and
icy. Yes, I had gone to bed Henry Jekyll, I had awakened Edward
Hyde. How was this to be explained? I asked myself; and then,
with another bound of terror – how was it to be remedied. It was
well on in the morning; the servants were up; all my drugs were in
the cabinet – a long journey, down two pair of stairs, through the
back passage, across the open court and through the anatomical
theatre, from where I <stood> ^was^ then standing horror-struck.
It might indeed be possible to <hide> cover my face; but of what
use was that, when I was unable to conceal the alteration in my
stature? And then with an overpowering sweetness of relief, it
came back upon my mind that the servants were already used to
the coming and going of my second self. I <was> ^had soon^

EUP 64.33–65.15

ND2 passed through the house (when Bradshaw stared and drew back
to see the etenal[22] Mr. Hyde at such an hour) and ten minutes later
Dr Jekyll had returned to his own shape and was sitting down <to
breakfast> with a darkened brow, to make a feint of breakfasting.

| 91 | Small[23] ...

MS dressed, as well as I was able, in clothes of my own size: had soon
passed through the house, where Bradshaw stared and drew back
at seeing Mr Hyde at such an hour and in such a strange array; and
ten minutes later, Dr Jekyll had returned to his own shape and was
sitting down, with a darkened brow, to make a feint of breakfasting.

Small indeed was my appetite. This inexplicable incident, this
reversal of my previous experience, seemed, like the Babylonian
finger on the wall, to be spelling out the letters of my judgement;
and I began to reflect more seriously than ever before on the issues
and possibilities of my double existence. That part of me which I
had the power of projecting, had lately been much exercised and
nourished; it had seemed to me of late as though the body of
Edward Hyde had grown in stature, as though (when I wore that
form) I were conscious of a more generous tide of blood; and I
<now> began to spy a danger that, if this were much prolonged,
the balance of my nature might be permanently overthrown, the
power of voluntary change be forfeited, and the <t>character of
Edward Hyde become irrevocably mine. The power of the drug
had not been always equally displayed. Once, very early in my
career, it had totally failed me; since then I had been obliged on
more than one occasion to double, and once, with infinite risk of
death, to treble the amount; and these rare uncertainties had cast
hitherto the sole shadow on my contentment. Now, however, and

| 55   in the light of that morning's accident, I was led to remark | that
whereas, in the beginning, <the very> ^the^ difficulty had been to
throw off the body of Jekyll, it had <lately,> ^of late,^ gradually
but de<d>cidedly transferred itself to the other side All things
therefore seemed to point to this: that I was slowly losing hold of
my original and better self, and becoming slowly incorporated
with my second and worse.

Between these two, I now felt I had to choose. My two natures
had memory in common, but all other faculties were most unequally shared between them. Jekyll<,> (who was composite) now
with the most sensitive apprehensions, now with a greedy gusto,
projected and shared in the pleasures and adventures of Hyde; but
Hyde was indifferent to Jekyll, or but remembered him as the
mountain bandit remembers the cavern in which he conceals

ND ...

MS himself from pursuit. Jekyll had more than a father's interest; Hyde had more than a son's indifference. To cast in my lot with Jekyll, was to die to those <pleasures> ^appetites^ <for> which I had long secretly <I> <allowed myself and which had> ^indulged and <recently> had of late begun^ to pamper. To cast it in with Hyde, was to die to a thousand interests and aspirations, and to become, at a blow and forever, despised and friendless. The bargain might appear unequal; but there was still another consideration in the scales; for while Jekyll would suffer smartingly in the fires of abstinence, Hyde would be not even conscious of all that he had lost. Strange as my circumstances were, the terms of this debate are as old and commonplace as man; much the same inducements and alarms cast the die for every tempted and trembling sinner; and it fell out with me, as it falls with so vast a majority of my fellows, that I chose the better part and was found wanting in the strength to keep to it.

Yes, I preferred the elderly and discontented doctor, sur-rounded by friends and cherishing honest hopes; and bade a resolute farewell to the liberty, the comparative youth, the light step, leaping pulses and <cherished> ^secret^ pleasures, that I had enjoyed in the disguise of Hyde. ^^24^I made this choice perhaps with some unconscious reservation, for I niether gave <aw>up the house in Soho<, discharged> ^nor destroyed^ the clothes of Edward Hyde, which still lay ready in my cabinet.^^ For two months, ^however,^ I was true to <these> ^my^ determination; for two months, I led a life of such severity as I had never before attained to, and <infal> enjoyed the compensations of an approv-ing conscience. But <the pas> time began at last to obliterate the freshness of my alarm; the praises of conscience began to grow into a thing of course; ^^I began to <grow> be tortured with throes and <tor> longings, <as> ^as^ of Hyde struggling after freedom^^ <and the clamour of mortified appetites to grow more instant>; and at last, in an hour of moral weakness, I once again compounded and swallowed the transforming draught.

| 56 | I do not suppose that, when a drunkard reasons with himself upon his vice, he is once out of five hundred times affected by the dangers that he runs through his brutish, physical insensibility<.>; <N> niether had I, long as I had considered my position, made enough allowance for the complete moral insensibility and insensate readiness to evil, which were the leading characters of Edward Hyde<;> . <and> ^Yet^ it was by <that> ^these^ that I was punished. <<My devil having been long caged, was in perhaps a stormier disposition. ^the more inclined to^>> My devil had

MS been long caged, he came out roaring. I was conscious, even when I took the draught, of a more unbridled, a more furious propensity to ill. It must have been this, I suppose, that <rage up> ^<raged> stirred^ in my soul that tempest of impatience with which I listened to the civilities of <that> ^my^ unhappy <man> victim; I declare at least, before God, <th> no man morally sane could have been guilty of that crime upon so pitiful a provocation; and that I struck in no more reasonable spirit than that in which <the> ^a^ sick child may break a plaything. But I had voluntarily stripped myself of all those balancing instincts, by which even the worst of us continues to walk with some degree of steadiness among temptations; and in my case, to be tempted however slightly, was to fall.

<With the first blow> ^Instantly^, the spirit of hell awoke in me and raged. With a transport of glee, I mauled the unresisting body, tasting delight from every blow; <until> and it was not till weariness had begun to succeed, that I I was suddenly [²⁵, in the top fit of my delirium,] [<pierced> ^struck^ through the heart] by a cold thrill of terror. <Hyde was quick enough to fear> <I>A mist dispersed dispersed; I saw my life to be forfeit; and fled from the scene of these excesses, <glorying in my act and trembling for the> <in the joys of cruelty> ^at once glorying and trembling, <at once revelling> my lust of evil gratified^ and stimulated, my love of life screwed to <its> ^the^ topmost peg. I ran to the house in Soho<;> , and (to make assurance doubly sure) destroyed my papers; thence I set out through the lamplit streets, in the same divided ecstasy of mind, gloating <i>on <what I> ^my crime^ <and>, light-headedly devising others ^in the future^, and yet still hastening and still <glancing behind me> ^hearkening in my wake for^ the steps of the avenger. Hyde had a song upon his lips as he compounded the draught, and as he drank it, pledged the dead man by name. The pangs of transformation had not done tearing him, before Henry Jekyll, with streaming tears of gratitude and remorse, had fallen upon his knees and lifted his clasped hands to God. The veil of self-indulgence was <thus> rent from head to
|57 foot, <and I beheld, in the holy place of> I saw my life as a whole: |
I followed it ^up^ from the days of <my> childhood, when I had walked with my father's hand, <<to the damned <incident> ^<horrors>^ of that night, and>> and through the self-denying days of my professional life, to arrive again and again, with the same sense of unreality, at the damned horrors of the evening. I could have screamed aloud; I sought with tears and prayers to smother down the crowd of hideous images and sounds with

ND ...

MS which my memory swarmed against me; and still, between <my> ^the^ petitions, the ugly face of my iniquity stared into my soul. As the acuteness of this remorse began to die away, it was succeeded by a sense of joy.<; Hyde was thenceforth impossible> ^The problem of my conduct was solved<:>^. Hyde was thenceforth impossible; whether I would or not, I was compelled to <the> ^my^ better life; and O, how I rejoiced to think it! <how> with what willing humility, I embraced anew the restrictions of natural life! with what sincere renunciation, I locked the door by which I had so often <come and gone> ^gone and come^, and <broke> ^ground^ the key under my heel!

<And> <t>The next day, <with> ^came^ the news that the murder had been overlooked, that the guilt of Hyde was patent to the world, and that the victim was a man <of> ^high in^ public estimation. It was not only a crime, it had been a tragic folly. I think I was glad to know it; I think I was glad to have my better impulses<,> thus buttressed and guarded by the terrors of the scaffold . <, for what temptation could now avail to make me choose the body> Jekyll was now my city of refuge; let but Hyde peep out an instant, and the hands of all men <were> ^would be^ raised to take <him> and slay him. <The long drawn hum of anger and horror that sounded through society upon the fall of their favourite crew, was>

I resolved in my future conduct to redeem the past; and I can say with honesty that my resolve was fruitful of some good. You know yourself how earnestly, in the last months of last year, I laboured to relieve suffering; you know that much was done for others, and that the days passed quietly, almost happily for myself. Nor can I truly say that I wearied of this beneficent and innocent life; I think instead that I daily enjoyed it more completely; but I was still cursed with my <infirmity> ^duality^ of purpose; and as the first edge of my penitence <wa>wore off, the lower side of me, so long indulged, so recently chained down, began to growl for licence. Not that I dreamed of rescussitating[26] Hyde; the bare idea of that would startle me to frenzy: no, it was in my ^own^ person, that I was once more tempted to <condescend with baser instinc> ^trifle with my conscience; and it was^ as an ordinary secret sinner, <and> that I at last fell before the assaults of temptation.

| 58 | There <is> ^comes^ an end <of> ^to^ all things; the most capacious measure is filled at last; ^and^ this <last condescension to> ^brief condescension to^ my evil finally destroyed the balance of my soul. And yet I was not alarmed; the fall seemed natural, like a return to the old days before I had made my discovery. <I sat on

ND ...

MS   a clear winter's> ^It was a fine, <J> clear January^ day, wet underfoot where the frost had melted ^but cloudless overhead^; and the <r>Regent's park was full of winter chirruppings and ^sweet with^ Spring odours. I sat in the sun on a bench; the animal within me licking the chops of memory; the spiritual side a little drowsed, promising subsequent penitence, but not yet moved to begin. After all, I reflected I was like my nieghbours; and then I smiled, comparing myself with other men, comparing my active goodwill with the lazy cruelty of their neglect. And at the very moment of that vainglorious thought, a qualm came upon me, a horrid nausea and the most deadly shuddering. These passed away, and left me faint; and then as <the> in its turn the faintness subsided, I began to be aware of a change in the temper of my thoughts, a greater boldness, a contempt of danger, a solution of the bonds of obligation. I looked down; my clothes hung formlessly on my shrunken limbs; the hand that lay on my knee was corded and hairy. I was once more Edward Hyde. A moment before I had been safe of all men's respect, wealthy, beloved – the cloth laying for me in the dining room at home; and now I was the common quarry of <the> mankind, hunted, houseless, a known murderer, thrall to the gallows.

My reason wavered, but it did not fail me utterly. I have more than once observed that, in my second character, my faculties seemed sharpened to a point and my spirits more tensely elastic; thus it came about that, where Jekyll perhaps might have succumbed, Hyde rose to the importance of the occasion. My drugs were in one of the presses of my cabinet; how was I to reach them? That was the problem that<,> (crushing my temples in my hands) I set myself to solve. The laboratory door I had closed<;> . <i>If I sought to enter by the house, my own servants would consign me to the gallows. I saw I must employ another hand, and thought of Lanyon. How was he to be reached? how persuaded? Supposing that I escaped capture in the streets, how was I to make my way into his presence? and how should I, an unknown and displeasing visitor, prevail on the famous physician to rifle the study of his colleague, Dr Jekyll? Then I remembered that of my original character, one part remained to me: I could write my own hand; and once I had conceived that kindling spark, the way that I must

|59   follow became | lighted up from end to end.

Thereupon, I arranged my clothes as best I could, and summoning a passing hansom, drove to an hotel in Portland street, the name of which I chanced to remember. At my appearance <,>(which was indeed comical enough, however tragic a fate these

ND2 | misfitting clothes rendered me so marked an object <that> in the
| 103 streets, that the danger of recognition was increased to something
close on certainty; and it was thus my wish to stay as long as
possible in the hotel<,>. <where> But at length I began to fear
<that> I <was> shuld be judged excentric, <and the> ^formed
another plan,^ called for my bill, <paid it,> ordered a four wheeler
^to the door^, and <concealing myself> ^sitting back^ in the
<darkest> corner, had myself driven to a remote part of London<,>.
<where> ^Here^ I stopped ^the driver^ at a door, asked for the
first name that came into my head, was of course refused admittance, and was then driven back to the nieghbourhood of Cavendish Square not very long before the hour of my appointment.

MS garments covered) the driver could not conceal his mirth. I
gnashed ^my teeth^ upon him with a gust of devilish fury; <that>
and the smile withered from his face, happily for him, yet more
happily for myself, for in another instant I had certainly dragged
him from his perch.

At the inn, as I entered, I looked about with me with so black a
countenance as <turned> ^made^ the attendants tremble; not a
look did they exchange in my presence; but obsequiously took my
orders, led me to a <si> private room, and brought me
wherewithal to write. Hyde<,> in danger of his life was a creature
new to me: shaken with inordinate anger, strung to the pitch of
murder, lusting to inflict pain. Yet the creature was astute;
mastered his fury with a great effort of the will; composed his two
important letters, one to Lanyon and one to Poole; and that he
might receive actual evidence of their being posted, sent them out
with directions that they should be registered.

Thenceforward, he sat all day over the fire in the private room,
gnawing his nails; there he dined, sitting alone with his fears, the
waiter visibly quailing before his eye; and thence, when the night
was fully come, he set forth in the corner of a closed cab, and was
driven to and fro about the streets of the city. He, I say – I cannot
say, I. That child of Hell had nothing human; nothing lived in him
but fear and hatred. And when at last, thinking the driver had
begun to grow suspicious, he discharged the cab and ventured on
foot, attired in his misfitting clothes, an object marked out for
observation, into the midst of the nocturnal passengers, these two
base passions raged within him like a tempest. He walked fast,
hunted by his <alarms> ^fears^, chattering to himself, skulking
through the less frequented thoroughfares, counting the minutes
that still divided him from midnight. Once a woman spoke to him,

EUP 70.12–71.2

ND2   You know already what occurred. Lanyon threw me off from
him with horror; it scarcely moved me; I was still so full of my
immediate joy. I was already so conscious of the perpetual doom
that hung above my head; and when I returned home, carrying
with me my precious drugs[27] |

...

MS   offering, I think, a box of lights. He smote her in the face, and she
fled.

When I came to myself at Lanyon's, the horror of my old
friend perhaps affected me somewhat: I do not know; it was at
least but a drop in the sea to the abhorrence <a> with which I

| 60   looked back upon these hours. A | change had come over me. It
was no longer the fear of the gallows, it was the horror of being
Hyde, that racked me. I received Lanyon's condemnation partly in
a dream; it was partly in a dream that I came home to my own
house and <went to> ^got into^ bed. I slept after the prostration
of the day, with a stringent and profound slumber<,> which not
even the nightmares that wrung me could avail to break. I awoke
in the morning shaken, weakened, <still haunted by the> ^but
refreshed. I still^ hated and feared the thought of the brute that
slept within me <and> <; I still> , and I had not of course
forgotten the appalling dangers of the day before; but I was once
more at home, in my own house ^and^ close to my drugs; <close
to the> ^and gratitude^ for my escape <was> ^shone^ so strong
<within me> ^in my soul^ that it almost <wore> ^rivalled^ the
brightness of hope.

I was stepping liesurely across the court after breakfast,
drinking the chill of the air with pleasure, when I was siezed again
with those indescribable sensations that heralded the change;
^and^ I had but the time to <fly> gain the shelter of my cabinet,
before I was once again raging and freezing with the passions of
Hyde. It took on this occasion a double dose to recall me to
myself; and alas, six hours after, as I sat looking sadly in the fire,
<lashed> the pangs returned, and the drug had to be re-
administered. In short, from that day forth it seemed only <In sh>
by a great effort as of gymnastics, and only under the immediate
stimulation of the drug, that I was able to wear the countenance of
Jekyll. <Whe> At all hours of the day and night, I <was> ^would
be^ taken with the premonitory shudder; above all, if I slept, or
even dosed for a moment in my chair, it was always as Hyde that I
awakened. <This condemned me to vigils in> ^Under the strain of
this continually^ impending doom and by the sleeplessness to
which I now condemned ^myself^, ay, even beyond <the> <p>

ND ...

MS what I had thought possible <, Jekyll fell into a state of dazed> ^to man, I became, in my own person, a creature eaten^ up and <exhausted> ^emptied^ by fever, languidly weak ^both^ in body and mind, and solely occupied by one thought: the horror of my other self. But when I slept, or when the virtue of the medicine wore off, I would leap <(> almost without transition (for the pangs of transformation grew daily less marked) into <that> the <<uncontrollable energies, terrors and angers <of> that rent>> possession of a fancy brimming with images of terror, a soul boiling with causeless hatreds, and a body that seemed not strong | 61 enough to contain the raging energies of life. The powers | of Hyde seemed to have grown with the sickliness of Jekyll. And certainly <if> the hate that now divided them was equal on each side. With Jekyll, it was a thing of vital instinct<;> . <h>He had now seen the full deformity of that creature that shared with him some of the phenomena of consciousness, and was coheir with him to death: <<more bonds he could not now recognise; the thought of him, like the <sight of something odious> ^<killing smell of ammonia>^,>> ^and beyond these links of community, <he did not stoop to recognise him>^, which <were> in themselves ^made^ the most poignant ^part^ of his distress <and horror>, he <but> thought of Hyde, for all his <ecstasy> ^energy^ of life, as ^of^ something ^not only hellish but^ inorganic. This was the <horror> ^shocking thing^; that the slime of the pit seemed to utter cries and voices; that the amorphous dust gesticulated and sinned; that what <ha> was dead, and had no shape, <shuld> ^should^ usurp<ed> the offices of life. And this again, that th<is>at insurgent horror was knit <by> ^to^ him closer than a wife, ^closer than an eye^; <a> ^<and>^ <went to and fro> ^lay caged^ in his <bosom> ^flesh^, where he heard it <growl> ^mutter^ and felt it <wrest> struggle to be born; <and was at all points conterminous with his life.> ^and at every hour of weakness, and in the confidence of slumber,^ prevailed against him, and deposed him out of life. The hatred of Hyde for Jekyll, was of a different order. His terror of the gallows drove him continually to commit <that> temporary suicide, and return to his subordinate station <as> of a part instead of a person; but he <ga> loathed the necessity, he loathed the despondency into which Jekyll <had> ^was^ now fallen, ^and^ he resented the dislike with which he was ^himself^ regarded. Hence the apelike tricks that he would play me, scrawling in my own hand blasphemies <upon> ^on^ the pages of my books, burning the letters and destroying the portrait of my father; and indeed, had it not been for his fear of

ND ...

MS   death, he would long ago have ruined himself in order to involve
me in the ruin. But his <fear> ^love^ of <death> ^life^ is
wonderful; I go further: <I think it touching> I, who sicken and
freeze at the mere thought of him, when I recall the abjection and
passion of this attachment, and when I know how he fears my
power to cut him off by suicide, I find it in my heart to pity him.

<W> It is useless , <, it is loathsome,> ^and the time awfully
fails me,^ to prolong this <picture> description; no one has ever
suffered such <a> torments, let that suffice; and yet even to this
<there> <time> ^habit^ brought – no, not alleviation – but a
certain callousness of soul, a certain acquiescence of despair; and
my punishment might have gone on for years, but for the last
| 62   calamity which has now fallen, and which has finally | severed me
from my own face and nature. My provision ^of ^ the salt, <had>
which had never been renewed since the ^date of^ first
experiment, began to run low. I sent out for a fresh supply, and
mixed the draught; the ebullition followed, and the first change of
colour, not the second; I drank it and it was without efficiency.
You will learn from Poole how I have had London ransacked; it
was in vain; and I am now persuaded that my first supply was
impure, and that it was that unknown impurity which leant
efficacy to the draught.

<Nearly a week has> ^<I have>^ ^About a week has^ passed,
and I am now finishing this statement under the influence of the
last of the old powders. This, ^then,^ is the last time, short of a
miracle, that Henry Jekyll can think his own thoughts or see his
own face (now how sadly altered!) in the glass. Nor must I delay
too long to bring my writing to an end; for if <this> ^my^
narrative has hitherto escaped destruction, it has been by a
combination of great prudence and great good luck. Should the
throes of change take me in the act of writing it, Hyde <would>
^will^ tear it in pieces; but if some time shall have elapsed after I
have laid it by, his wonderful selfishness and circumscription to
the moment will probably save it once again from <destruction>
^the action of^ his apelike spite. And indeed the doom that is
closing on us both, has already changed and crushed him. Half an
hour from now, when I shall again and f<u>orever reindue that
hated personality, I know how I shall sit shuddering and weeping
in my chair, or continue, with the most strained and fearstruck
ecstasy of listening, to pace up and down this room <,>(my last
earthly refuge) and give ear to every sound of menace. Will Hyde
die upon the scaffold? or will he find the courage to release himself
at the last moment? God knows; I am careless; this is my true hour

EUP 72.30–73.32

ND ...

of death, and what is to follow concerns another than myself<;> .
<and this moment when I shall> Here then, as I lay down the pen
and proceed to seal up my confession, I bring the life of that
unhappy Henry Jekyll to an end.

Robert Louis Stevenson.[28]

EUP 73.32–73.35

Notes

1 Cancelled *that* is restored by three dots underneath.
2 *the lawyer* (written once) is cancelled then restored by underlining with dots.
3 The cancelled catchword *This* at the bottom of p. 8 linked up with the top of p. 9; an inserted catchword *Hitherto* links with the new page 8A.
4 The order of *fogged face of the* (written only once) is changed by a stepped line, which is then crossed out.
5 At the bottom of p. 8A, the last word on the page *Now*, the catchword *he*, and the instruction *To p. 8B* are cancelled, and the new catchword *If* and the new instruction *to p 9* are substituted.
6 Four dots before indented *This* might indicate the deletion of a paragraph indentation. The following long deletion was made after the insertion of 8A, which reworks some of the same material.
7 Pages 33 and 48 are cancelled pages, belonging to what we have called *ND1*, probably corresponding to a completely different and earlier draft or phase of work.
8 Could be *Lewsome*. The same name also occurs in *ND2* f. 88.
9 The earlier cancellation of <," replied the lawyer> is inserted here by looped line.
10 Linehan has <; *and*>.
11 Not strictly speaking part of *MS* but a version discarded in the preparation of it. Stevenson probably decided to rewrite and rework 'the exploration of the cabinet' on a fresh sheet.
12 Written above 'globus hystericus', though the latter is not cancelled.
13 Inserted in the upper part of the left margin, beginning with an indent.
14 Written in the middle of the left margin beginning with an indent.
15 Linehan's transcription here (which could be right) is: *shame. And it was.*
16 Information for p. 85 comes from the catalogue of the Strong sale 1914, Item 321, which gives the first complete sentence only, presumably leaving out the last two words of the sentence carried over from the previous page: *doubtless* (which is the catchword at the end of p. 84) and *right*, which have here been taken from *MS*.
17 *ND2* text from here to the end of the paragraph is used a little later in *MS*.
18 The catchphrase on the previous page is: <*burning*> *trimming*.
19 The catchword at the bottom of the previous page is *Dr*, the first word at the top of this is *Doctor*; the compositor of *1886L* used the latter form.

20 In *genial respectability* the second word is not written out but recovered from the first version on the line beneath (... *liberty and respectability*) by a stepped line; then first and second version were both crossed out and Stevenson starts the sentence afresh.

21 Just the 'me' part of 'methought' is deleted and 'I' written above it.

22 Looks like the non-existent word *etenal* (but even 'the eternal Mr Hyde' would be strange here).

23 Catchword from previous page; new paragraph placed here following *MS*.

24 This sentence is written vertically in the margin.

25 The order of the two phrases in square brackets is inverted by a stepped line (*<pierced> etc.* was originally first).

26 The first two syllables of the word are underlined by a double stroke of printer's pencil, drawing attention to the misspelling.

27 *ND2* ends here in mid-sentence, half-way across the nineteenth line of the page with no catchword.

28 Ink colour and the slope of letters show that the author's signature was added separately, not immediately after finishing the last word of the text.

APPENDIX B

Early Editions and Translations

1. Editions after 1886

Apart from in the 1886 Longman and Scribner's editions, Stevenson's text was also published in English (in a volume with *An Inland Voyage*) at Leipzig in 1886 by Bernhard Tauschnitz (Collection of British Authors, 2387) and in the United States in numerous pirated editions. Norbert Spehner's list of 600 editions and translations 1886–1997 in *Jekyll & Hyde. Opus 600* (Roberval [Québec], Ashem Fictions, 1997) gives an idea of the wide diffusion of Stevenson's text. What follows is a short list of the editions in Britain and America that have been most frequently used as reference and copy texts together with some recent editions of critical interest.

New editions (most, if not all, based on post-1886 versions of the text) became numerous after the end of 'unrestricted copyright' on Stevenson's works in December 1924 (when republication was allowed, with 10 per cent royalty still payable to Stevenson's heir, Lloyd Osbourne, until 1944, when copyright ended) and concurrently with the film versions of 1920, 1931, and 1941. Electronic texts on the Internet (in January 2003) all seem to be based on post-1886 editions and contain additional gross errors due to imperfect character recognition and lack of proof-reading. A return to the use of *1886L* as the copy text had to wait until Watson (1986). Others who have used this (with minor differences in emendations) are Letley (1987), Dury (1993), Mighall (2002), Menikoff (2002) and Linehan (2003). Oates (1990) and Wolf (1995) use *1886NY*.

Britain: 1. The Edinburgh Edition, vol. 8, 1895; 2. *The Strange Case of Dr Jekyll and Mr Hyde with other Fables*, Longman, 1896; 3. The Pentland Edition, vol. 6, Cassell, 1907; 4. The Swanston Edition, vol. 5, Chatto & Windus, 1911; 5. The Skerryvore edition, vol. 4, Heinemann, 1924; 6. The Tusitala Edition, vol. 5, Heinemann, 1924; 7. *The Strange Case of Doctor Jekyll and Mr Hyde, and other stories*, Dent Dutton (Everyman Library), 1925, and many others, including 8. *Dr Jekyll and Mr Hyde and Other Stories*, ed. Jenni Calder, Penguin (Penguin Classics), 1979; 9. *Strange Case of Dr Jekyll and Mr Hyde. A Centenary*

Edition, ed. Roderick Watson, Edinburgh, Canongate, 1986; 10. *The Strange Case of Dr Jekyll and Mr Hyde and Weir of Hermiston*, ed. Emma Letley, OUP (World's Classics), 1987; 11. *The Strange Case of Dr. Jekyll and Mr. Hyde and Other Stories*, ed. Claire Harman, Dent (Everyman Library), 1992; 12. *The Strange Case of Dr Jekyll and Mr Hyde and Other Tales of Terror*, ed. Robert Mighall, Penguin (Penguin Classics), 2002.

United States: 1. The Thistle Edition, Scribner's, vol. 7, 1895; 2. The Biographical Edition, vol. 14, Scribner's, 1911; 3. The Household Edition, vol. 5, Lamb, 1906; 4. The Vailima Edition, vol. 7, Scribner's, 1922; 5. The South Seas Edition, vol. 10, Scribner's, 1925, and many others, including 6. in *Frankenstein, Dracula, Dr Jekyll and Mr Hyde*, intro. by Stephen King, Signet, 1978; 7. *Strange Case of Dr Jekyll and Mr Hyde*, ed. Joyce Carol Oates, University of Nebraska Press, 1990; 8. *The Strange Case of Dr. Jekyll and Mr. Hyde*, introduced and edited by Barry V. Qualls and Susan J. Wolfson, New York, Washington Square Press, 1995; 9. in *The Essential Dr. Jekyll & Mr. Hyde*, ed. Leonard Wolf, New York, Plume, 1995; 10. *The Strange Case of Dr Jekyll and Mr Hyde*, ed. Martin Danahay, Broadview, 1999; 11. in *The Complete Stories of Robert Louis Stevenson*, ed. Barry Menikoff, The Modern Library, 2002; 12. *Strange Case of Dr Jekyll and Mr Hyde*, ed. Katherine Linehan, Norton (Norton Critical Editions), 2003.

2. Early Translations

Part of the history of *Dr Jekyll and Mr Hyde* is its geographical and cultural diffusion via translations. The early translations (the first fifty years, until 1935) are given in the following list (in order of the first translation into the language – excluding, where possible, re-editions of the same translation). Information comes from the BOSLIT catalogue (National Library of Scotland), Norbert Spehner (op. cit.), and from the on-line catalogues of various national libraries.

French: 1. 1887 (tr. Jules-Paul Tardivel; in *La vérité* [Québec], January–April); published in book form in 1888 with *Le treizième fils de Jean-Pierre* by C. Buet (Québec, Drouin); 2. 1890 (tr. B.-J. Lowe [Berthe Low], Paris, Plon); 3. 1924 (tr. Fanny-W. Laparra, Paris, Stock); 4. 1926 (tr. Théo Varlet, Paris, Jonquières, ill. Constant le Breton); 5. 1931 (tr. Henri Tilleul, Paris, Hachette); 6. 1935 (tr. A. Declos-Auricoste and P. Courant, Paris, Didier).

Russian: 1. 1888 (St Petersburg, Izd. Suvorina); 2. 1916 (tr. M. Likjardopulo, Moscow, Izd. Akts. ob-va universal'naja biblioteka).

German: 1. 1889 (Breslau, Schlesische Verlagsanstalt); 2. 1910 (Hamburg, Vitus-Verlag); 3. 1910 (Berlin, Schottländer); 4. 1922 (tr. Wilhelm Emmanuel Süskind, Hanover, Steegemann); 5. 1924 (tr. Ilse Schneider,

Vienna/Leipzig, Herz-Verlag); 6. 1924 (tr. Marianne Trebitsch-Stein, Vienna, Steyrermühl); 7. 1925 (tr. Curt Thesing, Munich, Buchenau & Reichert); 8. 1925 (Stuttgart, Lutz); 9. 1925 (Munich, Medusa-Verlag, ill. Theo Scharf); 10. 1926 (Munich, Müller); 11. c. 1926 (Berlin, Helikon); 12. 1927 (Leipzig, Hesse & Becker); 13. 1927 (Stuttgart/Berlin, Neufeld & Henius); 14. 1930 (Berlin, Singer); 15. 1930 (tr. Grete Rambach, Leipzig, Insel Verlag).

Danish: 1889 (tr. 'K.', Rønne, Sørensens Boghandel).

Czech: 1. 1889 (tr. Josef Novácek, in *Vesna* [Velke Mezirici], vol. 9, April-September); 2. 1900 (tr. Josef Bartos, Prague, Tiskem a nákladem J. Otty).

Spanish: 1. 1891 (tr. Emilio Augusto Soulère, New York, Appleton); 2. 1920 (tr. José Torroba, Madrid, Calpe); 3. 1920 (tr. Carlos Pereyra, Madrid, Atenea); 4. 1920 (México, D.F., México Moderno, ill. Antonio Gómez); 5. 1930 (Madrid, Novelas y Cuentos); 6. 1931 (Santiago de Cile, Zig Zag).

Serbo-Croatian: 1. 1891 (tr. Iso Velikanoviâc, Zagreb, Jutarnji list); 2. 19– (tr. N. B. Jovanoviâc, Belgrade, Narodna knjiéznica, by 'L. R. Stivenson').

Polish: 1. 1895, in two numbers of *Czas* [Krakow]; 2. 1909 (tr. M. Rakowski, Warsaw, Bibl. Dziel Wybor; 3. 1934 (tr. B. Szarlitt, Warszaw, Biblioteka 'Echa Polskiego').

Swedish: 1. 1897 (tr. Anna Geete, Stockholm, Beijer); 2. 1908 (tr. Wilhelm Uhrström, Stockholm, Norstedt); 3. 1911 (tr. J. P. R., Stockholm, Wändahl & Anderson); 4. 1917 (Stockholm, Nord. förlaget); 5. 1921 (tr. Erik Karlholm, Svenska förlaget); 6. 1921 (tr. H. Flygare, Stockholm/ Helsinki, Björck & Börjesson/Söderström); 7. 1926 (tr. M. Drangel, Stockholm, Åhlén & Åkerlund).

Hungarian: 1899 (Vienna).

Finnish: 1. 1897 (Brooklyn, NY, Suomalais-amerikkalainen kustan-nusyhtièo); 2. 1911 (Helsinki, Otava).

Welsh: c. 1900 (tr. John Ashton, London, Cyhoeddedig gan yr Awdwr).

Italian: 1. 1905 (tr. A. Nichel, Milano, Libreria Lombarda); 2. 1925 (tr. Arturo Reghini, Roma, Voghera); 3. 1928 (tr. M. Malatesta, Milano); 4. 1929 (tr. I. Lori, Milano, Mondadori); 5. 1933 (tr. C. Meneghelli, Milano, Elit); 6. 1934 (tr. Gian Dauli, Milano, Aurora).

Esperanto: 1909 (tr. William Morrison and Willliam W. Mann, London, British Esperanto Association).

Yiddish: 1911 (tr. B. Rauz and A. Frumokin, London, Ferlag Kunst).

Dutch: 1913 (tr. Gonne van Uildriks, Amsterdam, Maatschappij voor Goede en Goedkoope Lectuur).

Norwegian: 1. 1917 (Kristina, Eriksen); 2. 1927 (tr. Helge Krog, Oslo, Gyldendal).

Estonian: 1920 (tr. H. G. Oras, Tallinn, Rahvaülikool).

Armenian: 1923 (tr. H. Tsovikean, Boston, Vahan S. Malkhasean).

Slovak: 1924 (tr. M. Kovaccik, New York, New Yorkskây Denmik).

Japanese: 1. 1925 (tr. Tsuneo Momoi, Tokyo, Kongosha); 2. 1928 (tr. Hoei Nojiri, Tokyo, Kaizo Bunko); 3. 1929 (tr. Saishi Tada, Tokyo, Tohoshoin); 4. 1934 (tr. T. Katta, Tokyo, Kembunsha).

Malay: 1925 (tr. W. E. Gregory, Tananarive, Impr. F.F.M.A.).

Korean: 1926 (Kyongsong [Seoul], Choson Yaso Kyosohoe, Taejong 15).

Chinese: 1926 (tr. J. S. Gale and Yi Wong Mo, Kyongsong [Seoul], Choson Yaso Kyosohoe, Taejong 15).

Hebrew: 1928 (Jerusalem, Mitspeh).

Irish Gaelic: 1929 (tr. F. W. O'Connell, Dublin, Ar na fhoillsiú do mhuinntir C. S. Ó. Fallamhain, i gcomar le hOifig an tSoláthair).

Portuguese: 1933 (tr. A. Victor Machado, Lisbon, Minerva).

Catalan: 1935 (tr. Josep J. Margaret, Barcelona, Quaderns Literaris; ill. Enric Cluselles).

NOTE

The Stevenson entry by Bradford A. Booth in *The Cambridge Bibliography of English Literature*, second edition, 1969–77, lists four translations not found by the present compiler: German 1887, Dutch 1909, Polish 1924, and Arabic 1927. It also lists translations that probably correspond to republications of earlier translations and are therefore not listed above: a German translation of 1928 (a repackaging of the 1927 translation), and a Spanish translation of 1921 (a republication of the 1891 translation). The updated entry by Roger Swearingen in the third edition (2000) includes these (as testified by Booth), as well as two new listings not found by the present compiler: a German translation of 1921, and a Finnish translation of 1921, possibly a confusion with the Swedish translation published in Helsinki in that year.

Textual Notes

Textual Notes

Description of Manuscripts

NDI MORRIS L. PARRISH COLLECTION, PRINCETON UNIVERSITY
LIBRARY

The first 'Notebook Draft' (*ND1*; 'Unpublished Portion of ... "Strange
Case of Dr Jekyll and Mr Hyde" ' in the Princeton Catalogue) consists
of two notebook pages, with the *JH* text crossed out and the backs used
for a letter to Stevenson's cousin Bob (mid-October 1885, *LETBM*, vol.
V, pp. 132–4) in which he says 'excuse the use of ancient scraps of M.S. I
have no other paper here'. Page numbers, inserted by Stevenson (33 and
48), are at the top centre of the two folios, in clear contrast to *ND2*. This
suggests (Stevenson being otherwise consistent in numbering style) that
the two pages belonged to a different sequence – probably earlier
('ancient'), and possibly chance survivors of the famous first draft
thrown in the fire, or trial attempts ('scraps') marked as separate.

    The two cancelled pages passed into the collection of John Gribbel,
sold in 1940, after which they came into the possession of Henry E.
Gerstley who subsequently presented them to Princeton University
Library.[1]

ND2 BEINECKE LIBRARY, YALE UNIVERSITY, B 6934, WITH A
FOLIO AT THE ROBERT LOUIS STEVENSON SILVERADO MUSEUM,
CALIFORNIA

The second Notebook Draft (*ND2*) consists of twenty-five folios of identical size and ruling to those used for *ND1* but numbered by Stevenson in the top left-hand corner.[2] *B 6934* consists of pp. 58, 67, 69–84, 86–90, 103; the Silverado p. 68 fits exactly into a one-page break in this sequence. The single p. 85 (fitting into another one-page break) was sold in 1914 but has since disappeared.[3]

This version (closer to the first printed edition than *ND 1*) seems to have been left incomplete: the last folio of the extant manuscript (numbered 103) ends on line 19 (where all other folios have 20 or 21 lines of writing), half-way across the page and in mid-sentence. Apparently unsatisfied with the way things were going, and able to see clearly to the end, Stevenson decided to leave the last part till the next draft (i.e. *MS*).[4]

The Silverado folio was given by Fanny Stevenson in 1898 to John E. Schermerhorn (an American traveller who had met RLS on board the *Mariposa* in 1893), and was eventually sold to the Museum in 1983. The rest of *ND2* (a twenty-four-page fragment 'found in an old trunk which had not been opened for a long time') was offered by Belle Strong to the collector J. Pierpont Morgan in 1911 without success.[5] It then came into Harry Glemby's Stevenson collection and, when this was auctioned in 1926, it passed into the collection of Edwin J. Beinecke,[6] who donated it, together with his whole Stevenson collection, to Yale University in 1951.

MS PIERPONT MORGAN LIBRARY, NEW YORK, MA 628, WITH A
FOLIO AT THE ROBERT LOUIS STEVENSON SILVERADO MUSEUM,
CALIFORNIA

Description

MS (Veeder's 'Printer's Copy') is Stevenson's final manuscript copy. It was used for setting up *1886L*, as shown by the marginal compositors' names, marks, and calculations.[7]

The incomplete manuscript of thirty-four folios covers just over half of the published text and consists of two continuous sequences covering the beginning and the end of the text, with the middle section missing. The first group of pages consists of fourteen folios (numbered 1 to 13 with an inserted f. 8A). These contain all of the first two chapters and most of the opening paragraph of ch. 3. The other group of pages consists of twenty folios (numbered 43 to 62), and contains the last two-thirds of ch. 9 and the whole of ch. 10. Both groups have been roughly folded in four, but the second group has been first shortened by folding a bottom strip upwards.[8] In both cases the pages were folded together, at the same time, no doubt in order to fit them in an envelope and send them by post to Stevenson together with the proofs. Probably, leaves 1 to 13 and the lost leaves 14 to 42 were returned together with the proofs of the first six sheets (i.e. that which would become signatures B to G, pp.

1–96) of *1886L* and the rest later. This we deduce from the printer's note on the first leaf of *MS*: 'proofs <u>immediately</u> / to R. L. Stevenson Esq. / Skerryvore / Bournemouth / per est [? per estenso, 'in full'] / (6 shts)'. The beginning of the seventh sheet is indicated by a compositor's mark in *MS* about a quarter of the way down f. 43, so this and the following leaves were probably held back and sent to RLS when the typesetting was finished.

The first folio of the second surviving sequence is written on the back of an earlier draft, numbered 39; this latter, however, is in pencil, is completely crossed through, and was not intended for the printer. Stevenson clearly wanted to try out details which he adds here to the *ND2* description (the tea things, the mirror), but then crossed through the text in order to write the final version with (assuming that this was close to *1886L*) even more changes and additions to the description of the tea things and 'pious work', and with added details of the reflections in the mirror.

History

The *MS* was in the possession of Isobel Strong, Stevenson's stepdaughter, in 1899–1900, less than six years after Stevenson's death. In 1899 she gave f. 47 to a friend, describing it as 'A page from the original manuscript of "Jekyll and Hyde" given me at Vailima by my step-father Robert Louis Stevenson';[9] and in an article in the *Bookman* 12(1), 1900, Eugene Limedorfer tells us that Mrs Strong had 'put the whole manuscript at my disposal' (p. 52 note).

This manuscript was probably the same incomplete fragment that exists today. It is true that Limedorfer refers to 'the whole manuscript' and even specifically to the lost central section, saying that 'the twenty-five ... pages' between pages 13 and 39 'show very little alterations' (*sic*) (p. 56). There are, however, various reasons for doubting his reliability. 1. He transcribes the cancelled p. 39, says that it is crossed out and that Stevenson used parts of it in the first edition, but fails to make any comparison with a rewritten p. 39 which would have existed in a complete manuscript and would have given him a striking example of the author's 'hard, painstaking labor' (p. 58). 2. He quotes what would be the last words of the lost p. 38 and the beginning of the extant cancelled p. 39, yet the equivalent words to those on the lost *MS* p. 38 in the extant versions that precede and follow it (*ND2* and *1886L*) are so similar to each other that Limedorfer's different intermediate version is unlikely. 3. He claims that the manuscript (citing extant pages) has marginal comments of which, however, there is no trace in *MS*, and which anyway sound improbable (authors do not normally write fully formed messages to themselves such as '"Threw him out of gear." I do not like that phrase'). 4. The passages discussed and the pages repro-duced all correspond to extant pages only. 5. The style of the article suggests an immature writer.

The bulk of the extant *MS* was sold by Isobel Strong to the collector J.

STRANGE CASE OF DR. JEKYLL AND MR. HYDE

Pierpont Morgan in December 1909.[10] It consisted of thirty folios, since four had been separated from the two main sequences. 1. Folio 47 had been given away by Mrs Strong to 'Dr. Kelseny' on 25 December 1899; the page was later owned by 'a member of the Quarto Club of New York' who allowed its reproduction in 1929 in the limited edition of *Dr Jekyll and Mr Hyde* published by Random House with illustrations by W. A. Dwiggins. 2. Folio 43 (with the cancelled pencil-draft p. 39 on the back) had also been previously given away, again possibly as a Christmas gift, judging from the annotation on the back: 'R. L. Stevenson's manuscript of Dr Jekyll and Mr Hyde / from Mrs Isobel Strong De[cember] 1905 to EWW'. These two folios (43 and 47) were probably acquired by Edwin Beinecke some time after February 1951 and then donated to the Morgan Library in 1960. 3. Folio 52 (perhaps overlooked at the time of the 1909 sale) was sold by Isobel Strong to Edwin J. Beinecke in 1941, who then donated it to the Morgan Library in February 1951.[11] 4. Folio 9, one of the pages included in facsimile in Limedorfer's 1900 article, was some time later given by Mrs Strong to 'Mr and Mrs Frank Norris' and was left as a gift to the Silverado Museum in 1970.

MANUSCRIPTS, PROOFS AND EARLY FORMS OF THE FRONT MATTER: BEINECKE LIBRARY, YALE UNIVERSITY, B 7551, B 7552, B 7007; MORRIS L. PARRISH COLLECTION, PRINCETON UNIVERSITY LIBRARY, C 0171; R. L. STEVENSON SILVERADO MUSEUM, CALIFORNIA, COLVIN'S GALLEY PROOFS OF LETTERS.

Proofs survive only for the preliminary pages. Yale *B 7551* and Princeton *C 0171* are first proofs of the title page with the author as 'R. L. Stevenson', the publication date as 1885, and date-stamped '14 Nov. 85'. On the Princeton copy, Stevenson has crossed out the two initials of his first names and substituted 'Robert Louis'. On the upper right-hand corner the printer has written (presumably after the return of the page with corrections) 'impose with halftitle dedication & contents'. This calls for the preparation of the multiple-page frames of typesetting to produce the first half-length signature of four leaves containing all the front matter (the first page of the text starts with the second, eight-leaf signature 'B').[12]

Second proofs of the title page (with author's name in full, publication date still 1885), together with contents page and (non-verse) dedication, are held by the Beinecke Library (*B 7552*). They are dated by hand '19/11/85' and bear the printer's request 'Kindly return for press by next post'. The printing must therefore have been concluded by the end of November, with the title-page dated '1886' printed – or reprinted – after the decision to postpone publication, on or shortly before 28 November (see below, p. 183), but with '1885' hand-corrected to '1886' on the paper cover.

It was probably when returning these last proofs that Stevenson inserted the verse dedication. This derives from the second stanza of a two-stanza poem given to Katherine De Mattos in May 1885 and transcribed in Colvin's galley proofs and printed in his *Letters of Robert Louis Stevenson to his Family and Friends* (1899, Vol. II, p. 6).[13] This poem also exists in a manuscript version (*B 7007*) with a single change in the direction of the Dedication, so it could be a copy made in the process of adapting the poem for this later use.

Notes

1 Gribbel Sale at Parke-Bernet, Sale 223 (30 October to 1 November 1940), Lot 720 'An Unpublished Portion of "Dr Jekyll and Mr Hyde" ' (Beinecke Uncat. MS vault 805, Collector's files relating to R. L. Stevenson, Box 1, Folder vol. II D).

2 The leaves are 199 mm high by 159–62 mm wide (depending on how the edge nearest the notebook binding has been cropped), with twenty feint blue-green lines and no ruled margin.

3 Sold at the 1914 Stevenson sale (Anderson Galleries of New York, 23–5 November 1914), Item 321. According to the catalogue, the page begins 'I have observed that when I wore the semblance of Edward Hyde ...' and (tantalisingly) it 'Differs from the printed text and has two long passages which have not been printed'. A copy of the catalogue in the Beinecke Library, has the following annotation: 'Owned by Wm Evarts Benjamin'. There can be no doubt that it is p. 85 missing from a sequence in *B 6934*: the last words on the extant p. 84 are 'And in so far I was' followed by the catchword 'doubtless'; *MS* and *1886L* have exactly the same words at this point followed by 'doubtless right' and then word-for-word the first sentence quoted in the catalogue.

4 Veeder thinks that Stevenson must have paused here and continued on a series of lost final pages in the whirl of 'his white-hot labors' (Veeder, p. 4). In support of this he cites *MS* p. 39, which similarly ends early and in mid-sentence, and claims that anyway there is no indication of any new draft. *MS* p. 39 is a cancelled rough try-out sheet, however, and there is no other example of Stevenson stopping mid-sentence, mid-line, short of the page end and then continuing on the next page. It is possible that Stevenson, close to the end of the text, felt the need to change the whole drift of the passage (notably different from the final version), so decided to tackle it directly on the final draft, *MS*.

5 1952 memorandum by George K. Boyce, curator of the Morgan Library referring to a letter from the dealers Dodd and Livingston dated 9 June 1911 (Morgan Library archives, qu. Veeder 1988, pp. 4–5).

6 Harry Glemby's book collection (more than a fifth of it Stevenson items) was sold at the Anderson Galleries, New York, 16 November 1926; *ND2* is Lot 475 (the catalogue is in the Beinecke Library *B 1794*).

7 *MS* is written on foolscap sheets of laid paper 330 by 200 mm, with (on both sides of the sheet) a top margin, thirty-six feint blue-green lines and a vertical red line creating a left-hand margin. The paper has two variants of watermark: crowned oval with Britannia (facing left) over copperplate lettering 'A&DP', and 'A & D PADON / EXTRA STRONG'. For more details, see Veeder, p. 4.

8 Folio 9 in the Silverado Museum has no signs of folding, but has no signs of ruled lines either, though size and watermark (the version without Britannia) are identical to the other folios: the lines have faded and the folding become

imperceptible because the sheet was framed and exposed to sunlight for many years.

9 Letter accompanying *MA 2075* in the Pierpont Morgan Library.

10 Memo by the curator of the Pierpont Morgan archives George K. Boyce, 5 May 1952 in the Morgan archives, qu. Veeder, p. 5.

11 For the sale, see letter dated 15 September 1941 to E. J. Beinecke saying that the page is being sent (Beinecke Library, Uncat MS Vault 805, 'E. J. Beinecke's Collector's Files relating to RL Stevenson': Box 3, File vol. VI, H). For the donation, see letter accompanying Morgan *MA 1375*, copy in Beinecke *B 6935*.

12 This page was sold by Anderson Galleries of New York in 1914 (Part I, Lot 583) and is reproduced in the catalogue following p. 68.

13 Presented to Katherine De Mattos at the Stevensons' fifth wedding anniversary dinner (at which each guest received a poem) in Bournemouth on 19 May 1885. The original manuscript is untraced, but it is printed together with this date in the galley proofs of transcribed manuscript letters that Colvin had made as working documents for his edition of the letters. He then printed it undated in the *Letters*, immediately after Stevenson's letter to Katherine (1 January 1886) that had accompanied a presentation copy of *JH*. Colvin thereby gives the erroneous impression that the full poem accompanied the letter; cf. also *LETBM*, vol. V, p. 168. For the full poem, see Explanatory Notes.

History of Composition and Publication

COMPOSITION

The year 1885 was important for Stevenson's career as a writer: he published three volumes, *The Dynamiter*, *Prince Otto*, and *A Child's Garden of Verses*, as well as 'Markheim', 'Olalla' and 'On Style in Literature: Its Technical Elements' – a collection of works that must have impressed contemporaries by its variety alone. Unfortunately, these publications did not bring in enough money for the expenses of a permanent household in Bournemouth and for his stepson Lloyd's education, and so most of the year was marked by worryingly uncertain finances.[1] This situation was made worse by Stevenson's poor health which led not only to doctors' and chemists' bills but occasionally prevented him from working and therefore from earning money: 'Doctor, rent, chemist, are all threatening; sickness has bitterly delayed my work', he writes in a letter of December 1884 (*LETBM*, vol. V, p. 45).

The year started with lung haemorrhages ('Bloody Jack') which kept him in bed over Christmas (ibid., p. 52 note). In the period of slightly better health that followed he was able to work hard ('I am a machine of work' he says on 27 January, and 'O, I am busy!' on 30 February; ibid., pp. 73, 80). Then in March he suffered from pleurisy and general exhaustion from overwork, and was unable to write. In this month he complains of 'dry-rot', by which he seems to mean a general run-down state.[2] On 7 April, just before moving house to Skerryvore (the Bournemouth house given to RLS's wife Fanny by his father), he coughed up blood and did so again in the second half of the month, 'the worst hemorrhage he has ever had in England accompanied by congestion of the brain'.³ The erratic 'mad' behaviour associated with the latter was probably caused by fever and possibly also by the ergotine used to stop internal bleeding.⁴ In the same letter Fanny says 'I had to lift Louis in and out of bed ten times in one night. He was quite off his head and could not be contradicted because he was bleeding at the lungs at the same time, and got into such furies when I wasn't quick enough.' And in late April/early May she writes to Colvin, 'Louis is much better today, but mentally more or less an idiot ... I am more than ever convinced that it is softening of the brain';⁵ and to Henley in the same period 'Ever since the slight congestion of the brain he has been absolutely unable as his mind at all [sic]'. She goes on to say that he had written twenty pages or so 'full of utter nonsense', which he said 'was his greatest work', but 'fortunately he has forgotten about it now'.⁶ Stevenson himself at the end of April admits 'I cannot write ... I don't know what has happened' and that he is 'once more dry rotten' (ibid., p. 106).

After recovering from this bout of debilitating illness, he passed the summer with numerous visits from family and friends but unable to do much writing (in November 1885 he says he is working hard 'to make up for my six months' uselessness', *LETBM*, vol. V, p. 153). All went well with his health until the start of an intended holiday in Devon, when he had a 'dreadful hemmorrhage' in Exeter on 27 August, again accompanied by erratic behaviour (ibid., pp. 125–6) and was forced to stay there to recover.

Some time after his return home on 12 September, *Jekyll and Hyde* was begun. The story of the composition can be reconstructed from Stevenson's letters of late 1885 and early 1886; from his newspaper interviews in New York 1887 and San Francisco 1888; and from his account in 'A Chapter on Dreams', written in October 1887.⁷ Stevenson's wife and stepson, Lloyd Osbourne (then seventeen), give brief but valuable information in letters in late 1885, but did not leave fuller accounts of events until 1900, in written replies to queries from Stevenson's biographer, Graham Balfour, and after that in versions published in 1905 (Fanny) and 1924 (Lloyd).⁸ Also present around the house at the time was Stevenson's doctor, Dr Thomas Bodley Scott, who gave an account published in 1922, and the maid Valentine Roch who gives some information in a newspaper interview of 1893.⁹ Some others give accounts based on what they heard from those present: Andrew Lang (from Stevenson) in 1886 and 1895; Stevenson's stepdaughter Belle (from Stevenson, Fanny and Lloyd) in 1944 (and from her, Limedorfer in 1900 and Elsie Caldwell in 1960); and Nellie Sanchez in 1920 (from Fanny).¹⁰ Stevenson's cousin Graham Balfour gives an account published in 1901 possibly based on conversations with Stevenson and certainly on conversations and correspondence with Fanny and Lloyd.¹¹ All these later accounts are open to the influence of imperfect memory (things get forgotten, confused with similar incidents, or misordered) and of narrative creativeness and the normal evolution of oft-repeated stories (things get simplified or emphasised, or influenced by similar stories).¹²

Back in Bournemouth from Exeter, then, Stevenson was searching for a subject for a story ('For two days I went about racking my brains for a plot of any sort'), aware that he urgently needed to make some money in the face of financial difficulties ('Dreams', *TUS*, vol. XXX, p. 52). He told his doctor that he was looking for a subject for 'a shilling shocker', a sensational or supernatural tale; and we may suppose he was thinking of the Christmas market for ghost stories for which he had supplied material in the past.[13] He says that 'I had long been trying to write a story on ... that strong sense of man's double being which must at times come in upon and overwhelm the mind of every thinking creature' (ibid., p. 51). This is confirmed by Andrew Lang, who says that Stevenson had talked about writing such a story ten or so years before.[14] Fanny says that early memories of the story of Deacon Brodie of Edinburgh ('respectable artisan by day, a burglar at night') and then years afterwards the deep impression made on him 'by a paper he read in a French scientific journal on sub-consciousness' combined to create an interest in the idea of the double life, expressed in the play *Deacon Brodie*,[15] 'Markheim' (1885) and finally *Jekyll and Hyde*.[16]

He had already used the theme of the double in 'Markheim' (1885), and in 'The Travelling Companion' (started 1881 but destroyed in 1886 or '87).[17] 'Markheim' also has elements of the Christmas story uncanny that can additionally be found (together with less explicit forms of doubling) in 'Thrawn Janet' (1881), 'The Merry Men' (1882), 'The Body Snatcher' (1884), and 'Olalla' (1885), the work he wrote in the period immediately after finishing *JH*.

For the first time since Fanny had known him, Stevenson's sleep became restless and he went through a period of headaches and nightmares.[18] It was during one of these (as he told Charles Longman), that he dreamed 'the main incident' of *JH*;[19] Lang in 1886 (p. 441) says that the 'central incident ... the awful effect produced on Hyde when he swallows the mysterious potion ... was beheld by the author in a dream' and in the 1887 newspaper interview Stevenson says 'all I dreamed about Dr Jekyll was that one man was being pressed into a cabinet, when he swallowed a drug and changed into another being'. In the fullest account, however, he says he not only dreamed this scene ('in which Hyde, pursued for some crime, took the powder and underwent the change in the presence of his pursuers') but also 'the scene at the window'.[20] The latter must refer to the glimpse of Jekyll's transformation at the window. Veeder's suggestion that it refers to the Carew murder is unlikely since this scene is viewed *from* a high window, it does not take place 'at' a window. In addition, in 'Dreams' he says that, apart from the scenes mentioned, the dream gave him 'the central idea of a voluntary change becoming involuntary', an element which can be seen as deriving from the 'scene at the window' corresponding to ch. 8.[21]

The nightmare made him cry out: 'cries of horror' for Fanny (Balfour 1901, p. 13), though Stevenson says that they were more like grunts of appreciation at a good story:

I am quite in the habit of dreaming stories ... They sometimes come to me in the form of nightmares, in so far that they make me cry out aloud. But I am never deceived by them. Even when fast asleep I know that it is I who am inventing, and when I cry out it is with gratification to know that the story is so good. So soon as I awake, and it always awakens me when I get on a good thing, I set to work and put it together. ('Dreams', p. 85)

When the alarmed Fanny woke him he said 'Why did you wake me? I was dreaming a fine bogey tale.'[22]

He started writing early next day: Fanny reports that 'At daybreak he was working with feverish activity on the new book', and when his doctor came on his visit that same morning he greeted him with 'I've got my shilling shocker', and he 'described a dream that he had had in the night' (Scott 1922). Stevenson's stepson, Lloyd Osbourne, learnt about the new story that lunchtime: 'he came down to luncheon in a very preoccupied frame of mind; hurried through his meal – an unheard-of thing for him to do – and on leaving said he was working with extraordinary success on a new story that had come to him in a dream, and that he was not to be interrupted or disturbed even if the house caught fire' (Osbourne 1924, pp. 62–3; *TUS*, vol. V, p. ix).

Stevenson's first reference to the new work is in an undated letter to Colvin (but it must be late September or early October): 'I am pouring forth a penny (12 penny) dreadful; they call it ... Dr. Jekyll' (*LETBM*, vol. V, p. 128). In the same period, and possibly earlier, Fanny writes to Colvin:

> Again Louis is better, and possessed by a story that he will try to work at. To stop him seems to annoy him to such a degree that I am letting him alone as the better alternative; but I fear it will be only energy wasted, as all his late work has been. For the last few days he has, however, seemed much cleared in his mind about things, but has been suffering from dreadful nightmares and headaches at night. (*B 3648*; qu. *LETBM*, vol. V, p. 128 note 2)

Since she makes no reference to the subject of the story, not even in relation to her fear that it might be unpublishable (presented here as a prediction based on recent experience of other writings),[23] it would seem that she has not yet read the story or heard it read. In all probability, therefore, she is here referring to the first (destroyed) draft, and the nightmares mentioned would therefore include the very one that set off the writing of the story.

On 4 October (the first dated reference) Lloyd writes, clearly after having heard the story read to him (so, as we shall see, after the first draft had been finished), 'Louis is doing very well though still weak. He has been writing a most terrible story which he said occurred to him in the night. It is certainly one of the most ghostly and unpleasant stories I have ever heard. He is still writing it' (*LETBM*, vol. V, p. 128 note 2). By 12 October the title of the story is known to the family as Stevenson writes to Fanny (in London) 'I drive on with *Jekyll*, bankruptcy at my heels'.

The first draft was furiously written in three days (RLS 1888: 'The draft I made in three days'). Lloyd says 'For three days a sort of hush descended on "Skerryvore"; we all went about, servants and everybody, in a tiptoeing silence; passing Stevenson's door I would see him sitting up in bed, filling page after page, and apparently never pausing for a moment. At the end of three days the mysterious task was finished' (Osbourne 1924, *TUS*, vol. V, p. ix). Although Fanny says in 1905 that the first version was of a similar length to the final version, the three days of writing suggest that it was a shorter or incomplete version. Belle Strong heard Stevenson tell the story of composition in Samoa on several occasions and insists that it was 'just a few pages ... What he had written was only a few pages' (Strong 1944).

Some time before 4 October, then, Stevenson read out to Fanny and Lloyd what he had written. Only Lloyd has left an account of the event (Osbourne 1900): 'I remember that first reading as though it were yesterday. He came down stairs in a fever; read nearly half the book aloud; and then, while we were still gasping, he was away again, and busy writing' (Osbourne 1900; Balfour 1901, p. 13). In 1924 he writes,

> At the end of three days the mysterious task was finished, and he read aloud to my mother and myself the first draft of *The Strange Case of Dr. Jekyll and Mr. Hyde*.
> I listened to it spellbound. Stevenson, who had a voice the greatest actor might have envied, read it with an intensity that made shivers run up and down my spine (Osbourne 1924, p. x).

Fanny then made her criticisms of this first version. Stevenson was not always happy with his wife's role as adviser, as Fanny herself reveals: 'He asked me, as usual, to make no criticisms until the first draft was done. As he didn't like to get tired by discussing my proposed changes to his work it was his custom that I should put my criticisms in writing' (FS 1900a, f. 158r; qu. Frayling, *Nightmare: The Birth of Horror*, p. 148). Clearly, at an early stage of their marriage, Stevenson had negotiated a limitation to her interventions in order to avoid disputes. Lloyd, writing many years afterwards in 1924, claims to remember a full-scale row after the first reading, sparked off by Fanny's negative criticisms and chary praise: 'the scene became so painful that I went away, unable to bear it any longer. It was with a sense of tragedy that I listened to their voices from the adjoining room' (Osbourne 1924, *TUS*, vol. V, p. ix). Afterwards he returned to the room to find his mother alone:

> Then we heard Louis descending the stairs, and we both quailed as he burst in as though to continue the argument even more violently than before. But all he said was: 'You are right! I have absolutely missed the allegory, which after all, is the whole point of it – the very essence of it.' And with that, as though enjoying my mother's discomfiture and her ineffectual start to prevent him, he threw the manuscript into the fire! Imagine my feelings – my mother's feelings – as we saw it blazing up; as we saw those precious pages wrinkling and blackening and turning into flame! (ibid., p. xi)

This artistically shaped melodramatic scene of entry, declamation and irreversible act would seem to be an invention of Lloyd's who was writing more than thirty-five years after the event. It certainly contradicts his mother's earlier version written to Graham Balfour:

> I left my paper [of comments] with Louis, who was in the bedroom writing in bed. After quite a long interval his bell rang for me, and Lloyd and I went upstairs. As I entered the door Louis pointed with a long dramatic finger (you know) to a pile of ashes on the hearth of the fireplace saying that I was right, and there was the tale. (FS 1900a; Balfour 1901, p. 13)

It seems clear that both Lloyd and Fanny were present at the first reading which was followed by Fanny's verbal and written criticisms; they were both present at the first news of the burning of the manuscript and of the indication of the ashen evidence for this which probably took place in Stevenson's bedroom (where he wrote most of the first version). Graham Balfour adds a further pictorial detail (either from conversations with Stevenson in Samoa, where he lived from August to November 1892 and again from June to October 1894, or from conversations with Fanny then or afterwards) when he says that Stevenson did not even speak when the burning was revealed: 'She gave the paper to her husband and left the room. After a while his bell rang; on her return she found him sitting up in bed (the clinical thermometer in his mouth), pointing with a long denunciatory finger to a pile of ashes. He had burned the entire draft' (Balfour 1901, p. 13).

What were Fanny's criticisms? In 1900 she says

> In this tale I felt, and still feel that he was hampered by his dream. The powder – which I thought might be changed – he couldn't eliminate because he saw it so plainly in his dream. In the original story he had Jekyll bad all through, and working for the Hyde change only for a disguise. I wrote pages of criticism, pointing out that he had here a great moral allegory that the dream was obscuring. I didn't like the opening, which was confused – again the dream – and proposed that Hyde should run over the child showing that he was an evil force without humanity. (FS 1900a; Balfour 1901, p. 13)

So Fanny thought that the character of Jekyll should not be 'bad all through', using Hyde 'only for a disguise', and that the story could become 'a great moral allegory' (perhaps of the struggle against temptation and sin). In 1905 she repeats her idea that the dream had too great an influence on the writing: 'the first draft ... was ... re-written from another point-of-view, – that of the allegory, which was palpable and had yet been missed, probably from haste, and the compelling influence of the dream' (FS 1905; *TUS*, vol. V, p. xiv).

Concerning the opening, Fanny's words tell us that in the first draft there was probably a vague and allusive encounter between Hyde and 'the child' – the child that was already in the original version (if she had suggested both child and trampling, it would have been more normal to say 'I proposed that Hyde should run over a child').

Fanny claims that she objected to 'the powder' (a chemical source of change – rather than, perhaps, the intervention of an uncanny supernatural force) but, in a later letter to Balfour, she admits that this was not strictly true: 'I had an afterthought about the powder, but after the burning scene dared not mention it'[24] – she was here probably influenced by Henry James's criticism in 1888 where he criticised 'the business with the powders'.[25]

After the burning of this first draft, Balfour says 'It was written again in three days' and 'after this he was working hard for a month or six weeks in bringing it into its present form' (Balfour 1901, p. 14). A few months after publication (1 March 1886) Stevenson himself says '*Jekyll* was written, rewritten, re-rewritten, and printed inside ten weeks' (*LETBM*, vol. V, p. 216), and in 1888 he says 'I think I occupied about six weeks, or something like that, in writing it. The draft I made in three days' (RLS 1888).

These various clues to the overall period of composition correspond with one another: there are exactly eleven weeks between the return from Exeter on 12 September and the dispatch from London of the second proofs of the title page, dated 19 November and containing the request 'kindly return for press by next post', a period containing 'inside ten weeks' but not much more. This suggests that the famous nightmare took place in the week or so following the return from Exeter. The period from such a date for the nightmare to completion of *MS* on (or just before) 28 October would therefore be about six weeks, which ties in with Stevenson's three days and six weeks.

The number of more-or-less complete drafts must have been three, corresponding to the 'written, rewritten, re-rewritten' sequence of Stevenson's 1886 account. These should be the destroyed three-day first draft, *ND2* and *MS*. The existence of a three-day post-burning draft is attested only in later accounts by Fanny Stevenson (1905), Lloyd Osbourne (1924), and (on their testimonies) Graham Balfour (1901, p. 14). There may well have been partial drafts after the burning (the fragment we have called *ND1* may be a relic of such a try-out), though there is no strong evidence for a full-length version before *ND2*, which we may take to have been the penultimate draft and in front of Stevenson as he wrote *MS*.

It is unlikely that *ND2* is this three-day post-burning draft: it consisted of 103 notebook leaves which could not have been written in three days, since this would mean an unlikely thirty-four leaves (or 7500 finished words) a day.[26] To get an idea of the improbability of such a speed, we can compare it with some cases where Stevenson expressed satisfaction at the amount of writing he managed to do. The first fifteen chapters of *Treasure Island* were written with great facility in the autumn of 1881 at the rate a chapter a day (cf. RLS's essay 'My First Book'), which makes 2000 finished words a day (plus those that were cancelled). In December 1884, Stevenson shows satisfaction with his speed in writing 'On Style in Literature: Its Technical Elements', when he says, 'I have sent off a long, long, elaborate article on style. The work of five days in bed. Five days, sir!' (*LETBM*, vol. V, p. 55). This essay is 6600 words long – so 1300 finished words a day. If we double this to allow for two full drafts in the same period we get to 2600 words a day.

From these testimonies we can say that Stevenson thought it an achievement of note when he managed about 2000 words a day, a total that is so far short of the 7500 words a day needed to write *ND* in three days as to exclude this possibility.

The accounts of Fanny and Lloyd also exaggerate the brevity of the overall period of composition. In his 1924 account, almost forty years after the events, Lloyd claims that Stevenson worked on the first draft 'for three days', burnt and rewrote it in 'another three days' and finally 'copied out the whole in another two days, and had it in the post on the third!' (Osbourne 1924, p. xi). This 'three days plus three days plus three days' reminds us of how myths tend to accumulate repeated elements, and is possibly influenced by Fanny's erroneous version of events published in 1905: 'In three days the first draft ... was finished, only to be entirely destroyed and immediately re-written ... In another three days the book ... was ready for the press' (FS 1905, *TUS*, vol. V, p. xvii). The calculation of two writings-out of the book, already slightly exaggerated in Fanny's account, 'sixty thousand words' (when the single text is just over 25,000 words), is further inflated to 'Sixty-four thousand words' in Lloyd's account. The unconscious (and quite normal) aim of both writers would seem to be to emphasise the exceptional nature of the text and to encourage its reading as a tale dictated by the subconscious in a furious episode of composition.[27] As we have seen, Stevenson in 1888 said that he took about six weeks, his letters show a period of continuous composition from late September to the end of October,[28] and if we needed further proof, there is Thomas Sullivan's report of his conversation with Stevenson in 1887, when the latter told him that '*Jekyll and Hyde* was written very slowly, and much material was discarded'.[29]

Concerning the circumstances of composition, it is notable that Stevenson himself does not mention the criticisms of his wife or the burning, nor does he underline the rapidity of composition: the first perhaps too painful, the second irrelevant, and the third not really true. He does, however, mention the dream: he tells Charles Longman about it in a letter (cf. Lang 1895b), he gives his permission for Lang to mention the fact in his review in his 'At the Sign of the Ship' column in *Longman's Magazine* in February 1886,[30] and centres 'A Chapter on Dreams' around the origin of the tale in a dream and in the unconscious workings of the imagination (his 'Brownies'). The foregrounding of the dream origin of a literary work that explores the unconscious belongs to a long tradition: while Horace Walpole describes such an origin of *The Castle of Otranto* (1765) only in a private letter,[31] Mary Shelley publicly informs the reader of the dream origin of *Frankenstein* (1811) in her 1831 'Introduction' and (as in Stevenson's story) has a *mise en abyme* nightmare in the text itself, and Coleridge attaches a 'Preface' to 'Kubla Khan' from its first publication in 1816, explaining the dream origin of the poem and presenting it as a 'psychological curiosity'.

The completion of the final version (*MS*) is reported in a letter dated 28 October ('a story being done, I am at some liberty to write', *LETBM*, vol. V, p. 143) and the publisher, Charles Longman, acknowledged receipt of it in a letter of 31 October.[32] Stevenson offered the story for publication in *Longman's Magazine* and (probably working on two fronts as a hedge against unforeseen difficulties) he had also mentioned it to Charles Gray Robinson as a possible contribution to the Christmas number of his *Court and Society Review*. Longman's reply must have included acceptance to publish, as in a letter postmarked the day after, 1 November, Fanny tells Robinson 'A note has come from Longman which makes it impossible for Louis to propose the taking back of "Jeckyl"'.[33]

When Charles Longman had read it, he immediately decided (and probably said so in the 31 October letter) that it was unsuitable for magazine publication, as he wrote to Graham Balfour in October 1900:

> I read the story with intense interest, and could not put it down till I had finished it. Naturally I regarded it as an admirable story for the magazine, but it would have been necessary to divide it into two or more parts, and I thought that it was a tale which should be read straight through not at an interval of a month. I accordingly wrote to Stevenson asking him if I might publish it complete as a shilling book instead of running it through the magazine. He wrote back that he would have no objection, but that the lack of ready cash was of importance to him and that he knew I should pay him so much at once if it appeared in the magazine, whereas if it was issued separately it might fail & bring him in nothing. This difficulty was early met by making him an advance payment on account of royalties. (NLS *MS 9895, Balfour Biography Notebook*, ff. 111–12)

Negotiations must have taken place with a rapid exchange of letters because the contract was dated 3 November, the cheque for the advance on royalties was paid on 6 November, and on 12 November Stevenson was already correcting the proofs.[34]

The decision to publish in book form created another problem, since Stevenson had promised his next book to Chatto and Windus. On 7 November he writes to Andrew Chatto saying that 'I shall have the air of playing fast and loose with our agreement', but 'Considerations with which I have nothing to do made Mr Longman rather object to put the story in the *Magazine*, and he offered me instead, which was quite foreign to my intention, to bring it out as a volume'. Since 'hunger was in the bank account' he accepted the offer rather than delay further by offering it to Chatto as agreed (*LETBM*, vol. V, p. 152–3).

Stevenson was to receive one-sixth of the cover price (2d. a copy, 3d. for the cloth version), and Longman agreed to pay an advance payment of royalties on the first 10,000 copies (i.e. £83 6s. 8d.), plus half the proceeds of overseas' sales. Longman's agent in New York then made a separate agreement with Scribner's Sons on 16 December 1885 that specified royalty payments of 10 per cent on the retail price of the cloth edition only (but apparently omitted to state that these were to be shared equally between publisher and author, a condition of the London contract signed with RLS)[35] and £20 to Longman for advanced sheets of the London edition (to allow publication of the 'Authorised Edition' in New York slightly before London and give Scribner's some advantage over inevitable pirate editions).[36]

The original idea to publish the book for Christmas was still the plan on 17 November when Longman sent Scribner's a set of uncorrected proofs and proposed an American edition (on the request of Stevenson himself),[37] though not for 'simultaneous publication' as the work was to be published 'very shortly in this country'. The decision to publish after Christmas was made on or just before 28 November for, on that date, Longman sent Scribner's a telegram and a letter asking them to postpone any publication until January and (in the new circumstances) offering them simultaneous publication.

The change of publication date is explained by Charles Longman: 'The little book was printed but when it was ready the bookstalls were already full of Christmas numbers &c., and the trade would not look at it. We therefore withdrew it till after Christmas.'[38] In the letter to Scribner's of 28 November, however, Longman had said the postponement was 'on account of the pressure of business in other directions'. In any case, Longman had decided right from the end of November to put off publication until after Christmas.[39]

FIRST EDITIONS

The first London edition was published by Longmans, Green, and Co. (on 9 January 1886) in two formats: 1. with light-brown (buff) paper wrappers, rather crude blue ornamental lines and blocks, and with blue and red lettering on the front, with at the bottom '1885 / Price One Shilling', the last number of the date being neatly changed in pen to 6;[40] 2. bound in boards covered with salmon-coloured cloth, without the year and the price on the front and with flower and leaf endpapers, which sold for 1s. 6d. These two versions (which differ only in the cover), though showing no attempt at elegance, have spacious typesetting with good margins and chapters beginning on a fresh page – they therefore distance themselves from cramped cheap editions with small type and little spacing. The first printing (December 1885) was of 10,000 copies (cloth and paper wrappers together); of the 10,000 printed for the 'Second Edition' (January 1886), 1000 were probably in cloth.[41]

The first New York edition was published by Charles Scribner's Sons four days earlier on 5 January 1886 in two equivalent formats: 1. in yellow paper wrappers with 'Price Twenty-five Cents.' (the equivalent of about 6d., so slightly cheaper than the London edition) and '1886' on the front, with a more studied layout and typography than the London edition; 2. bound in boards covered in olive-green cloth. This latter was sold at $1, equivalent to about 2s., so more expensive than the equivalent London edition. It was also prepared with greater care: the thicker laid paper (the London edition uses lighter wove paper) makes it into more of a 'book' than the slim London booklet; the lettering on the cover is in gold not black; it has title, author, and publisher on the spine (where the London edition is blank); and the top edge of the pages are gilt. (The two main New York formats were therefore distinct in both paper and binding, while the pages printed in London, being identical, could be used to produce either of the two versions.) The first New York printing was of 3000 copies in paper and 1250 in cloth.[42]

By the Longman annual accounts' day of 1 June, they had produced (in seven printings) a total of 43,000 copies (2200 of which were bound in cloth), of which they had sold 39,572.[43] As this figure shows, sales soon passed the number corresponding to the advance on royalties and so Stevenson received what must have been very welcome cheques in February, April, and June for a total of £255 7s.[44] By his death, Stevenson had earned £690 from the Longman editions.

In the following year to June 1887, Longman printed a further 9000 (reaching the 'Eleventh Edition') and sold 10,962. Sales then quietened down, apart from a secondary peak in printing and sales in the year to June 1889 (with 23,000 copies printed between March and August 1888 for the 'Thirteenth' to the 'Sixteenth Edition' and over 18,000 sold, numbers which suggest a bulk purchase). Sales also revived with Stevenson's death (6000 being printed in December 1894 in the 'Nineteenth Edition'), after which Longman also began producing a range of other versions: *Strange Case of Dr Jekyll and Mr Hyde with Other Fables* (1896), in an edition of 500 copies, with the same text issued in the 'Silver Library' from the following year; a 'Special Edition' (1901) at 5s.; and editions in the Pocket Library (1908) at 2s. (cloth), and 3s. (leather).[45]

On 24 February, seven weeks after publication, Scribner's sent Stevenson a royalty payment of £60 11s. 10d. Calculating five dollars to the pound,[46] this would have been just over $300; if Stevenson was paid a tenth of the $1 cover price of the cloth format only, then this would represent royalties on 3000 copies, which would mean that Scribner's reprinted the cloth version very quickly. If, by some misunderstanding, paper wrapper sales were included (the Scribner's annotation, see note 35 below, mentions only "10% to Stevenson"), then it would represent sales of over 7000 copies (about the rate of sales per month of both versions of the London edition in the first six months). Almost 20,000 had been sold by April, and printing of the fortieth thousand was reached in 1887.[47]

By 1900, Longman had sold just under 94,000 copies in various editions. The pirated American editions (of which there were at least sixteen before 1900)[48] together with the Scribner's editions probably sold 'not less than a quarter of a million copies', according to Graham Balfour.

A few corrections of obvious mistakes in typesetting were made to these 1886 editions in later printings,[49] but no entirely new settings of the text were made by Longman or Scribner's in Stevenson's lifetime.

Notes

1 Financial troubles are already referred to in letters of November 1884, when he mentions 'some bills outstanding; Scott [his doctor] not paid' (cf. *LETBM*, vol. V, p. 21; cf. also pp. 23, 26, 33), and then in 1885 (pp. 64, 93), including the period of composition of *Jekyll and Hyde* (pp. 128, 135, 136, 141, 216); Stevenson repeats the story of financial hardship during the composition period in 'A Chapter on Dreams', and in an interview in the New York *Herald* on 8 September 1887 in which he says 'I was very hard up for money, and I felt that I had to do something' (J. A. Hammerton [ed.], *Stevensoniana* 2nd ed., Edinburgh, 1907, p. 84).

2 In October 1884 he complains of 'the feeling of illness and prostration and mental imbecility and giddiness and rot'; in March 1885 he says 'I am so dry-rotten that I can do nothing' (*LETBM*, vol. V, pp. 16, 90). In May he says 'I am suffering from marine cachexia: which I used to call dry rot'; this type of cachexia (a word from the Greek for 'bad condition', now usually applied to conditions of uncontrollable weight loss) was hypothesised by Dr Dobell of Bournemouth and seems to refer to a state of liver and associated digestive disorders (*LETBM*, vol. V, p. 109 and note).

3 Letter from Fanny to Colvin (*B 3640*; second half of April 1885; published in E. V. Lucas, *The Colvins and their Friends*, London, Methuen, 1928, p. 161, where Mrs Sitwell is mistakenly described as the addressee). Prolonged intellectual exertion or anxiety was believed to cause increased blood flow in the brain leading to congestion and from this a variety of disorders (insomnia, mental confusion, manic behaviour, excitability, irritability etc.), cf. William Hammond, *A Treatise on the Diseases of the Nervous System*, New York, Appleton, 1893. Stevenson suggests that 'congestion of the brain' might be the cause of the 'exhilaration, nightmares, pomp of tongue' of those staying in the Alps – although these symptoms might equally be caused by 'a return of youth' since the 'blessedness of boyhood' has effects that are 'strangely similar' ('The Stimulation of the Alps', *Pall Mall Gazette*, 5 March 1881; *TUS*, vol. XXX, p. 158).

4 Commenting on Stevenson's 'mad behaviour' during his haemorrhage in Exeter five months later (see below) Fanny writes 'I think it must be the ergotine that affects his brain at such times' (*LETBM*, vol. V, p. 126). Ergotine is toxic and can have the following results:

> The nervous system is markedly affected, a series of nervous phenomena being the result. The patient first complains of creeping sensations in the limbs, as if an insect were running along the skin; sudden painful cramps or twitchings of the legs follow; the gait becomes staggering (ataxic); and convulsions, with loss of sensibility and motion, may ensue. These nervous effects are chiefly seen in cases of chronic 'ergotism', where the drug has been consumed in large quantity in rye bread; they have been met with clinically, and their origin has not so far been fully explained. (J. M. Bruce and W. J. Dilling, *Materia Medica and Therapeutics*, London, Cassell, 1921 [12th ed., 1st ed. 1884], p. 397).

5 *B 3641*, Lucas, *The Colvins and their Friends*, p. 162.

6 Beinecke Library, Uncat. MS Vault File (in 2001), acc. No. 20010222–j; parts of the text given in the Phillips catalogue (*Books, Atlases, Photographs & Manuscripts*, sale No. 30999, New Bond St, London, 17.11.00) and in *TLS* 3.11.00, p. 20. The 'utter nonsense ... greatest work' referred to in this letter is wrongly identified with *Jekyll and Hyde* in the sale catalogue: Ernest Mehew

in the *TLS* points out that this is impossible since there is a reference to Henry James still coming every evening (May–June 1885) and *JH* cannot have been begun before September. The letter was probably written in early May and refers to the illness of late April.

7 (a) *LETBM*, vol. V; (b) New York *Herald*, 8 September 1887, reprinted in Hammerton, *Stevensoniana*, pp. 84–5 (henceforth RLS 1887); San Francisco *Examiner*, 8 June 1888, cutting in Scrapbook 3, 1887–90 (Monterey Stevenson House), p. 60, (henceforth RLS 1888); (c) 'A Chapter on Dreams'. *Scribner's Magazine* 3 (January 1888; written October 1877, cf. Roger G. Swearingen, *The Prose Writings of Robert Louis Stevenson*, Hamden, CT, Archon, p. 117) (henceforth 'Dreams').

8 (a) Letters in the Beinecke Library, in part quoted in *LETBM*, vol. V and in Lucas, *The Colvins and their Friends*; (b) (i) Fanny Stevenson (May 1900), answer to Graham Balfour's list of questions, Balfour, *Notes and Papers of Sir Graham Balfour: Balfour Biography Notebook*, NLS MS 9895, ff. 157–8 (FS 1900a); (ii) Fanny Stevenson annotations on Balfour's typescript, *Notebook, n.d., used by Balfour in writing his biography* NLS MS 9903, p. 217 (FS 1900b); (iii) Lloyd Osbourne (*c.* 1900), untitled note in Balfour *Notebook*, NLS MS 9895, p. 217 (Osbourne 1900); all three of these notes are quoted in part (with a few inessential variations) in Balfour 1901, vol. II, pp. 12–13, and the two by Fanny Stevenson are quoted (in part, but at greater length) in Christopher Frayling, *Nightmare: The Birth of Horror*, BBC Books, 1996, p. 148; (c) Fanny Van de Grift Stevenson, *Registration Prefaces to Robert Louis Stevenson's Works*, New York, Scribner's, 1905, reprinted in Scribner's Biographical Edition of the works of R. L. Stevenson, vol. XIV (1911), and *TUS*, vol. V, 'Prefatory Note', pp. xv–xviii (as well as in the equivalent Skerryvore and South Seas Editions of the Complete Works) (FS 1905); (d) Lloyd Osbourne, *An Intimate Portrait of R.L.S.*, New York, Scribner's, 1924, pp. 62–7, reprinted in *TUS*, vol. V, 'Preface', pp. vii–xiv (and in the Skerryvore and South Seas Editions) (Osbourne 1924).

9 (a) Dr T. Bodley Scott in Rosaline Masson (ed.), *I Can Remember Robert Louis Stevenson*, Edinburgh/London, Chambers, 1922, p. 213 (Scott 1922); (b) interview not traced but referred to by Elsie Noble Caldwell, *Last Witness for Robert Louis Stevenson*, Norman, University of Oklahoma Press, 1960, p. 101; Caldwell's book is based on conversations with Belle Strong 1930–53.

10 (a) Andrew Lang, *Longman's Magazine*, vol. VII No. 40 (February 1886), in his 'At the Sign of the Ship' column, pp. 441–2 (Lang 1886); Letter to *The Athenaeum*, No. 3507 (12 January 1895), p. 49 (Lang 1895a); Letter to *The Athenaeum*, No. 3511 (9 February 1995) p. 186 (qu. in part in *LETBM*, vol. V, p. 150 note) (Lang 1895b); (b) the memorandum dictated by Stevenson's stepdaughter, Isobel Field (previously Strong), 'Mrs R. L. Stevenson's part in the writing of Dr Jekyll and Mr Hyde' (*B 7372*), printed in part in Frayling, *Nightmare: The Birth of Horror*, p. 149 (Strong 1944); (c) Eugene Limedorfer, 'The Manuscript of Dr. Jekyll and Mr. Hyde', *The Bookman* 12(1), 1900, pp. 52, 58 (Limedorfer 1900); (d) Caldwell, *Last Witness*, p. 101 (Caldwell 1960); (e) Nellie Van de Grift Sanchez, *The Life of Mrs Robert Louis Stevenson*, London, Chatto & Windus, 1920, pp. 118–19 (Sanchez 1920).

11 Balfour 1901, vol. II, pp. 12–14.

12 Doubtless many people who met Stevenson would be curious about the writing of his most famous work. Belle says 'I heard R.L.S. tell this story not only to me, but to several others, such as visiting poets and literary men who came to Samoa' (IF 1944). Such questioning may have become unwelcome: Eugene Limedorfer (with information from Belle, though we must remember

his unreliability) says 'In his later years Stevenson did not like to refer at all to Jekyll and Hyde. He always said that the writing of the story was such a strain on him he could never forget it' (Limedorfer 1900, p. 58).

13 Oral 'winter's tales' of the supernatural, traditionally associated with hearthside narration (represented in the frame situation of Henry James's 'The Turn of the Screw', 1898), inspired the nineteenth-century literary genre of the 'ghost story'. An important early example is Scott's 'Wandering Willie's Tale' inserted in *Redgauntlet* (1824). Dickens also has an inserted ghost story in Chapter 29 of *The Pickwick Papers* (1836), 'The Story of the Goblins', where publication of the relevant monthly number, embedded narration, and the narrative itself are all located at Christmas. This temporal coincidence of narrative levels continues in *A Christmas Carol* (1843) and the annual series of novella-length Christmas Books and their imitations in the 1840s and '50s, which married a sentimental celebration of Christmas charity with the traditional supernatural elements. These supernatural themes, but without Dickensian sentimentality, continued to inspire shorter Christmas tales, 'the Christmas ghost story', set at Christmas or inserted in a framing narrative situation at the Christmas-night hearthside, published in annuals and in the Christmas numbers of magazines especially between about 1880 and 1930, and continuing at Christmas time today in broadcast versions on radio and television. Stevenson himself supplied four works for this market in this period: 'The Body Snatcher' for the 1884 *Pall Mall Christmas Extra*, 'Olalla' for the Christmas 1885 number of the *Court and Society Review*, 'Markheim' originally intended for the 1884 *Pall Mall Christmas Extra* but then published in Unwin's 1885 Christmas Annual entitled *The Broken Shaft: Tales of Mid-Ocean*, and 'The Misadventures of John Nicholson. A Christmas Story' for *Yule Tide ... Cassell's Christmas Annual* (1887). 'Markheim' and 'The Misadventures of John Nicholson' continue the Dickensian tradition of setting the narrative itself at Christmas time. The unresolved, uncanny narrative of *Jekyll and Hyde*, its promise of 'a strange story', and its mainly cold and night-time settings fit in with the Christmas tradition, and the reviewer in *The British Weekly* of 2 November 1888 claimed it as 'the greatest triumph extant in Christmas literature of the morbid kind' (Scrapbook 2, p. 87, Monterey Stevenson House). Its final exclusion of supernatural and external forces (despite the false scents of them in the narrative) would have made it atypical, however (for, while ghost stories like those of Le Fanu (d. 1873) leave uncertain whether the disturbances suffered by the haunted protagonists are of diabolical or psychological origin, they never exclude the uncanny supernatural as contribution or cause of the inner disturbance).

14 Andrew Lang in 1886 (for references, see note 10 above) says that after the dream, Stevenson

> instantly saw that his sleeping self had presented his waking sense with the keystone (so to speak) of an idea for a romance which had, at intervals, been present to his waking consciousness for many years. Long ago – ten years ago – Mr. Stevenson told some one, in conversation, about this idea as he had then conceived it.

The 'some one' was undoubtedly Lang himself who met Stevenson in Menton in 1874 and at intervals afterwards at the Savile Club in London. In 1905, Lang suggests it was in London that Stevenson told him about his idea: '... at the old Savile Club, in Savile Row, which had the tiniest and blackest of smoking-rooms. Here, or somewhere, he spoke to me of an idea of a tale, a Man who was Two Men' ('Recollections of Robert Louis Stevenson', *Adventures Among Books*, Longmans, 1905, p. 46, qu. R. C. Terry, *Robert Louis*

Stevenson. Interviews and Recollections, Iowa University Press, 1996, p. 59).

15 Written with Henley 1878–80, though Stevenson had written earlier versions 1864–9 (Swearingen, *The Prose Writings of Robert Louis Stevenson*, pp. 3, 4, 36–8).

16 FS 1905, *TUS*, vol. V, pp. xv, xvi. Fanny's reference to a paper on subconsciousness could easily be confusing a paper read afterwards. RLS says that he read the paper by Myers on the multiple personality case of 'Louis V[ivet]' after the publication of *JH* (interview in *The Argus*, 'Wellington, April 11 [1893]', Scrapbook 5 pp. 163–64, Monterey Stevenson House). Even assuming Fanny is correct, the article cannot be identified as there were too many French scientific periodicals with too many articles on subconsciousness and double personality in the period before 1886. The most likely case, however, would be that of the much-discussed Félida described by Dr Azam in four articles, the first three on the front page, of the *Revue scientifique*: two in 1876, and then in 1877 and 1878; the case is also described in the *Revue philosophique* in 1876. In 1886 F. W. H. Myers says that 'Felida's name ... is probably familiar to most of my readers' ('Multiplex Personality', *The Nineteenth Century* 20 [November 1886]: p. 648).

17 'I had even written one [a story on the strong sense of man's double being], *The Travelling Companion*, which was returned by an editor on the plea that it was a work of genius and indecent, and which I burned the other day on the ground that it was not a work of genius, and that *Jekyll* had supplanted it' ('Dreams', *TUS*, vol. XXX, pp. 51–2).

18 FS 1905, *TUS*, vol. V, p. xvi; *B 3648*, qu. in *LETBM*, vol. V, p. 128 note 2.

19 Stevenson to Charles Longman, *c.* 1 November 1885 (qu. in Lang 1895; cf. *LETBM*, vol. V, p. 150).

20 RLS 1887, qu. Hammerton, p. 5. Andrew Lang in 1886 tells how Stevenson was given the 'keystone' of his story in his dream: 'He saw Hyde chased into a mysterious recess, saw him take the drug, and was awakened by the terror of what followed.' Fanny says that she woke Stevenson 'at the first transformation scene' (Balfour 1901, p. 13).

21 William Veeder, 'Children of the Night', in *VH*, p. 112; 'Dreams', *TUS*, vol. XXX, p. 52.

22 Balfour 1901, p. 13; for a similar account, see also FS 1905, *TUS*, vol. V, p. xvi.

23 She is probably referring to the 'utter nonsense' written when Stevenson was 'off his head' due to fever and medication in late April and early May (see note 4 above).

24 FS 1900b; Frayling, *Nightmare: The Birth of Horror*, p. 148.

25 James probably made his criticisms known to RLS earlier, since already in 'Dreams' (written October 1887), Stevenson uses the identical phrase employed by James in his 1888 article when referring to 'the business of the powders, which so many have censured'.

26 The twenty-six-leaf fragment of *ND2* contains about 4500 uncancelled words or an average of about 175 finished words a leaf; 103 leaves would therefore have contained about 22,600 words.

27 William Beckford claimed that he wrote the Gothic novel *Vathek* 'at one sitting, and in French. It cost me three days and two nights of hard labour. I never took my clothes off the whole time.' Unfortunately, his correspondence shows that he spent 'years rather than days' in writing the book (E. Denison Ross, 'Introduction', *The History of the Caliph Vathek*, London, Methuen, 1901).

28 'I am very hard at work' (mid-October), 'I drive on with *Jekyll*' (20 October) (*LETBM*, vol. V, pp. 133, 135). In a letter postmarked 22 October RLS

complains of 'my work still moving with deliberate slowness – as a child might fill a sandbag with its little handfuls' (ibid., p. 136).

29 Thomas Russell Sullivan, *Passages from the Journal of Thomas Russell Sullivan, 1891–1903*, Boston, Houghton Mifflin, 1917, pp. 124. It is true that in a letter of 1886 RLS refers to the 'white-hot haste' of writing *JH* (*LETBM*, vol. V, p. 216), but this is in order to excuse himself for what his correspondent saw as a mistake.

30 Andrew Lang, letter to RLS (18 November 1885), in Marysa Demoor (ed.), *Dear Stevenson*, Leuven, Peeters, 1990, p. 91.

31 Letter to Wiliam Cole, 1765, qu. In *The Castle of Otranto*, ed. Michael Gamer, Harmondsworth, Penguin, 2001, p. xxiv.

32 *LETBM*, vol. V, p. 150 note 1. Charles Longman's reply has not survived but is referred to by Andrew Lang in a letter to the *Athenaeum*, 12 January 1895.

33 Fanny Stevenson to Charles Gray Robertson, *B 3726*, postmarked 'NO 1 85'; qu. (with italics and normalised spelling for 'Jekyll') *LETBM*, vol. V, p. 152 note.

34 For the contract, see Reading University Library, *The Longman Archive*, MS A 21 (another copy is in the Society of Authors Archive, British Library Add. 56638, f. 27); for the date of the cheque, *The Longman Archive*, Royalty Ledger R1, p. 317; for the correction of proofs, *LETBM*, vol. V, p. 153. All the first proofs had been printed by 17 November when an uncorrected copy of them was sent to Scribner's (cf. letter in Scribner's Archives, Princeton).

35 The information on the agreement (untraced) comes from an annotation in the Longman Royalty Ledger R1, p. 184: 'C. Scribner's Sons to pay £20 for early sheets and will publish in two formats viz. cloth @ $1 & in paper @ 25 cents. They will pay Royalty of 10 per cent on retail price of the cloth edition only. See their letter of Dec. 16/85 (with Agt.).' The source of the subsequent mix up about royalties can already be seen in the annotation made by the Scribner's office on the letter from Longman of 18 December 1885 asking for an offer for publishing *JH* (that had crossed in the post with theirs): 'Burlingame wrote Dec. 16th '85 offering £20 & 10% *to Stevenson*' (emphasis added). On receipt of Scribner's offer, Longman sent a postcard 'In reply to your letter of Dec 16 we wish to say the accounts for Dr Jekyll and Mr Hyde are to be settled with us', but Scribner's overlooked this. As the result of an enquiry made on 9 May 1887, Longman learned that Scribner's had paid royalties directly to RLS. Scribner's then paid royalties for the latest period only, and by accounts day on 1 June Longman had received £19 6s. 8d. which was divided in two with the author (Ledger R1, p. 318; RLS later seeks information from Scribner's in order to pay Longman their share of earlier payments, *LETMB*, vol. VI, p. 52). If this sum from Scribner's corresponds to $100, then it would represent sales of 1000 copies of the cloth edition, but the period of sales is not known (it was certainly after February 1886, when Stevenson had already received a cheque for £60 11s. from Scribner's). The correspondence from Longman proposing the American edition (November to December 1885) and then clarifying the royalties question (September to November 1887) is in Princeton University Library *C0101* (Scribner's Archives), Box 142, Folder 1, and Box 143, Folder 7; for letters from RLS to Scribner's on the matter, see *LETBM*, vol. VI, pp. 41 and note, 50 and note, 52 and note.

36 The first US pirate edition was published on 1 February 1886 (in George Munro's 'Seaside Library'). The fact that the United States repeatedly avoided granting international copyright protection had been a bone of contention since the early part of the century (Dickens expounded the iniquities of the situation when in America in 1841). The United States did not recognise

British copyright until the Chace Act of 1891, and this did not enter into effect until after Stevenson's death (N. N. Feltes, *Literary Capital and the Late Victorian Novel*, Madison, University of Wisconsin Press, 1993, p. 95–6).

37 In March 1885 RLS had promised to offer Scribner's 'the sheets of my next book' in gratitude for their generous offer to publish *A Child's Garden of Verses* (*LETBM*, vol. V, p. 86).

38 NLS MS 9895, *Balfour's Biography Notebook*, f. 112 (letter of Charles Longman to Graham Balfour, 25 October 1900), qu. in part in Balfour 1901, p. 14.

39 Feltes (*Literary Capital and the Late Victorian Novel*, pp. 89–102) suggests that the London edition may have been delayed to make sure of profits from an American edition, but Longman decided to defer publication on 28 November when they had not yet heard if Scribner's were willing to publish the American edition (Princeton *C0101*, letter of 28 November).

40 The wrapper was probably printed earlier as it not only has the earlier planned date of publication (where the title page has 1886), but also the author's name in the form 'R. L. Stevenson' rather than with the full first names that Stevenson had time to substitute for the initials on the proofs of the title page. For a full bibliographical description of the London and New York first editions see McKay, vol. II, *B346–8*, and W. F. Prideaux (*A Bibliography of the Works of Robert Louis Stevenson*, London, 1917), pp. 44–5. For a reproduction of the cover, see Linehan (ed.), *Strange Case of Dr. Jekyll and Mr. Hyde*, p. 3, and (in colour) Gilles Menegaldo and Jean-Pierre Naugrette (eds), *R. L. Stevenson & A. Conan Doyle. Aventures de la Fiction*, Rennes, Terre de Brume, 2003, pl. V.

41 University of Reading Library, *The Longman Archive*, Impression Books, vol. XXIII, p. 23: for the second printing of January 1886 only 9000 blue and red paper wrappers were printed.

42 McKay, vol. II, *B 346–7*. Stevenson thought the cloth edition 'very handsome' (*LETBM*, vol. V, p. 179).

43 *The Longman Archive*, Royalty Book R1, p. 317. These sales were considered 'enormous' by *Book-lore* in June 1886 (Jason A. Pierce, 'Penny-Wise and Virtue-Foolish': Robert Louis Stevenson and the Late Victorian Publishing Industry', PhD dissertation, University of South Carolina., 1999, p. 156).

44 For production and sales numbers (paper and cloth versions combined), see *The Longman Archive*, Impression Books, vol. XXIII, pp. 23, 33, 36, 49, 62, 69; Royalty Ledger R1, p. 317; these confirm Charles Longman's figure of 'close on forty thousand' for the first six months, cf. Charles Longman to Graham Balfour (25 October 1900), NLS MS 9895, f. 112, qu. Balfour 1901, p. 13. For royalty payments to Stevenson, see Royalty Ledger R1, p. 317.

45 Scribner's also issued volumes in their Thistle edition as single volumes; in this case *The Merry Men and Other Tales and Fables. Strange Case of Dr. Jekyll and Mr. Hyde*.

46 Linda Ekins in a message to the VICTORIA discussion list 23 October 1998 quotes the economic historian Sheila V. Hopkins (in Carus-Wilson, *Essays in Economic History*, 1966): 'To arrive at dollar figures, convert pounds into dollars by multiplying by five' and adds 'The ... rate of conversion is valid until the first world war.'

47 *The Book Buyer* (New York), April 1886 (Stevenson's Mother's Scrapbook 3, p. 12, Robert Louis Stevenson Cottage, Saranac Lake, NY); George L. McKay, *Some Notes on Robert Louis Stevenson: His Finances, and His Agents and Publishers*, New Haven, Yale University Library, 1958, p. 18.

48 McKay, *Some Notes on Robert Louis Stevenson*, p. 19, lists seven 1886–91 and

the *National Union Catalog, Pre-1956 Imprints* contains a further nine 1886–1900.

49 In April 1887 (the 'Eleventh Edition') the type of the Longman edition was stereotyped so no further changes were possible (University of Reading Library, *The Longman Archive*, Impression Books, vol. XXIII, p. 164).

The Present Edition

CHOICE AND TREATMENT OF THE COPY TEXT

MS has not been adopted as the copy text (apart from the fact that it covers only half of the text) for a variety of reasons: RLS received and read the proofs; he was a meticulous proof-reader and particularly objected to his punctuation being changed by the printer; there are only a few differences between *MS* punctuation and that of *1886L*, and many of the new points can be seen as typically Stevensonian. In short there is no indication at all of the *MS* punctuation being substituted by that of the compositors.

That Stevenson received the proofs is shown by the printer's instruction written on p. 1 of *MS* to send them to him immediately. On 12 November RLS says that 'I am just now literally off my head with work ... I am writing a story against time; and correcting the proofs of another' (*LETBM*, vol. V, p. 153), which must refer to the writing of 'Olalla' and correcting the proofs of *JH*. That he read the proofs is corroborated by the several substantive changes made between *MS* and *1886L* which can only be authorial.

Although the above letter shows Stevenson under pressure, it gives no clue as to whether he thought he was being forced by lack of time to accept printing-house changes. Evidence from before and after November 1886 suggests that this would be unlikely. At the end of March 1885 he writes to Henley 'A desperate lark the *Arab* proofs have been: every stop was changed; and I came near an explosion' (*LETBM*, vol. V, p. 98), which suggests a violent protest at the changes. At Saranac Lake in early November 1887 he returned proofs (probably of 'A Chapter on Dreams') with the note 'If I receive another proof of this sort, I shall return it at once with the general direction: "See MS." I must suppose my system of punctuation to be very bad; but it is mine; and it shall be adhered to with punctual exactness by every created printer who shall print for me' (*LETBM*, vol. VI, p. 51). This, too, was a period of hectic work ('I am up to my neck in attempted papers', ibid., p. 50), yet he finds time to dedicate to the job of restoring the proofs to his original intentions. Edward Bok of Scribner's, who saw him at work in 1887, reports that 'No man ever went over his proofs more carefully than did Stevenson; his corrections were numerous; and sometimes for ten minutes at a time he would sit smoking and thinking over a single sentence, which, when he had satisfactorily shaped it in his mind, he would recast on the proof'.[1]

The changes between *MS* and *1886L* are not many: apart from thirty-seven substantive changes, ten others involve compounds and hyphens, and thirty-two involve punctuation. The nine inserted hyphens (in six cases where RLS had two separate words, the others where he had one) could well be a house-style change that was merely accepted by Stevenson, but the case of the thirty-two changes to punctuation is not so clear. First of all, these changes do not represent a general substitution of one system by another but only about 2 per cent of all non-sentence-final pointing in the extant manuscript. Secondly, many of the changes seem to be typical of RLS's own pointing. I refer here to examples such as the three semicolons substituted for commas in the description of Utterson (p. 7), e.g. 'No doubt the feat was easy to Mr. Utterson; for he was undemonstrative at the best', added to the eight others in this short passage. Note how in the angry letter to the compositor he seems to be illustrating his fondness for the semicolon in the message itself ('I must suppose my system of punctuation to be very bad; but it is mine; and it shall be adhered to ...'). Even cases which could be conventional pointing like 'I smiled to myself, and, in my psychological way, began lazily to inquire ...' (p. 64), where *1886L* adds a comma after 'myself', could also be seen as authorially motivated (in this case, contributing to the slow, musing tone of the narration which imitates the thought processes narrated). In short, total changes are few and we cannot draw a line between cases that may have been printer's pointing that were merely accepted and changes that we can see as conforming to authorial style. In view also of Stevenson's careful and exigent proof-reading practice, *1886L* (and not *MS*) must be taken as representing the author's final intentions.

The 1886 New York edition was set up from printed sheets of *1886L* and includes some variant readings, some of them corrections of obvious mistakes (they include, for instance, all seven of the emendations that have been made in this edition). These corrections and other changes must have been made independently by Scribner's because, if any authorial or editorial changes had been transmitted via Longman to Scribner's on the sheets they sent them, they would naturally have been noted for the second London printing, and the only *1886NY* variant found there is the substitution of a semicolon for a piece of faulty type (p. 63.3 of this edition). In fact, spot checks in the second London printing for these *1886NY* variant readings, together with a series of candidates in *1886L* for possible 'correction' (spelling inconsistencies, unusual punctuation, etc.), show that the first two Longman printings are identical except for this one correction.

The text of *JH* in the Edinburgh and Thistle Editions of Stevenson's Works, published in 1895, have no special authority: Stevenson's abundant surviving correspondence from the end of his life when the two collected editions were being planned and prepared contains no instructions for changes, and no request to take the text in hand. A collation of the first chapter in *1886L* and in the Edinburgh Edition shows 8 per cent of non-final punctuation changed (twenty cases) and five new hyphenations added as well a change in spelling ('storey' to 'story') and one substantial change ('It was' to 'He was'). In contrast, Scribner's Thistle Edition (lacking the contribution of Sidney Colvin) was prepared with no such policy of editorial 'improvement': text and punctuation of ch. 1 are identical with *1886NY* apart from one unfortunate typo ('friendship' for 'friendships'). None of the variations in the two 1895 editions is in the direction of *MS*.

The exact typographic format of text titles in *1886L* has not been reproduced in the present edition: for example, '*STORY OF THE DOOR.*' in *1886L* ('Story of the door' with double underlining in *MS*) is 'Story of the Door' here, following the style of the Centenary Edition. The full stop has also been omitted here and after other text titles. Otherwise, within the text, the present edition follows *1886L* in spelling, capitalisation, and punctuation. Even that which would today be regarded as misspellings and unusual punctuation and capitalisation has been retained as interesting attestations of the state of the language in 1885.

The occasional uses of the full form 'Doctor' rather than the abbreviated 'Dr.' have not been standardised;[2] nor have we standardised variation here in the titles to ch. 6 and ch. 9: hence we have 'Remarkable Incident of Doctor Lanyon' as a title at the head of the chapter, even though the same chapter title on the contents page has 'Dr.'.

Styles of capitalisation in street names such as 'Regent's park' and 'Portland street' have been kept alongside 'Cavendish Square', 'Gaunt Street', 'Queer Street', since there was much variation in this area in the nineteenth century: for example, Kelly's *London Directory* for 1843 and 1851 and the Post Office Directories for the same two years both use the 'Oxford street' style.[3]

The variation of 'storey' (ch. 1) and 'story' (ch. 8) (in the sense of 'floor of a building') is retained as the spelling was not yet fixed at this time: the *OED* (1919) actually has 'story' as the main entry, with a cross-reference from the alternative spelling, which (though now the standard British English variant) was much less frequently used in the nineteenth century (cf. also Fowler, *A Dictionary of English Usage*, 1926).

Another problematic point is Stevenson's strange use of the diaeresis. It seems as though he wanted to distinguish a prefix ending in a vowel (*re-, pre-*) from the root of the word beginning in another vowel and in four cases uses a diaerisis on the prefix vowel (as in 'rëinforce'); he decided this at a late stage (such spellings exist in *MS* but not in *ND2*), and elsewhere has used a hyphen ('re-administred') or no distinguishing sign at all ('reindue') with this prefix.[4]

Emendations include four clear cases: one case of faulty type that did not print in *1886L*, two cases of a lack or misplacing of a quotation mark, one case of a comma inserted within an adverbial phrase (a seeming erroneous anticipation). There are also three other cases of a missing comma where I judge usage to be so codified as to qualify the lack as a mechanical slip, one missing in front of a question tag (present in *MS*, and a comma is present in the only other question tag in *MS*), and two missing in front of a parenthetical vocative (where the text contains scores of other vocatives set off by commas), both close together, suggesting an inattentive compositor.

VARIANT READINGS

The reading to the left of the square bracket is that of the present edition (with page:line reference) as well as the reading of those members of the set of reference texts (*MS*, *1886L*, *1886NY* for the first and last sections, just *1886L* and *1886NY* for the central section) that are not explicitly identified with the variant reading to the right of the square bracket. Apart from the choice made at 48:16, the seven other cases where *1886L* is to the right of the square bracket indicate an amendment to that edition that has been made here. Cases where *MS* is to the right of the bracket show changes that were made at the proof-reading stage. Cases where *1886NY* is to the right show changes made in setting up that edition. The swung dash (~) is an abbreviation to show that the variant reading agrees with the present edition for a word or an understandable sequence of words.

All *1886NY* variants have been noted, but non-problematic changes between *MS* and *1886L* have been omitted: 1. repeated house-style and formatting changes (stops added after 'Mr' and 'Dr'; quotation marks changed from double to single; chapter titles written all in capitals; the first word of each chapter and 'signatures' at the end of quoted documents set in capital and small capitals); 2. corrections of scribal errors (obvious mis-spellings, repetitions, omissions, word-order confusions).

Differences between the cancelled *MS* f. 39 and *1886L* have not been listed, unlike in Veeder, as the former was not part of the text to be set in type. Veeder's list of variants is also unreliable because he compares *MS* not with *1886L*, but with a much later edition.[5]

Dedication

TO / KATHERINE DE MATTOS] TO / KATHARINE DE MATTOS / THIS TALE / IS AFFECTIONATELY DEDICATED / BY JEKYLL / NOT BY HYDE, *B 7552* (which lacks the dedicatory verse)

It's ill to] We cannae *Colvin* (*Galleys* and *Letters*), <We cannae> ^It's ill to^ *B 7007*
loose the bands] break the bonds *Colvin* (*Galleys* and *Letters*), *B 7007*
bind;] ~, *Colvin* (*Galleys* and *Letters*), *B 7007*
Still will we] Still we'll *Colvin* (*Galleys* and *Letters*), *B 7007*
countrie.] ~! *Colvin* (*Galleys* and *Letters*), *B 7007*

Pages corresponding to the first section of MS:

7.4	lovable] loveable *MS*
7.7–8	after-dinner] afterdinner *MS*
7.12	others;] ~, *MS*
7.13	misdeeds;] ~, *MS*
7.15	I incline] I rather incline *MS*
7.18–19	to such as these, so long as] to these, as long as *MS*
7.21	Utterson;] ~, *MS*
7.23	good-nature] good nature *MS*
8.1–2	well-known] well known *MS*
8.3	other] ~, *1886NY*
8.7	put the greatest store] set ~ *MS*
8.21	well-polished] well polished *MS*, *1886NY*
8.32	the recess] its shelter *MS*
9.4	voice, 'and] voice. "And *MS*
9.25	one look, so ugly that] one look so ~ *MS*
9.32	sight. So] sight; so *MS*
10.17	but to that place] but that place *MS*
10.28	rest," says he, "I] rest," says he. 'I *MS*
10.34	it.] it, sir. *MS*
10.36	Tut-tut] Tut—tut (dash) *1886NY*
11.4	suppose;] ~: *MS*
11.12	place, isn't it?] place isn't it? *1886L*
11.14	about – the place] about the – place *1886NY*
11.18	judgment] judgement *MS* (same change at 65.23)
11.37	Yes,] Yes, sir, *MS*
13.13	it provided] and it provided *MS*
13.23	him both as] him as *MS*
14.13	dining-room] dining room *MS*
14.25	must be] will be *MS*
15.17	also was engaged] was also engaged *MS*
15.21	a nocturnal city] the ~ *MS*
15.38	mind] ~, *MS*
16.7	clauses] clause *1886NY*
16.7	And at least] At least *1886NY*
16.13	plenty] ~, *1886NY*
16.13–14	face of the fogged] fogged face of the *MS*
17.19	let me see your face] look me in the face *MS*
17.27	Good God!] Good God, *MS*
17.27	can he too] can he, too, *1886NY*
17.29	acknowledgement] acknowledgment *1886NY*
17.37	cried Mr. Hyde, with a flush of anger. 'I] cried Mr Hyde, "never, never told you. I *MS*
18.32	fan-light] fanlight *MS*
19.1–2	dining-room] dining room *MS*
20.3	doing, yet] doing yet *MS*
20.12	wheel – if] wheel, if *MS*

Section for which the MS pages are missing:

24.1	October] ~, *1886NY*
24.5	upstairs] up stairs *1886NY*
24.12	experience)] ~, *1886NY*
25.8	under foot,] ~ *1886NY*
25.20	victim;] ~: *1886NY*
26.1	longer:] ~; *1886NY*
26.2	recognised] recognized *1886NY*
27.8	Very well then,] Very well, then, *1886NY*
27.27	lockfast] lock-/fast *1886NY*
29.5	dissecting rooms.] ~ *1886NY* (faulty type)
32.11	house;] ~, *1886NY*
32.27	he said;] ~: *1886NY*
33.9	safe] ~, *1886NY*
37.1	bracketed] bracketted *1886NY*
38.11	back way to] back way, to *1886NY*
39.16	bystreet] by-/street *1886NY*
40.27	'What] What *1886L*
42.18	unlooked-for] unlooked for *1886NY*
42.32	voice;] ~: *1886NY*
43.22	Every time] Everytime *1886NY*
44.26	his avoidance] the avoidance *1886NY*
45.12	me, sir,] me, *1886NY*
45.13	That is] That's *1886NY*
45.18	know, Poole,] know Poole, *1886L*
46.3	O,] 'O, *1886L*
46.25	he led] led *1886NY*
46.31	sound] sounds *1886NY*
46.38	ears, Mr. Utterson] ears Mr. Utterson *1886L*
47.31	besiegers,] ~ *1886NY*
48.6	gone;] ~: *1886NY*
48.16	bystreet] by-/street *1886L*
48.16	this,] ~ *1886NY*
48.20	empty] ~, *1886NY*
48.23	door,] ~ *1886NY*
50.12	solemnly.] ~, *1886NY*
50.14	follows.] ~: *1886NY*
51.7	the formality] formality *1886NY*
51.16	my fortune or my left hand] my left hand *1886NY*
51.27	forced;] ~: *1886NY*
52.19	Five minutes afterwards,] Five minutes, afterwards, *1886L*
52.26	labouring] laboring *1886NY*
53.27	manufacture;] ~: *1886NY*
53.30	half-full] half full *1886NY*

Pages corresponding to the final section of MS:

54.6–8	How ... ? If ... ? And ... ?] How ... ? if ... ? and ... ? *MS*
54.7	sanity,] ~ *MS, 1886NY*
54.15–6	I went myself at the summons,] I opened it, of course, myself, *MS*
54.18	Dr.] Doctor *MS*
54.20–1	a searching backward glance] a search ~ *MS*
54.27	before,] ~; *MS*
54.33	incipient rigor,] incipient rigor or what is called goose-flesh; *MS*
55.9–10	moving me to laughter.] tickling the cacchinatory impulse. *MS*
55.19	cried.] ~, *MS*
55.35	the hysteria] the hysteric ball *MS*
57.23	faded] melted *MS*
57.30	say but] say, but *1886NY*
57.33	hunted] now hunted *MS*
58.3	fellow-men] fellow men *MS*
58.16	shame. It was] shame, and it was *MS*
58.18	was and, with] was; and with *MS*
59.1	reäcted] reacted *MS* (diaeresis in *MS* is cancelled, possibly by the printer)
59.3	and from both sides] and both sides *MS*
61.22	Again] And again *MS*
61.22	life,] ~ *MS*
61.22	been,] ~ *MS*
61.28	Evil] ~, *MS*
62.1	evil:] ~; *MS*
62.16	diabolical] diabolic *MS*
62.19	time] hour *MS*
63.6	Doctor] Dr *MS*
63.16	complete.] ~, and I could snap my fingers. *MS*
63.20	mirror;] ~: *MS*
63.24	undignified;] ~. *MS*
63.24	term. But] term; but *MS*
63.27	I was often plunged] I soon began to be plunged *MS*
63.30	centred] centered *1886NY*
64.3	entering;] ~ *1886L* (faulty type)
64.5–6	I shall no more than mention.] I mention only in passing. *MS*
64.12	name, of] name of *1886NY*
64.18	out for] out on *MS*
64.23	frame;] ~: *MS*
64.26	myself, and,] myself and, *MS*
64.30	eye] eyes *1886NY*
65.8	journey,] ~ *1886NY*
66.25	any tempted] every ~ *MS* (*1886L* could be a misreading of this)
66.32	pulses] impulses *1886NY*

66.34   Soho, nor] Soho nor *MS*
67.17   I declare at least,] I declare, at least, *1886NY*
67.23   tempted,] ~ *MS*
68.1   pledged the dead man.] pledged the dead man by name. *MS*
68.7   toils] days *MS*
68.15–6   now confined to the better part of my existence] compelled to
          my better life *MS*
68.31   earnestly] ~, *MS*
68.38   license] licence *MS*
69.9   clear,] ~ *MS*
69.9   under foot] underfoot *MS*
69.10   melted,] ~ *MS*
69.11   Regent's park] Regent's Park *1886NY*
69.12   Spring] spring *1886NY*
69.18   over me] upon me *MS*
69.33   moment] occasion *MS*
70.15   face – happily for him –] ~, ~, *MS*
71.8   Hyde] ~, *MS*
72.10   co-heir] coheir *MS*
72.38   these,] this *MS*
73.31   the courage] courage *1886NY*

Hyphenation

Of the line-end hyphenations in this edition, only the following
correspond to hyphenation in *1886L*: after-dinner (p. 7); well-known,
by-street (p. 8); dining-room, Jack-in-the-Box (p. 19); light-hearted (p.
21); well-founded (p. 24); pocket-handkerchief (p. 41); knife-boy (p. 42);
double-dealer (p. 58); mid-London (p. 64); self-denying (p. 68). One
line-end hyphenation in *MS*, 'by-/street', transcribed here as 'bystreet'
(p. 48), could also be hyphenated.

Notes

1 Edward Bok, *The Americanization of Edward Bok: The Autobiography of a
  Dutch Boy Fifty Years After*, New York, Scribner's, 1923; extract at http://
  www.uta.edu/english/danahay/bokextract.html (accessed 15 January 2003).
2 "Are you come from Doctor Jekyll?" (*MS* f. 43) becomes 'Are you come from
  Dr. Jekyll?' in *1886L*, indicating an effort to change to the abbreviation.
  Stevenson's own variation is shown clearly on *MS* pp. 50–1, where the
  catchword at the bottom one page is 'Dr', but the first word at the top of the
  next page is 'Doctor' (and this latter has been followed by *1886L*).
3 Paul Lewis in VICTORIA discussion list <http://www.indiana.edu/ ~victoria/
  index.html>, 28 August 2001; Keith Ramsey (28 August) reports that *Kelly's
  Directory of Bristol* was using the 'Oxford street' style as recently as the 1970
  edition; Peter Shillingford (private communication) says that in editing
  Thackeray's works he found 'Oxford Street', 'Oxford street' and 'Oxford-
  street' styles. The 1899 Baedecker *Londres* has the 'Oxford street' style (also
  Regent's park) exclusively in the index, but 'Oxford Street' on the engraved

maps and 'Oxford-street' (and sometimes 'Oxford-Street') in the text.

4 There are two similar cases in 'Markheim', spelt 'rëarise' and 'rëinspired' in the manuscript written in November 1884, but spelt 're-arise' and 'reinspired' when printed in 1885 from a (lost) revised manuscript that was prepared in the same general period as the writing and publishing of *JH* (cf. Barry Menikoff [ed.], *The Complete Stories of Robert Louis Stevenson*, New York, Modern Library, 2002, p. 793). In this case, therefore, Stevenson changed in the direction of more normal spelling or accepted the changes made by the printer. The *OED* (1903) says the use of the diaeresis with this prefix is 'much less frequent' than the hyphen.

5 Despite Veeder's column heading 'first printed edition' (p. 54), page numbers and variants coincide exactly with the 1979 Penguin edition (not cited). Spot checks of the latter show that it probably takes its text from the Tusitala edition.